Shade Infinity

A Thriller

by Steve DeWinter

Summary

What does it mean to be an individual?

Someone else has Michele's face, her name, and is reliving her life down to the smallest detail, including sleeping with her husband.

She is determined to discover what is happening and return to her happily ever after. What she uncovers is something that could change humanity forever.

And not for the better.

SHADE INFINITY is a thriller about human cloning in a world that is coming sooner than we thought.

This book is also available serialized under the following titles:
One Shade of Black
One Shade Darker
Shade Tolerance
Shade Mask
Shade Cover
Shade Element

Ramblin' Prose Publishing
Copyright © 2015 Steve DeWinter
All rights reserved. Used under authorization.
www.stevedw.com

eBook Edition
ISBN-10: 1-61978-098-4
ISBN-13: 978-1-61978-098-9

Paperback Edition
ISBN-10: 1-61978-106-9
ISBN-13: 978-1-61978-106-1

Chapter 1

The whole world changed on a Wednesday. Unfortunately, nobody knew it but me.

You see, that was the day I watched myself die. Then again, that was only the trigger for something larger. Much larger. Something big enough to bankrupt companies hundreds of years old, topple governments, and threaten the very idea of what it meant to be human.

But I'm getting ahead of myself.

Maybe it's best if I started at the beginning so you can understand why I did what I did. Why I had no other choice.

That day started out like any other.

I woke up beside my husband to see him watching me in the faint light of the morning.

He smiled as soon as my eyes fluttered open.

"Morning sleepyhead," he said as he pushed some stray hairs to one side of my face.

I smiled back up at him.

He leaned down and kissed me tenderly.

I welcomed the love and wrapped my arms around his neck, keeping him close. After nearly three years of marriage, there was still that spark that reminded me of why I fell in love with him.

His cell phone buzzed on the nightstand, its vibrating hum echoing in the hollow wood.

"Ugh," he complained.

"Leave it," I whispered and nibbled his ear.

He pulled away grudgingly. "I can't."

"Just this once," I said as I batted my eyes at him.

He gave me a quick peck on the lips and rolled away to answer his phone. "This is Robert."

His back straightened as the tinny reply came over the phone. He glanced at me and winked as he responded to the demanding voice.

"No, I'm already in the car. The traffic is heavy. Looks like some construction, so I might be a little late. Okay. Hold the plane. Bye."

He switched off the phone and gave me a pitiful look as he stood up and started dressing.

"No," I whined as my shoulders dropped.

"Somebody's gotta pay the bills around here."

"I could get a part time job."

He knelt next to me on the bed as he buttoned up his shirt. "You already have a full time job."

I sat up and slid my hands into his shirt, stopping him from finishing. "I can do both."

He tenderly pulled my hands away and secured the final two buttons. "I want you to get better. I want you to remember us, like I remember us."

"I'm trying."

He smiled as he expertly whipped his tie into a perfect knot. "I know you are."

He stood up and donned his jacket.

"I've got to get going. Promise me you will make it to the doctor's on time this week."

"I promise."

He cocked his head to one side and smiled playfully. "Say that one more time. And mean it."

I sat up straight and held up three fingers together in the Boy Scout salute.

"I promise."

He smiled and gave me another kiss. I wrapped my arms around his neck and held him in the kiss longer. He pulled away slowly and peered into my eyes, the spark very much alive.

"I can't miss my plane."

"It's a private jet. They'll wait for you."

He laughed as he stood up. "If only I had that kind of influence."

He grabbed the handle of the suitcase he had packed the night before and paused at the bedroom door. "I'll call you when I'm settled into the hotel."

"I'll miss you," I said.

His smile returned. "Not as much as I'll miss you. Now, don't be late for your appointment."

"I won't," I said, and meant it.
Well, I meant it when I said it.

Chapter 2

As usual, I was running late.

I was taking the detour through the park, the one I took only when I wanted to be very late. Ever since my car accident four years earlier, I had not held a driver's license. There was some stupid rule about extended loss of consciousness and getting the "all clear" by a litany of doctors and psychiatrists before being allowed behind the wheel again.

So now, when I wanted to go anywhere, I had to walk, take the bus, or call a taxi.

It's not terribly convenient, and it's a slow way of getting around the city, but it's not like I had much of a choice.

So there I was, walking over one of the hundreds of bridges in Pittsburgh on my way to my weekly appointment hoping that this was the week she finally signed off on me and I could start driving again.

And as usual, I was running late.

But that is not why my life changed that day.

I remember watching transfixed as a young woman climbed up on the ledge of the bridge, preparing to jump.

I dropped my backpack and ran toward her.

"Don't!" I screamed as my feet pounded across the metal mesh surface. She stayed frozen on the railing until I reached her. She turned and looked me in the eyes.

I froze in place as a chill ran up my spine colder than the waters below.

She looked exactly like me.

She appeared to be a few years younger than I was. But it was still like looking in a mirror. A magical mirror that reflected a more youthful me.

But unlike the surprise on my face, her expression suggested that she expected to see her mirror image standing before her.

"How many more?" was all she said as she stepped backward off the bridge railing.

If I had known then what I know now, I would have followed her over the edge and into the sweet embrace of death offered by the icy waters below.

Instead, I lunged forward, reaching for her outstretched hand as she dropped out of sight. I reached the ledge and peered over in time to see her break through the surface and quickly sink into the shadowy depths. Within moments, the concentric rings expanding out across the surface of the water were the only indication that someone had just plunged deep into the river.

I should not have been on the bridge at that moment in time. I was supposed to be at my shrink's office, dealing with the demons in my head and trying to convince her to finally sign off on my driver's license application.

But I wasn't.

Instead, I was in the one place I never expected to find myself.

At the scene of my own suicide.

As I watched, the rolling river below smoothed out the undulating waves that were the only proof of what I had just witnessed.

But, what had I just witnessed?

Had I really seen myself jump off the bridge, or had I projected my own face onto some other girl, wishing I was the one who had the nerve to end it all?

Let's add psychotic episode to the list of reasons why I was on my way to a shrink. My psychiatrist was going to have a field day with this new development.

I glanced around but, in a city with nearly half a million people living in it, I was alone.

I saw my backpack lying right where I had dropped it. There wasn't even anybody around to steal it.

My eyes were drawn to a red object on the bridge, just below the rail where the girl had jumped.

It was her purse.

I glanced around again.

There was still nobody around.

I snatched up the purse and dug through it for a wallet. Finding it, I pulled it out and opened it quickly to see if there was a phone number written down of someone to call and tell them what had happened.

I flipped past a dozen credit cards, all platinum or black, until I reached her driver's license; and froze.

I stared at the picture for only a second before closing my eyes tightly.

I opened them again and glanced at the name. It said her name was Michele Gardner.

I reflexively dropped the wallet.

Her name was Michele Gardner?

But my name was Michele Gardner.

Or at least it was before I married Robert Black.

What the hell was happening?

Was I having a mental breakdown?

Maybe I shouldn't have missed today's appointment. Maybe none of this was happening and I was lying on the ground in the middle of the park having a seizure. I looked at my backpack that was still lying by itself on the ground where I dropped it. I wasn't lying next to it. If I was having an out-of-body experience, wouldn't I see myself lying on the ground?

My heart pounded against my ribcage and I could taste the adrenaline coursing through my bloodstream.

I pinched myself and winced, passing the tried and true dreaming test.

I was not dreaming. Nor was I having an out-of-body experience.

This was actually happening.

I picked up the wallet and inspected the picture from several different angles.

It might as well have been me who posed for this picture. It looked exactly like me. It even had my name.

I held it closer and only then noticed the words "IDENTIFICATION CARD" instead of "DRIVER'S LICENSE" next to the state name.

This other Michele didn't drive either.

I stuffed the wallet back into the purse and tucked it under an arm as I headed quickly back to my backpack.

I stooped down, grabbed the strap on my backpack, and

swung it up onto my shoulder without slowing down.

The last thing I needed right now was to be questioned by the police as a witness to my own suicide.

I opened my backpack and shoved the purse deep into it, hiding it under the change of clothes I kept in it for reasons unknown to me. It was Robert's idea to always have a spare change of clothes, in case anything happened.

I glanced at my phone and noted that I was now fifteen minutes late for the start of my appointment, and I was still another ten minutes away by foot.

I had a choice.

Be very, very late or just go back home.

I didn't think I could keep from talking about what had just happened, and I really didn't feel like discussing anything right now, so I turned back the way I had come.

I knew I would completely miss my appointment but I wasn't going to call the receptionist to cancel. I hated talking to her anyway. She always treated me like I was crazy.

Chapter 3

I made it home before I risked inspecting the purse further.

Pulling it out from the deep recesses of my backpack, I emptied the contents on my coffee table and pushed them around with a finger.

Lipstick.

Wads of used tissue; gross.

A ring of keys.

And the wallet.

I picked it up and popped open the second clasp to be rewarded with several hundred dollar bills staring back at me.

I pulled the bills from the wallet and tossed it back onto the coffee table. Fanning them out, I quickly counted eighteen bills.

She had almost two thousand bucks in her wallet.

With that kind of pocket change, why had she jumped?

This Michele was rich, if the money in her wallet was any indication.

I looked down at the fanned-out hundred dollar bills on the coffee table. This was her money and I was actually considering keeping it.

I finally convinced myself she didn't need it anymore and scooped the money up off the coffee table.

I stood and went to the kitchen to hide the money in an old cocoa powder box with the rest of my rainy day money. It was Robert's idea. He was always worried that burglars would break in and steal cash from the house. So, during the first few months we were together, he had cleaned out a used box of cocoa powder, wrapped it in flower print tissue paper with a bright red bow on it, and gave it to me.

I ignored last night's dishes sitting in the sink as I tucked the eighteen hundred dollars into the box and put it back in the cupboard next to the baking soda box that was actually filled with baking soda.

I never bothered to clean dishes on Wednesdays. That was Robert's day to travel for his job. My loving husband wouldn't be home until late Thursday night, so I didn't bother with them until right before bed on Thursday.

Wednesday was my one full day of rest.

If you could call discussing your problems with a shrink as restful.

I didn't even know why I had to endure those weekly sessions. In the four years since the car accident that took my memory, nothing she had done had helped bring it back. I requested, no pleaded, with Robert to let me stop, or at least see someone else.

He insisted I be patient.

Let her continue to work with me and I would eventually remember who I was.

I just had to give it time.

Now I know that will never happen.

If the ID in the wallet sitting peacefully on my coffee table was to be believed, I wasn't Michele Gardner despite everyone trying to convince me otherwise.

I had watched her die today and, despite not feeling anything other than that brief moment of terror at seeing her up on the bridge, I knew that I had died right along with her.

Chapter 4

I didn't remember falling asleep on the couch, but I woke with a start when the phone rang.

I glanced at the clock on the DVR above the TV.

It was three-fifteen in the afternoon.

That would be Robert. Right on schedule.

I grabbed the phone with one hand while wiping away the sleep from my eyes with the other.

"Hey Honey. How was the flight?"

"Hi Sweetie. Long and exhausting, as usual."

His voice was a smooth baritone. It was the one thing that had attracted me to him when we first met.

That and the fact that he was chiseled from the same stone as a Greek god. At forty-eight, he was exactly twice my age, but I considered myself mature for my years and I fell head over heels for him instantly.

There was nothing I could do to forget him once I had seen him in the supermarket staring perplexed at the watermelon in his hands.

He had been traveling on business and was only in town one day a week, but he insisted on seeing me that one day next week, and every week since.

After nearly a year of our "weekly dates", he convinced his company to relocate him and we were quickly married.

We had spent every day together since. At least we had until last year when his job started requiring weekly travel out of town. And his company, being the ultimate cheapskate, made him travel in the middle of the week when airfares were discounted.

It was the one caveat to allowing him to relocate permanently to the City of Bridges.

But he said I was worth it.

And with how well he treated me, I believed him.

We talked for half an hour before his yawning became more pronounced. If he didn't get to sleep soon, he would not be awake enough to broker the all-important international deals his company demanded from him.

Our conversations always ended the same.

"I'll be home before you know it."

"It already feels like you've been gone for days. I miss you. My body misses you."

I could hear him smile through the phone.

"My body will be against yours soon."

"I don't want to wait."

"Waiting is half the fun."

"We're married now. We shouldn't have to wait."

"I'll be home tomorrow night. I can sleep on the plane and be awake for you when I get home."

"I'd like that."

"What do you have planned for the rest of the day?"

He asked that same question every week. Only, this time, it caught me by surprise as my eyes fell on the dead woman's wallet.

I said what I always said, but my mind was already planning something else.

"Probably just some TV and then to my empty bed for an early night. You know, the usual Wednesday."

"I have to go. I love you."

"I love you too."

We made kissing sounds to each other and then the phone went silent.

I set the phone down and picked up the wallet.

I slid out the Pennsylvania ID and looked at the address.

It was on the other side of town, but a taxi could get me there in under twenty minutes.

I retrieved a couple of twenties from the cocoa box for cab fare and grabbed the wallet, keys, and lipstick, shoving them back into her purse.

I would just go and return everything. And maybe while I was there, I could get some more answers as to why she and I had the same name and the same face.

I glanced at the cupboard above the sink in the kitchen.

Everything but the money.

I didn't consider myself a thief, but there were just some things that had no purpose, and returning a dead person's money was high on that list.

I just wanted to see how this other me lived, and then I'd come right back home after I had some answers that were niggling in my brain.

At least, that was the plan.

Chapter 5

A little over an hour after calling for a taxi I paid a twenty to the driver, giving him a good tip, and waited for him to disappear around the corner before crossing the street toward the house with the same address on the identification card.

I looked around, but nobody was paying me any attention.

I fumbled with the keys when I heard my name being called from across the street.

"Michele!"

Busted.

I froze, my hand holding the keys just in front of the lock. Nobody should know who I am in this neighborhood. I was miles away from my house. And I generally kept to myself.

I could hear someone running across the street toward me, getting closer.

I held the keys tightly in my fist, letting several poke out between my fingers like the claws of the iconic comic book character Wolverine, and turned slowly.

A pudgy young man ran up the walkway and stopped in front of me. He was smiling, and I didn't recognize him. How had he known my name?

He pressed a fist into his side and breathed heavily as he winced and bent in half. He was, apparently, very much out of shape. Maybe being forced to walk everywhere had given me the stamina that lazy drivers never achieved.

He wheezed as he straightened back up.

"Glad I caught you."

I gripped the keys tighter.

"Do you think you can feed my dog this weekend?"

I loosened the grip on my keys.

Of course. He knew the Michele that lived here. He didn't know who I was.

There was no way for him to know Michele was dead and wouldn't be around to feed his dogs. I couldn't do that to someone's pets so I shook my head. "Sorry. I won't be around this weekend."

His face registered surprise.

"Simone said you were staying home all weekend to work on a project. Some scrapbooking thing or whatnot."

"Simone?"

"Uh... your roommate?" he said in a tone that indicated he thought I was losing it.

I looked back at the front door of the house. It suddenly terrified me. I was about to break into someone else's space. I was an unwelcome intruder.

"I asked her before she left this morning and she didn't think you would have a problem with it."

My head spun with the new information.

The pudgy fellow from across the street was shaking his head.

"If it were me, I'd make you get the hotel."

I looked at him in surprise.

"What?"

"I still think she got the raw deal, with you making her spend every Wednesday night in a hotel so you can entertain your gentleman caller."

"Gentleman..."

I let the words trail off. What type of person was this other Michele?

"So, can you feed my dogs? I'll leave the key under the planter by the back door like usual."

I was having a hard time focusing on the conversation, and I guess he decided I had agreed because he smiled.

"Thanks," he said as he headed back across the street. But instead of walking into his house, he stayed outside and picked up some massive shears and began trimming his bushes.

I felt the sharp edges of the keys in my hand. I couldn't leave now. He would see me leave without going inside and might come back over to find out why.

It would raise too many questions.

Questions, I didn't have answers to.

I spun around and started trying the keys, hoping it didn't take too long to find the right one.

I actually got it on the first attempt and the door opened

inward.

As I went in, I turned back and he waved at me as I shut the door.

Chapter 6

I twisted the knob for the deadbolt and placed my head against the back of the door.

My hands were trembling and I wiped the sweat pouring out of them onto my jacket. I looked through the peephole at the nosy neighbor across the street.

He was still out there tending to his yard.

I would have to wait until he went inside before I could escape.

I took a moment to slow my heartbeat and focused on the sounds of the house. Was the roommate still here?

I strained in the silence for any indication that I was not alone.

Just then, from across the street, the sound of a gas powered mower shattered the silence and I jerked to full attention, nearly crying out. There was no way to hear anything now. I had no choice but to venture deeper into the house.

I suddenly remembered that he mentioned Simone spent every Wednesday in a hotel. Maybe she had already left.

There was only one way to find out.

"Hello?" I asked into the empty house.

Silence replied.

I walked down the hallway and stopped just before the living room.

"Hello?" I said, bolder this time.

After another half a minute of silence, I was certain I was alone.

I walked through the house, noting the pictures of me with another girl spread around the living room. I recognized myself in the pictures, and guessed the black girl with the puffy afro had to be the roommate. I stopped at the TV and inspected one of the pictures on the shelf above it.

It was of me standing on the beach at sunset. I felt the surge of adrenaline fill my body again. I knew I was not in my own house looking at my own pictures, but I remembered when that picture was taken.

I could smell the salt infused breeze that blew through my

hair. I could feel the tightness of the bikini I was wearing. It was a bit too snug around my breasts, but I squeezed into it anyway.

It had been a gift from Robert on our fist vacation to Florida and I wanted him to see me in it.

The memories flooded back and my heart skipped a beat as I grabbed the picture off the shelf and looked at it closely.

This one had a lifeguard station in the background.

How could that be?

The station had caught fire a week before we had arrived, and there was a big local story about how with an entire ocean of water only a few feet away, it had still burned down to the ground. The local news reporters said that it would be a couple of years before the city had the funds to build another one, so instead of a lifeguard at that section of beach, a sign had been erected warning people they were on their own.

This picture showed a freshly built lifeguard station behind a rusted sign that had warned people about the lack of a lifeguard.

That sign had been brand new when we had been there.

This picture was more recent. Except for the station and the sign in the background, it was exactly the same as the one in my house.

What was going on?

Now, more than ever, I was convinced I was still lying on the ground having an epileptic seizure and hallucinating while I died.

Or maybe I was already dead.

And this was heaven?

I looked around at other pictures that were of me and remembered posing for half of them.

I felt sick.

I dropped the picture and ran to the sink in the kitchen and lost what was left of breakfast into it. After washing the bile from my mouth, I spotted the cabinet above the sink.

No.

It was too much to expect.

I reached up and opened the cabinet slowly.

There it was, mocking me from the top shelf.

The cocoa box sat like a bright red beacon on the shelf.

I pulled it down and poked a finger through the opening just enough to feel the edges of dollar bills inside.

This wasn't heaven.

This was hell.

Chapter 7

I ran to the door and stopped as I heard the roar of the lawnmower from across the street.

That damn neighbor was still outside.

And I was still trapped in my own personal hell.

I slammed my hands on the door. "Why the fuck won't you go away?!"

I dropped to the floor with my back against the door and hugged my knees.

I could just wait him out.

A part of me wanted to explore more of the house, but the part of me terrified at what I might discover won out and I sat there against the front door listening to the droning of the lawnmower across the street.

I didn't know how long I sat there, but the sun had crawled across the sky and was invading the living room through the windows at a low angle.

After all this time, it finally sounded like he was done. I peeked through the peep hole in the door and saw him still out there tending to his damn bushes again.

"Bastard," I cursed at him under my breath.

A blinding light streaked across the peep hole and I tried to blink away the spot that was burned onto my retina.

I looked through with my other eye.

I could see the back end of a car that had stopped in the driveway just as the engine went silent.

A car door slammed and I jerked back as soon as I saw someone step around the edge of the house, heading toward the front door.

I backed away and ran for the hallway just as I heard keys jangling outside.

I was a trespasser in this house.

Was this the roommate coming back?

Or was this the gentleman caller the neighbor had mentioned visited every Wednesday night?

Either way, I didn't want to stay and find out.

I reached the sliding glass door in the kitchen that led out to the back yard and yanked on it.

It wouldn't budge.

I heard the key being slid into the deadbolt.

I had to get out.

I fussed with the latch and it snapped up.

I tugged again, but the glass door refused to move.

It was no use, I had to do something else.

I had to go somewhere else.

I ran down the hallway toward the back of the house.

The house wasn't all that big. From what I had seen, there was the front hallway, living room, kitchen, and rear hallway that led to the two bedrooms at the back of the house.

I darted into the back bedroom and closed the door silently, holding the knob to keep the door from making that click sound just as I heard the front door swing closed followed immediately by a set of keys and a phone hitting the top of the hallway table.

I scanned the room.

Dammit!

There wasn't a sliding glass door back here. I looked at the window that sat over the head of the bed. I could pop out the screen and jump out of it and be gone before…

"There you are," a deep voice said behind me.

My heart leapt into my throat.

I had been discovered.

I spun around to confront the homeowner and nearly collapsed at seeing who stood before me.

Chapter 8

"Robert?" I stammered as relief washed over me. I rushed forward and wrapped my arms around him tightly.

"How did you…? How did you find me?"

"It wasn't hard. You weren't in the kitchen or the living room. The house isn't really that big."

My brain was in fight or flight mode and I took too long to comprehend his response.

I hugged him tighter, not wanting to look him in the eye. "No. I mean, how come you're here?"

"You mean early? I convinced my boss to let me sneak out. I wanted to spend more time with you."

I kept my face pressed against his warm chest. His answers did not make sense. I could feel my muscles quivering from the dissipation of adrenaline from my system.

He held me close. "You're trembling. Are you okay?"

"I'm okay," I lied. How could anything about what I had seen and done today be okay?

I had to risk looking him in the face.

I slowly released him and leaned back.

He smiled sweetly at me, his eyes searching mine.

"I've missed you," he said as he placed his hands on the side of my face and drew me in. Out of instinct from doing the same thing with my husband for the last four years, I closed my eyes and returned his warm kiss.

He pressed his lips deeper into mine, his tongue flicking out tenderly. He hadn't kissed me like that in a long time and I melted in his arms, hungry for the attention. I opened my mouth and returned the affection.

We kissed passionately for half a minute before he pulled away, keeping his arms protectively around my waist.

"I'm starving. How about we get Chinese takeout tonight and continue this later?"

I wanted him to take me now. He hadn't treated me like this in nearly a year. Lately, he had been acting as if I was fragile and he might break me, he had been so careful and tender with me.

I guess I accepted it as falling into the standard relationship rut that everyone falls into. We were in love, and none of that had changed.

I wanted to confront him right then and there and bust open the charade, but then he kissed me again.

Maybe we hadn't fallen into a rut after all.

My resolve for a confrontation melted away as I hung in his arms, helpless to do anything but whatever he wanted.

We fell to the bed and reacquainting ourselves with every crease and curve on each other's body.

As I lay panting, drenched in a fragrant concoction of his sweat mixed with mine, he perched on his side, rising up on one elbow.

He smiled down at me and pushed some matted hair out of my face.

"I should order the food before they close."

I reached for him, but he was too quick. He paused at the bedroom door and looked hungrily at me. I hadn't seen that look from him in over a year.

"I'll be right back. Don't you go nowhere."

I patted the bed next to me.

"Don't let this get cold."

He headed down the hallway and I heard him pick up the phone.

As the heat from his body faded among the bed sheets, so did my confidence that everything was alright.

What was I doing?

How could this be right?

I thought about how the real owner of this house looked exactly like me.

Had the same name.

Posed for the same pictures.

Even kept the same mad money cocoa box.

It was surreal.

Even more surreal was that my husband had a key to this house and had walked in without a moment of hesitation.

He was cheating on me!

With me!

What were the odds that there was someone else in the world with the same name as you?

Who looked like you?

And was fucking your husband?

There were no odds that could predict this.

This could never happen by coincidence.

"You okay?"

I jumped, startled by not realizing he had returned to the room after calling in our dinner order. He hadn't even asked me what I wanted.

At that moment, I would be willing to bet anyone he had ordered Kung Pao chicken, with no green onions, for me. It was a bet I was very certain I would win.

He let his robe drop to the floor and I could instantly see that he was still interested in me.

But instead of lying down beside me again, he retrieved his boxer briefs from the floor and slid them up his legs.

"China Palace said that they are down to one car for deliveries and it would be a couple of hours. They promised to give me a discount if I picked it up myself. I'll be back in half an hour."

He leaned down and kissed me deeply. I closed my eyes, taking in his essence.

He pulled away.

"Be right back."

He disappeared down the hallway and I heard the front door lock with a faint click.

I leapt from the bed and grabbed up my clothes strewn about the room.

I had to go!

I couldn't keep pretending. I no longer wanted any part of this and I also didn't want to know why it was happening.

I just wanted to get back home.

I no longer felt safe in this strange, yet familiar, house. Everything I looked at was familiar to me as if I had lived here, yet I knew my house was on the other side of the city.

This was not my house.

I dressed hurriedly, not even concerned about lining up the buttons on my sweater, and ran out of that infernal house and into the cool night.

I reached in my sweater pocket for my cell phone.

It was missing.

I spun back around and stared at the house. It was lit from within and looked more inviting than it should have.

I had no choice but to go back in for my phone. There were no longer any payphones in the city and there were most certainly none in this quiet suburb on the outskirts of Pittsburgh. And I wasn't going to leave my phone in a stranger's house.

I ran back into the house and began looking around. I couldn't find it anywhere. I checked every room, which shouldn't have taken long since there were only three.

But I spent way more time double checking, and triple checking, everywhere in the house. I even tossed the couch cushions around, knowing I had not once sat on the couch, but there was nowhere else left to look.

I was on my stomach, peering into the darkness under the bed at empty space when I heard the engine of Robert's car pull back into the driveway.

I had used up all my time searching for a phone that was not here. Where had I left it?

I then remembered fumbling the twenties out of my pocket to pay the cab driver. Maybe my phone had fallen out then.

It made sense, but it didn't help me now.

As I listened to the front door open and close, I knew I had to pretend to be the other me for a little longer. I would stay the night and then go home, never to return to this nightmare ever again.

At least that was the promise I made to myself. My biggest problem, according to my shrink, was that I had a hard time keeping my promises. She said I was too good at lying to myself.

Chapter 9

We ate dinner in silence. It was not the same type of silence as the dinner we had last night, with Robert reading the financial news on his iPad while I read a romance novel on my Kindle.

I knew he loved me and that we had settled into a comfortable pattern. Words weren't needed for us to express how we felt for each other.

But last night was so very different from tonight. Today, I had noisily lived that romance novel rather than just reading it quietly at the dinner table.

Tonight, words still weren't needed, but so much more was being said as we watched each other eat by the flicker of amber light coming from the fireplace. We alternated taking bites of Kung Pao chicken and smiling like we were making eyes at each other from across the cafeteria in junior high.

The television was off and there was not a smartphone or tablet to be seen.

There was nothing but the two of us sitting on the white faux tiger rug by the fire.

I had forgotten how much fun it was to sit and say nothing with this man.

How had we lost this?

I closed my eyes tightly.

I had to remind myself that Robert thought I was someone else. I felt like I was in an episode of The Twilight Zone, one where we lived in an alternate reality where we were still giddy in love. I was being shown what was missing from my life. I hadn't noticed it was gone because it had happened so slowly.

We had been exactly like this when we were dating and for a few years after we were married. But the transition to taking each other for granted had been gradual and unintentional.

Maybe I was partly to blame.

I had become sick and spent two months in the hospital right around my birthday last year. After coming home, Robert had treated me with kid gloves, like I would shatter at his very touch.

I should take some of the energy I showed tonight and prove

to him that I am stronger now.

I was not some fragile porcelain doll. I could dish it out as well as I could take it. And I had to admit it, I was enjoying myself. We had both dished it out with wild abandon.

I would take that back to my real life and rekindle the flame I knew was still there. After all, our rut had only developed after my stay in the hospital. My strength was back and we could return to a better life together. I just had to show him it was still there.

My birthday was coming up again. I would be turning twenty five and this time I felt much better than I did last year. That would be my birthday present to him. I would return what had been missing from our lives for the past year.

After dinner, we cuddled on the couch and talked about everything; and nothing. I made sure not to be too specific, but spoke in generalities. It wouldn't be good to let Robert find out that I wasn't his other Michele.

It felt strange talking about some of the same things that I knew Robert and I had discussed when we were dating.

It seemed that this relationship was still in the early stages. It felt like I had gone back in time to when my Robert and I were still dating.

Was all this really happening?

Or was I still lying by the side of the road hallucinating?

On the off chance that this was real, I had to maintain the charade until I could get away cleanly and return to my real life.

Chapter 10

I felt a presence beyond my closed eyelids right before lips touched mine.

My eyes fluttered open to see Robert, fully dressed, pulling away. He noticed me looking up at him.

"Oh, sorry. I didn't mean to wake you."

I yawned and sat up, stretching in the bright morning light and looked at him.

"You're back early. Wow, I had the strangest dream last night."

Robert sat on the edge of the bed and placed his hand on my thigh. I shuddered from his touch and opened my leg slightly to give him access should he want it.

He kept his hand in place and gave a light squeeze.

"The best thing about dreaming is that anything can happen."

I smiled at him.

"You're telling me. I dreamed that I saw myself jump off a bridge."

His look shifted instantly to one of concern and he leaned in closer, removing his hand from my thigh.

"You're not having suicidal thoughts again, are you?"

What did he mean, again?

"No," I said. "It was just a dream."

He placed the back of his hand against my forehead.

"You're a little warm."

I brushed his hand away a little too forcefully.

"I'm fine."

He sat up and pulled his phone out of his pocket.

"I should call the doctor and get an appointment for you."

I pulled the blankets up around my chin.

"I'm fine. I don't need a doctor."

He set the phone to his ear and looked at me like I was a child.

"Not that kind of doctor. I'm calling Dr. Westcott."

Every muscle in my body tensed.

Why was he calling her?

He spun away from me and began talking.

"This is Robert Black calling in for Michele. I'd like to set up an appointment with Dr. Westcott for today. I know this is not her regular day, but it's important."

He looked at me and then walked out into the hallway and spoke quietly, but I still heard him clearly.

"Tell Dr. Westcott that we have a code five."

He looked back at me while he waited for his message to be relayed. I was stunned into silence as we stared at each other. He saw the concern on my face.

"It's okay sweetie, everything's going to be fine."

He looked away from me quickly and spoke into the phone.

"Yes. Is that the earliest? Okay, fine. I will bring her in personally. I understand that, but I want to stay with her. No. No. I know what to do. Everything will be fine. No. I'm not jeopardizing anything, just clear your schedule for the rest of the day."

He thumbed his phone off and stuck it back in his pocket before pulling it back out again.

"I got you an appointment at noon. I'm going to go with you but I need to make a call to my boss and let him know I won't be in today."

From my angle on the bed, I watched him go out through the front door and close it behind him as he placed the phone to his ear.

A buzzing sound emanated from the metal radiator against the wall next to the bed.

Wait a minute. I didn't have a radiator next to my bed. I looked around me, confused for a brief moment right before my heart started beating faster in response to what my subconscious realized before I did.

I wasn't in my bed.

I wasn't in my room.

I wasn't in my house.

I was still in the other Michele's home.

And I had almost blown it.

The radiator buzzed again and my phone rumbled into view

next to one of the metal feet. That's where my phone had disappeared. I lunged out of the bed and reached for it, turning it right side up to see the screen.

Robert was calling me.

I slid my finger across the display and stuck the phone to my ear.

"Hello?" I said barely above a whisper.

"Hey Honey, it's me. Did I wake you?"

"No. Where are you?"

I pinched my eyes closed and scrunched my face up as soon as the words came out of my mouth. Between the two of us, I was not where I belonged.

"Sorry to call so early, but something came up at work and I'll need to stay an extra day."

My eyes popped open and I immediately looked down the hallway at the front door.

There was a moment of silence, and then, "I will be home tomorrow morning, first thing. I promise."

I played along like normal.

"Why can't you come home now?"

"This negotiation has become complicated and I need to stay to work it out. There's a big bonus attached to this contract. I almost have them nailed down and then we can afford that trip to Italy you've always wanted. I love you, Michele. You know that, right?"

"Yes," I replied, all the emotion stripped from my voice.

"You are my world, Michele. I'll be home soon, I promise. I have to go. I'll try to call you on my next break."

"Okay," I said quietly.

"I love you," he said and then waited for me to respond.

I hear the neighbor's dogs across the street bark a delayed half-second before I heard them again through the phone.

"I love you too," I said and the call disconnected with a faint beep.

Chapter 11

My dream was becoming a nightmare. I wanted to scream. I wanted to cry. I wanted to run down the street naked and let everyone see the real me.

Instead, I fell silent and let Robert direct the rest of the morning. The animal lover of last night had been replaced by a gentle caretaker.

He started my shower.

He toweled me off.

He selected my clothes and assisted me with getting dressed.

He even walked me to the car and belted me in as we made our way to the doctor.

He treated me like a helpless child without hesitation, just like at home.

When I dared look Robert in the eyes, I could see them filled with worry. He cared about her. That much was evident. He undertook his caretaker responsibilities without question. He seemed comfortable in his new role with Dead Michele, like he had done before with me.

But none of this answered the mass of questions swirling in my head.

First and foremost, why was he cheating on me?

Did it matter that it was someone who looked exactly like me?

Had this other woman undergone plastic surgery? Was her name even Michele Gardner or had Robert insisted she change it when he altered her face?

Why does she see the same psychiatrist as me?

Did she know about me?

Is that why she killed herself?

I shuddered at the thought that had crossed my mind unexpectedly and looked over at Robert with alarm.

He was focused on the road, honking at slower cars, crossing onto the shoulder of the road to go around them.

He looked like the same Robert I had met, fallen in love with, and married.

Nothing about him screamed "sick bastard."

But maybe that was what had made it possible for him to find some random woman and convince her to change her name; and her face.

But for what?

I thought about the money in her wallet.

From what the neighbor had said, and from everything Robert had said, he only came around once a week to have a fling with his mistress. It was the same day he was away from me on business every week.

Had he been doing this since I nearly died in the hospital last year? Was this some bizarre attempt of his to return to the relationship we had before I fell sick?

I finally found my voice.

"How long?"

He honked at another driver and swung onto the shoulder. He glanced at me for a brief moment before returning his eyes to the road and honking at another car.

"We're almost there."

"No. How long for us?"

"What?"

I wasn't ready to let him know who I really was. It was best to let him think I was his mistress.

"How long have we been together?"

"I don't know, a few months," he replied and swung out onto the shoulder again to go around a slow moving truck. He darted back onto the road just before the next bridge. A couple of seconds later and we would have gone into the river. I didn't know what his hurry was to get to a psychiatrist. It was not like I was bleeding out in the back seat.

"Has it been a year?"

He frowned and slowed down to match the speed of traffic and blared his horn at the stopped cars in front of him. I had never seen him behave like this... ever.

"You're right," he said and smiled over at me. He could pay me more attention now that he was dealing with sluggish traffic on the bridge. "Are you wanting to do something for our first anniversary?"

I looked outside. I had my answer and nothing more needed to be said.

Thankfully, he accepted my silence and drove us to the doctor's office without another word.

He parked in the spot nearest the stairs and helped me out of the car. I leaned on him, both to keep up the act that I was frail, and because I still wanted to be close to him despite everything I had learned.

I guess it could be considered flattering that your husband only wanted to cheat on you with yourself, but it was still super creepy. I would even hazard that it was to the level of serial killer creepy.

We had been together for four years, and I was only just discovering that he had a mistress in the same fucking town we lived in that he saw every week instead of flying out of town on business.

What more about him was there to learn?

Unfortunately, I was going to find out.

Chapter 12

Robert set me down in a chair in the waiting room where Dr. Westcott's rude receptionist could keep an eye on me while he went in to talk with the doctor first. I didn't know why he wanted to talk with her, but with the receptionist watching me, I couldn't sneak up to the door and listen in.

Instead, I sat there and glared at her. Her nose hooked forward and down like the beak of a hawk, so it was only fitting she regarded me like one watching a mouse. Her head even bobbed back and forth in bird-like motions.

She pretended to be interested in something on her computer while we sat in silence. I wasn't fooled. I knew I had her full attention.

After only a few minutes, the door to the office opened and I sat up as Robert came out. He smiled and crouched down in front of me.

"Are you doing okay?"

I nodded, still maintaining the illusion of being in a weakened and vulnerable state. It seemed to be what he was expecting, so I kept it up.

Dr. Westcott appeared at her door and looked down her nose at me, appraising me with her eyes.

"Please come in, Michele."

Robert nodded to me as he stood up.

I didn't turn around as I went into the office, but I was sure he watched me the whole time until the door closed behind me.

Dr. Westcott smiled and motioned to the chair in front of her massive mahogany desk.

"Please, have a seat and tell me about your dream."

I sat down and laughed nervously.

"It was just a stupid dream."

"Robert tells me that you committed suicide in your dream."

I shook my head. Of course, Robert had panicked and got it all wrong. Then again, it wasn't even a dream. It had actually happened.

"No. I saw someone else jump off the bridge, but she had my

face."

Dr. Westcott's brow wrinkled and she leaned forward to jot a note down on the open notebook in front of her. She set her pen down with a snap and leaned back.

"Tell me about this other person who looked like you. Did she speak to you?"

My pulse quickened as I thought about what the woman had said before she stepped backward off the bridge. She had asked me, "How many more?", but I wasn't about to tell that to the shrink.

I shook my head again.

"It happened too fast. I saw someone standing on the edge of the bridge, and when I got close enough to see she looked like me, it was too late. She jumped."

Westcott nodded.

"You mean you jumped."

It was better to agree with this doctor. I had spent one day a week for the past four years with this woman. I knew her better than she knew me.

"I guess you can say it was me."

Westcott flipped through her notebook and made a couple of notes before removing her reading glasses and leaning back comfortably in her chair.

"Good. Now have you been experiencing any dizziness or muscle weakness since we last met?"

This time I was able to speak the truth.

"No. I feel fine."

"Good. And you are taking the medication like I prescribed?"

"Like clockwork."

Dr. Westcott sat up suddenly, her eyes flashing a startled look at me that I didn't understand.

"What?" she asked sharply.

I stammered my response, not sure what had just happened.

"I... I'm taking them every day."

Westcott's eyes became slits as she regarded me closely. It was more scrutiny than I wanted to be subjected to while pretending to be a dead woman.

I looked around the room and back to the doctor who was furiously scribbling in her notebook.

Had I said something that the other woman never said? Did I just expose myself to the one person who was trained to spot the difference?

She finished writing and held the pen tight enough in her grip to force the blood from her knuckles.

"Have you missed any sessions with me in the past few months?"

What was she driving at?

"I don't think so."

"Can you remember what we discussed at our session on Monday?"

She knew and was fishing for proof of what she had just guessed.

How was I going to convince someone who logged down every little detail of our time together in her notebook; documented everything I did and said like she was studying me for a science project?

In a flash, I saw the picture on the mantle at the dead woman's house that repeated Robert and I's vacation in Florida. If this other woman was repeating my life, for reasons unknown, then maybe the doctor was talking about the same things with her.

My mind reeled as I thought back to one of my early sessions with Dr. Westcott.

There was one driving point that she never failed to discuss during the first year we were together. She held onto it like a bulldog with a new bone. If Dead Michele was repeating my life, this was my one chance to protect my false identity.

I mustered up all the courage I could to look Westcott directly in the eyes.

"It's the same thing we talk about every week. I still can't remember anything before the accident and I don't think the medication is working."

Westcott visibly relaxed and wrote a quick note in her book.

Had I passed her impromptu test?

Did it matter even if I did?

I might have allayed her suspicions temporarily, but she would keep digging given the chance. I had already done something to alert her to my charade and I decided I wouldn't give her that chance again.

I had to distract her, and from what Robert had mentioned earlier that morning, I knew exactly what to say. While I never had expressed my feelings with Westcott during any of our sessions over the years, I knew what the other Michele was feeling if she truly was replaying my life.

"Last night was not the first time I had the dream about jumping from a bridge."

Westcott stopped writing and looked over the rims of her glasses at me.

"You haven't mentioned this before."

"It was just a dream. I thought we were here to talk about my real life."

"Then why tell me about it now?"

"This time it felt so real. And when I woke up, I wished I was the one who had jumped."

"Do you know why?"

"The new medication. It makes me feel drowsy."

"You've been on it for months now."

"I started having the dream soon after starting the new pills."

"I've already adjusted your dosage and switched to a more selective brand because of your earlier complaints."

"It's not working. I've been having the bridge dream nearly every night for the past couple of months."

It was becoming easier to lie.

Westcott removed her glasses with the same hand that still clung to her pen and let out an exasperated breath.

"I guess I can see if there is something else I can do."

I let my shoulders drop in an attempt to show that I was relieved she was listening to my concerns like a good doctor should.

She pointed at me with her glasses.

"In the meantime, I want you to keep taking the medication

exactly as I prescribed until I can find a suitable alternative."

I nodded vigorously.

"Of course," I lied again.

I had stopped taking the medications this woman had prescribed to me after spending two months in the hospital without them. Despite almost dying in that hospital, I had felt better than ever once I was released.

The hospital was like a rehab center for me, forcing me to stop everything cold turkey, although not by choice.

Robert and I were on vacation in Florida. It was the second time we had visited and we even took pictures of the area being cleared to rebuild the lifeguard station that had burned down years before.

When I collapsed during dinner at a restaurant, I had been rushed to the nearest hospital where they immediately connected me to every machine they had.

Despite Robert's insistence, the head doctor refused to let me be relocated to our hospital in Pittsburgh. He said that I might not survive the night, and that my death would be assured if they disconnected and moved me.

I did survive that night, and every night for the next two weeks until they woke me up from the medically induced coma. Slowly I recovered and was able to come off the machines after only a month.

By the end of the second month, I was released and allowed to come back home. But ever since then, Robert had treated me with kid gloves; and I didn't blame him. I had almost died. But once I was released, I had never felt better.

Being off the medications I had taken since the car accident had improved my mood, my health, and my mind. Coming out of the hospital was like a rebirth. The world was more colorful and clear than I had ever remembered.

The same day we came home, I started dumping the meds down the toilet to keep anyone, even Robert who laid the pills on my nightstand by our shared bed every evening, from knowing that I had stopped taking everything. I promised myself that if I started to have problems, I could always start taking them again.

Every day I dumped the medication down the plumbing. And every day I felt a little stronger and was becoming whole again. I was no longer getting tired and falling asleep before the end of every movie.

I hadn't recovered my memories from before the accident, but I no longer felt like I was wasting away. I had proven to myself that I didn't need the medication.

It was the only lie in our marriage.

Or at least, the only lie I had brought into our marriage.

Robert had many more lies surrounding our lives. They swirled around in my head while I listened to Dr. Westcott, but did not hear a thing she said.

How could Robert lie to me like that?

He called me from the front yard of his whore's house and lied to me without giving it a second thought. It had come so naturally for him, how long had he been lying to me?

Our short life together played through my mind like a movie on fast forward only to be interrupted.

"Michele?"

I blinked and looked at the puzzled face of Dr. Westcott.

She leaned forward, her elbows resting on her expansive desk.

"Have you been listening to me, Michele?"

"Sorry. It's this medication you have me on. My mind wanders too easily."

She frowned.

"It shouldn't be affecting you like that."

I sat up straight, adopting a defensive posture.

"Well, it is!"

Her eyebrows shot up in surprise and then she scribbled in her notebook again.

She removed her glasses and placed them on the desk.

"I will get a new prescription that is better for you by the end of the week, but I mean it when I tell you to keep taking them every day until I get it changed. Do you understand? Stopping them will be far worse for you."

I nodded silently.

She squinted at me.

"Say it."

I took a quick breath to steady my nerves.

"I will keep taking the meds."

"Because…"

"Because you know best."

"And…"

"And you have my best interests at heart."

"I'm not the only one. Robert loves you and wants you to get better. We have to work together to make that happen. That means you have to work with us. Is that clear?"

"Yes, ma'am."

She smiled and then, as if remembering something important, looked at her watch.

"I'm afraid I have another appointment and our time is up."

I stood up and Westcott came around the desk and placed her hand on my arm.

"I promise that the new medication will stop your nightmares. Do you believe me?"

"I do," I said.

I didn't.

Chapter 13

Robert stood as I came out to the waiting room. He and Dr. Westcott exchanged a look and then he guided me to a chair.

"I just need to speak with the doctor for a minute. Then I can take you home."

I watched the door to her office close behind him leaving me with hawk face. While I sat there, I avoided making eye contact with her. I didn't want to give her the chance to figure out I was here pretending to be someone else.

Even if that someone else had been pretending to be me.

The door finally opened and Robert came out. Without a word, he collected me and we left the office quickly, taking a back stairwell down to the ground floor rather than the elevator.

Robert was not as frantic on the drive back as he had been when driving me to the doctor's office. He only leaned on his horn once when a delivery truck changed lanes unexpectedly. The driver even returned a one-finger salute, but Robert ignored him and turned off the freeway well ahead of our normal exit.

Oh, right. We weren't going back to our real home. We were headed to Dead Michele's house.

I watched him as he drove.

How many more lies were inside that head of his? Would I be able to get through them all to find the truth?

I was lost in thought when he pulled halfway in to the driveway and cursed.

There was another car blocking him.

He backed out and pulled along the curb.

Who had parked in Michele's driveway?

I was about to find out.

The front door to the house opened and a young black woman, with a frizzy afro twice the size of her head, peeked out. I recognized her from the pictures in the house. This had to be the roommate.

She saw me, flung the door open all the way, and ran toward me. Robert quickly got out and met her on my side of the car.

"Simone, wait."

She looked at Robert.

"I stopped by on my way to work and neither of you were here and her room looked like it had been tossed."

"She had a bad dream and I took her to see her doctor, that's all."

She leaned around Robert to look at me.

"Is she okay?"

"She's fine now. We just need to adjust her medication again."

The young woman put her hands on her hips.

"That shit's gonna kill her."

"It's what's keeping her alive."

"You don't know that."

"She's been through…"

Simone cut him off.

"You've told me all this before. She suffered a major head trauma, can't remember her bad self, blah, blah, blah. There are better ways to help her than pump her full of chemicals."

"That's why I took her to see the doctor."

Simone darted around Robert and opened the car door.

"Come on Michele. What you need is some herbal tea and rest."

She helped me out of the car.

Robert moved in and reached for me. Simone nudged him away with a flick of her hips.

"I think you've done enough Robert. Let her roommate take over."

Robert looked ready to challenge her when his eyes softened and he stepped back.

"I have to go… to work."

His irregular pause did not go unnoticed by me. I knew where he would be headed, and it wasn't work. He wasn't supposed to be coming home, to our real home, until tomorrow morning. But with the danger over, and Simone taking over as my caretaker, I could tell he was planning to go there now and surprise me.

I had to get there before him somehow.

Simone guided me into the house and waved at Robert, dismissing him like the Queen of England dismissing one of her royal subjects, right before she closed the front door. She made it clear by her actions that his day at their house was over and he was no longer needed.

She set me down at the small dining room table and then looked through the cupboards, pulling down various boxes of tea.

As she filled the teapot, she glanced over her shoulder at me.

"Is Robert treating you okay?"

I looked at this stranger who behaved like my sister.

"He treats me just fine."

"You can tell me anything, especially all the delicious parts. I love the delicious parts."

"There's nothing to tell," I lied.

She finished filling the teapot and placed it on the stove, twisting the knob. She waited with her hand on the knob while the sparks ticked repeatedly until the flame burst to life under the pot.

She set the burner to high and faced me, leaning back against the edge of the stove.

"If you can't be honest with me, who can you be honest with?"

Now that was a good question.

Unfortunately, I didn't have time to ponder this, or any other good questions; and there were plenty of good questions bouncing around in my head right now.

Robert was heading back home and I had to be there. I wasn't ready to explain to him where I had been. Especially since I had been with him. I didn't fully understand it myself, and knew I could never find the right words to demand the truth from him yet.

I wasn't sure if I was ready for the truth but, ready or not, he was on his way home.

I had to see how he would behave once he was back home.

Our home.

Our real home.

I looked up at Simone.

"He asked me to go away with him."

Simone couldn't hide the shock on her face.

"Who? Robert?

I bobbed my head up and down, confirming her question.

"When?"

"Today," was what popped out of my mouth.

She glared at me.

"Shit. Fucking up your life once a week not good enough for that asshole?"

I stood up.

"It's not like that."

"Oh, sure. You're in love, and all that."

"We are."

"Honey, I've heard it all before. And from better men than that forty-something pervert who comes over to boff you once a week. He probably has a slut in every major city up and down the coast."

Her face suddenly softened as she realized what she had just said.

"Sorry. No offense. I meant all those other women are sluts. Not you, of course."

"Robert's not like that."

Simone stepped forward.

"You're suffering from Stockholm Syndrome, Sweetie. You don't have to defend that bastard with me. I know what he wants."

Simone looked around the room. I hadn't had time to clean up after our amorous evening before he had rushed me out of the house.

She looked back at me as if she had just smelled something disgusting.

"And so do you, if you'd only just admit it. Stop lying to yourself and you will be much better off. Believe me. I've been right where you are now."

I doubted that.

Behind her, the teapot whistle started low and quiet before quickly building in pitch and volume.

As she turned around to tend to the pot, I took the opportunity to dash back to my room and gather enough clothes to keep up the charade I was going on a short vacation.

As I tossed random clothes onto the bed, Simone appeared at the door.

"How long this time?"

I looked at her, my brain in overdrive.

How long should it be? I knew she would expect me back once the time was up. But her Michele was never coming back. I had to give myself enough time to figure out what was going on before the world discovered Michele Gardner's disappearance, starting with Simone.

"A week," I replied. "I'll call you with the details."

I guess I was planning to come back here next Wednesday, since Robert had no idea I was supposed to be with him all week, even though I would be. But it would be as his wife and not as his mistress.

I doubted I could keep this up for very long, but I had been backed into a corner and had to say something to give myself time to figure out what was really going on.

Since I didn't know where this Michele kept her luggage, I pulled up the edges of the bedspread and wrapped it around the small pile of clothes. I guess, my next trick would be to shove a stick through the knot and hop an open railcar on a passing train.

Simone gave me a withered look.

"Fine, you can borrow my luggage. All you had to do was ask. You don't have to be so dramatic."

She walked into her room and returned with an empty suitcase.

"If you plan to travel more often with that old fart, you might want to hit him up for your own set of luggage."

I stuffed clothes I was not going to wear into the suitcase, along with the wallet that was sitting in plain sight to keep Simone from getting suspicious, and shut it. I hefted it off the edge of the bed and looked at the girl who would not have been treating me so well if she knew the truth.

"Thank you. For everything."

Simone made another face.

"You act like you're never coming back."

A sly smile spread across her face.

"You're not running off and getting hitched, are you?"

How could I tell her that I had already done that years ago?

Instead, I shook my head.

"Of course not, he's twice my age. But can't a girl have a little fun before she settles down."

Simone's mouth finally turned up at the edges in a wider smile.

"You are a cheeky one. Don't get pregnant."

A wave of memories flooded me unexpectedly. Robert and I had more than our share of close calls in the heat of passion, but not once had I gotten pregnant. I originally thought we were lucky, but in light of this new state of affairs, affairs in more than one way, I wasn't so sure.

Simone snapped her fingers in front of my face.

"Hey. Hey. Where'd you go?"

I blinked and returned back to the present. I smiled warmly to disarm Simone and keep her from pressing me further.

"We should be back next week. Can you keep your hotel reservation for Wednesday, just in case we aren't done with our vacation, so to speak?"

Simone rolled her eyes.

"When I agreed to the lower rent, I didn't think it was because I was going to be spending the difference on hotels every week."

"You won't find a cheaper price anywhere in town." I was taking a risk that this discount was significant enough to more than offset the hotel charges.

Simone let out long sigh.

"You're right. I guess I can put up with it for a while longer. Besides, I have the whole house to myself the rest of this week, don't I?"

"And part of next week. Feel free to throw a week-long party for all your friends."

What did I care? This really wasn't my house and I wasn't coming back. I was going to have it out with Robert and he wouldn't be coming here next Wednesday after I was through with him.

I dragged the suitcase toward the front door, Simone tagging along right behind.

"What friends?" she asked. "I just moved here six months ago."

"What about the guy across the street?"

Her face scrunched up again as if the invisible putrid smell invaded her nostrils again.

"You mean Hubert? It's bad enough he's always watching us from across the street. No way in hell am I inviting him over here."

I opened the front door and turned back.

"Oh, I almost forgot. He needs you to feed his dogs this weekend."

"I sent him to you."

"And I won't be here."

Her eyes rolled up into her head again and her mouth turned downward.

"You're a bitch. You know that don't you?"

I smiled.

"Thanks Simone. I really mean that."

I hurried down the front path and out of sight. I ditched the suitcase into the bushes around the corner and pulled out my phone to call for a taxi.

If I was lucky, I would make it home before Robert. For some reason, I knew I wouldn't be so lucky.

Chapter 14

As the taxi pulled up in front of my house, I could see a light on upstairs that I hadn't left on. The driver popped the trunk before he climbed out.

I met him at the back of the taxi and pulled grocery bags out of the trunk. I made sure to only buy enough that I could carry on my own.

The driver held the second bag and we swapped his payment for the bag.

He tipped his hat and returned to the taxi.

I waited until he drove off before walking up to the front door. As I struggled with the keys, the door opened inward with a rush of wind.

I tried to look startled, like I hadn't been expecting him.

Robert looked at me like I had returned from the dead.

"Where have you been?" he snapped.

I held the grocery bags up.

"Where do you think?" I snapped back.

He took one of the bags from me.

"Why haven't you been answering your phone?"

I looked at him, trying to put on my confused face.

"Were you calling me?"

I took my phone out with one hand and looked at it. I had heard the phone ring on every one of the twelve missed calls. But before coming home, I had shut off the ringer.

I showed him the screen on my phone.

"I guess the ringer was off."

"Why'd you go shopping anyway? I thought you hated having to spend money on a taxi just for grocery shopping. You usually wait for me."

"You weren't going to be home until tomorrow."

His look softened and he turned away from me to take his bag into the kitchen.

"They signed one hour after I called you, so I caught the next flight home. I wanted to surprise you."

I followed him into the house and set my bag down next to

his on the counter.

I placed my arms around him.

"Well, this is the kind of surprises I like."

I moved in for a kiss and he pulled away quickly, turning his attention to the bags.

"Is there anything perishable?"

"Just the milk."

He reached for one of the bags, but I beat him to it and yanked the milk out.

"I'm not an invalid. I can handle it."

I opened the fridge and stuck the new carton of milk way in the back behind the orange juice. I didn't want him to see that I had two other cartons of milk already in there.

He started to remove other items and place them on the counter.

I placed a hand on his.

"I can take care of this. You must be tired from your flight along with the time change. Why don't you go rest?"

He left his hand under mine and looked deeply into my eyes. There was a sadness there for a brief moment before he turned away.

"You're right. I didn't sleep well last night."

I knew all too well why he hadn't slept last night. I had seen a fire in him that I thought had burned out long ago.

After he disappeared upstairs, I finished putting away the groceries, stuffing them into places they wouldn't fit since we hadn't needed them, but I needed a cover as to why I wasn't home when he arrived.

I looked around. The dishes were still in the sink from two nights before. I hadn't expected to spend last night away from home. I was just going to return the other Michele's purse and come straight back.

It hadn't turned out that way.

It was time to see if that fire still burned as brightly in this house as it had in the other Michele's house.

I crept upstairs and thought I heard Robert's voice. Was he talking to someone?

I stepped over the creaky step to avoid telegraphing that I was almost at the top of the stairs and slunk to the closed bedroom door. I pressed my ear against the hollow wood and strained to hear what he was saying.

"No. She was shopping. No. I don't think that... What was I supposed to do? No. I won't do that. No. I'm not going to leave her..."

I stumbled backward from the door.

Leave me?

Was he talking to the other Michele?

No. That wasn't possible.

I saw her jump.

If not her, then who was he talking to?

I moved back toward the door only to have it open suddenly and Robert and I both yelled out in surprise.

Robert recovered quicker than I did.

"Michele. What are you doing?"

"I was just coming up to spend some quality time with you. You're home early and I want to take advantage of that."

I smiled slyly at him.

"I want to take advantage of you."

He looked around him, as if I had just propositioned him in public. His eyes lingered on the picture hanging in the hall before they snapped to me.

He moved forward, all his apprehension gone as his smile spread to his eyes and he snatched me up in his strong arms.

"Now that sounds like a plan."

He spun me around and carried me into the bedroom. Setting me down gently on the bed, he leaned in and kissed me. It was the same depth of passion that I had experienced with him last night.

He slipped his warm hands under my clothes and met me skin to skin.

We shed our clothes off and soon we were entwined with each other.

I could feel his passion building, and then he would ease up, his hesitation spreading to other parts of him. His body responded to his reluctance to treat me that same he had the night before.

I bucked against him, bringing his hardness back and clung to him, wordlessly enticing him to release inside me. In that moment I decided that we had been married long enough.

It was time to build our family so that he didn't need to go looking anywhere else for what was missing from ours.

I was not worried about the other woman in his life. I knew she was gone forever. I knew that he still had it in him to treat me like a lover first and a wife second.

I could feel him building up, his thrusts getting faster and stronger.

"Yes. Right there." I whispered into his ear, letting him know I was as ready as he was.

Suddenly, he pressed into me and I felt him shudder with release.

We were both breathing heavily as he slid sideways and flopped onto his back, panting for air. I rolled over and placed a hand on his chest, leaning forward to kiss him deeply.

He looked at me.

"Where did that come from?"

"It's always been there. You just had to be reminded."

As the blood returned to his head, he looked at me in alarm.

"Uh oh," he said.

I smiled and stroked his chest hair.

"It's okay. It's time we start."

He sat up suddenly and looked at me.

"We can't."

I sat up on one elbow.

"What? I thought that's what you wanted?"

"It is. It's just that…"

He tossed the covers aside and stepped out of bed in a single motion.

"I have to get to the office."

I sat up, pulling the sheets up to my chin.

"Right now? You just got back."

He opened his dresser and pulled out a pair of boxer briefs

and pulled them on.

"I'm sorry, Honey. I promised my boss that I would give him an early debrief on the contract negotiations, since there was trouble."

He was lying to me again.

Was he fantasizing about being with the other woman? Was that why he had just made love to me like we used to before I went to the hospital?

I had to prove to him that I was still strong. I was still vibrant and could be the woman he wanted me to be. He didn't have to try to recreate me with someone else.

I was right here.

He finished dressing and dropped down to the bed and gave me a quick peck on the cheek.

"Please don't think I didn't enjoy that. I did, really. But I promised my boss…"

I grabbed his head in my hands and pulled him down for a full kiss.

He let it linger longer before pulling away.

"I just have to go in and do this one thing. I'll come home early tonight, I promise."

I gazed into his eyes, still holding his head in my hands and then kissed him even more deeply. I pulled away, not releasing his face.

"Was that as strong as a promise to your boss?"

He smiled.

"Stronger."

We kissed again and then he left the house as if it were on fire.

I stayed in bed until I heard the garage door rattle closed.

I flung the sheets off and dressed quickly.

As I stepped from the bedroom, I paused and looked at the picture Robert had been looking at. I went to remove the picture and found it stuck to the wall. It wasn't just hanging by a wire on a nail. It was glued to the wall.

I dug my fingers into the edge of the frame and tried to pry it loose but it wouldn't budge. I thought about getting the hammer and using that to rip the picture off the wall, but how would I explain why I did that to Robert. I guess it depended on what I found behind the picture.

I went around to the other pictures in the house. They were all glued to the walls. Why the hell were they glued to the walls? Was this normal?

Robert had hired an interior decorator before we moved in. Maybe picture frames glued to the wall was the latest trend. I hadn't noticed it in anyone else's house, but then again, when was the last time I had tried to pry pictures from the walls of other people's homes?

Hell, when was the last time I had ventured into someone else's home in the past year? Robert had been so careful with me after my hospitalization, like I would get every disease known to man if I went anywhere but the grocery store, the drug store, and my shrink's office.

I hadn't realized I was under house arrest, but now that I thought about it, I was.

Maybe Robert hadn't been looking at the picture upstairs as much as he was trying to delay making eye contact with me?

And he had plenty to feel guilty about.

Chapter 15

After Robert had returned home from "work" I had his dinner hot and ready like the good wife attending to his needs.

We made love again that night, but this time he had been slow and careful, despite my attempts to draw out the animal I knew was in there.

Our lives quickly fell back into the rut and the next week went the same as always.

Within a day of his return we were back to our silent meals; he with his iPad and me with my Kindle. He was pulling away this time even further.

I wanted to confront him about the other woman, but it never seemed the right time.

As it got closer to Wednesday, when he would be leaving on his supposed weekly business trip, he grew more and more distant, as if his mind were elsewhere.

I knew exactly where his mind was.

It was with her.

The other me.

I decided I would become that other woman for one more night before telling him I knew about everything.

Tuesday night was the last night we had together as husband and wife before he would go to her and let his animal out of its cage.

I was already in bed when he came into our bedroom. He went straight to the bathroom to brush his teeth.

He came back out and I watched him strip down to nothing. Except for my T-Shirt, we both slept in the buff.

When he switched off the light and climbed in bed next to me, he rolled to one side and faced away from me.

I scooted closer and reached down to stroke him. He was limp in my hand and twisted his hips to pull away from me.

"Not tonight, honey. I have to meet with those same guys as last week. They pulled back on the contract and I need to convince them to return to the negotiating table."

I leaned into him and nuzzled his ear.

"I'll do all the work."

He rolled over and faced me.

"I love you, but I'm just not feeling it tonight. My mind's too distracted with the mess at work."

I knew he was lying to me.

He was worried about her.

If he only knew.

Finding out she had killed herself would tear him apart. I knew how he would feel if I had killed myself.

But how could he feel the same about her as he did about me? Why had he distanced himself from me only to redirect his feelings to my double?

And how had he convinced her to become someone else?

None of it made any sense.

He rolled away from me and I lied perfectly still on my back, unable to sleep. I was listening to his breathing and could tell the moment he fell asleep from his steady shallow breathing.

I knew every little intimate thing about this man, yet at the same time, I knew absolutely nothing about him.

Chapter 16

I woke before Robert and prepared breakfast. As he came down the hall fully dressed, his luggage in tow, he spotted the dining room table set with a country style breakfast spread complete with eggs, pancakes, two kinds of potatoes, sourdough toast, and crispy bacon; just the way he liked it.

His puzzled expression met my smile.

"What is all this?"

I approached and wrapped my arms around his waist and looked up into his deep brown eyes.

"Just my way of letting you know that, no matter what happens at work today, I am here for you. I will always be here for you."

He looked down at me, his puzzled expression more pronounced.

For some reason, finding out my husband was cheating on me should have made me want to leave him. But the circumstances around how I found out kept me from blaming him until I could figure out exactly what was going on.

The mystery was too enticing to make snap judgments. Besides, I had thoroughly enjoyed my time with Robert last Wednesday, and after a few days of benign neglect, I was starved for his undivided attention.

He reached around me, selected a piece of toast, and gave me a quick kiss before grabbing the handle of his luggage and heading for the front door.

"That's a beautiful breakfast, sweetheart, but I'm late for my flight. Please don't think I'm rude for not being able to stay and eat it with you."

I pasted on my warmest smile.

"I was hoping you had more time."

He scanned the steaming dishes before returning my gaze.

"I wish I did. It looks great."

"While this piping hot breakfast might not be here for you when you get back, know that I will always be here for you."

His forehead furrowed and his eyes darted toward a picture

on the wall for the briefest of moments. If I had not already been suspicious of his actions, and paying attention to where he was looking, I would have missed it.

He turned away from me quickly and opened the front door.

"Am I the only woman for you?" I said.

He paused with his hand on the door and slowly turned. He was inspecting my face with scrutinizing eyes.

"Why would you ask such a thing?"

"I have the same insecurities of any woman. I want you to tell me that I am the only woman for you."

He let go of the suitcase handle and crossed the space between us in two large strides.

He wrapped his powerful arms around me and held me tightly. I leaned into his embrace, taking in his scent.

"There is no one else for me. There never has been and there never will be."

"Then stay with me," I said with my head still leaning against in his chest. "Forget about the job. Forget about the business trip."

I felt his muscles tense.

"I can't," he answered softly.

"Just this once."

He held me tighter.

"I want to, but…"

"But what?"

He held me out at arm's length and looked directly into my soul with his gorgeous coffee-brown eyes; no cream, extra sugar.

"Tell you what. Let me talk to my boss and see if I can get a couple of weeks off from having to travel on business. If I ask nicely, I might even be able to get as early as next week off."

"What about starting right now?"

"There is no one else who knows those guys like I do."

He was lying to me again.

"Tell me again I'm the only woman for you."

"You are the only woman for me."

I didn't feel like he was lying when he told me I was the only one for him. But how was that possible? He had someone else on the side. Someone whose bed he traveled to every week.

Had he started to believe that by changing this other woman's name and face that he had found a loophole in the system? Did he not consider what he was doing every damn week cheating on me?

"Am I the only man for you?" he asked, catching me by surprise.

I smiled quickly.

"There could be no one else."

He gave my shoulders a squeeze and grabbed his suitcase.

"I will call you this afternoon at the usual time. And I want you to promise to keep your appointment with the doctor this morning. Don't skip like you did last week."

With everything churning around my head, I had actually forgotten all about my meeting with Dr. Westcott. She hadn't forgotten, and neither had her hawk-nosed receptionist who had called several times during the past week to verify that I would not be missing another scheduled appointment.

Robert squinted one eye at me.

"I know that look. Promise me you'll see her."

As much as I wanted to, I couldn't lie to Robert as easily as he could lie to me, so I told him the truth.

"I promise. I'll go."

At least it was the truth at that moment.

Chapter 17

I dumped the entire breakfast down the disposal and ran the water as it was ground to a fine paste and delivered into the sewers that ran below the city.

It was probably the best breakfast the City of Bridges had ever had.

I couldn't shake the feeling that, even though Robert had left in his car half an hour before, I wasn't alone.

I replayed our conversation several times in my head and kept focusing on that one action of his that seemed out of place.

It hadn't been my imagination.

I had seen him do the same thing before.

He had looked at the picture hanging on the wall, like he was looking to it for approval.

Was there someone watching from behind the picture? I didn't mean a full human person, but maybe a camera that was transmitting video to someone else.

And did Robert know they were watching.

If there were cameras hidden behind our pictures, why were they there?

I shook my head. I couldn't even begin to think about that. I had to first find out if there were cameras before I even started to contemplate a reason for them being there.

As I stood at the sink, scraping food off each plate, I looked at the window that led into our backyard. But I wasn't looking through the window. I was looking at its reflection of the room behind me.

I stared hard at the picture mounted on the living room wall. I had already discovered a few days before that it was glued to the wall. If I wanted to find out what was behind it, I would have to pry it off the wall.

I wouldn't be able to hide my actions. I had to be sure that I was committed to taking such drastic measures, because if I found nothing I would have to come up with a plausible reason for the destruction that would surely accompany what I planned to do.

When the last plate of food was fed into the bottomless belly of the sewer beast, I shut off the water and stopped the grinder.

It was now or never.

I slid along the counter, keeping my back to the picture. If someone was watching, I didn't want them to know what I was up to until I knew for sure that I was committed.

I opened the junk drawer at the end of the counter and pulled out a hammer. The claw on the back of the head was excellent at prying nails out of wood. I hoped it was just as good at prying glued picture frames off of walls.

I tucked the hammer into my pants and pulled my sweater over the top of it, hiding it from view. I turned back around and walked purposefully out of the kitchen and through the living room. I walked past the picture without giving it a second glance.

I was looking to see where all the pictures in my house were placed. To my dismay, I discovered that most of them were in view of other picture frames.

If there was a camera behind each one, my house had better coverage than the one on the reality show Big Brother. More importantly, I wouldn't be able to sneak up on a picture from the side without being spotted by another camera across the room.

I suddenly remembered the picture at the top of the stairs. I climbed the steps slowly, my hand running along the banister, and observed the angles and placement of every picture frame from where I was at any given moment.

The picture frame at the top of the stairs was more isolated than any of the rest. If I shut the doors to the bedrooms, the hallway picture was far enough from the stairs that it was not fully visible by any of the pictures in the living room; or the front hallway.

This was the one.

It was also the first one I had noticed Robert look to when I had surprised him with a suggestive proposition in the hallway of our home.

I went to the bedroom and shut the door. I then went to the other bedroom and the upstairs bathroom, and shut those doors. There was a small picture above the toilet, so it never paid to be too careful.

With the hallway picture separated from the herd, it was time to move in for the kill. I pulled out the hammer and crept along the wall, being careful to stay well out of sight of the stairs and the pictures below.

I wedged the buck teeth of the hammer into the bottom edge of the picture frame and pushed down on the handle like a mad scientist throwing the switch to bring his monster to life.

The picture frame splintered right before the hammer popped out and fell to the floor.

I picked it up quickly and stuck it in again and began working away the edge of the frame until I had a good half inch gap all along the bottom.

I dropped the hammer and tucked my fingers into the space between the frame and the wall.

I stuck my foot on the wall and pulled on the frame.

It came off the wall easier than I had expected and I fell backward as the frame broke in half, ripping the picture straight up the middle in the process.

I landed hard on my ass, half of the shattered frame still in my grasp.

I looked up and my mouth fell open in disbelief. I shouldn't have been surprised. It was the whole reason I had taken an implement of destruction to the painting, but there it was.

Laughing at my naiveté.

A thin red wire snaked out of a hole in the wall and led to the edge of the torn picture.

I stood up and grabbed the ragged edge of the canvas and pulled it away, exposing the polished surface of a tiny camera lens.

Chapter 18

The next hour went by in a whirlwind blur. I had grabbed my cell and ran out of the house with no real destination in mind.

When I finally stopped running, I found myself standing at the same bridge as the week before.

The one the other Michele had used to end her life; and mine.

She would never know it, but that woman had taken my life with her over the edge of the bridge.

I stood facing out over the river and closed my eyes while my mind replayed the event as if it was happening in real time.

I remembered my shock when I was close enough to recognize that she looked exactly like me. But there was no surprise on her face when she looked at me, like she didn't find it unusual to see her perfect double standing in front of her.

Since that time, I had attributed her lack of amazement to the knowledge that Robert had changed her appearance to match mine.

But then, what she said still didn't make sense. I focused on that moment in time and listened again to the only words she spoke to me. I heard them clearly as if she were still standing on the ledge.

"How many more?"

I opened my eyes again and watched the river slither away at a constant pace from where I stood.

How many more of what?

I thought about the cameras in my house. Robert had to have known about them. It was his unconscious actions that led me right to them.

Why were they there?

Had this other Michele discovered cameras in her house too?

Is that why she killed herself? She had discovered that she was being watched.

Maybe she wanted to know how many were watching. Were there cameras at the doctor's office, the stores she visited, or the restaurants she frequented?

I had found cameras behind one picture. I didn't doubt there were ones behind every picture, and now I had the same question she did.

How many more were there?

Was I being watched everywhere?

Was there any place I could go to escape the prying eyes of unknown watchers?

And who else was being watched?

I knew then where I had to go and who I had to warn.

Chapter 19

I stood alongside the fence at the corner half a block away from Simone's house where her car sat in the driveway.

Last week, I had come to the house in the late afternoon, so I never saw when she usually left. Maybe her being home at this hour was normal.

Still, I had no way of knowing for sure.

Despite who Simone had thought I was last week, in reality I was a complete stranger. The only thing I knew was that she was expecting me back today. I had told her that much when I had rushed from the house, suitcase in hand.

The suitcase!

I couldn't come back without it.

I stepped away from the fence, keeping my profile turned away from the house in case she, or the nosy neighbor, were looking this way.

I walked the couple of blocks to the thicket I had stashed the suitcase. I glanced around to ensure I was alone before pulling the dense bushes apart and peering inside.

The suitcase was gone.

I stepped back and looked up and down the block. This was where I had left the suitcase. It was exactly as I remembered it. I had left everything in these bushes, fully out of sight.

I pulled apart another section of shrubbery and glanced at the empty space.

Well, not entirely empty.

There were broken beer bottles and torn potato chip bags littering the ground in the natural space below the stand of thick bushes.

My heart sank.

I had ditched the suitcase in the local underage drinking hideout.

I should have been paying more attention, but I was blinded by my haste to get home before Robert.

Oh well, there was nothing I could do about it now. I would just have to come up with some plausible reason as to why I didn't have Simone's suitcase; or my keys to the house.

Whatever excuse I invented, I prayed Simone would accept it without asking too many questions.

I still had to warn her about the cameras that were no doubt cataloging her intimate and private actions.

As I turned the corner of the block, and Simone's house came into view, I stopped short in my tracks.

Whoever was watching those cameras must have noticed the other Michele's disappearance. They certainly wouldn't let an entire week go by without doing something to find her.

I made a mental note to ask Simone if anyone had stopped by in the past week to ask about me.

I glanced across the street and relaxed when I noticed that the neighbor who had asked me to watch his dogs was not home. His car was not in the driveway and I remembered seeing his garage door opened last week. The space inside was filled to capacity with boxes and junk.

If his car was not visible, it stood to reason that he was gone as well.

I hurried down the street and walked up the front path to the front door.

I racked my brain for the excuse I knew I needed for why I was ringing the doorbell instead of using my keys to let myself in.

I suddenly realized the irony of my situation. Simone being home meant I could actually get inside the house. With the suitcase missing, along with the other Michele's belongings, I had no other way in.

I finally settled on what I would say and pressed my finger against the dimly lit button next to the door.

As I heard the sound of muted bells chiming inside in response, I had no idea I would never be given the chance to lie to Simone.

Chapter 20

Standing on the front porch, I took a deep breath and let it out slowly, calming my nerves.

Through the frosted glass next to the door, I could see her dark shape coming from the living room to answer.

She opened it and looked at me. Her eyes were puffy and red, as if she had been crying.

My heart broke.

Simone was already crying over something and here I was about to give her some lie about how I lost her suitcase.

"Look Simone, I…"

Her face contorted into abject terror and she let loose the most blood curdling scream I had ever heard.

Before I could react, she slammed the door in my face and I heard the deadbolt engage.

"Simone?" I called out.

She was still screaming as she ran from the door. I cupped my hands against the frosted glass and tried to peer inside.

"Simone!"

It was no use. I couldn't see anything, and she was far enough away that I couldn't make out where she had gone.

I rang the bell twice more, only to be rewarded with more screaming. I distinctly thought I heard the word "police" and "go away" among the rest of her unintelligible shrieking.

It sounded like she was nearer the back of the house.

I ran around and pushed my way through the gate and into the side yard along the house. I stopped at the window to her room and looked inside.

I jerked back reflexively when Simone screamed again and ran from the room.

"Simone! Wait!" I hollered after her.

I had to get in there and calm her down. What had I done? Could I even defuse the situation?

I ran around until I spotted the sliding glass door that led into the small breakfast alcove next to the kitchen. The last time I tried to escape the house through it, I had been defeated.

To my relief, this time it was open halfway.

On the other side of the water stained glass, Simone and I locked eyes as she made the same discovery.

We both rushed for the door at the same time.

She was closer, and managed to start the door closing before I reached it.

I kicked my foot forward and stuck it in the shrinking gap. The door stopped short and pinched my shoe between metal rims.

I grabbed the handle and pulled as Simone pressed all her weight on the other side.

The door was crushing my foot and the pain was telling me in no uncertain terms to remove my foot as soon as possible. I ignored those messages and focused on Simone's reddening face.

"Listen to me Simone…"

She kept all her weight on the door and looked away from me.

"I've called the police. They'll be here any second."

I winced from the pressure on my foot. Even if I wanted to, I was trapped and wasn't going anywhere until Simone let up.

"My foot's trapped," I hollered.

She released the door slightly.

That was all I needed.

I forced myself into the widening gap and pushed the door open enough to wriggle inside.

Simone backpedaled away from me into the kitchen.

"The police are coming!" she screamed.

Now that I was inside, I slid the door fully closed and flipped the lock.

Simone's breathing came in spasmodic gasps as she backed herself into the corner of the kitchen, knocking a clear plastic bag with a red and yellow label on the floor between us.

Her hand bumped a half-open drawer and she yanked a fork out, brandishing it in front of her and slashing at the air as if it were a machete. She kicked the bag aside as she moved forward.

My hands shot up and I took a step backward.

"Easy Simone."

She jabbed the fork in the air to punctuate her words.

"Who are you?!"

I kept my hands up. If I lowered them, she might think I was going for a weapon of my own and do something we would both regret.

"I'm Michele."

She shook her head, the tears flowing down her cheeks.

"No you're not!"

She jabbed at the air again with her fork to keep me back. I had to keep Simone calm if I wanted to find out what she knew.

"Why do you say that?"

She lowered the fork as she stared at me, the fear and sadness in her eyes fighting for dominance.

"Because Michele's... you're... she's dead."

Chapter 21

I kept my eyes glued to the fork in Simone's hand. She knew my dirty little secret. Well, half of it anyway. But how had she found out?

"Who told you I was dead?"

She gripped her fork and looked at the floor.

"The police. They found your body in the river two days ago."

Her head jerked back up to look at me.

"They made me verify the body. I saw you…"

Her face scrunched up in pain from the memory of what she had been forced to do and the tears ran freely down her cheeks.

"Michele's dead."

Her head drooped and she sobbed briefly. Then just as quickly as she had started, she stopped crying. She lifted her head and focused her eyes on me.

Her fingers fiddled with the fork in her hand.

"If she's dead, then who are you?"

That was a good question. It was one that I had an answer for until last Wednesday. Now, I wasn't so sure.

Simone tilted her head and regarded me quizzically.

"You knew, didn't you?"

There was no sense in lying to her. She had already called the police and they would be here soon. If I was to find out what she knew, and hopefully get away before the police arrived, I had to get the ball rolling.

I slowly lowered my arms.

"Yes. I tried to stop her from jumping."

Her eyes scanned my face.

"So, that was you last week in my house?"

I nodded.

"What were you doing here?"

"I was returning her purse and wallet. She left it on the bridge when she… I didn't want someone to steal it."

I left out the fact that I had removed a sizeable sum of cash from her wallet.

"Why didn't you tell me what happened? Why did you

pretend to be her? And why do you look exactly like her?"

"I don't know why we look the same, but it has something to do with my husband who, I found out while I was here, was cheating on me with your Michele."

Her eyebrows knitted in confusion.

"Cheating on you?"

I remembered the camera.

"I don't know what is going on, but I do know you are being watched."

She glanced around her quickly.

"Not like that," I said. "Let me show you."

I headed for the living room and spotted the large hanging picture above the couch. Simone remained in the kitchen, but stayed where she could see me.

I looked at her.

"Do you have a hammer or crow bar?"

"What do you want with a hammer?"

"To pry the picture off the wall. There is something behind it you should see."

"You don't need a crowbar. Just take the picture off the wall."

"I can't. It's glued down."

"No, it's not."

I looked at the picture and, for the first time, noticed that it was hanging slightly askew. Not by much, but enough to not be considered hanging straight.

I leaned over the couch and pulled on the frame. The picture came away easily. It was not glued to the wall like every picture in my house.

And even more surprising, the wall behind it was empty.

There was no camera behind this picture.

I ran across the room to the large picture above the fire place. Ignoring all the pictures of me on the mantle, I pulled back the painting.

Nothing.

I looked at Simone.

"Where are they?"

"Where are what?"

"The cameras."

She looked alarmed.

"Cameras?! Why would there be cameras?"

"There were cameras in my house. I assumed this Michele was being watched too."

The sound of sirens echoed in the distance.

I didn't have much time.

I ran from one room to the next, which didn't take long in the small two bedroom house.

None of the pictures hid a camera.

I started feeling the walls for a hole or depression that might indicate something hidden in a hole that had been drilled and then covered up again before being painted.

There was nothing.

I was even more confused than before. I was so sure there would be cameras here, and then I could convert Simone into an ally.

Instead, she looked at me like I was a crazed intruder.

Which I was.

The sirens were coming from multiple directions and were close enough to drown out my own thoughts. If I stayed any longer, I would never be given the chance to find out what was really happening. I had no answers for the police as to why I didn't report the suicide.

Or why I had come to her house and pretended to be her.

Or more importantly, why she and I had the same name; and the same face.

The doorbell rang.

We both looked at the frosted glass next to the front door that showed several dark shadows. The muted crackle of radio chatter invaded the house.

"Police department," a deep male voice shouted through the door followed by loud knocking.

I looked at Simone. She still gripped the fork in her hand, ready for what I might do if she made a move to let in the police.

"I'm sorry," was all I said as I ran for the sliding glass door, flipped up the lock and yanked it open in a single motion.

I was already straddling the back fence when I finally glanced back. Simone was opening the front door and shouting to the uniformed officers which way I had gone.

Chapter 22

I dropped down into the neighbor's yard and ran for the side gate. I heard shouting and men with overstuffed officer utility belts scrambling over the fence after me.

I darted into the street, shifting my angle to keep from being hit by the car suddenly skidding toward me. It narrowly missed me and collided with a parked car as I continued across the street. I ignored the angered shouts from the driver as I shoved my way through the next side gate and into another back yard.

I was over the fence before I heard the clatter of police belts after me.

I hit the ground running and crashed through another side gate, this time crossing the street without incident.

I glanced back just as I opened the next gate.

A uniformed police officer was just coming through the gate and he spotted me.

I darted into the back yard and kicked the fence loudly before ducking down into some thick bushes along the side of the house.

I hoped the pursuing officers would think I went over and keep after me.

The officer who had spotted me from across the street appeared suddenly from around the corner of the house. He ran full speed through the backyard, launched himself into the air, and was over the fence with a quick nimbleness I thought was not possible with everything strapped to his waist.

I stayed low as two more officers entered the backyard and followed their comrade over the fence.

I sat down in the soft dirt and waited.

I must have waited for a couple of hours in that spot without moving.

I couldn't see anything from my hiding spot in someone's back yard, but it was clear from the less frequent fly-bys of the police helicopter circling overhead, Pittsburgh's finest had determined that I must have escaped and were starting to expand their search radius.

I would need to proceed carefully if I were to get away.

I rolled to my knees and peered out from the bushes into the empty back yard. I decided it was best to wait for the next pass from the helicopter before making my move.

Where would I go?

Home?

Robert wouldn't be back until tomorrow.

My heart pumped faster as I realized where Robert would be in a couple of hours.

He was coming here.

And this time, there would be police waiting for him.

Simone knew I had spent last week with him, and he just might become the primary suspect in the other Michele's death.

I had to keep him from coming here.

I pulled out my cell phone and stared at the cracked screen. It had been destroyed during my daring escape from the police. I pressed the power button repeatedly, but nothing happened.

"Dammit!" I said aloud and stuck it back into my pocket. The phone was useless, but I still had to warn Robert.

I closed my eyes and pictured the way he had drove back to this house from the psychiatrist's office last week.

My eyes popped open. I knew which way he would use to get here, and where I could easily run into the street to stop him before he got too close.

I crawled out of the bushes and was just starting to stand up when a voice broke the silence.

"Freeze!" someone shouted at the same moment I heard the sound of a gun being pulled from its leather holster.

My heart stopped and my hands shot to the sky as I looked at the barrel of a gun pointed at me from the corner of the house.

"Lie down and keep your hands where I can see them," the voice demanded.

I did exactly as asked and had only just settled into the grass when a knee dug into the center of my back and rough hands yanked my wrists back to slap handcuffs on them.

"Control, this is twelve. I have the suspect in custody."

The officer lifted me up by my arms and shoved me ahead of

him.

"Lucky thing I decided to check the last place I knew you were before I lost sight of you. I must have run two more blocks before I realized you hadn't kept going."

I glanced back and was surprised to see a ruggedly handsome face, with a five o'clock shadow developing on his sharp, angular features, looking at me.

His eyes did not burn into me with anger but instead transmitted a hint of excitement as if he were thanking me for presenting him with a worthy challenge.

"I mostly chase around thugs and addicts who can barely keep one foot in front of another, let alone run very far. It was a pleasure to try to keep up with someone in such good shape."

I didn't have the heart to mention how I had become so sick a year ago that I nearly died.

He walked me back around the block rather than take us through the numerous yards I had used to get where he found me.

As I walked down the street toward the other Michele's house, I spotted Simone standing on the front lawn talking with two detectives in their requisite wrinkled beige overcoats.

Her eyes found mine across the short distance. We looked at each other for a moment before she looked away. The officer stopped at the back of a squad car and opened the door for me.

"Watch your head," he said and carefully placed his hand on me to ease me into the back seat.

Just as I settled into the car, I recognized the man driving through the small police blockade, peering in at who was being arrested.

Robert and I locked eyes as he followed the instructions of the police officer directing traffic around the menagerie of official vehicles parked haphazardly in the street around Simone's house.

I watched him turn the corner and disappear from view. Would I ever see him again? And if I did, would we ever be able to go back to the life we had before? As soon as he was back at our real house, he would see the torn picture and the camera that I had discovered.

The life that I had known was over and there was no going back to it now.

Even after almost dying last year, I felt like I had reached the lowest point of my life.

I had no idea that it was about to get worse.

Chapter 23

Thanks to a hit television show, everyone is saying that orange is the new black.

Well, I still feel like the same old Black.

Michele Black.

My life was officially over, but I wasn't dead yet. I was still alive, if you could call wearing an oversized bright orange jumpsuit, and being crammed into a cell smaller than the guest bathroom of my house, as living.

The arresting officer had turned me over to processing as soon as we arrived at the police station and I hadn't seen him since.

I guess I watched too many TV cop shows where the perps were constantly harassed by the police. I guess dramatic television was as different from the real world as my life had become.

I had spent the last several hours being moved from one person to another as I was fingerprinted, photographed, recorded, and then paraded on to the next level of embarrassment.

I even had a nurse come and scrub a cotton swab against the inside of my cheek; twice. The second time, I got up the nerve to ask why they were taking DNA samples without my consent. The nurse looked at me, but never said a word as she finished and left the room.

Even more strangely, another nurse came in to my room and made a dental mold of my teeth. I had never heard about this being done as part of the booking procedure. None of the police procedural TV shows ever showed it.

When they were done, and led me away from the processing room, I thought they would put me in a large communal cell where I would be propositioned by some huge butch woman for sexual favors in exchange for protection.

Instead, I was ushered to a tiny room with no windows and a slot in the door where they could pass food to me during the mandated eating hours.

I guess I should have been grateful that I was not in the large cell, huddled in a corner under constant threat of being beaten up by real criminals, and waiting for Robert to bail me out.

But then again, I was left alone with my own thoughts. I really wasn't sure which was worse.

In the solitude of my tiny cell, my mind kept returning to the message Robert had left on my cell phone. With my cell phone shattered during my ill-fated attempt to flee, his call was never heard by the police after they had confiscated my belongings. It had taken lots of convincing to allow me to make a second phone call after Robert never answered the "one phone call" that I was allowed.

When Robert hadn't answered, I didn't bother leaving a message and instead dialed my own number. According to the time stamp, his message on my phone was left shortly after my arrest.

He told me that the negotiations were not going well at all and didn't know how long he would need to stay. He promised to keep in touch and call again soon.

He thought it was Michele Gardner who had been arrested. Why wouldn't he think that? It had happened in front of her and Simone's house.

But Simone had told me that they had fished the other Michele out of the river a couple of days ago. Why didn't whoever made her look like me know that she was dead? Were they not watching her as much as they had been watching me?

By now, they should have noticed I tore the picture away and exposed one of their cameras. Why weren't they charging into the police station with warrants and official government documents trying to get me back before I talked?

Even if I did talk, what would I say?

That my husband had convinced someone to change their

appearance so that he could cheat on me without technically cheating on me?

That I was being constantly watched in my own home? But if I was being constantly watched, where were the watchers now?

Unless, no one monitored the cameras. Had my life become so boring that whoever "they" were had stopped watching?

A tear welled up in the corner of my eye. Robert and I had too easily fallen into a boring rut. The most exciting thing to happen to us hadn't even happened to us. It had happened to him and his mistress. Or so he thought.

His message to my cell phone had confirmed as much. He was abandoning our marriage to be here for his mistress in her hour of need.

But it was my hour of need.

What would he do when he discovered I wasn't his other Michele? Would the news of her death destroy our relationship?

Was there anything left to destroy?

I looked at the slate-grey cement walls of my prison cell. Was this all that was left of my life?

I heard a ring of keys rattle right before the lock on my cell door made a loud clunk sound and creaked on untended hinges as it swung inward.

I blinked against the bright light that spilled in from the hallway as a guard filled the open doorway. Her unusually high pitched voice was in stark contrast to her girth; which stretched her uniform at the seams.

"Get up."

I stood and let her shackle my hands together.

"Where are we going?"

She smiled at me, the gap between her two front teeth whistling softly as she sucked in a quick breath before speaking again.

"Your attorney's here."

Chapter 24

I followed the guard through brightly lit hallways and to a closed door.

She opened it and motioned for me to go into the room ahead of her.

She followed me in and pointed to the chair on the other side of the small metal table in the middle of the room.

After I sat down, she leaned heavily on the table, the metal legs groaning under the pressure.

"When you are done, wait here until I come get you," she squeaked at me.

I nodded and she left me alone in the room.

It wouldn't be for long. My mind barely had the chance to resume my earlier track when the door opened again and a man in a finely pressed pinstripe suit entered.

His face was clean shaven, yet he had a noticeable scar running along his jaw line on one side. His chest stretched at the fabric of the suit and, while I could see that it was tailored, he didn't look comfortable in it. Not the image I would have expected for an attorney.

He moved with a practiced grace as he stepped into the room and moved to the side to let another man in.

My heart skipped a beat.

It was Robert.

I started to react when Robert shook his head briefly, motioning for me to stay quiet as he closed the door behind him.

The attorney stayed against the back wall and sidled sideways up to the camera mounted in the corner of the ceiling. He reached up and unplugged the cable from the back of the camera, leaving the room unmonitored.

That one action seemed strange. As far as I knew, he could have requested the camera turned off, citing client-attorney privilege and privacy concerns. Why had he bothered with sneaking up under the camera and physically unplugging it?

The attorney, finished with his initial task, turned to me with a deadly gaze that probably won him every case he took to trial. I knew if I were on a jury, and he looked at me like that, I would vote whichever way he told me to.

He sat down quickly at the metal table and placed his hands softly on the surface, his face never showing any emotion as he settled into the metal chair.

"What have you said?"

I looked at Robert, who was still standing by the door.

Like a cobra striking at its prey, the attorney snapped his fingers in front of my face and drew my attention back to his serious face. My heart pounded as I looked into those dark eyes that failed to give any indication that there was a caring human behind them.

"Miss Gardner. I need to know what you have told the police."

He had called me by my maiden name, so they were still under the mistaken conclusion that I was Dead Michele.

"Umm. I haven't talked to anyone."

The attorney smiled again.

"Good. Let's keep it that way. Do you know why you were arrested?"

The attorney leaned over to get into my field of vision. The movement brought me out of my reverie and I focused on him as he smiled sweetly. Too sweetly. It seemed unnatural for his face.

"Have they told you what you are being charged with yet?"

I shook my head.

"They haven't told me anything."

He leaned back.

"Good. According to the report, you are being held under Pennsylvania Code Chapter 5100, but nobody can tell me why they have done that."

"Chapter 5100? What does that mean?"

"It's their mental health regulations. It means they can hold you longer without pressing charges and are legally able to conduct involuntary examinations."

He squinted at me.

"Have they examined you?"

I frowned.

"Examined me?"

"Have they taken any blood or DNA samples?"

"They scraped cotton swabs on the inside of my cheek. Isn't that for DNA?"

The attorney sat back and studied my face. He sat still, like a statue and regarded me for a long moment. There were no emotions in his features.

"Since they are using the mental health code to stall for time, we will take full advantage of that. I want you to remain silent. Don't answer any questions, no matter how hard they push. Do you understand?"

"Yes," I said.

I didn't.

I looked at Robert. Our eyes met and I knew instantly that I wanted to go home with him. Not to the Dead Michele's home, but back to our real life, our real home.

The attorney reached into his pocket and extracted a small paper envelope. He opened the envelope and leaned forward, shaking a small red gel capsule onto the table from the envelope.

"Take this."

I looked at it.

"What is it?"

"It's a sedative. Take it. Now."

"A sedative?"

"I will be sending someone to get you out of here tonight, and I need you to be relaxed."

"Why?"

He reached forward with the speed of a cobra again and grabbed my wrists, pulling me forward over the table. Our faces were inches apart.

"If you want to get out of here, you do exactly as I say. Now you pick up that pill and put it in your mouth, or I will do it for you."

He let go of me and I jerked my hands back quickly, hopefully out of his extended reach. His grip had been so tight, and I could sense the anger through his cold touch.

His eyes darted from the pill back to my face. I didn't want to see how he planned to force me to take the pill, so I picked it up and stuck it in my mouth before he decided I was taking too long to comply.

His eyes squinted at me.

"Swallow it," he commanded.

I swallowed.

His eyes glistened as he ignored the loud shouts from the hallway.

"Good girl."

He stood up and faced Robert, nodding his head. Robert unlocked the door and opened it.

The attorney walked out of the room, leaving Robert looking at me sorrowfully.

"Don't worry, Michele. You'll be out of here before you know it."

"Mr. Black," the attorney said forcefully from the hallway and Robert followed him out of the room, closing the door and leaving me alone.

With no one in the room with me at that moment, I spit the gel cap onto the floor and placed my foot on top of it, smashing it into the carpet.

I would have liked it if Robert could have stayed, but the gel capsule tucked into the side of my cheek was starting to dissolve and the one side of my tongue was feeling numb.

I don't know what the attorney meant when he said he needed me relaxed when I was released, but I didn't trust him and was not about to eat anything he gave me.

Despite everything, I trusted Robert. But when he let the attorney take the lead, I knew that he was not in charge of what was happening. Why hadn't Robert come to see me sooner?

And why had he deferred to the attorney?

Why hadn't he defended me, or come to my rescue, when the attorney demanded I take the pill. He hadn't even made a move to help when the attorney had grabbed me by the wrists and pulled me over the table.

Was Robert not able to help me?

Or was he unwilling?

I had more questions than answers as I sat in the room. My eyes noticed the dangling cable.

Did they even know my attorney was gone?

As previously ordered, I sat waiting for the guard to come and get me, no matter how long it took. Eventually, they would check this room when they noticed the camera didn't work.

I jumped slightly, caught by surprise when the door opened and a man poked his head into the room and smiled at me. Shivers ran up and down my spine as I recognized him.

He stepped into the room, a thick file tucked under one arm, and closed the door before turning to face me.

"Name's Detective Janssen. You were my last catch as a beat cop and I've been lucky enough to get you assigned to me as my first case as a detective. Small world, huh?"

Janssen's suit was not as polished as the attorney's had been, nor was it as perfectly fitting, but it complimented his body, leaving little to the imagination as to how well it fit.

While not grossly bulked out, Janssen looked like he exercised regularly and was probably maintaining less than five percent body fat. I felt my heart flutter as his shoulder muscles flexed while he thumbed through the pages of the folder in his hands.

When he finally looked at me, all the posturing and alpha male supremacy was gone, replaced by a softness that I was not prepared for.

I glanced at the camera mounted in the corner, the cable still dangled from the hole in the wall. He glanced at the disabled camera and then back at me.

"That asshole actually did me a favor. I don't want what we are about to discuss to be recorded either."

My heart raced. What was he going to do to me that he didn't want recorded?

Chapter 25

I flinched as he took a step closer.

His eyes softened and he smiled warmly at me. It melted all my reserve and I instantly trusted him.

He set the folder on the table and sat down across from me. He didn't remain standing to place himself in a position of power over me.

"I am hoping that you can help me make some sense out of my first case as a detective."

What was he doing? Was he trying to gain my trust by treating me as an equal? I didn't have the heart to tell him that his disarming smile had already started to chip away at the walls I had instinctively put up. It had happened so quickly and easily, I didn't know what to make of it.

With us sitting so close, I breathed in his scent and looked him in the eyes. His piercing blue eyes, with flecks of green, drew me in.

I knew from reading the various magazines at my shrinks office that enlarged pupils meant that someone was interested in you. I felt moisture form along my forehead and under my arms as he peered deeply into my soul. I knew I could never lie to those eyes.

"I don't know how I can help you. I'm not a detective. Should you even be showing me a case file?"

He flipped through several pages and studied a page filled with handwritten notes before looking back at me again.

"I think you can bring a unique perspective that will help me make heads or tails of what it says right here on this report."

He accented his last two words by stabbing at the page with his index finger.

"Okay, I'll bite. What does it say?"

He glanced back and forth, as if checking that we were still alone, and then leaned forward.

When I stayed where I was, he wiggled his finger, silently asking me to get closer.

We were close enough to kiss and all I could see were the

large pupils swimming in the bluest ocean.

He whispered as if, despite the camera already disabled, someone might still be listening in.

"This report is trying to convince me that the person sitting here with me now is the exact same person I have on ice down in the morgue."

Chapter 26

My mouth went dry.

"In fact," Detective Janssen continued. "According to this report, the two of you are identical in every way except for three things."

He ticked off the items on his fingers as he looked me in the eyes.

"Your vital status, your age, and your tattoo."

The room spun as I tried to comprehend what he had just said. It was no use. I was utterly lost as if he had spoken to me in a foreign language.

"What?"

He glanced down at the paper.

"According to this, the body I have downstairs is about five years younger than you and, while she had the same tattoo you do, this says it is different, but not how it is different."

I glanced at the tattoo imprinted on the underside of my wrist. Being a small tattoo, it was partially concealed by the handcuffs still wrapped around my wrists. It was no more than half an inch wide and portrayed the infinity symbol with four tiny dots above it and three tiny dots below.

I never knew what it meant, and without the benefit of the memories of my life before the accident, I thought I never would.

I looked up at the detective.

"You said she had the same tattoo?"

He flipped through the thick case file, pulled out a black and white photo, and slid it across the desk to me.

I looked down and my mouth fell open.

It was a close-up picture of a tattoo like mine, but not exactly like mine.

My eyes recognized the difference immediately. This tattoo had the same infinity symbol with four dots above it. But instead of three dots below, there were four. I touched the lower four dots on the picture.

Michele's words echoed to me from beyond the grave; and they were starting to make sense.

"How many more," I whispered.

"How many more what?" Janssen asked softly.

I suddenly remembered where I was and looked up at him. My mind whirled with the implication of what I had just realized and I didn't care that he heard what I said aloud.

"She was number eight. I am number seven."

Detective Austin Janssen's forehead wrinkled as he looked me.

"Seven? Do you mean the little dots?"

He grabbed the picture and looked at it again.

"There are eight dots on the woman in the morgue. And you have seven?"

Janssen grabbed my wrist sending electric shivers up my arm and into the rest of my body. Even after three years of marriage, I had never felt the same when Robert touched me.

Janssen either didn't notice, or didn't care, about my discomfort as he pulled my wrist closer and inspected my tattoo.

I did my best to keep my breathing at an even rhythm even as my heart raced at his touch.

Chapter 27

Janssen studied my wrist for a long moment before focusing his bright blue eyes on mine.

"What does it mean?"

"I don't know."

For once, I was telling the god-awful truth.

I had no idea what any of it meant. Then I remembered something else the detective had said.

"The report said she was younger than me?"

He flipped through several pages and then nodded while reading one page more thoroughly.

"By five years."

"How do you know?"

He flipped the page over and read it for a few more seconds.

"According to this, your wisdom teeth have already come in, and the deceased was still a couple of years away from having hers erupt."

He looked up at me.

"Is that right? They actually use the word, "erupt" to describe your teeth coming in?"

I shrugged. "I'm not a dentist. I wouldn't know."

He shuddered.

"Sounds more like they are describing a volcano rather than regular old teeth."

A thought occurred to me.

"Could she have been my sister?"

He shook his head.

"According to our lab specialists, a bit of a know-it-all if you ask me, the latest studies have demonstrated that even identical twins don't have the exact same DNA sequence."

I looked him in those deep blue eyes.

"Then what are we talking about here?"

"I was hoping you could answer that for me."

"I don't know."

"You must know. I mean, according to the roommate, you took over her life once she was out of the picture."

He looked at me strangely.

"How long did you two know about each other?"

I thought back to the first moment I laid eyes on her at the bridge. It felt like a lifetime ago.

"I wasn't even supposed to be on the bridge then. I was late for an appointment and saw a woman about to jump."

"I take it she did jump?"

I nodded silently and looked down at my hands. For some reason, I knew deep down inside that Detective Janssen didn't think I had killed the other Michele.

"Why didn't you report it?"

"I don't know. I didn't know what was happening."

I looked up at him.

"I mean, she looked exactly like me. What would you have done?"

"I may be biased, but I would have called the police."

We stayed looking at each other for a long minute, neither of us saying a word. It was strange, but he didn't look at me with malice or accusation. Instead, I could see that he trusted me, which was good since I had not lied to him once since he caught me in that backyard.

How did he know he could trust me?

Was this some form of interrogation technique that helped him get more confessions from criminals? I thought they always brought in another officer for a game of good cop, bad cop? That's what they did on all the cop shows.

Unconventional interrogation technique or not, I found I trusted him and hoped the trust I saw in his eyes directed toward me was not an act to get me to confess to a crime I knew nothing about.

He was the first to break contact and looked down at the file. I thought I saw a hint of discomfort right before he broke away.

Or was it a hint of attraction?

Was he attracted to me?

It seemed unlikely. He was my arresting officer, and was now interrogating me for a possible crime, for which I had not been charged with yet.

The attorney's words echoed in my head as I waited quietly for Janssen to finish reading another page in the file. I wasn't going to be the first to break the silence. I had read somewhere once that criminals who had something to hide hated uncomfortable silence and would usually confess to everything if the room stayed quiet long enough.

I had no problems with letting the silence expand between us. I had plenty of practice eating dinners in silence with Robert nearly every night. I would not let the still of the night break me.

Besides, I had nothing to hide.

Or did I?

I still had no answer as to why the other Michele looked like me. Or had my maiden name. So far, everyone had been calling me Michele Gardner. I was even booked under that name. Nobody had yet made the connection with my real self.

Robert had even come in with an attorney and didn't let anyone know that he was my husband. The attorney had even called me Ms. Gardner, and Robert hadn't corrected him.

Detective Janssen closed the file with a loud slap and looked up at me suddenly.

"Who are you?"

"Excuse me?" I stammered.

He stabbed at the folder in front of him with an index finger.

"The comments from the roommate and the body in the morgue confirm that Michele Gardner died recently and that you took her place. The processing staff used your fingerprints to determine your identity. I have purposely kept the identity of the woman we pulled out of the river from the papers and the public record. Booking has no idea they pulled the dead woman's identity up as your own."

He opened the file again and pulled out a form.

"According to this, you were identified by your fingerprints as Michele Gardner with a perfect match."

He pulled out another form and laid it side-by-side with the first form.

"According to this, the woman in the morgue was identified by her fingerprints as Michele Gardner. Your fingerprints are a perfect match to hers."

He looked deeply into my eyes as he continued.

"I would like to say that one of the people who ran the query made a mistake, but I can't, and do you know why?"

I shook my head.

"Because I ran both queries myself against the database. At first, I thought the database had duplicate records, but there was only one match found with both sets of fingerprints. You have already admitted to me that you took over Michele Gardner's life after she jumped from the bridge. So, if you are not Michele Gardner, then who are you?"

His eyes darted back and forth as they probed mine.

"You are right. I'm not Michele Gardner. But I used to be."

Detective Janssen gave me a quizzical look, so I continued.

"Before I married, my name was Michele Gardner."

"What is your name now?"

"Michele Black."

He flipped quickly through various pages in the file.

"How come I can't find any record of your alias?"

"It's not an alias. I changed it when we got married."

"Legally, that is considered an alias. Why is this not part of your fingerprint record?"

"I didn't know it wasn't."

"And this hasn't come up before now?"

"I've never been arrested before now."

Chapter 28

I was back in my windowless cell and enjoying a wonderful meal of fetid water and stale bread. I'm sure that the food was better than that, but it felt more appropriate to think of them in terms that matched where I was eating it.

After giving Detective Janssen my real identity, he left the interrogation room and had me sent back to my cell.

I had no way to gauge how long I had been in there. There were no windows to see whether the sun or moon was in the sky, and there was no clock to at least tell me the time regardless of whether I knew it was day or night.

All I knew was, it had been several hours since Janssen and I had spoken. He no doubt had contacted Robert by now.

Robert would have no choice but to admit what he was doing. Even if it came filtered through my next interrogation, I would finally get at the truth.

The truth about the other Michele.

The truth about the cameras in our house.

The truth about me.

I looked at the tattoo on my wrist and focused on the dots. The seven tiny dots. The other Michele had eight dots, and was younger than me. She had somehow figured out that she was not the first of something, but the eighth.

I traced the dots with a finger.

And I was number seven.

But seven of what?

I was the seventh, which meant that there had to have been others before me. But how was that possible?

I inspected my fingerprints.

I don't care how good a plastic surgeon considered themselves, nobody could alter fingerprints to match someone else perfectly.

Janssen had said that both the other Michele and I were perfect matches for the fingerprints on record.

There was only one answer.

Whoever Robert was working for, whoever had installed the

cameras in my home, was connected enough to alter the records in the police database. They had somehow altered the database to make someone think they had found the same record with both sets of fingerprints.

There simply wasn't any other plausible solution to the puzzle presented by two different prints matching to the same record. There had to be a duplicate record with all the same information in it. Whatever checks and balances the police put in place to avoid this from happening had been circumvented by Robert's mysterious watchers.

There was no other way they could change a person's fingerprints, so they just changed the database records.

My tongue found a smudge of the materiel that they had used to make an impression of my teeth. Janssen had mentioned that they were also a match, only Dead Michele's were at a younger state than mine in age.

I ran my tongue over my teeth. Had they surgically moved my teeth around to match the others? The ones who had come before me?

I looked at the seven dots on my wrist. If I was number seven, then there had been six before me. But if that was the case, why had the other Michele asked, "How many more?" right before she jumped.

Surely, she had to have known about me. She wasn't surprised to see me when I came running up. She had to have known exactly how many came before her.

Maybe she wasn't asking how many more came before.

Maybe she was asking how many more would come after?

After what?

A chill ran up my spine.

I had been so focused on being number seven of something; I hadn't even considered where the other six were that came before me.

What had happened to them?

Robert's work schedule scrolled through my mind, and I saw it with a new understanding.

He had been dating the other Michele for only one day a

week. The day he was gone from me. I thought back to when Robert and I started dating.

He could see me only once a week because he traveled so much on business. Was that the same excuse he gave the new Michele?

After we had been dating for a year, he had convinced his boss to eliminate his travel completely, and we moved in together; marrying shortly after.

Things were perfect, until a year ago when I had gone into the hospital and nearly died. Not soon after I came back out, Robert's company required that he start traveling again one day a week.

That had to be when he started dating the other Michele. I had discovered that much when he took me to see Dr. Westcott last week.

Everything about her life was a complete reproduction of my life. Even the pictures on the mantle above her fireplace were re-dos of my vacations with Robert. She was reliving my life down to every detail.

What did he have planned for me when it came time to move in with the new Michele and be home every day for her? Was there another Michele out there waiting for him to stumble across in a grocery store somewhere years from now?

When he had stumbled across me nearly five years ago, and we began dating, what had he done with the Michele before me?

What had become of Michele number six?

I looked at the too-close walls of my windowless cell. Would I ever be given the chance to find out?

I lied down on the bed and closed my eyes, willing myself to drift off to sleep.

I don't know how long I slept when a loud popping sound brought me fully awake. My heart pounded heavily inside my ribcage and I glanced around in a panic, completely disoriented, before I remembered where I was.

The windowless walls of my cell gave me very little comfort. They meant that everything that had happened to me recently was not a dream.

It was a nightmare.

And, as far as I could tell, it wouldn't be ending anytime soon. There would be no waking up from this nightmare. I was already fully awake.

Two more loud pops just outside my cell door made me flinch involuntarily. I jumped out of the small bed when the electronic door lock clicked loudly. I backed away, pressing myself up against the far wall, as the door swung inward.

Highlighted by the brighter light of the hallway, Detective Janssen filled the open doorway with his gun drawn. He had blood splattered all over the front of his torn shirt and a crazed look in his eyes.

I cried out in terror, slid down the wall, and curled into a ball. Something had driven the detective mad, and now he was on a killing spree throughout the police station, with me as his next target.

I refused to make eye contact for fear that would be seen as a challenge and make him kill me sooner. If I was lucky, and stayed small and quiet, maybe he would move on and leave me alone.

I wasn't so lucky.

Chapter 29

Detective Janssen lunged forward and grabbed my arm, yanking me to my feet with a strength I hadn't expected.

"You're coming with me," he growled through clenched teeth as he spun me around and shoved me toward the door.

We stopped at the open doorway right before exiting the cell. He slammed me against the wall with one hand and stuck a finger in my face.

"Don't move."

I could smell the blood mixed with sweat that drenched his shirt. I couldn't tell if he was covered in his own blood, or someone else's.

He held me against the wall with his hand against my throat and peeked out into the hallway, quickly looking both directions.

He jerked back in and twisted his fist to gather up the collar material of my bright orange jumpsuit.

He leaned in close, his hot breath washing over me as he exhaled heavily.

"Move when I move. Stop when I stop. Do you understand?"

I nodded. What else should I have done with a crazed maniac who had a death grip on the collar of my jumpsuit? If he had asked me to jump off a bridge, I would have done it.

He yanked on me, wrapped his arm around my neck from behind, and pushed me ahead of him as we entered the hallway.

I tried my best to keep from stepping on his toes as he kept his body pressed against mine and walked us forward down the hallway.

A man dressed all in black, complete with a very large assault rifle with an extended barrel, appeared around the corner. He spotted us and raised his rifle, pausing for a brief moment when he saw me.

Janssen took advantage of the man's hesitation and fired three rounds.

I tried to shy away from the deafening sound, but Janssen held me tightly and kept me in place.

The man jerked from the impacts, pulling on the trigger of his assault rifle reflexively as he pitched backward. The wall to my left side erupted as a line of bullets chewed into it as the man fell onto his back.

The assault rifle wasn't as loud as the detective's handgun, and I realized that the extended barrel was a silencer attached to the end of the rifle.

It was then I knew why Janssen hadn't killed me back in the cell.

I was to be his human shield.

He walked me forward toward his latest victim. I tried not to look at the man he had just killed but, like when you came across a car accident and couldn't look away, I found my eyes examining the carnage.

He wasn't dressed like a police officer, but looked more like a military soldier. But there were no insignias or badges on his fully black uniform. He also wore a black knit cap and had a thin wire leading to his ear from under his jacket. He looked more like a mercenary rather than a police or military officer.

The mushroomed ends of three bullets were lodged in his bulletproof vest. Janssen pushed me forward until we stood over the groaning man. He kicked the man in the face and was rewarded with silence.

He shoved me face-first into the wall and leaned heavily against me, his warm hand holding my arm tightly. I don't know if this was what they meant by Stockholm Syndrome, where victims become enamored with their captors, but when his hand gripped my arm forcefully, I felt a surge of unwarranted desire well up inside me in response to his electric touch.

"Stay," he hissed.

I did as he asked, but turned my head slightly to watch him. He leaned down and picked up the assault rifle, stuffing his comparatively tiny police revolver back into its holster.

He checked the rifle quickly. He ejected the spent magazine and pulled another one out from a pocket on the man's vest. He slapped it into the rifle and pulled on the charging handle, loading the first bullet into the chamber.

He grabbed two more magazines and shoved them into the

front of his pants before turning back to me.

"Let's go."

He grabbed the collar of my jumpsuit with his clenched fist and moved me through the hallway in front of him.

I didn't like being his bulletproof vest, but I was in no position to complain. I still had no idea what was going on. Was I still asleep in my cell and only dreaming this?

Another black-clad mercenary poked his head around the corner. Janssen fired from my hip and forced the mercenary back out of sight.

Janssen pushed us to the floor and behind a desk. He pointed his rifle around the corner of the desk and waited.

Bullets impacted with the top of the desk, ricocheting over us, forcing a panicked scream from my throat as I shielded my eyes from debris raining down on us. Janssen returned fire and the bullets whistling overhead stopped.

He grabbed my bare arm, more electric sparks firing making my heart beat faster, and lifted me back up. The mercenary on the other side of the room was lying face down in a growing pool of blood that expanded out from his head.

I looked at Janssen with alarm.

How was a city police detective holding his own against a group of mercenaries?

I didn't know much about how the mercenary world operated, but I was sure if they planned to openly attack a metropolitan police station, they were probably well armed and highly organized.

Janssen had arrived already torn and bloody. He had come across at least one mercenary before coming for me and I had watched him dispatch two in as many minutes without batting an eye.

I was being rescued by my own Bruce Willis from Die Hard, a movie made before I lost my memories, but thanks to Netflix was able to see again, along with a lot of movies that helped pass the time while Robert was at work.

Did Robert know about this attack?

I thought back to the mysterious reply from the attorney

when I questioned taking the sedative. He had said I needed to be relaxed because they were getting me out of jail tonight.

Was this how he had planned to get me out?

Send in a private army to take me by force?

If I had taken the sedative, I would have not been able to keep up with Janssen as we made our way down some stairs and into the basement of the police station.

He paused at the bottom of the stairwell and pointed to a door on the other side of the hallway that stretched in both directions.

"Through that door is the motor pool. My car is the second to the last one in the first row. It's a grey Toyota Prius. As soon as I say go, you run for my car, get in, and stay down."

I nodded, not sure if I could convince my legs to run out into the open space, exposed to whatever dangers lurked in the parking garage.

He peeked around the corner and jerked back quickly.

"Okay. The hallways clear. On the count of three, run through that door and get to my car. It's already unlocked, so just get in and stay down out of sight."

He peeked one more time down the hallway and motioned with his hand.

"Go."

I knew it. My legs failed to obey. I was frozen in place. He looked back at me, his frustration with my inaction evident on his face.

"Go!"

My legs finally responded and I darted out across the hallway, pushed on the bar to open the metal door, and stepped into the parking garage.

It swung open quickly, swinging all the way to slam into the cinderblock wall with a loud bang.

A black-clad mercenary poked his head from around a car at the far end of the parking area, lifted his assault rifle, and fired.

The muzzle flash had barely registered in my brain before bullets pinged off the cement all around my feet. I screamed, running in circles while protecting my head from the flying shards of cement with flailing arms.

As soon as the shooting stopped a dark shape charged at me from the side and tackled me to the ground.

I was rolled roughly onto my back. A mercenary straddled me and held my arms against the floor with his knees. He smiled when he saw my face and pinched the front of his neck with two fingers.

"This is Blue Five, target acquired."

Chapter 30

I struggled under the mercenary's weight, but it was no use. He was twice my size and easily three times my weight. I wasn't going anywhere until he decided I could.

"Let her go!"

The command was punctuated by the sound of a revolver hammer being pulled back.

The mercenary's smiling face darkened and he looked away from me.

I followed his gaze. Detective Janssen was standing inside the doorway, out of view of the other mercenaries at the far end of the garage.

He leveled his gaze at the mercenary pinning me down while holding his revolver steady.

The mercenary grinned at him, but didn't move to let me up.

"I suggest you drop your gun and surrender."

"And why should I do that?" Janssen countered.

"Because you've lost."

"I'm not the one with the gun pointed at my head."

It was then I saw the shadow on the stairs. Someone was coming down quietly behind Janssen. I took a breath. Without even looking at me, the mercenary placed his hand over my mouth and muffled my warning.

"You're dead. You just don't know it yet," the mercenary said, a hint of humor entering his voice.

Janssen shuffled forward slightly, but stayed just behind the doorway and out of sight. "Oh, yeah? Why is that?"

"You should have listened to your orders. You aren't supposed to be here. But since you are, we can't let you live. Not after you've seen my face."

"Did I just step into some kind of low-budget cliché-filled movie?" Janssen asked.

The mercenary chuckled.

"If you had, this would be your big death scene."

Janssen fired without hesitation or warning, the mercenary's head exploding and spraying blood all over me. His headless body slumped on top of me as two more shots echoed through the doorway and into the underground garage.

Janssen darted out and rolled the headless mercenary off me. The reply from the other end of the garage was immediate.

Cement and sparks exploded all around me, drowning out my screaming as Janssen pulled me behind a car. From this angle, I could see that he had killed the mercenary coming down the stairs behind him.

Who was this guy?

I was beginning to think that he was better than Bruce Willis in any of his movies. He was like all the best heroes from every action movie all rolled up into one very attractive package.

I looked at his sweaty, blood covered, face and my heart fluttered like a maiden catching her first glimpse of the knight in shining armor charging at the dragon.

He hadn't shaved all day, giving him a grizzled and raw expression as he peeked through the tinted rear windows of the car we hid behind; looking for the next dragon to slay.

He dropped back down next to me.

"It looks like there's only one guy still protecting the exit. My car is right there."

He pointed and I looked at the grey Prius parked a few spaces away, but might as well have been a thousand miles. I looked back at him, my heart pounding out a steady beat, ready to protest when he put a hand up.

"Don't worry; I'm not making you run for it."

My heart slowed slightly as relief washed over me. And then he stuck the rifle in my hands.

"You are going to provide the cover fire while I run for it."

I was stunned to silence. I had never fired a gun before in my life. Didn't you have to start out with pellet guns and then work your way up from there? He couldn't very well expect me to fire an assault rifle on my virgin try?

He peeked over the top of the hood and dropped down quickly as sparks exploded where his head had just been.

"Okay, that guy is pretty trigger happy. I'm going to need you to start firing first before I run to my car."

I was shaking my head.

He pointed to the extended barrel on my assault rifle.

"This sound suppressor also helps dampen some of the upward force, but not all of it. You will need to keep applying downward pressure while firing to keep from shooting at the ceiling."

I stared at the alien contraption in my hands.

"There's no way I can hit anything I shoot at with this thing."

"You don't have to. As soon as you start firing, that guy down there's going to duck into hiding."

"Do you know how to reload?"

I stared at the finely milled black metal in my hands. I was lucky I knew about the trigger, my life was so sheltered. I looked at him, confusion written all over my face.

"That's what I thought," he said. "That magazine's gonna empty fast, and you won't have the chance to fire again, so I have one shot at getting to my car."

I looked at him, tears welling up along the edges of my eyes. He moved forward and cupped my face in his hands. It caught me by surprise, and was too intimate a move for the situation we found ourselves in.

I looked into his eyes. The last time Robert had done this, he'd thought I was someone else.

I was so starved for that kind of contact; I guess that's why I talked myself into becoming the other Michele. To feel like a woman again.

Janssen moved his face close to mine and looked deeply into my eyes. Had he realized that we wouldn't be surviving the night and wanted to go out in a blaze of sexual glory?

Instead of kissing me, he said, "Do you trust me?"

Still comfortably held in his grip, I moved my head up and down.

"Good."

He still had my head in his hands. He gave me an odd look, and then tilted my head down to kiss me warmly on the forehead.

He released my face slowly and backed away. I don't know if it was the threat of impending death or the fact that he had saved my life repeatedly tonight, but my body ached for his touch again. This had to be the most inappropriate place for these types of feelings, but matters of the heart always had a big problem with timing.

"Now, you just point this in that direction and hold down the trigger. We'll be out of here before you know it."

He angled close to the front of the car and looked back at me. He held up three fingers and started counting down silently. I felt like a school girl who had been promised a kiss by the football quarterback if they won the next game.

On the count of one I jumped up, pointed the assault rifle at the mercenary standing at the entrance, and screamed as I pulled the trigger.

I was rewarded with a faint click, but nothing else. No missiles of hot searing death propelled out the front of my rifle. The mercenary at the entrance gave me a strange look and then smiled at me as he swung his own rifle in my direction and fired.

Chapter 31

I dropped out of sight, the rifle clattering to the ground at my feet. Sparks exploded above my head and tinted glass rained down on me.

What had happened?

Why hadn't the damn thing fired?

I looked over at Janssen for guidance on what went wrong, but he was gone.

He had abandoned me. I crouched all by myself on the side of the car with nothing, and no one, to protect me. The mercenary at the entrance stopped firing. His voice boomed across the distance, with the hint of a South African warlord speech pattern to it.

If I ever made it out of this alive, I vowed to watch fewer action movies on Netflix.

"Detective Janssen! Turn over the girl and I will let you live."

I scanned the parking garage all around me, but I couldn't find Janssen anywhere. I peered under the car and could see the mercenary's black boots slowly coming down the slope of the parking lot entrance as he continued talking.

"My associate misspoke when he said he would kill you because you saw our faces. He paid for that mistake with his life, but you don't have to do the same. I used to be a police officer myself in Johannesburg, so I get it. What else were you supposed to do when a group of heavily armed thugs entered your station? Your actions are totally understandable and, whether you believe it or not, I do live by a code of honor."

From my angle under the car, I could see the mercenary was fully in the garage and checking between every car as he slowly progressed toward me.

"But I will only give you one chance to give the girl to me. If you surrender yourself right now, you have my word that you will not die tonight."

Janssen didn't respond. I wasn't even sure he was still in the garage. Maybe he had used me as his distraction to escape and save himself. He had used me as a human shield earlier, so it was in line with his tactics. Bastard!

"Do you hear me, Janssen? Give up now or the deal is off the table."

I glanced over at the rifle. It was useless, but maybe I could still use it to survive the night on my own. Janssen had abandoned me, and there was no way I could escape, so I had no other choice. I grabbed the rifle and stood up quickly, holding it high over my head in surrender.

The African mercenary instantly crouched and pointed his rifle at me.

"Toss the gun to the side."

I threw it into the aisle between the parked cars. The mercenary glanced around.

"Are you alone?"

I nodded.

"What happened to the detective?"

"He left me."

The mercenary laughed heartily and stood up straight.

"I thought he had more backbone than that."

"Me too."

My only hope was that he would take me to Robert and not kill me. I wanted to know what was happening and Robert was my only way to find out.

"If he's hiding at your feet with a gun, I'll kill you both."

"I promise you, he's not with me."

"Where did he go?"

I shrugged.

"I don't know, and frankly, I don't care. Take me to Robert."

The dark mercenary's eyes squinted as he kept creeping closer to me.

"Who?"

"Robert sent you here to get me, didn't he?"

"I'm not at liberty to discuss who sent me. My orders are to collect you and the dead one."

"The dead one?"

He wasn't given the chance to reply. He had just reached Janssen's grey Prius when it shot out in near silence, the only warning that the car was about to move was the sudden white flare of reverse lights.

The mercenary screamed and started firing into the back of the Prius as it slammed into him, pushed him across the aisle, and crushed him into the side of a police cruiser.

Janssen pulled forward quickly, and then reversed again, smashing the mercenary between his bumper and the side of the police cruiser once more for good measure.

Janssen pulled out, swung the car wide and then backed up to where I was still standing with my hands in the air. He leaned over and opened the passenger door.

"Get in!"

He hadn't abandoned me after all. My feet were in motion before I realized that I was going to keep trusting the detective who had saved my life yet again.

As I jumped into the car, he punched the accelerator and we shot forward out of the parking garage; the forward movement closing my door for me.

At this speed, the incline leading up and out of the garage became a stunt ramp and we took to the air. Bullets pinged on the sides of the car as more mercenaries tried to prevent our escape.

"Stay down," Janssen screamed as he shoved me toward the floorboards.

Tires squealed in protest as he skidded around the first corner and then we rocketed down the street, fewer and fewer bullets hitting the car as we escaped with our lives intact.

Chapter 32

We continued in silence through the night as Janssen drove north along Pennsylvania Route 66. I leaned my head against the window. Only the rear window had been shattered, so we didn't look too out of place among the other cars on the freeway. What few cars there were at this hour probably never even bothered looking at our bullet hole-riddled car anyway.

Janssen finished his call abruptly and tossed his cell phone onto the dashboard.

"Damn battery died. At least Dalton knows I'm coming."

"Where are we going?"

"I'm taking you somewhere safe for the night."

I twisted in my seat to face him.

"How do you know it's safe?"

"I have a friend who works where we're going. I've known him since grade school, so I can trust him."

"Could you trust your police captain?"

He gave me a sideways glance.

"What's that supposed to mean?"

"That mercenary said you weren't even supposed to be there. What did he mean by that?"

"I don't know. I'm still working that through my head."

"How did they know your name?"

Janssen shot me a look.

"I said I don't know, okay!"

I turned away and watched the road ahead lit by the one working headlight.

The car started to sputter and jerk slightly.

"Shit!" Janssen muttered under his breath.

"What's the matter?"

"I filled up this morning, and we're almost out of gas. A bullet must have punctured the tank."

"This is a hybrid right? How long can you go on the electric engine after you run out of gas?"

"It doesn't work like that."

Up ahead the lights of a small town came into view.

"We're going to have to ditch this somewhere and find another way."

"Maybe there's a gas station up ahead."

He shook his head.

"Won't do any good if the tank is full of holes."

"You don't know that."

"I do know I filled up this morning. I should have been able to take us all the way to Canada and back, twice, before I needed to full up again. We've been driving for less than an hour and the needle is already on empty."

The lights on the dash dimmed and the car sputtered again. He tapped the touch screen display and switched to the car graphic that showed we had less than a mile left of electric charge.

He turned on his hazard lights and we slowed down, trying to coax as much juice from the batteries to get us all the way to the lights of the town up ahead.

Soon, red lights began to come to life all around the dash, trying to warn us of imminent engine failure.

He tugged on the wheel and guided the car slowly off the two-lane highway and rolled to a stop in front of a corrugated steel building right before the car jerked to a stop.

He shifted the car into park and let out an irritated breath.

"Well, that's it."

He grabbed his cell phone and held down the power button. It refused to turn on as well.

He tossed it back onto the dash.

"Dammit!"

He sat back and covered his face with his hands.

And started to laugh.

I didn't say a word, and let him work through whatever was going through his mind. He had just killed several people, and that was finally hitting him. People reacted differently to intense stress, and what we had just been through was very extreme.

He stopped laughing and rubbed his face quickly before turning to face me.

"Let's walk up to the town and see about getting a ride."

I looked at him. He was disheveled and torn, with dried blood clotting the wounds of his face. Then I remembered I was still wearing a bright orange prison jumpsuit.

Who in their right mind would give either of us a ride, let alone both of us at the same time?

He seemed to notice the same thing and looked himself over in the rear view mirror, trying to smooth his wild hair into some semblance of order. All he ended up doing was making himself look even more deranged.

"Okay," he said. "Hitchhiking is out. I guess we will have to borrow a car."

I couldn't believe what I was hearing, from an officer of the law no less.

"You mean steal a car?!"

"I said borrow. I will make sure it gets back to the owner."

"Can't you just call for help?"

He held up the cell phone, as if showing it to me would make me understand better.

"Battery's dead."

I looked down the street at the lights reflected on the low clouds.

"There has to be a payphone or something in town."

He laughed.

"That 'town' is nothing more than a gas station and a truck stop diner."

"I'm sure they have a phone."

"I don't think it's a good idea to call anyone until you're safe."

"You don't think I'm safe yet?"

He looked at me; his serious expression caused my heart to skip a beat.

"Not until you are at Forest."

"What's Forest?"

He smiled.

"It's a surprise."

I didn't have the heart to tell him I hated surprises because, for the past week, my life had been nothing but one surprise after another. I didn't think he would even believe me.

A bug tried to fly into my right ear. I waved it away with a hand, but it stayed right next to me. I swatted again, rubbing up against my ear.

The buzzing grew louder as if the bug had flown into my ear. I stuck my finger in and swished it around.

Janssen looked at me strangely.

"Are you okay?"

The bug buzzed even louder, and my head started to ache.

"I think a bug flew into my ear."

He leaned over and swiped at the air around my head.

"Is it gone?"

"It's in my ear," I said in a panic and dug my finger deeper into my ear.

Janssen opened his door, the overhead light dimly glowing from whatever juice was left in the car battery. He grabbed my hand and pulled it away before I dug all the way to my brain.

He twisted my head and peered in my ear.

"There's nothing in there," he said.

I could barely hear him over the increasing buzz saw that sounded like it was cutting my skull in half.

"Make it stop," I screamed.

"I don't see anything," Janssen yelled.

Suddenly, everything went deathly silent.

He noticed my face changed and I had stopped struggling against him, so he let go of me. I looked around and then over at Janssen with a smile on my face.

"It's gone," I said.

And then the world went white.

Chapter 33

It was dark, but slowly my senses were returning. The first sensation I discerned was of a slight rocking, like a boat on the ocean in a light breeze.

I felt the light breeze lift my hair and brush it across my face.

The next sensation was of my body pressed against someone else. It felt like I was draped over them. My inner ears instantly re-oriented my body and I realized I was being carried sideways.

My eyes popped open and I saw Janssen's face next to mine as he carried me across his shoulders like a road kill deer.

He heard my audible gasp and his head snapped to look me in the eyes. I saw his concerned face shift instantly to relief.

"I thought you were going to die on me."

He lowered me down and I stood unsteadily on my feet, leaning heavily on him while my inner ears struggled to stabilize me.

"What happened?" he asked, the concern on his face making me feel warm all over.

"I don't know. There was a buzzing sound, and then nothing."

"Have you ever passed out like that before?"

"No. Never," I replied.

I looked around at the unfamiliar surroundings. His car wasn't anywhere near us. Neither was the town that we had stopped near. In fact, there was no road. It seemed we were in the middle of the woods.

"Where are we?"

"As soon as you collapsed, I gathered you up and was ready to find a car to borrow…"

"Steal," I corrected him.

"Well, anyway. I had just reached the gas station when a helicopter appeared out of nowhere and hovered over where I had left the car, shining a bright light down on it. I carried you off the road and hid in a drainage pipe while several black SUV's screamed past. I've stayed off the road ever since. Every now and then, I stopped to duck down as the helicopter made another pass overhead."

My mouth hung open. Janssen asked the same questions that were swirling around in my head.

"Who are these guys? Why do they want you so bad? And how did they know where we were?"

I didn't have an answer to any of his questions. Everything that happened only made everything else make less sense. I racked my memories for something to hold onto that would bring clarity to everything else.

There was nothing.

"How long was I out?"

"About four hours. I figure we are less than a couple of hours away from my friend. Now that you are awake, we can move faster, that is if you think you can walk."

I felt fine, as if nothing had happened.

I nodded and let go of him.

"I can walk on my own."

He looked around and pointed into the thicket of trees.

"I passed a dry creek bed a couple hundred feet back that way. We can make better time following that."

As we walked, every now and then Janssen would suddenly crouch down to one knee and hold his hand up in a fist. I quickly learned that was his silent hand signal instructing me to stop, get low, and stay quiet.

As I followed him through the rough terrain, Janssen seemed to be comfortable with the harsh environment. No, more than comfortable. He seemed to be at home in the middle of the forest.

Despite never being more than a mile from a house, or the road, it felt like we were in the middle of uncharted territory that had never had been trod on by humans before.

Janssen moved through it noiselessly while I crashed through the forest behind him, snapping every twig on the ground in my path and rustling every leaf in a three foot radius around me. He had given up on trying to make me walk quietly through the middle of the wild countryside.

It was still dark when we reached the edge of the forest next to railroad tracks. He gave the stop signal and I crouched next to him.

He leaned in close and whispered in my ear.

"Stay here until I come back."

"Where are you going?" I whispered back.

"This is where my friend works. I need to make sure we can get in."

He started to stand up and I grabbed his arm to stop him, electricity shocking my whole body as our skin touched.

He crouched back down and I looked into his eyes in the darkness. Even in the pale light of the moon, they shone brightly.

"What if you don't come back?"

He looked out of the forest and then back at me, letting his warm smile spread to his eyes. It was mesmerizing. I wanted to stay just like this; lost in his eyes forever.

"I'll be back. I promise."

"How long do I wait?"

"Until I come back."

I gripped his arm tighter.

"But what if you don't?"

He placed a hand on my hand. Despite the cold air around us, my whole body warmed at his tender touch.

"Do you believe me when I tell you that nothing could keep me from coming back?"

My mind replayed everything he had done to keep me safe at the police station, and after. I had my own personal John McClain, Jason Bourne, and Jack Bauer all rolled up into one.

"I believe you," I said barely above a whisper.

He smiled and my body quickly heated up even more. He gently peeled my hand off of his arm and pointed into the woods.

"Stay out of sight until I come for you."

I crashed noisily deeper into the woods and waited. The longer I sat there, the colder I got. I longed for the warmth from Detective Janssen. I wanted him to be here with me. I wanted him to always come back for me.

Did he want to come back for me?

Janssen had been confused by the reports that showed the

other Michele and I were identical in every way, except for age and the tattoo on our wrists.

He had mentioned that even identical twins weren't identical at the DNA level. There were still differences. But, according to his lab reports, the other Michele and I were the same person.

Only, one of us was dead, and the other was still very much alive and on the run.

On the run from what?

From who?

Robert?

The mercenary didn't know who I was talking about when I demanded to be taken to Robert. I had assumed Robert was behind everything.

Maybe I was wrong and he was caught up in something he had no control over.

But why me?

I had seen enough movies to know that the only way to get two people with identical DNA was to clone them.

Robert had been replicating my life with the other Michele up until she took her own life. Had he replicated her body as well?

But why had Robert cloned me to make another Michele?

I glanced at the tattoo on my wrist.

Maybe he hadn't cloned me.

I glanced at the seven dots on my wrist around the infinity symbol.

I still didn't fully understand how or why, but the only thing that made sense was;

I was a clone.

Chapter 34

In the cold darkness of the forest I huddled next to a tree with my knees drawn up trying to stay warm.

Leaves rustled close by and I looked up to see a dark shape near me. Right before I cried out for Janssen to help me, the shadow rushed forward and clamped a hand over my mouth.

The dark shape angled to let the moonlight hit his face and I relaxed in his grip.

Janssen smiled as he released his hand.

"Told you I'd be back."

I wrapped my arms around his neck and buried my face into his chest. I breathed in his scent. It still had the rustic smell of blood mixed with dried sweat, but at that moment it was the sweetest smell I had ever experienced.

"What's that for?" he asked softly.

I clung to his warmth and safety.

How can I tell him I missed him?

He gripped my shoulders and held me at arm's length.

"How would you like a warm shower and clean clothes? Something other than that ugly orange jumpsuit?"

I looked down at my brightly colored prison attire and smiled back.

"I don't know. Orange is the new black you know."

He helped me to my feet and we walked out of the forest down the railroad tracks until we reached a crossroad.

I looked at the barbed wire running along the top of the chain link fence that stretched away from us in both directions. The gate on the road was open and a man stood near it in denim jeans and a plaid shirt.

He waved to us to come forward.

I turned to Janssen.

"Where are we?"

He placed his arm around my shoulder and walked me forward toward the open gate.

"Forest State Correctional Institute."

I stiffened in his arms.

"Is this a prison?"

"A maximum-security male only prison."

"You're not taking me in there are you?"

"No. You will stay in one of the houses used by senior correctional officers, of which Dalton is one."

"Who?"

"The friend I was telling you about. He is a supervisor at Forest."

I stopped walking and Janssen gave me a curious look.

"It's okay. This is not a trick."

I looked from the open gate that led to prison, and then back over my shoulder to the wide open world where shadowy soldiers were trying to kill me.

I was frozen with indecision.

Janssen placed a finger on my chin and turned me to face him.

"Still trust me?"

"I do."

My heart leapt into my throat as I said those words and my mind instantly showed us standing before a priest, with him in a black tuxedo and me, all in white.

His eyes sparkled as he held my chin.

"Let's get cleaned up and get some rest. Everything will be better in the morning."

I let him lead me through the gates. His friend, Dalton, looked at me with appraising eyes.

"Now there's something you don't see every day around here," Dalton said.

Janssen twisted me away from Dalton.

"You promised me she would be safe here."

Dalton gave a mock look of shock.

"There is no safer place for a girl in the world. Nobody in their right mind, or even off their rocker, would ever think to look for her here."

Dalton shut the gate and climbed into an electric golf cart, waiting for us to join him.

He drove less than five hundred feet before turning off the road onto a small street with three houses encircling the cul-desac.

Dalton pointed to the one house on the left.

"Mine's the big one on the end. Perks of being senior management."

He pulled into the driveway and shut off the electric cart, stepping out in a fluid and practiced motion before the cart had fully stopped.

Dalton's house was filled with all sorts of computers, all connected together with cables. It looked like the inside of a computer hacker's den rather than the lead supervisor of a correctional facility.

It was hard to not trip over the cables that stretched back and forth across every inch of the floor.

Janssen guided me through the jungle of computers and cables, looking around him at the absolute mess.

"What is all this?"

Dalton beamed as he brushed Ding Dong boxes and wrappers off a dining room chair in the middle of the living room. He smiled as he held his arms wide, taking in the whole room.

"I monitor all sorts of satellite communications. It's sort of a hobby of mine. Not only can I access every television satellite circling the globe, I can even eavesdrop on the NSA's eavesdropping. It's like meta-eavesdropping."

He picked up a printout that was filled with nonsense characters and looked sullenly at it.

"I don't have the encryption codes, so I don't know what is being said, but I can still listen."

Janssen looked around at the mismatched equipment that had been cobbled together with wires.

"That doesn't sound very legal?"

Dalton rolled his eyes.

"You of all people shouldn't lecture me on what is legal."

Janssen laughed.

"I'm a cop now."

Dalton nodded.

"So you say. How is the quiet life of a cop treating you these days?"

Janssen and I exchanged a glance before he responded to Dalton.

"Not too quiet. An extraction team tried to take her from my station."

Dalton raised an eyebrow.

"Extraction team? Whose?"

"They didn't have any insignia, but I recognized one of them. Whoever hired them didn't go for the best on the market; which was lucky for us."

"Lucky!" I blurted. "They nearly killed us."

Janssen laughed. It seemed odd that he was taking what had happened so lightly.

"If I hadn't had the element of surprise on my side, and they were a little more organized, they would have killed both of us."

He turned to Dalton.

"Any chatter about who might have attacked a downtown Pittsburgh police station."

Dalton shook his head.

"I checked all my backups and printouts. I couldn't find anything remotely like that."

He snatched up a graph printed out on form-feed paper.

"But I did notice something strange."

He held the paper up. It showed a line graph that drew a line along the bottom of the paper and then suddenly spiked to the top of the page before settling back down to the bottom of the page.

"This is from an unregistered satellite I picked up a few months ago. Since I never got more than a steady baseline signal from it, I decided it was some cheap Chinese communications satellite that had failed."

He pointed to the peak of the spike.

"And then, about five hours ago this happened. I've never seen anything like it, and it hasn't done it again."

Janssen regarded the printout.

"How do you know?"

Dalton pointed to a printer that had been quietly spitting out reams of paper ever since we had arrived. He ripped out a section and held it up.

"The signal has gone back to the baseline."

I suddenly noticed the stacks of boxes of printer paper that served as stands for half of the computer monitors.

"Have you been printing this one satellite's signal this whole time?"

Dalton shook his head.

"I started about a month after I found it."

"Why?" I asked.

A smile spread across his lips.

"Because it's different. If it was really broken, there wouldn't be any signal at all. I've been watching it to see if there was any pattern, but there never was any change in the signal until earlier tonight."

He looked at Janssen.

"I probably never would have noticed if you hadn't called me."

My bladder suddenly urged me to deal with something I had been ignoring for far too long. I looked at Dalton.

"Is there somewhere I can go to the bathroom?"

Dalton placed his hands on the side of his head.

"I'm an idiot. You guys look like hell and all I've been doing is blathering on about failed Chinese satellites."

Janssen nodded.

"I think we can both use a little refreshing."

Dalton pointed to a room that, thankfully, had no cables leading to it.

"There is a washroom with a shower in the master bedroom. I found some clothes for you, Control, but I wasn't able to find much for your lady friend."

I tugged at the jumpsuit.

"That's okay. Anything will be better than this."

"You two go on in and get cleaned up. Feel free to turn on the TV in there. I get every channel."

Janssen followed me into the master bedroom and shut the door behind us. For the second time since we had met, we were alone in a room together. Only, this one had a bed in it.

I instantly blushed and he jabbed a thumb at the door as he stammered.

"I can wait outside with Dalton while you get cleaned up if you want?"

I looked at him in the bright light. He was even more ruggedly handsome than before, if that was possible with what he had been through along with the lack of sleep.

I gave him a half-smile.

"I'm still technically under arrest. You probably shouldn't leave me alone in a room with windows."

He smiled back, understanding my playfulness.

"I think you are right. Should I turn around at least?"

I walked closer to him and studied the cuts on his face caused by tangling with hired killers. Hired killers with me as their target. I didn't want to be alone right now, and I needed to find comfort from someone. Robert was not around, and I wasn't sure I would find comfort from him ever again.

I took Janssen's hand and led him to the bathroom and turned on the sink, pulling up the stopper lever to let the basin fill with warm water.

His eyebrows knitted together.

"What are you doing?"

I placed a finger on his lip.

"It's the least I can do for saving my life; repeatedly."

I dunked a washcloth in the water and twisted the excess water from it. I wiped away the grime from his face and neck that had accumulated while he was keeping me out of harm's way.

I rinsed the washcloth and then wiped away the dried blood and sweat from around his forehead.

He gave me a confused smile.

"I don't think I need…"

I raised my arm with my hand balled into a fist. He understood the silent command and his mouth snapped shut.

"Let me do this for you, Detective Janssen," I whispered and slowly unbuttoned his shirt.

"Please," he said. "Call me Austin."

Smiling, I pulled off his shirt, spun him around and began to clean his back. I carefully wiped away the sweat from his muscled torso. I had been married to someone twice my age for four years. While I was not turned off by him, his body had shown its age. Now I was with a perfect specimen closer to my own age.

Wiping his back with the wet towel ignited a fire deep inside and made me hunger for what he could do to me. I could tell, as I wiped the grime from his shoulders and back, he would not treat me like I was about to break.

I stood on tiptoes and brushed my lips against his ears.

He nuzzled me at first and then pulled away slightly.

"You sure you want to do this?"

I had never wanted anything so much in my life. I pressed my body against his and nibbled his earlobe lightly.

He spun in my embrace and looked me in the eyes before running his gaze down my body. He suddenly smiled and a chuckle escaped his perfect lips.

I frowned at him for breaking the mood and looked down at myself.

I was still in the orange prison jumpsuit that was covered in dried blood.

Not the sexiest of attire.

He reached for the zipper at my neck and slowly zipped it down; exposing the exercise bra and panties I wore underneath.

He placed his forehead against mine and placed a hand around the back of my neck.

His warm breath enveloped my face and I closed my eyes in anticipation of what came next.

"We shouldn't do this," he whispered.

"I want to," I whispered back.

He let out a fast breath of air and moved back, away from me.

"I want to, but all of this is just leftover adrenaline from earlier."

I shook my head.

"No. I know what I want."

"You don't know what you want."

"Yes I do. I want you."

His hands squeezed my arms gently and he looked into my eyes.

"In another place and time, maybe there could have been something."

He let me go and grabbed a towel from the rack. He walked away, drying himself off. I watched him dress in the new shirt that his friend had left on the bed along with another full set of clothes for me.

"No way!" Dalton exclaimed loudly from the living room.

Austin looked toward the closed door and back to me.

"As soon as you are dressed, come on out so we can decide what to do next. As he closed the door behind him, leaving me alone in the bedroom with an empty bed, I knew exactly what I wanted to do next.

I turned toward the mirror, and for the first time, noticed the dried blood caked on the side of my face from when Austin had shot the mercenary that had me pinned to the ground.

He had killed so quickly and effortlessly.

There was no remorse in his eyes for what he had been forced to do to get me safely away from the police station.

I used the same washcloth to wipe the blood from my face. Behind it was a person who was as unfamiliar to me as a stranger on a train.

I laughed quietly at my reflection.

Strangers on a Train.

I really shouldn't have treated my Netflix queue as a personal challenge.

After I put on the boy jeans and checkered flannel shirt, I wadded up the orange jumpsuit and stuffed it into the trash can under the bathroom sink.

I took one last look at myself in the mirror. With the boyfriend clothing, I thought I looked even more alluring. Without the blood all over my face, and the prison jumpsuit, maybe Austin would look at me differently.

A bug buzzed by my ear again.

I refocused my attention and waved at the air, but I didn't see any bugs flying around the vanity lights above the mirror.

Fully dressed, I walked out to the living room where Dalton and Austin were huddled over the printer as it ground away with its dot matrix print head on more of the green and white striped form-feed paper.

"What's so exciting?" I asked as I waved at the air next to my right ear to shoo away the bug that wouldn't leave me alone.

A beep sounded from a monitor to one side. Dalton looked at it like it had suddenly turned into a pink elephant with yellow polka dots.

"Wow," he exclaimed.

"What?" Austin asked.

"It's happening again."

"What's happening again?" I asked.

He looked from me to the computer screen, and then back at the paper spitting from the printer.

"That satellite, the broken Chinese one I told you about, it's doing that thing again."

The buzzing got louder and I winced as pain shot through my jaw just below my right ear.

Austin looked at me, his mouth opening slowly.

"What's the matter?"

I slapped at the side of my head.

"Those damn bugs are in my ear again."

Dalton pointed to the monitor that mirrored the printout.

"Look!"

The line on the bottom of the graph was slowly climbing higher. I tried to concentrate on why this was so exciting to him, but the bug had gotten in my ear and I went after it with a finger.

Dalton was alternating his attention between a wrinkled sheet of paper in his hand and the monitor. He looked at Austin, hopping up and down with excitement.

"If the new signal matches the last one, it should peak in about ten seconds."

Austin was watching me with rapt attention. I flinched again as the buzzing in my head grew to a fever pitch.

The last thing I saw was the room tilting wildly as Austin rushed toward me, obviously realizing what was about to happen before I did.

"There it is," Dalton shrieked. "Just like I said."

And then everything went white.

Chapter 35

This time, my senses returned more quickly and I opened my eyes first. I found myself staring up at the ceiling of a car, the sensation of moving almost making me seasick.

The sun was low in the sky, but it was a bright light which meant it was morning and not sunset. Dalton's face came into view, looked at me with a smile, and then looked away.

"She's awake," he said.

The car jerked to one side and skidded to a halt. Austin's face came into view and looked down at me.

"Are you okay?"

Dalton helped me sit up, the world spinning wildly around me.

"I think so. What happened?"

Dalton was hopping in the seat next to me like a little kid.

"You were triggered by the satellite signal. It was fuckin' awesome."

Austin reached over the back of the seat and punched Dalton in the shoulder.

"Don't be an asshole, Alt. That thing almost killed her."

Dalton frowned and rubbed his shoulder.

"It never would have killed her. My guess, it was designed to transmit her location and then knock her out for recovery."

I looked at Dalton in alarm.

"Knock me out? Recovery? What are you talking about?"

Dalton held up a grain of rice in his hand and inspected it.

"This was embedded under the skin behind your right ear, although I've never seen one this small. We used to use them all the time in…"

"Alt!" Austin interrupted.

Dalton snapped his mouth shut and a litany of silent looks shot back and forth between the two men, ending with what looked like Austin winning the soundless argument.

I reached up and felt under the band aid stuck to my ear. I didn't feel any pain as I poked at it and pulled off the plastic strip, wincing as it pulled some hair out with it. There was no blood on the cotton square. I would have expected there to be some after cutting into my scalp.

I touched the space behind my ear, but felt nothing. I couldn't even find where they had cut into me.

"Where was it?" I asked Dalton.

I turned my head and let him inspect behind my ear.

"Huh," he said. "You heal fast."

"Alt, please," Austin said from the front.

I leaned back. I guess having Dalton around was good if his hand was so steady as to make a precise cut that healed quickly.

But what history did these two have? It seemed to be stronger than just growing up together as kids, and seemed to include something far more recent that Austin didn't want told.

I decided to let them have their secrets and decided to ask a more innocuous question.

I turned to Dalton.

"Alt?"

Dalton's eyes flicked to Austin and then back to me while he replied in a reserved monotone.

"It's short for Dalton."

Austin turned around and started the car back up. Dalton mouthed, "Tell you later" to me silently as Austin pulled the car onto the road.

We rode in silence for a few minutes before Dalton leaned forward over the front seat.

"Can I show her the video?"

Austin thought about that for a minute and then pulled to the side of the road, shutting off the engine.

"Might as well. Maybe she will recognize someone."

I looked at Dalton.

"What video?"

Dalton pulled a cell phone from his pocket and tapped on it excitedly as he spoke.

"Less than an hour after we left, my automated security systems recorded this."

He held the phone sideways. Thankfully, he had a large-screened phone and I was able to see the interior of his living room clearly.

"What am I...," I started to say when he wiggled a finger at me and pointed at the screen.

"Just watch."

I leaned over and watched his empty living room. Well, empty except for the hundreds of cables that stretched from the dozens of computers.

The front door suddenly exploded inward, or more accurately it was reduced to splinters as it knocked several computers over from the concussive blast. Several black-clad soldiers rushed in and fanned out through the room, all pointing in different directions.

I looked at Dalton. He could see the fear written on my face. They were coming for me and, if Austin and Dalton hadn't left when they did, we would have been caught by now.

"Keep watching. Let me know if you recognize anyone."

I studied the movie playing on Dalton's phone. Two of the mercenaries broke from the group and rushed through the doors into the bedroom. After a few seconds, they returned to the living room with their rifles lowered, the second one tossing my orange jumpsuit into the middle of the room.

The rest of the mercenaries all stood up as they remained vigilant, but visibly relaxed.

One of the mercenaries kicked over a computer monitor in frustration and started yelling at the other mercenaries. The movie played like an old silent film and I couldn't hear anything the lead mercenary was screaming at his subordinates. I looked at Dalton.

"Is there sound?"

Dalton winced and closed his eyes briefly.

"I installed the camera to see who kept unplugging computer cables while I was at work. Turns out a raccoon had dug a hole under a printer stand and was yanking out cables every time he left. The system wasn't designed to survive a dynamic entry like that. I was lucky the camera still works after all the C4 they used on the door."

On the screen, all the mercenaries snapped to attention when the front doorway darkened. A man I recognized entered the room. It was someone I had just met yesterday at the police station. I pointed at the screen.

"That's my attorney."

Dalton laughed.

"An attorney. That's a new one. Even for him."

I looked at Dalton.

"Do you know him?"

Dalton's face grew somber, but Austin answered for him.

"Yeah. We know him. He's not an attorney, I can tell you that. When did he tell you he was your attorney?"

"He was in the room right before you came in."

Austin banged a fist on the steering wheel.

"That son-of-a-bitch. He walked right in and I had no idea he was there."

"Who is he?" I asked.

Dalton cleared his throat.

"He's someone you don't want to find you."

"Why not?"

"Because, the next time he has you in his sights, you will probably end up dead."

"Alt!" Austin snapped.

Dalton held his free hand up.

"Hey, just letting the lady know what she's got herself into and how serious this is."

"How serious is this?" I asked.

Dalton and Austin exchanged a glance. Austin nodded his head, apparently giving Dalton the all clear to bring me into the loop.

"If the people who are after you hired that guy," Dalton pointed at my attorney on the screen. "They don't want to capture you. They want to kill you."

"Who is he, and how do you two know him?"

Dalton's eyes looked away from mine.

"He's not someone you want to be tangling with. Keep watching. There's more people for you to see."

On the phone screen, the doorway darkened again and my jaw

fell open involuntary as I saw who entered the room and looked around at the destruction wrought when the mercenaries had blasted their way in.

I should have guessed he would be there, but up until that moment, I had wanted to believe he was as innocent as I was in the entire situation.

There was no denying, based on how everyone treated him as he walked around the damaged computers that he was heavily involved in what was happening to me.

The man stepped closer, the top half of his body filling the frame. Dalton tapped the screen to pause the video.

"I take it, from your reaction, you know this guy?"

I nodded and looked at Dalton, but I didn't really see him. My mind was elsewhere as I answered.

"He's my husband."

Dalton and Austin exchanged another look, but stayed silent as two other people, a bald man and woman with grey hair tied up in a bun, entered the room and spoke with Robert and my killer attorney.

"Do you recognize either of these two people?" Dalton asked.

I squinted at the small screen.

I shook my head.

"Think hard. Have you ever seen them before? In the waiting room at the dentist? In line behind you at the grocery store? Sitting near you in a restaurant?"

I studied the faces of both the man and the woman as they walked around the shattered computers. Nothing came to mind.

"No. Never."

On the screen, the attorney suddenly looked right at the camera.

He moved closer until his whole face filled the screen.

As he smiled, the scar on the side of his face tugged awkwardly at the skin of his cheek. He pointed directly at the camera with two fingers on his left hand and one finger on his right hand and then the screen went blank. Dalton turned off the phone and stuck it in his pocket.

"That's all there is."

I thought about what the attorney had done right at the end. I looked at Dalton.

"What was that thing he did right before the camera died?"

Dalton looked out the window.

"He was sending us a message."

"What message?"

Austin turned back forward and started up the car. Dalton held three fingers up in the same configuration that the attorney had as we headed back out on the road.

"These are the fingers you use on a keyboard to hit the keys Ctrl-Alt-Delete."

"Why did he do that to the camera?"

"He letting us know he will find us and kill us unless we do what he wants."

Chapter 36

I sat in silence as Austin drove us in circles across half the state. He turned on the radio and kept switching from one news station to another every few minutes.

After half an hour of this, Dalton was snoring loudly beside me and I was no longer listening to the announcers who all sounded like the same person as they regurgitated the same news over and over.

I still had no idea why someone would want to kill me, other than being part of some secret cloning project, I had no enemies.

Cloning? It's like I had stepped into a science fiction movie.

What little I knew about cloning, which was admittedly nothing beyond an article in TIME Magazine, was that scientists were decades away from actually cloning humans, and that research was delayed even further due to moral and legal implications and restrictions.

I absentmindedly rubbed the tattoo on my wrist.

I was number seven.

My doppelgänger was number eight.

What else could it be but cloning?

Why had Robert become involved?

And why was he working with a ruthless killer to come after me?

If what Dalton said was true, I was more valuable dead than alive to whoever Robert was working with.

I envisioned the bald man and the older woman and racked my brain for any semblance of a memory that I had seen them before.

My memory!

Ironically, I had forgotten that I had lost my memory four years ago. Did that have something to do with what was happening to me now? Had I seen something that mattered to the people Robert worked with?

Or worked for?

As I thought back to my first meeting with him, I saw everything with a new perspective.

Now that I looked back, everything had seemed a little quick. A little forced.

Our chance encounter in a grocery store.

Our weekly dating that resulted in an unexpected proposal and hasty marriage within a year. I wasn't a prude, by any stretch of the imagination, but going from single to married in the space of a year was fast; even for me.

Had I seen something before I lost my memory that someone didn't want me to remember?

Was that why Robert was sent to keep an eye on me? Was Dr. Westcott involved?

I thought about the long list of medications she was constantly subscribing. When I had stopped them, I had started to feel better and could think more clearly.

Were the doctor and my husband working together to keep me from actually getting my memories back?

Had I even lost my memory?

Or had Robert's associates taken it from me?

Even if they had, none of that answered why there was another Michele who was repeating my life with Robert.

Austin's DNA tests had proven we were the same person inhabiting two separate bodies. I studied the dots on my wrist that bordered the infinity symbol on the top and bottom. Was my tattoo a label that told somebody what or who I was, like the serial number on a computer to uniquely identify it?

Had somebody manufactured me in a lab?

Was I somebody's property?

But I was almost twenty-five years old. According to everything in TIME's report, we were still decades away from cloning humans. I had to have been cloned twenty-five years ago, long before the technology was good enough to clone Dolly the sheep.

Is that why someone wanted me dead?

Was I the first clone to escape from their protective net?

I stared at the seven dots in my tattoo.

I wasn't the first.

What happened to the others?

Chapter 37

I shook my head, forcing the dark thoughts out and looked up as Austin steered the car into a parking lot behind a truck stop restaurant.

He shut off the engine and spun around to look at Dalton asleep next to me in the back seat. He leaned over and smacked Dalton's knee.

Dalton bolted upright and looked around.

"Are we there?"

Austin shook his head.

"There's been nothing on the news about the attack at the police station last night, or anything about the actions at Forest."

Dalton wiped a hand across his face and dug the crust out of the corners of his eyes.

"Forest likes to keep a low profile; I can imagine how that wouldn't get into the news."

Austin frowned.

"I exchanged dozens of rounds with several of Nick's mercs. We shot the place up to hell. Surely something would have leaked out when the next shift arrived."

"Who's Nick?" I asked.

Dalton ignored me and rubbed his face one more time, stretching out his chin with a hand as he continued his conversation with Austin.

"How come you were the only one to see Nick's mercs?"

"Who's Nick?" I demanded louder.

They both looked at me.

"He's the guy who pretended to be your lawyer," Dalton replied, as if I should have already known that. "For some reason, he's also the guy who emptied a police station of all personnel before going in."

"I've been wondering about that. When I went to the station, it was just to pick up a copy of the file to study at home. Instead, I came across unmarked soldiers removing a body from the morgue."

Austin looked at me.

"As soon as I saw who they had, I knew they were coming for you too, so I got you out of there as easily as I could."

I snorted an uncomfortable laugh.

"You call that easy?"

"My point exactly. I left plenty of damage and dead bodies on my way out. Why hasn't someone on the radio mentioned it?"

Dalton leaned forward and placed his arms over the back of the passenger seat.

"Maybe they are keeping it under wraps. The press would go crazy if it came out there was a major shootout between unknown assailants and a hotshot detective at the Pittsburgh Police Department."

Austin held his hand out to Dalton.

"Give me your phone."

Dalton tilted his head to one side.

"Why?"

"I'm calling the station to see what's going on."

Dalton fished the phone from his pocket and handed it over.

"I'd like to go on record saying I don't think it's a good idea."

"Duly noted," Austin said as he took the phone and started dialing. He pressed the speakerphone button and held the phone between us as it rang.

The phone was answered on the second ring.

"Pittsburgh Police Department. How may I help you?"

"This is Detective Austin…"

"One moment Detective," the operator interrupted him; right before ringing could be heard again.

This time, the phone was answered on half a ring.

"Captain Styles."

Austin looked at Dalton, the confusion in his eyes shifted to concern as he held the phone closer.

"Captain, this is Detective Janssen."

"Janssen, where the hell have you been?"

"Sir?"

"Last night was your shift to man the switchboard. You were gone when the morning duty officer arrived. I will not tolerate any excuse for leaving the station empty and unmanned."

"I don't understand. I wasn't on the roster for last night."

The sounds of papers being rustled echoed from the tiny speaker on the phone.

"Says so right here on the duty roster. You were supposed to be on the switch. Where the hell were you?"

"Captain, before I tell you, can I ask a question?"

The captain let out a rush of air to show he wasn't happy with his staff members shirking their responsibilities.

"Sure."

"What happened last night?"

"You should be thanking your lucky stars nothing major happened last night. We came in this morning to a few calls on the voicemail for domestic disturbances."

"What about the body in the morgue?"

"What?"

"Can you please check to see if Miss Gardner's body is missing?"

"If her body was missing, the coroner would have informed me immediately. You should be thankful nothing's missing or I would be demanding your badge and not just an excuse. Anyone coming here last night after you took off doing god-knows-what would have had the run of the place."

Austin hung up and dialed again.

The same operator answered on the second ring.

"Pittsburgh Police Department. How may I help you?"

Austin pinched his nose and spoke in a high tone.

"Coroner's office. Please."

"One moment."

I looked at Austin in surprise.

"What are you…?"

Dalton clapped his hand over my mouth and whispered into my ear.

"Shh. Daddy's working."

He slowly took his hand away and I quietly listened.

"Coroner's office, this is Willy."

Austin kept his nose pinched.

"Hey Willy, this is Sergeant Harris over at five. I think I found some more personal effects from the body we fished out of the river. Do you still need them?"

There was rustling noises before Willy responded. He sounded distracted as he continued to make background noises while he talked.

"Have you checked with the case officer?"

"You mean Janssen?"

"Yeah, Janssen. Check with him."

"I already talked with him and he said to see if you wanted anything."

"Why would I want anything? The body was transported out before I started my shift. And I'm not too happy about that. I was promised final approval on all transfers."

"Transferred? Who ordered the transfer?"

More rustling sounds.

"According to the transfer order, Janssen approved the order and then signed for it last night while on duty. That guy's gonna get an earful from me when he gets in. It looks like I needed to run more tests."

"More tests? Why?"

"There was an inconsistency between two of the reports regarding the body temperature."

"What kind of inconsistency?"

"Nothing major, but according to the second report, the temperature had increased from the first reading. My assistant probably just needs a kick in the ass for sloppy work, but I would have liked the chance to verify that before they took the body."

"Where did the body go?"

"What am I? The information booth? Look, there was a major drug exchange that went south last night in The Hill and I'm up to my elbows in fresh bodies here. Between you and me, I think the Russians are making a play on our little neighborhood."

"Why do you say that?"

"Two of the guys brought in this morning had tattoos written in Russian."

"What about the other three?"

"Hey? How did you know how many there were?"

Austin hung up quickly and redialed again.

On the second ring, the familiar voice echoed in the car.

"Pittsburgh Police Department. How may I help you?"

Austin didn't bother plugging his nose this time, but adopted a Southern drawl.

"Holding, please."

"One moment."

After a few rings, the phone was answered.

"This is Hastings."

"Yes, I have an order signed by a Detective Janssen to accept a prisoner from your department, but for the life of me, I can't make out the last name. The first name looks like Michele, but that might not be right."

"One moment."

There was more rustling sounds, and then the snap of a sheet of paper being straightened out one-handed.

"According to the movement report only one person was transferred out last night, a Michele Gardner."

"Can you tell who signed for her release into transport's custody?"

"Yeah. It was Detective Austin Janssen himself."

"Thanks."

Austin was about to hang up when Hastings said something that made him stop.

Austin moved closer to the phone.

"Can you repeat that again," Austin said with his Southern drawl.

"Yeah. I still have a box of Michele's stuff that was collected from her apartment before Janssen was given the case. Where do you want me to send it?"

Austin and Dalton had a lightning fast silent conversation with their eyes before Austin replied.

"I'll send one of my guys to pick it up. Can you leave it at the front?"

"Sure. Whose name should I put on it?"

Before he answered, there was a faint click that echoed from the phone. Austin and Dalton both looked at each other in alarm, and then Dalton's shoulder's dropped as if in defeat.

"I'll send Casey Bloom. She should be there tomorrow morning to pick it up."

"Okay. Will do."

Austin hung up the phone and handed it to Dalton with a sorrowful look in his eyes.

"Sorry about that."

Dalton took the phone and shrugged.

"I was up for an upgrade soon anyway."

Dalton opened the car door and stepped out. He dropped his phone on the ground and stomped on it repeatedly until it was no more than shattered glass and broken plastic.

I looked at him in shock.

"What did you do that for?"

Austin touched my arm, sending electric sparks up and down my spine. Despite everything that had happened, my body had one thing on its mind, to be near his.

"That faint click we heard was someone tapping Dalton's phone and putting a trace on it. They must have been monitoring every call into the station. Unfortunately, they were able to record that last bit of conversation and will be waiting for us tomorrow to pick up the package."

"Then, let's not get that package."

"Unfortunately, I think some of the items in that box can help us figure out what is going on."

"How?" I asked as Dalton got back into the car. Austin nodded to Dalton and then looked back at me.

"Michele had a bunch of old articles in a picture album. I think she knew you existed and had started researching how. She might have stumbled across something that led to her jumping from the bridge. We have to get that box of evidence and see for ourselves if it holds any answers."

My heart fluttered with the realization that Austin believed me and that I had nothing to do with the other Michele's death. Now he was including me in trying to figure out what had caused hard men to come looking for me in the middle of the night in a deserted police station. But this time, the station wouldn't be deserted. And there might be more mercenaries waiting for him to come back.

I suddenly feared for his life as much as mine.

"But you said they would be waiting for us."

"They will, but not until tomorrow morning."

Austin turned around and started up the car.

"That's why we are going to collect it tonight."

"Does Casey Bloom live nearby? Can you get her to pick up the package tonight?"

Dalton looked at me with a twinkle in his eye.

"There is no Casey Bloom."

"What? But Austin said he was sending her to pick up the box."

"He did. And she will," Dalton said.

"But you just said she doesn't exist."

"She doesn't. But she'll be getting that box for us in a couple of hours."

"How?" I asked, unsure if I really wanted the answer.

My suspicions were confirmed when Dalton pointed at me.

"You are Casey Bloom."

Chapter 38

I kept my eyes closed as Austin and Dalton both worked on me, applying makeup and fitting me with a wig they had purchased at a drugstore on the way back to Pittsburgh.

I felt them both pull away.

I opened my eyes and Dalton smiled at me.

He reached over the back of the car seat and adjusted the rear view mirror.

"Meet Casey Bloom."

I looked at my reflection in the mirror and my mouth fell open.

I hardly recognized myself. They had applied the differing shades of makeup to alter the natural lines of my face, making me look thinner and with a more pronounced forehead.

I touched my cheek with a hand.

"You did all this with just makeup."

Dalton nodded, his grin splitting his face from ear to ear.

"It's all tricks with shadows and perception."

I turned to face them both.

"What did you guys used to do that taught you how to do this?"

They looked at each other and Austin smiled wide as he replied for them.

"We were in theater."

"What kind of theater?"

Dalton stopped smiling and grew serious.

"The theater of war."

I looked back and forth between the two men who had just changed my appearance using store-bought makeup and a cheap wig. What section of the military gave them this type of training?

"You guys were in the army?"

Dalton shrugged.

"Of sorts."

They both turned away from me and I knew this conversation was over; for now. But I wasn't ready to let it go completely. I had to know everything about Austin.

No, not had to.

I wanted to.

We drove in silence until we were parked around the corner from the police station where I had nearly lost my life.

I looked again at my reflection in the mirror. If I didn't know I was looking at myself, I wouldn't know it was me. But would it work?

I looked at Dalton.

"So, are you going in with me to get the box?"

"Nope. This mission is yours alone."

Fear suddenly gripped me.

"I don't know if I can do this."

Austin gripped my arm and all my fears melted away with his touch. He leaned over the back of the seat and kissed me.

It caught me by surprise and I froze, barely returning his sudden public display of affection.

He pulled away and pushed the stray hair from the long wig away from my face with a finger.

"For luck," he said.

Dalton clapped his hands together.

"Aaalrighty then. Let's get this show on the road."

I turned to him.

"Are you sure you won't go in with me?"

Dalton shook his head.

"You don't need me. You've got that kiss from Romeo here to keep you going."

Austin smiled at me.

"Now, what is your name?"

I squared up my shoulders.

"Casey… Casey…"

"Casey Bloom," Austin reminded me.

"Right. Casey Bloom."

Austin held my shoulders in his warm grip. I didn't want him to let go of me now that he had me.

"Just go in there, say you are picking up the effects of Michele Gardner, and bring the box they give you back out to the car."

"Got it."

"Don't look around while you are walking. Just go on in, get the box, and come back out."

"Don't look around."

"If you do, you will draw attention to yourself. Nobody looks around as they are walking, and if you do, you'll stick out like a sore thumb."

"Draw attention from whom?"

"The people watching for me or Dalton."

My heart skipped a beat and my mouth went dry.

"You said they wouldn't be here until tomorrow."

"They don't expect us until tomorrow. But there is definitely someone watching the station right now."

I started shaking my head.

"I can't do this."

Austin grabbed my chin and forced me to look into his startling blue eyes.

"You can do this. You said it yourself, nobody will recognize you, and they won't be expecting you. They are looking for Dalton or me."

"How do you know?"

"Nick would make sure to put someone in place who knows us on sight. We've probably even worked with whoever is watching for us. You can do this Michele. Just go in there, and, what's your name again?"

"Casey Bloom."

Austin smiled.

"Excellent. You've got this."

Dalton opened the side door and beckoned me out of the car with a wave of his hand.

As I stepped out, he shut the door again and looked up at me from the passenger's seat.

"Remember, don't look around. Just walk in like you own the place, and then come out as if you are thinking about what you want for dinner and are upset with your boss for making you drive across town to pick up a stupid box for a dead girl."

I flinched at his callousness toward the situation.

"Sorry," Dalton said with a grimace. "I misspoke. Just act

natural. And not like you are pretending to act natural. Just act natural."

I nodded and looked at the corner ahead. Around it was the police station where I would be walking into, pretending to be someone who doesn't exist, and steal the possessions of someone who had died in front of me.

And I was doing all of this while someone who wanted to kill me was waiting and watching.

How much worse could it get?

Chapter 39

Tomorrow will happen just like today.

The words of the Information Society song from a time long before I had lost my memories echoed in my head as I walked away from Dalton's car. If it weren't for Pandora on my iPod Touch, I might never had heard that late 1980's song.

I don't know why that particular song entered my head at that moment, but after it had, it was the perfect song to play in my head.

I was about to enter a police station posing as someone else and steal evidence right out from under the noses of the establishment.

I was about to lie for Detective Janssen.

Did I trust him enough to go this far for him? To lie and steal for him?

Did I really know anything about him?

I remembered watching in horror as he easily killed the men who had come after me the night before at this very same police station.

He was keeping secrets about his past from me that his friend, Dalton, had been more than willing to share until Austin stopped him.

What was he keeping from me?

Was he worried that I would think less about him if I knew? What had he done before he had become a police officer? Did it have something to do with the man that worked with Robert to find me? Both Austin and Dalton seemed to know who he was. They had mentioned how dangerous he was, but that didn't explain how they knew him.

I paused on the corner outside the police station to gather my thoughts.

To keep from looking out of place just standing there, I leaned against a streetlamp and adjusted my shoe while my mind reeled.

Could I trust Austin? I knew I could trust Dalton. He had been ready to share all sorts of intimate details about their past life together. It was Austin who had stopped him.

I found myself strongly attracted to Austin, and had even tried to make the first move last night. After seeing the video this morning where Robert was coming after me with armed soldiers, I knew that we were over; if there was ever anything in the first place.

But with Austin, I had the chance for a new beginning. Ever since I had met Robert, all my tomorrows had happened like every day before them. Even more unnerving, all my yesterdays were becoming the new Michele's todays before she had killed herself to escape.

I didn't have to kill myself to get away from the cycle I was trapped in. I had another avenue of escape.

I had Austin. Together, we could make tomorrow happen differently from today.

He was my way out, so I was willing to do whatever he asked if it made that happen.

"Psst," a harsh voice hissed to my right.

I looked toward the sound.

Austin was pressed up against the edge of the building, trying to stay as much out of sight as possible.

"What are you doing?" he whispered loudly. "Get going or you will draw attention to yourself."

He motioned for me to keep going. He was right. I had been leaning against the lamp post too long adjusting my shoe.

I took it off completely and shook an imaginary rock out of it before replacing it and continuing down the sidewalk toward my destiny.

Chapter 40

I walked into the police station and paused, looking around.

Not twelve hours before, I had been running through here as death occurred all around me.

Bullets had been flying, and blood had been spilled, in the battle for my life between Austin and a team of assassins.

Despite their coordination, and obvious skill, Austin had defeated them and whisked me away to relative safety.

How had he been able to do that?

I wanted to know everything about him.

"Can I help you?"

The voice broke through my concentration and drew me out of my head and back to the desk sergeant who looked down at me from his high perch on the other side of the front counter.

"Umm, yeah. I'm here to collect a package."

He grabbed a clipboard and looked at it.

"Your name?"

My mind went blank.

Austin and Dalton had worked to drill everything into me so that I wouldn't freeze up. But that is what was happening to me right now.

"Bloom," I blurted out, my mind clicking like a gear finding the teeth of the opposite gear and catching. And then it slipped again. I couldn't remember the rest of my name.

The desk sergeant frowned at the list.

"Casey Bloom?" he asked.

That was it!

I nodded and he looked at me critically.

"You don't look like a Casey," he said.

My heart exploded rhythmically, trying to rip itself out of my chest.

I swallowed dryly and smiled at the sergeant, my brain running at top speed.

"Do I look more like a Deborah," I asked.

He squinted at me and then waggled a finger at me.

"Yeah. You look much more like a Deborah."

"That's my middle name," I replied.

Here I was, sneaking into a police station to remove evidence under false pretenses, and for the first time since I walked in, I wasn't lying.

Deborah was my middle name. Michele Deborah Black. Of course, I was finding out that everything else about my life had been a lie.

Maybe my middle name wasn't Deborah and I was still lying to an officer of the law.

He bent down and lifted a small cardboard banker's box sealed with packing tape.

"This is for you, Deborah," the sergeant said with a wink as he handed me the box.

I took it and smiled sweetly.

"Thank you. Do I need to sign?"

"Yes. Right here."

I signed as Casey Deborah Bloom and the handed the pen back to the sergeant.

He took it and smiled back at me.

"Have yourself a great day."

"You too," I said before I spun around and headed out of the police station.

Once outside, I resisted the urge to drop the box and start running down the street away from Austin, Dalton, and one possible future.

I wanted to run home.

But home to what?

To Robert?

We were through. He had to have known that the other Michele was dead by now. He might also already know that I had found the camera in our home. There was nothing he needed to keep from me, and that terrified me. What had he been hiding from me all these years?

I wanted to find out, but I didn't want Robert to be the one to tell me. I wanted to learn the truth with Austin by my side.

He had, after all, kissed me for luck.

My lips warmed with the memory of that kiss. Austin seemed

to be just as interested in what was happening to me as I did. It was why he sent me in to collect Dead Michele's belongings. There might be something in there that would lead us closer to the truth.

That made me feel safe and secure. The closer we could get to the truth without involving Robert, or that guy with him, the better.

As I descended the front steps of the police station, my eyes connected with the eyes of a stranger who watched me from a parked car across the street.

I looked away quickly and continued down the sidewalk toward refuge, toward Austin and Dalton. As I walked, I resisted the urge to look around me.

I had to look like someone late for work forced to make a detour from my daily life by an asshole boss.

I glanced behind me without thinking and locked eyes with the man in the car again.

He must have been watching me the whole time, because his face darkened and he immediately climbed out of the car.

I increased my pace as I neared the corner.

I glanced back to see the man heading my way, still waiting for a break in traffic to get to the same side of the street I was on.

He alternated between watching the moving wall of cars that blocked his progress and watching me. There was no sense in pretending to hide anymore. I was fully exposed and he was already coming after me.

So I ran.

I hit the corner and darted around it, preparing to yell for help as soon as I saw...

I skidded to a halt, nearly twisting my ankle as I struggled to keep the evidence box from tumbling out of my hands.

I was unsuccessful and the box hit the sidewalk, one corner caving in as the contents shifted.

The car was gone.

And along with it, Dalton and Austin.

Chapter 41

My heart hammered in my chest as I spun around, my eyes searching everywhere for something familiar. Maybe they had moved the car. Maybe they were waiting nearby.

There was one face I did recognize, but it wasn't the one I was looking for.

The man who had spotted me coming out of the police station appeared at the corner and noticed me immediately.

The smile that slowly spread across his face told me more than I wanted to know about his intentions.

I scooped up the box and started running.

I stumbled briefly on the sidewalk and wished I hadn't let Austin convince me to wear heels. Sure, it made the look of lab assistant more complete, even with the low heels I had on, but it made running from murderous thugs quite a challenge.

I kicked my way out of my shoes and was able to run faster.

I glanced back in time to see a meaty hand swinging at my head.

I tried to duck, but the man's arm smacked against my shoulder, knocking me off balance.

I fell to the sidewalk, tearing my slacks. I rolled, losing the box of evidence as it flew from my grip.

I came to a stop on my stomach, but as I raised myself to my elbows, big hands grabbed my sides and lifted me off the ground.

"Put me down!" I yelled, swinging balled fists at the face of my attacker, who was massive enough to be a Hollywood nightclub bouncer.

He squeezed me, causing me to cry out in pain. But I did what he wanted and stopped punching him in the face.

He carried me two steps and slammed me into the side of a building, holding me pinned to the wall with his hand around my neck. My feet could barely touch the ground, and my breathing was restricted by his vice grip on my throat.

I clawed at his hands. He ignored the pain I had to be inflicting on him and leaned in close.

"Where are your friends?"

Even if I knew the answer to his question, I would never have been able to get it out before I blacked out from the lack of oxygen.

"Right here pretty boy," a loud voice interrupted.

The big man turned his head, and as he angled away from me, I could see the same thing he could as Dalton swung a long metal pipe.

The pipe pinged dully as it connected with the large man's skull and he released his grip from my throat.

I fell to my knees, Austin appearing out of nowhere and caught me before I pitched forward face-first onto the sidewalk.

"Come on," Austin said as he helped me to my feet. "Alt's got this one."

Dalton was already swinging a second time. The large man's head snapped backward and he went down hard. I swear I felt the ground shake when he landed on his back. Dalton dropped the metal pipe and caught up to us.

"What..." I choked out before coughing from attempting to speak after the rough treatment of my throat; literally at the hands of my attacker.

"Don't speak," Austin said as he led me down a back alley.

Dalton caught up and fell in step next to us.

"The box," I croaked.

Dalton held it up.

"Got it."

I craned my neck to look back down the alley and could see a small crowd gathering around the unconscious attacker. One man was looking in our direction and pointing at us.

"Po..." I started before another fit of coughing overtook me.

"Just stay quiet."

I shook my head and tried to speak again.

"Police," I managed to get out before my throat burned too much to speak.

Dalton looked back.

"She's right. The police are headed our way."

I looked back again to see a uniformed officer talking into the radio mic strapped to his shoulder.

Austin secured his arm around my waist and picked up speed.

Dalton was running beside us.

"Do you want me to slow him down?"

Austin shook his head.

"We don't need to add to our troubles. Let's just concentrate on getting out of here in one piece."

With Austin's arm around me, I felt a calming warmth spread throughout my body. I was under his protection, and that made me feel safe, even while we were running from the police after stopping someone from nearly killing me.

I knew that, no matter what happened, Austin was more than capable of keeping me safe.

Austin yanked me sideways as we rounded the corner. Dalton's car came into view. He had parked it just around the corner.

They must have known that something would happen, and had planned ahead. More likely, they knew I would screw up and bring unwanted attention to myself.

They weren't wrong.

At least they had been able to stay one step ahead of our unknown enemy.

Dalton tossed the box into the back seat next to me as he hopped into the driver's seat.

I looked at the brown banker's box as we sped away.

Maybe the answers to the questions we didn't even know to ask were all in there.

Or maybe it was just a box of a dead woman's stuff that would be of no use to us.

Chapter 42

Dalton stuck a single ear bud from a set of headphones in his ear and twisted the tuning dial on the walkie-talkie tucked into the space between the front seats.

Every now and then, he would slow down and make an unexpected turn. A couple of times, he came to a full stop before backing up and taking another direction at the intersection we had just passed through.

Austin turned in his seat to face me.

"Sorry about letting that bruiser get his hands on you."

"What happened back there? How did he know who I was?"

"We told you to walk in and walk out as if you did it every day. He noticed you behaving differently from everyone else in front of the station. It is what he was trained to do. Spot the difference. Nine times out of ten, that is the target. Especially if they know they are a target."

I nodded to Dalton who was making another sudden directional change with the car, ignoring the honks of other drivers.

"What's he doing?"

Austin looked at Dalton and then back at me.

"He's listening in on the police band and keeping us away from everyone looking for us."

I stared deeply into Austin's bright blue eyes.

"Who are you guys?"

Dalton shot him a look.

"Tell her."

Austin never took his eyes off me. I could see the war raging inside his head as he debated what to say to me.

He closed his eyes.

"Tell her," Dalton said again.

Austin's eyes popped open and stared right through me.

"Not yet."

"Fine," Dalton exclaimed. "I'll tell her."

"No, Alt. I'll tell her when we get to the hotel."

I looked from Dalton to Austin.

"What hotel?"

Dalton ignored my question as he placed his hand over the ear bud stuck in his ear and slowed the car down. There was angered honking from the cars directly behind us.

Austin gave me a weak smile.

"We need a place to go over what's in that box. I am hoping it will give us some answers."

I looked at him.

"And if it doesn't?"

He looked at me for a full fifteen seconds in silence before turning back around and facing out the side window.

Our conversation was apparently over. I decided to give Austin the space he needed rather than push it.

He had just saved my life after all.

Again.

I guess I owed him that much.

Chapter 43

Dalton got us out of the city proper without getting spotted by a single police cruiser. Once outside, he put the pedal to the metal and we made it halfway through Pennsylvania before he pulled off the highway and into the parking lot of a dingy ten-room motel.

Austin opened his door and looked at Dalton.

"I'll get us checked in."

"Be sure to ask for the end unit," Dalton added.

Austin gave him a withering look and then headed to the lobby.

Dalton pulled the car to the end spot, and then we walked back to the third room from the main lobby, a full seven rooms away from the one he had asked Austin to rent.

Austin hadn't returned from the main lobby yet, but Dalton produced a set of metal objects from a small zippered case and bent down to fiddle with the door lock to Room 3.

"What are you doing?"

Dalton remained focused on the task at hand as he replied to my obvious question.

"Unlocking the door."

"I thought you asked Austin to rent the end unit?"

"I did."

"Why are you going into this room?"

"This is the one we'll be staying in tonight."

"I'm confused. Why are you breaking into a room when we are about to rent one?"

"If anyone spots the car, they will focus on the room closest to it. They might even ask the front desk what room we rented. That should give us ample time to escape while they are focused on the other end of the hotel. That little buffer of opportunity often means the difference between escape and capture."

I looked at the car in shock.

"Someone's going to find us way out here?"

Dalton made a satisfied sound in response to the lock clicking and the door swinging open.

He stood up and stepped into the room, switching on the light.

"Of course not. But it never hurts to be prepared for every eventuality."

I looked into the room.

I had been the most straight-laced person in the world until a week ago. Until I saw myself go over the edge of a bridge.

Since then, I failed to report a suicide, stole money, committed identity theft, cheated on my husband, with my husband, and entertained thoughts of cheating on my husband with someone more my age.

Now, I was about to spend the night in a stolen motel room with two perfect strangers.

Austin appeared right behind me and placed a hand on the small of my back, guiding me into the room ahead of him. My body tingled at his comforting touch.

Dalton closed the door once we were inside.

"Any trouble with the clerk?"

Austin shook his head.

"I gave the guy an extra twenty for housekeeping to be late tomorrow morning."

Austin looked around.

"Where's the box?"

Dalton palm-slapped his forehead.

"In the car."

Austin headed for the door.

"I'll get it."

Dalton moved so quickly, all I saw was a blur as he came between Austin and the door.

"Why don't I get the box, and you can tell missy here how come she's still alive."

The tension in the room ratcheted up as the two men stared at each other, their neck muscles flexing as they stood stock still.

Austin finally broke away and looked at me with a sigh.

"Fine."

Dalton smiled and slapped a hand on Austin's back.

"It's about time. I'll take, what, ten minutes to get the box and give you a chance to give her the civilian summary."

"Five minutes," Austin said through gritted teeth.

Dalton shrugged.

"If you think you can do it justice in five minutes, then fine. I like to add a little finesse when I bring someone into the fold."

Dalton smiled with his hand on the open door.

"Don't do anything I wouldn't do, keeping in mind that the list is pretty short."

"Out!" Austin barked.

Dalton was laughing as he closed the door.

Austin turned to me. His face was serious. All the merriment in the room had left with Dalton.

He motioned to the bed.

"Have a seat."

I sat down as he pulled the only chair at the small desk over in front of me and sat down in it, leaning forward.

"What I am about to tell you is known only by a select few at the highest level of our government."

I tried to inject a little of Dalton's humor into the conversation.

"And if you tell me, you will have to kill me?"

Austin didn't smile as he responded quietly.

"Yes."

My smile faded when Austin didn't take the joke for what it was.

"I'm sorry," I said just as quietly.

"Don't be. I get what Alt always does to lighten the mood. But this is serious."

"Why do you call him Alt?"

"You will understand once you hear what I have to say."

He looked down at his hands and I swallowed dryly. He hadn't even said anything significant yet and my heart was already pounding.

Maybe it was the intimacy we were about to share that had pushed my body into overdrive.

He looked up at me, his pupils large as he drilled deep into my soul.

"This is your last chance to stay out of this. Tell me you don't want to hear any of it, and I can get you somewhere safe and that will be the end of it. Do you want out?"

Did I want out?

How could I stay out?

This was all about me.

Austin, and now his friend Dalton, had been sucked into whatever I was already entangled in. I should be giving this speech to him.

What made him think that he could keep me out of whatever was happening? Was it because he and Dalton were involved somehow already? Had I walked into a trap that was coordinated by the men after me in cooperation with Austin?

Was this all a setup designed to make me trust him implicitly? Was he and Dalton working with Robert as well, and now that they knew I was clueless as to what was really happening, were they having a change of heart?

Even if they were working with Robert to trick me into giving up what I knew, I no longer cared.

I looked into his piercing blue eyes and gave my answer.

Chapter 44

"No," I said. "I want to stay with you."

Austin smiled.

"I'm glad to hear that. It's only going to get more difficult from here on out."

"Why? Are you working with Robert?"

"No. I got caught up in this when I showed up at the police station when I was off duty."

"But how come you know that guy working with Robert?"

"We have… history. It is only coincidence that Dalton and I know him and are working on opposite sides. But before we can do anything, I need to know what you know."

"I don't know anything."

"Just tell me everything, starting from the beginning."

I told him about the accident that erased my memory. I told him about the psychiatrist who I met with every week to try and recover my memories. I told him about almost dying, and then giving up the medications.

I told him about the other Michele on the bridge. I told him about the pictures of her and my husband repeating my life. I told him about the camera in my home. There was nothing else I knew, the rest was all guesswork and conjecture.

I wasn't about to say out loud what I had decided was the only possible answer to who I was. It was a ludicrous hypothesis.

When I was done, it was his turn.

He ran a hand through his hair and looked at me.

"Last chance."

I shook my head.

"I want to know everything about you, no matter what."

He laughed. When he did that, his face softened and I was attracted to him even more.

"No matter what," he said. "I like that."

He took a deep breath and glanced at the door. When Dalton didn't walk in, he looked back at me.

"Dalton, Nick, and I were part of an elite squad who would be sent in to nations to destabilize them. As the leader of the squad, my call sign was Control, Dalton was Alt, and Nick was Delete. Together, we caused all sorts of changes all around the world. Remember when Nick did this with his fingers?"

He motioned with two fingers on one hand and one finger on the other.

I nodded.

"That is the way to force a computer to shut down and restart. That was what we were sent in to do to nations that made things difficult for the U.S. Government. Our unique skills were used to start a revolution, or just wipe clean an existing government. We were the Control, Alt, Delete in the real world for things our government wanted eliminated or reset."

"But, how come Nick is working with Robert?"

Austin shrugged.

"When we were deemed no longer a necessary option in international relations, and discharged with accommodations, Dalton and I went into the civilian sector and got regular nine-to-five jobs. I had no idea where Nick ended up, but it looks like he is selling his services to anyone willing to pay."

"Why? How did my husband know to hire someone like Nick?"

"I've watched the video from Dalton's house several times. I don't think Nick is working for your husband. I know how Nick behaves around his superiors, and he behaved like he was in charge. I think your husband is working for the same people that hired Nick."

"Who hired my husband?"

The door opened and Dalton walked in with the evidence box. He held it up.

"We are hoping to get a clue to that from in here."

Austin frowned at Dalton.

"Were you listening in?"

Dalton tossed the box onto the bed and gave me a wink.

"I had to know if I would be interrupting anything."

Austin grabbed the box and pulled away the tape.

"Nothing was going on."

Dalton ignored his comment and looked at me with a smirk.

"So, are you afraid of us yet?"

"Why would I be afraid of you?" I asked.

He held up his fist and poked his pinky up in the air.

"Because I could kill you with this?"

I looked at Austin in a sudden panic.

Austin ripped open the top of the box.

"Alt won't hurt you, but he likes to joke a little too much. Now, let's see what we have in here."

He overturned the box and spilled the contents on the bed. I stood next to them and looked at the multitude of labeled evidence bags. Every one of them was transparent except for the red letters spelling the word "EVIDENCE" on a yellow band across the front of the bag.

"Why do you think there might be a clue among the other Michele's belongings?"

Austin began arranging the bags.

"According to your report, and what you've told me, she asked 'How many more' before killing herself."

I nodded. As he said it, I heard it in her voice and the image of the scene on the bridge flashed in my mind.

Austin continued as he sorted and lined up the evidence bags.

"She had to have found something that made her decide to kill herself. I'm hoping that it is somewhere in here."

Austin finished lining the evidence bags next to each other and stood back, frowning at them.

"There's one missing."

Chapter 45

I stared at the bags that stretched across the length of the bed.

"One missing? How can you tell?"

"When a case is first started, they label the bags with letters instead of numbers. There were only twenty bags, so the last one should be labeled with the letter T. T is right there on the end, but there are only nineteen bags, and C is missing. I could hazard a guess, and probably be right, that what we are looking for is in the missing bag."

I gawked at the row of evidence bags. I had almost been killed getting these and now it was possible that the whole reason we wanted to get them wasn't even here. How could this be happening to me?

"We have to go back," Austin stated matter-of-factly.

I looked at him like he had sprouted antennas.

"Go back! They could still be waiting for us, and now they know we are together. We can't go back."

Dalton lifted the first bag and inspected it, peering at the contents through the transparent plastic.

"Maybe there's still something to find in one of the other bags."

Austin nodded.

"It's worth a shot. Start opening them."

Dalton tore open his bag as Austin picked up the next one and tore it open. He picked up the next bag and tossed it to me.

I caught it and looked at him.

"What am I looking for?"

Dalton was removing items from his bag and placing them on the desk as he looked at me.

"I guess this is a case of we'll know it when we see it."

I looked down at the evidence bag in my hands. It looked like it was filled with socks of varying colors. What significance could these actually have as to why she had killed herself and why everyone was after me?

I ripped open the top of the bag carefully. The glue was stronger than the plastic, and the bag tore in chunks as I winced from permanently destroying an evidence bag.

Austin placed his hands on mine, sending electrical sparks up and down my spine.

"Don't worry about the bags. What we are doing is so incredibly illegal, nothing else we can do will be any worse."

I smiled weakly at him hoping that this was the worst we would be doing. After what I had witnessed him do at the police station less than twenty-four hours before, I doubted he was telling me the truth.

But, technically, he wasn't lying to me either.

Chapter 46

After emptying every evidence bag, we had a small pile of items on the desk that Austin had deemed important. At least, more important than the socks, bras, and other items of clothing that filled most of the bags.

At the center of the select items was a wrinkled piece of newspaper I had found wadded up inside a sock.

Dalton picked up the torn paper and inspected it closely. It showed a blurry picture of me coming out of somewhere. The picture had been torn down the middle, so we couldn't see who held onto my arm.

Dalton held it out to me.

"Are you sure you don't remember when this picture was taken?"

I had studied that picture the first time I had seen it, but to humor Dalton, I looked at it closely again.

The jacket I was wearing was one I didn't recognize. It had short lapels and large brass buttons. And it was white, or a light color. It was hard to decide the color exactly in the black and white photograph printed on cheap newspaper.

The jacket looked out of style from anything I wore. It almost looked like something from before the turn of the millennium.

I looked up at Dalton.

"I don't remember owning a jacket like that."

"What about the location? It looks like you were coming out of a large building, like an office complex or something."

I stared at the picture. Unfortunately, too much of the rest of the picture had been ripped away and there was no way to tell where this picture was taken.

I held it out to Dalton with a shake of my head.

"I don't know."

Dalton inspected the picture closely, leaning under a lamp for more light.

"That looks like a wheelchair in the background."

Austin snatched it from his hands and looked closely before handing it to me.

"Could this have been taken in front of a hospital?"

I held the picture up and studied it, trying to recall being anywhere like the place in the picture. I came up with nothing.

When I lowered the picture, Austin was looking at me strangely.

"Hold that up again."

I looked down at the section of torn newspaper in my hand and held it back up.

"Like this?"

Austin tilted his head to one side and pointed to the back of the newspaper.

"Does that look that an advertisement for a gun show to you?"

Dalton tilted his head the other way.

"Yea. And look, there's the date of the show."

Their faces changed and they both looked at me.

Dalton was the first to speak.

"How old are you?"

It seemed a strange question, but I answered honestly anyway.

"Twenty-four. Why?"

They looked at the back of the newspaper.

Dalton whistled.

"You, girl, have stumbled on the fountain of youth."

I frowned at him and turned the newspaper clipping over to see what they were looking at.

It was a flashy gun show advertisement that encouraged everyone to attend on the second weekend in October.

Twenty-eight years ago.

Chapter 47

I gawked at the date and then flipped back to the picture that showed me about the same age I was now. It was a blurry photograph on wrinkled paper, but I was still easily identifiable as the person in the picture.

I looked up at Austin.

"What is this?"

He took it from me and he and Dalton took turns flipping the newspaper back and forth as they studied other areas on the paper.

Austin looked back up at me, a smile slowly spreading on his face.

"We can narrow down when this photo was taken and find the rest of this picture."

"How?"

"The newspaper archives at the Carnegie Library. They've digitized every newspaper going back into their microfilm archives now that the internet has taken over."

Dalton was nodding.

"Shouldn't take long to find this if we all search at the same time."

Austin grabbed me by the shoulders and kissed me excitedly. He pulled away and looked at the torn photograph.

"We can find this full page; see who is standing next to you. Maybe the article will shed some light on what was happening when this picture was taken."

I barely heard what he had said. Our second kiss had taken me by surprise even more than our first.

Dalton winked at me as Austin gathered up all the evidence strewn around the room and shoved it back into the box. As soon as the room was relatively clean, he looked at us.

"I'll get something for us to eat."

He looked at Dalton.

"The usual?"

"Of course."

He looked back at me.

"What do you like on your burgers?"

"Where are you going," I asked.

He and Dalton exchanged a knowing glance as he responded.

"Dairy Queen. It's a beat policeman's best friend."

Dalton laughed.

"I would think, even if you became a fry cook at McDonald's, you would still eat at Dairy Queen every chance you got."

Austin mocked looking hurt.

"I exercise. I can afford it."

Dalton shook his head.

"Garbage in is still garbage in."

Austin hooked a thumb in Dalton's direction.

"He's a health nut. Just ignore him."

"I'm not a health nut, but I try to take care of what I stuff down my gullet, unlike some people."

Austin smiled.

"Still the usual, right?"

Dalton smiled.

"You know it."

Austin perched the box on the side of his hip.

"He talks a big game, but when push comes to shove, he will happily eat just like I do."

"So says a self-professed social junk food consumer."

"Hey, I can't be a social eater if I'm doing it alone."

Dalton was shaking his head and laughing.

"So you see, it's my fault if he doesn't get his junk food."

Austin punched Dalton in the arm and looked at me.

"What do you want on your burger?"

"The works," I said.

He looked at me appreciatively.

"A woman after my own heart."

He spun around and exited the hotel room, leaving Dalton and I alone.

Dalton jumped on the bed and leaned his back against the wall.

"He likes you."

My heart skipped a beat as I pretended I hadn't heard him.

"What?"

He smiled knowingly as he unwrapped the mint he had snatched off the nightstand.

"I can tell by the way he looks at you. Also, by the way he keeps kissing you."

I felt my face grow hotter.

He pointed the empty cellophane wrapper from his mint at me.

"And you like him back. I can tell by the way you're blushing."

My face got even hotter.

I was embarrassed, but this was my chance to find out more about Austin. Who knew him better than his best friend?

"Is he seeing anyone?"

Is he seeing anyone? I mentally kicked myself for blurting out the first stupid thing that came to my head.

Dalton smiled as he swished the mint around in his mouth, letting it clatter against his teeth.

"Nope. He's free and clear. How about you? Any baggage other than the ones trying to kill us?"

I laughed. Mostly from nervousness. Dalton was taking being targeted by highly trained assassins way too well. It was almost like he was glad for it.

He waggled a finger at me.

"I know what you're thinking, and yes. I am never more alive than when I am on a mission. Even if it's not sanctioned by the people who retired me way before my time."

I sat down on the edge of the bed.

"You look so young."

"Yep. Austin and I are both twenty-eight. Hell, we've known each other since fourth grade. We plan to be together on the day we both die in a blaze of glory."

"Kind of hard to do with you both working separate jobs. How come you aren't still in the army? From what I saw, you are both still in perfect health."

Dalton flexed his arm muscles.

"Thanks. I guess we are in tip-top shape."

"Then why did you guys leave?"

Dalton got a faraway look.

"It wasn't by choice."

"Does the army retire soldiers before they're thirty or something?"

"Not normally, no."

"Why were you guys discharged so young?"

"Remember that guy from the video?"

"Nick?"

"Yeah. And I'm sorry you know his name."

"Why?"

"Because, if he ever gets to you, he won't be happy about it."

I clasped my hands together to keep them from shaking.

Dalton leaned forward.

"Don't worry. Neither Austin nor I will let that bastard get anywhere near you."

I know he was trying to make me feel better, but I had also seen how many more trained soldiers Nick had at his command. No matter how good Austin was, everyone had their limits.

Dalton was shaking his head and muttering under his breath. I thought I heard him curse after saying Nick's name again.

"Is he the reason you were kicked out?"

Dalton got that faraway look again.

"Yeah. I guess you could say that. He really screwed it up for the rest of us."

"What did he do?"

Dalton laughed heartily.

"Jesus. What didn't he do?"

Dalton noted my eyebrows knitted in confusion.

"Nick was the same age as we were and came from some school in the Midwest. When he was assigned to our squad, we worked so well together, he might as well have grown up with Austin and me."

"What happened?"

"I'm not entirely sure. We had just come off a short holiday to work in some redacted country doing classified things and he just snapped. I guess the stress got to him."

"Weren't you all under the same level of stress?"

"I would say Austin had the most. He was our leader and no matter what happened, he was ultimately responsible for it; good or bad. But he was always good at suppressing his feelings, and I use humor to let off steam. Nick? He used killing to solve his problems. It's why his call sign was Delete. He was exceptionally good at killing. Once you got in his sights, like a badger, he never gave up until you were dead."

My heart thudded against my ribcage.

"What about me?"

Dalton focused on me and smiled, speaking in a thick Texas drawl.

"Don't worry, darlin'. We ain't gonna let nothin' happen to ya."

"But you just said…"

I wasn't able to finish my sentence. I couldn't believe we were talking about my life as if it was cheap and meaningless, like a bag of stale marshmallows.

"Okay, you got me. I can't guarantee that Nick won't get to you, but I can promise that it will be over Austin's and my dead bodies."

I looked at him with fresh eyes. I had only just met this man, but he was willing to lay down his life to protect mine. Why?

"Why are you and Austin doing this?"

His eyes sparkled as he looked at me.

"I'm doing it because it beats the drudgery of being a prison guard. And because if Austin said he was headed to hell and needed a driver, I would be the first volunteer. He's not related by blood, but he's my brother and I would die for him with a big smile on my face."

"But why is he helping me?"

He chomped on the mint, crushing it with his teeth, and grunted as he jumped up out of the bed.

"You'll have to ask him."

Dalton headed into the bathroom and closed the door. I guess our conversation was over, just like that.

The shower started up, so I knew I would be by myself for a

while. In fact, it was the first time I had been truly alone since I had been arrested. There were no guards or cameras watching me. I could do anything or go anywhere, and nobody would know.

It was a strange taste at freedom and surprised me that I thought about running.

I glanced at the front door and then back at the bathroom door. Dalton was in the shower and Austin was away getting food.

I could just walk out the hotel room and disappear forever.

I laughed out loud.

How could I disappear? I didn't have the skills that both of these guys possessed.

I could run, but I couldn't hide.

I pulled back the cuff on my sleeve and stared at the tattoo.

I still had no idea who I was.

Dead Michele's final words haunted me.

How many more?

She had died not knowing the answer to that question.

I picked up the newspaper clipping and looked at my picture, wearing clothes that had gone out of style two decades ago.

I flipped the paper over and looked at the gun show ad.

Did the Michele in the picture ever find out who she really was?

Had she asked the same questions Dead Michele had; and was replaced?

I had never questioned my life. Was that the reason I was still alive? I had accepted the reasons given to me for my memory loss. I had welcomed my relationship with Robert, despite our age difference.

Was I the first Michele to accept her life as-is? Dead Michele had started digging into who she was, and whatever she found made her kill herself.

How had someone gotten to some of the evidence before we did?

And what was in Evidence Bag C?

Whatever it was must have been the answer to questions

Dead Michele had, but it hadn't answered her final question.

Would I live long enough to finish the quest that she had started?

Chapter 48

I jolted awake when the door to the hotel room slammed shut.

I sat up in the chair I had fallen asleep in and looked around, disoriented for only a moment until I saw the smiling face of Austin carrying three large white fast food bags with the DQ logo emblazoned on the side.

He handed one bag to me while Dalton seized the other one and tore into it like a rabid wolverine.

I had barely opened my bag when Dalton was cramming fries into his mouth and unwrapping his burger. I guess the one thing they never taught you in the military was how to eat like a civilized human being.

Watching him tear into his burger so hungrily triggered a noisy growl from my stomach in anticipation of what was coming.

I opened my burger and took a small bite. My mouth instantly filled with saliva and I took a second, bigger, bite. The three of us ate in silence, focusing our full attention on the food.

Before I knew it, the burger was gone; and so were half my fries. With the constant ebb and flow of adrenaline, I hadn't realized how famished I was.

It was probably why I had also fallen asleep in the chair while waiting. Now that I had eaten, I was more awake than ever.

Dalton let out a huge burp, breaking the silence as rudely as humanly possible, and patted his bulging stomach.

"Now that was what I would call the worst meal I ever had."

Austin stuffed the last of his fries into his mouth, but didn't let that stop him from keeping up the conversation.

"What about Skuon?"

Dalton burped again, placing the back of his hand against his mouth to prevent anything from escaping.

"Remind me to pack a lunch if we ever pass through Spiderville again."

I looked at Dalton.

"Spiderville?"

Dalton burped again, doing his best to keep his food down as he recalled past events.

"They are popular for their fried spiders as big as your hand."

Dalton shivered from the memories no doubt running through his head.

"Blech! Give me greasy burgers from a fast food joint any day."

Austin was laughing.

"They weren't that bad."

I looked at Austin in shock.

"You ate one?"

Austin stuffed more fries into his mouth, letting them stick out like the legs of the spiders they were talking about, and smiled mischievously.

"You want spiders with that?"

I shut my eyes and did my best to picture something else, anything else, before my dinner came back up.

"Can we try to keep the conversation civilized, please?"

Austin poked the fries into his mouth.

"Sorry about that. Alt and I are not used to having a girl around."

I shot him a stern look.

He raised his hands in defense.

"Easy. That's not what I meant."

I crossed my arms and stared him down.

"And what exactly did you mean?"

Dalton crumpled his grease-stained fast food bag and tossed it across the room, landing a perfect shot into the trash bin.

"She got us, Austin. I don't know much about women, but I do know when it's best to let it go before you dig yourself a deeper hole."

Austin's mouth clamped shut and he gave me a sorrowful look. My heart melted. It would take a lot to keep me mad at him, even though I wasn't really mad. Who could be mad at the man who was the only reason they weren't dead?

Not me.

I decided to let him off the hook by changing the subject.

"So, when do we go the library to look up the newspaper

article?"

Austin's face softened. He looked relieved to be able to discuss something else.

"It's getting late, but we should be there first thing in the morning. We'll call for a taxi an hour before they open."

"A taxi?" I said. "What about the car?"

Dalton was shaking his head.

"Someone probably saw it when we dealt with that guy who assaulted you outside the police station. If I know Nick, that guy wasn't operating alone, and that means Nick already has the make, model, and license plate number of our car."

"So what do we do while we wait?"

Dalton pointed to the bed.

"You, of course, get the bed. Austin and I will take turns keeping watch. If anyone pokes around the motel, or my car, we can make a swift, and decisive, response."

I looked at the bed. I wasn't tired.

Austin seemed to be reading my thoughts.

"I know you just got a boost of energy from the food, but we have had a rough twenty-four hours and need to be ready for the next twenty-four. Whatever happens, we take it one day at a time…"

Dalton finished Austin's sentence.

"And we sleep and eat every chance we get, because you never know when you will get another opportunity."

I looked at the single bed in the small motel room.

"Where are you guys gonna sleep?"

Dalton kicked at the single chair with his leg.

"We can take turns in the chair or the floor. Trust me when I tell you we've fallen asleep in far worse places."

Austin glared at Dalton.

"Yeah. You try falling asleep when your partner keeps ripping out fried spider-induced farts. I'd rather sleep in a decomposing cow."

My stomach churned with the image painted in my head by Austin.

"Conversation…" I reminded him before my stomach flipped

entirely over.

Austin looked at me with concern.

"Oops. Sorry. I know it's early, but we should try to rest. I anticipate a big day ahead tomorrow."

"Why?" I asked as I sat on the bed.

He shrugged.

"I've never known Nick to let up, and we are going right back into the area he is confident he controls."

"You think he's at the library?"

"Not specifically, but he won't leave the city unwatched. He knows we know about him, so he will be a little more covert about watching the city and try to force us to do something drastic."

My eyes popped out in surprise.

"Drastic? Like what?"

Dalton cracked his neck and flexed his shoulders as he settled into the chair.

"Like going back into the same city where they are waiting for us to find what we didn't get the first time."

Chapter 49

I couldn't sleep. I lay on the bed and watched the light increase incrementally as Austin opened the door, letting the light from the parking lot spill into the small room.

I peeked through half-closed eyelids as Austin and Dalton silently switched positions. It was amazing to watch them work flawlessly together without so much as a single quick glance between them as if they were two halves of a single organism.

After Dalton left, I rolled over to face Austin who had settled into the chair with his eyes closed.

In the partial darkness, his eyes popped open and he looked right at me.

"I'm sorry. Did we disturb you?"

"No," I replied. "I wasn't asleep."

"You need to rest."

"I am resting, but I can't sleep. Too much going on in my head."

There were plenty of things swimming around in my brain, but there was one burning question that kept bubbling up to the surface that needed to be answered before I fully gave my trust to the man who had already earned it.

I perched up on an elbow in the darkness.

"Why are you helping me?"

He sat up and switched on the light.

We both blinked at the sudden brightness.

The front door opened slowly and we both looked at Dalton peeking inside.

When he saw we were okay, he opened the door wider.

"I saw the light go on."

Austin put his hand up.

"We're fine."

Dalton gave me a shrewd smile, winked at me, and closed the door; returning to his vigilant watch over the motel grounds to keep anyone from sneaking up on us.

Austin rubbed his face with both hands and then watched me for a long moment. He lowered his eyes and stared at the floor for another long minute.

I decided to give him all the time he needed before pressing him for an answer. He looked up at me and let out a rush of air between his pursed lips.

"I took you to Dalton's place last night because it was the one place I could think of where the mercenaries would never look for you. Before we even got there, I had already decided to turn you over to the FBI first thing in the morning."

I studied his face. He was having a hard time telling me this. I scooted to the edge of the bed and reached over, placing a hand on his knee.

"Why didn't you?"

He looked at my hand, his expression contorting from the flurry of emotions flooding across his face.

I sat up, faced him, and gripped his hands in mine. He didn't shy away from my touch and instead seemed to inch closer in his chair to be nearer to me.

He tilted his head up and I saw a look in his eyes I had never seen before. It was fear.

"Nick."

My eyebrows raised in surprise as he continued.

"After Dalton found the tracking device behind your ear I decided not to wait until morning to turn you over to the FBI. We were headed to the closest field office when Alt's phone told him someone had triggered his security cameras."

He looked at the floor again.

"When I recognized one of the mercs that blew through Alt's front door as one of the ones from the police station, I knew that you were the one they were after. And then Nick walked in. Anything he is involved in can't be good. And if Nick was after you, I knew that there was nowhere safe for you but with me."

He looked up at me.

"I could never live with myself if I let him get you."

Warmth filled my inner core and I leaned closer, my lips parting as I closed my eyes.

I paused just before his lips, letting his warm breath wash over me. We didn't stay barely touching each other for very long. He leaned the rest of the way and pressed his mouth against mine.

I felt his apprehension mirror my own as we kissed slowly before he pulled back and leaned his forehead against mine, our eyes still closed.

"I can't," he whispered.

"Yes you can," I whispered back.

Our eyes opened at the same time and we gazed deeply into each other's souls looking for a truth we knew was there.

I closed my eyes again and I felt his lips brush against mine when the door to the room opened suddenly.

Dalton was out of breath, as if he had been running laps around the parking lot.

"We've got to go," Dalton said, his eyes wild with excitement. "Now."

Austin was on his feet, the vulnerability he had allowed himself to reveal was instantly locked away.

He was back to all business.

Whatever intimacy we were about to share was gone like a wisp of smoke on a blustery day.

I stood up as Austin grabbed my arm and led me out of the room.

"What's going on?" Austin asked.

Dalton held the door open as we ran out of the motel room.

"I decided to listen to some police band, you know, for shits and giggles, when I heard a call sending some units to this very motel on a tip from the clerk. You were right that they got the license plate. They put out an APB on the car."

Austin opened the back door and removed the evidence box.

"Any mention of us?"

Dalton shook his head.

"None."

Austin was lost in thought. I looked between them as we hurried across the parking lot and toward the woods behind the motel.

"What's that mean?"

Dalton answered since Austin was apparently lost in thought.

"It means they want to keep our identities off the record."

"What?"

I was more confused than before he had answered.

Austin held the box close to his chest as he pushed his way through the bushes lining the parking lot. Dalton stomped down on a large branch and made a small path for me to follow.

"Everything's discoverable in court proceedings. If things don't go as planned, they don't want any record of looking specifically for us. It also means that when they do find us, we can disappear without any connection to them. We will just become another missing person statistic."

"What do we do?"

Dalton grabbed my arm as I stumbled in the darkness and kept me from falling on my face. He guided me as we moved quickly through the forest.

"Austin and I do what we do best. Make sure everything doesn't go as planned for the bad guys."

Chapter 50

We ran for over an hour, Austin scouting ahead while Dalton helped me navigate the dark forest. It was like he had cat eyes. Somehow he managed to see every hole or tree root in the darkness before we tripped over them.

At some point, we got close enough to Austin that I noticed the evidence box was no longer in his hands. I hadn't even seen him ditch it as we moved through the overgrown brush, but he no longer had it in his possession.

I guessed he still had the only significant thing we had discovered. The partial newspaper photograph. I wondered if we were still planning to go to the library in the city and see if we could locate the rest of the article and find out what the picture was about. And maybe even discover who was attached to the arm holding on to me in the picture.

My muscles ached and I wished I had taken their advice and at least tried to sleep. How was I supposed to know we would be running through the middle of the night in the wild countryside after only a few hours of rest?

They had told me to take advantage of every opportunity to eat and sleep when it presented itself during a mission because you never knew when you would get the chance again.

I silently promised myself I would take full advantage of the next opportunity; if it ever came up.

I prayed that the opportunity would come soon. My arms and legs were all scratched up from charging through nature like a bat out of hell. What I wouldn't give for a hot bath and a glass of wine right now.

Or at the very least, a smoothly paved sidewalk.

Up ahead, Austin stopped and dropped to one knee, holding his fist in the air. I remembered what that meant and I joined Dalton next to a tree as we both simultaneously stopped and crouched in place.

Austin was too far away to ask why we stopped, and when I looked over at Dalton, he was busy listening to the police radio chatter through the ear bud stuck in his ear.

I stayed quiet, and was glad I did when I saw a flash of light up ahead between the trees.

I looked at Dalton just as he spotted the light too. He switched off the radio and stuck it back in his pocket; pulling the ear bud out of his ear with the other hand.

He stuck a finger to his lips reminding me to stay absolutely silent. Then he pointed at the ground, telling me to stay put.

I nodded and he moved away in the dark. I knew, from the noise I had been making as we ran, that the ground was covered with dry and crumbling leaves. Yet, Dalton moved away from me just as silently as Austin had traveled through the forest the night before.

How did they do that?

If we ever made it out of this alive, I would have to get one of them to teach me how to move like a ninja.

A cloud blew across the moon, throwing the forest into darkness. Up until now, the moon had enabled us to see where we were going, despite the deep shadows cast by the trees.

With the moon gone, I would never be able to walk around without tripping on everything in my path. Could Dalton see just as well as he had before? I didn't think that was humanly possible, but then again, the very fact that I was still alive meant that these guys were used to doing the impossible.

I squinted into the blackness, trying to locate Dalton or Austin. I couldn't see anything except the sweeping light that bobbed back and forth deeper in the forest.

Dalton had been gone for what seemed like forever when someone suddenly moved in close next to me. I jerked in surprise, but a hand clamped over my mouth before I could cry out.

Dalton's face moved in close enough for me to recognize him in the dim light. I relaxed in his grip and he let go of me, leaning close enough to my ear that his lips were practically touching me.

It didn't send the same uncontrollable impulses coursing through my body like it did when Austin got that close.

He spoke so softly, I could barely hear it over the rustling of the leaves on the trees above us. And the wind was barely blowing.

"It's just some guy looking for his dog. Austin's going on ahead and will meet us at the library tomorrow morning."

I twisted my head to the side to look at him, forcing him to jump back before I bashed his nose with my cheek.

He clamped his hand over my mouth again and then guided my lips to his ear.

"Why isn't he waiting for us?" I whispered.

Still gripping my head in his hands, he turned me and spoke softly into my ear.

"We stand a better chance of not being noticed if we split up. Nick will expect us to stay together, so if we travel separately, we just might slip through his net."

I pulled against his grip, so he guided my head around until I was staring into his ear.

"Why aren't I with Austin?"

I could see Dalton's smile as he passed my face on his way to my ear.

"He has a couple of things to do before we meet at the library. Besides, we both agreed that you are too much of a distraction for him."

I jerked my head out of his hands and looked away just as the moon moved out from behind the clouds and the pale light increased all around us.

After the relative darkness, it was like the sun had finally come out after a long storm, but for me, the darkness would be ever present until I was by Austin's side again.

Chapter 51

I sat silently in the woods, my butt freezing in the cold mud, while we waited for the man to find his dog and return to his home.

That took almost an hour. Dalton had helped me shift to a sitting position after five minutes of waiting, which relieved the burning in my legs, but the chill in my ass started soon after and never let up until ten minutes after we had been able to stand up and continue through the forest.

Before we had set out again, Dalton reminded me to stay quiet unless I was in imminent danger, whatever that meant. I hoped it didn't mean we would be running into bears or wolves in the middle of their home turf.

Unfortunately, having already been placed under a strict gag order, I wasn't able to ask what he meant until we exited the woods at the edge of a small town.

Once we had crawled our way out of the Pennsylvanian jungle and were walking along the smooth blacktop, passing signs of civilization that stated "Food, Gas, and Lodging", Dalton visibly relaxed.

He pointed to the glow in the clouds ahead.

"Once we get to that town, we can call a taxi to take us into the city."

I thought back to how much driving we had done to get out here, not to mention the past few hours of walking through the woods.

"Won't that be expensive?"

Dalton whipped out a small black card from the front pocket of his jeans.

"Not to worry. I have Austin's Amex Black."

I had never seen a metal credit card before and gawked at an exclusive tool of the ultra-rich. Why did Austin have one of those? He didn't appear to have much money, let alone be exceedingly rich. And why did he let Dalton have it?

"He gave that to you?"

"Gave, took, it's all semantics."

It only took another hour to reach the town. Calling it a town was being generous. It was little more than an intersection with a gas station on one side and a truck stop diner on the other.

Dalton noticed me eyeing the painted pictures of food on the backlit windows of the twenty-four hour diner.

I looked at him, imagining the drool running out the side of my mouth as I spoke.

"When in the middle of a mission, you've got to take every opportunity to eat or sleep when it presents itself."

He smiled, pressed his hands together like he was about to pray, and bowed.

"You are learning, Grasshopper."

Chapter 52

I shifted uncomfortably on the cracked vinyl seat and held a hand against one side of my stomach. It felt like it was going to burst.

Dalton burped quietly next to me and picked at his teeth with a toothpick in the back seat of the taxi that had picked us up outside the diner.

"Whew," he exclaimed. "I never thought I would meet anyone who could match me bite for bite. Either I am getting soft or you are chock full of girl power."

I breathed in and out slowly, trying not to let the motion of the taxi jar my swollen belly too much.

"Why does it have to be either of those things?"

"Well, for one, a girl half my size was able to keep pace with me at the feeding trough. That doesn't happen without a major disturbance in the force."

I had no idea what he was talking about, but I was in too much happy pain to let it bother me. Besides, despite only knowing Dalton for less than a day, I knew he joked when things got uncomfortable.

With how much we had both eaten at the all-you-can-eat buffet, he had to be in as much pain as I was, if not more.

Dalton wedged the toothpick between his front teeth and dislodged a chunk of meat. He chewed on it for half a second before swallowing it.

"You know what the worst thing that could happen to us right now is?"

"There's something worse than this?"

"Maybe not much worse, but a little worse."

"What?"

"The worst thing right now would be if Nick found us like this."

My heart skipped a beat. Didn't this guy ever let up with inducing terror and panic in me on a constant basis?

"You couldn't fight him like this?"

Dalton started to shake his head, and thought better of it

when his face turned a lighter shade of pink, puffing his cheeks out as he burped.

"Nope. I could still take the bastard. But I'd probably vomit all over him in the process. And nobody wants to see that after what I ate."

I regarded Dalton. He never hid what he was thinking, not for a moment. It was refreshing after the growing silence and apparent lies from my own husband. It was nice to see that there were still people in the world who cherished honesty and bravery.

Bravery. That was what I needed right now, and I had it. I had two brave knights working to protect me from a dragon.

And we still had no idea how big this dragon was. We had seen snippets of the enemy but were still, more or less, completely in the dark.

It was a stroke of luck that put Austin in charge of my case after my arrest. He was not only more than capable of protecting me, but he knew the enemy intimately.

Unfortunately, the reverse was also true.

Nick knew as much about my two protectors as they knew about him. But he had resources at his disposal that my knights in shining armor lacked.

We were truly on our own and stumbling around in the dark.

I reached into my pocket and felt the folded up newspaper article hiding in there.

Maybe finding out what the article said would bring us out of the darkness and into the light?

I watched out the window as the sun burst from the horizon and slowly rose while we headed back into the dragon's den.

Dalton said they would be watching for us, so we had to be careful about how much exposure we allowed as we entered the city.

The plan was to stop directly in front of the library, climb out of the taxi, and walk right into it. This time, I promised not to look around and bring attention to myself. I just had to walk straight in, like I was a student heading in to do some research for a class I never really wanted to take in the first place.

As we pulled up to the street in front of the library, Dalton handed the credit card to the driver.

"Give yourself a good tip. I mean, a really good tip."

The driver smiled and punched in a bunch of numbers before swiping the card through a card reader stuck into the headphone jack of his iPhone.

He handed Dalton the phone for signature.

Dalton looked at the screen and smirked at the driver.

"Now Aunt Mable can get that operation, huh?" he said as he signed with his fingertip on the touch screen.

"Do you need a receipt?" the driver asked, taking back the phone.

"Naw," Dalton replied and climbed out of the taxi. I open my door and followed him out. The driver took off before I had even closed the door, no doubt worried that Dalton might change his mind about the generous tip.

As the taxi sped away, Dalton pointed to the library steps.

"You go straight in and wait for me inside."

"What are you going to do?"

"I'm going to take a stroll and see if anyone is watching the library."

I headed down the sidewalk and up the main steps of the library. This time, I didn't pause to adjust my shoes or look around. It was hard not to, but I had learned my lesson. I wasn't about to draw any attention to myself.

I hit the top stair and headed for the main doors of the library. As I got closer, I noticed that I was the only person heading for the doors, which were still closed.

I grabbed the handle and tugged, but the door didn't budge. I pulled again, but the door remained closed.

I looked to one side and saw the sign that displayed the hours of the Carnegie Library of Pittsburgh.

They didn't open until ten in the morning, and the sun had just come up. I couldn't get into the library for another couple of hours.

What was I supposed to do?

I scanned the sidewalk in both directions, looking for Dalton. He was nowhere to be seen.

Had he abandoned me?

After everything that had happened, it seemed unlikely. But as I walked back to the top of the stairs and checked in every direction, he was gone.

He couldn't have just vanished.

At the same moment that thought crossed my mind, my eyes fell on a black panel van with tinted windows parked directly across the street from the library entrance.

I must have stared too long at it because the back doors opened and a man, dressed in black combat gear and holding a pistol with an extra-long barrel down against his leg so as not to draw attention to the fact he had a gun in his hand, jumped out into the street and focused on me.

Chapter 53

I didn't wait to see if he was actually looking for me or not. Any hesitation on my part meant a speedy capture for him, and if he wasn't there for me, he wouldn't bother chasing me.

I kicked off my heels and darted to my left, running through the grass along the edge of the library.

I ducked instinctively when bits of wall shattered near me and exploded outward as I ran. I hadn't heard any gunshots. The extended barrels on the gun must have been a silencer, and he was firing at me.

That settled it.

He was definitely here for me.

I didn't slow down as I rounded the corner. There was only one of them, and only one of me. But I wasn't dressed appropriately to win a foot chase.

Nor was I trained in hand-to-hand combat, which, I surmised with a sense of irony, didn't really matter.

He had a gun, skills, and training.

The only thing I had going for me was…

Nothing.

Well, I did have Dalton; but he had vanished.

Where had he gone? And how had he missed the obvious black van with tinted windows parked on the street? Hadn't we split up so he could scout for any problems and prevent what was happening to me right now?

A chunk of grass exploded near my foot, leaving a small crater where the bullet had impacted.

I yelled out involuntarily and dashed around the back of the building as a chunk of the corner exploded near my head, spraying plaster and cement dust into my eyes and mouth.

I coughed and sputtered, spitting out the grit that covered my teeth. I would never be able to outrun the man chasing me as long as I was barefoot. I had to outsmart him if I was going to survive this encounter.

Besides, how many times could I circle the library before others joined in on the chase or he doubled back and came at me from the front?

Since running away was out, I had to hide from him. The bushes that lined the edge of the library property just might work.

I angled my trajectory and propelled myself across the grass, crashing into the bushes with wild abandon.

To my surprise, the bushes turned out to be the tops of trees. I realized this a heartbeat too late as the ground fell away from me and I tumbled end over end, slamming into tree trunks that spun me in different directions as I somersaulted out of control.

I splayed my arms and legs, trying to regain control as I tumbled violently down the hill.

I didn't stop until I hit the bottom and landed on my side. Fortunately, I hadn't been knocked unconscious.

I moved one arm and leg at a time, fearing the worst. I felt pain as I moved them, but nothing severe enough to indicate I had broken anything.

I rolled to my stomach and raised myself to my hands and knees. The world spun as I sat up and leaned back on my heels.

When it slowed enough to see clearly, I leaned against a tree for support and stood up unsteadily on my feet.

I shook my head to clear it and looked around me for the bushes I thought were here. All around me were tree trunks reaching for the sky. There was nowhere to hide.

Across the small street was a thicker stand of trees surrounded by bushes. I could hide in there if I could reach it before the assassin followed me down the hill.

I stumbled forward, leaning on trees as I walked and focused on putting one foot in front of another, increasing my speed with each step.

By the time I reached the road, I no longer needed support, which was good since there was none.

I checked both directions and jogged across the street and slipped into the bushes. I didn't bother to look to see if the mercenary had seen me. If he had, I was already caught. If not, then I hadn't given him the chance to discover me through my hesitation.

I hunched down and sat in the thickest part of the bushes,

peering back the way I had come.

My breathing had finally returned to normal by the time I spotted the mercenary sliding down the hill. He traversed the same path under much more control than I had.

His eyes were scanning the disturbed dirt, easily following the path I had made when I behaved like a pinball and hit nearly every tree trunk on the way down.

He followed my trail like a bloodhound, all the way to the edge of the street; directly across from me.

He looked back and forth along the street, tucking the pistol behind his back every time a car passed.

I stayed perfectly still, afraid to move. I didn't even risk shrinking farther back into the shadows of the bushes I was hiding in. By the way he was scanning the road in both directions, he obviously hadn't seen me enter the bushes and I didn't want to give away my position.

The mercenary alternated between both directions for nearly a minute before he decided I had headed for the bridge.

I remained frozen in place for ten minutes after I lost sight of him. I finally decided it was time to see if I could find Dalton. Unless someone had killed him.

I stamped down that thought as unproductive and brushed my hair away from my eyes. I slowly parted the bushes, aware of the noise they made with each movement, and crept out of the bushes.

I hurried across the street and climbed back up the way I had fallen, slipping a few times on the loose dirt of the steep hill.

As I crested the top of the hill, I crouched and scanned the open space between me and the library. I slowly turned my head, looking to see if anyone else was looking around instead of just going about their day.

Nobody triggered my spidey senses as I looked at them from my hiding spot. But then again, I wasn't a trained soldier like Dalton or Austin. I was an unemployed housewife who had to take the bus wherever she went.

My heart sank as I realized that I hadn't done anything to deserve what was happening to me. Then my heart hardened as I remembered that Robert was part of it.

Had my entire life been a lie? Or at least, the part that I remembered? Who had I been before the accident that had taken my memories? Had there even been an accident, or was this all part of the plot against me?

I was beginning to doubt everything I had ever been told. With the exception of flushing my meds, I had still trusted that Robert was looking out for me. I had believed that up until I found the camera behind the picture.

I had no idea who he was looking out for, but it certainly wasn't me.

Motion along the far corner of the building drew me out of my head and back into the real world.

Dalton was running a hand along the corner of the library, feeling the chunk that had been taken out of it by the bullet that had almost split my head in two. His other hand clutched the shoes I had abandoned at the top of the steps of the library.

He glanced in my direction, following the trail of footsteps in the grass I had left when I sprinted for the boundary of the library grounds.

I half-stood and waved at Dalton. His face registered relief and he smiled. He started to take a step in my direction when his smile twisted in agony and he spun violently around, sprawling on the ground at the same moment bright red liquid splattered across the wall next to him.

Chapter 54

I ducked back down and slid below the edge of the hill. With my head the only thing visible, I watched in horror as the man who had chased me around the library walked slowly up to Dalton's still form lying face down in the dirt.

He held his gun straight out in front of him, ready to finish the job should Dalton still be alive. I looked around at the few people walking on the sidewalks or driving by. Every pedestrian had headphones on their ears and were lost in their phone as they walked.

Nobody was paying enough attention to the world around them to see an armed gunman walking around the city in broad daylight. Even the homeless man, dressed in a gray hoodie that covered his head and torn jeans, digging through the garbage can on the corner was too involved in his own problems to see what was happening.

It was up to me to save Dalton. And if I didn't do something quick, Dalton would be dead; if he wasn't already.

I banished those thoughts from my brain. As long as I was still breathing, there was always something I could do.

I ducked out of sight and let out a blood curdling scream. I took another deep breath and let out another scream.

I poked my head up to see the assassin headed straight for me.

Well, that hadn't actually worked in my favor. Behind the gunman Dalton stirred on the ground. Whatever happened to me, at least I had kept him alive.

My focus returned to the cold-blooded killer whose attention never wavered from me. He was so focused on keeping me in his sights this time, he neglected to notice the homeless man rushing at him until he was tackled from the side.

I let out a cry of relief and watched as the hooded homeless man delivered a swift kick of justice to the assassin's face and rendered my executioner unconscious. He crouched next to the body and relieved him of the silenced pistol, tucking it into the back of his pants.

Great! I had just unwittingly armed a hobo.

The homeless man looked at Dalton and then over in my direction. He pulled back his hoodie and my heart pounded heavily in my chest as soon as I recognized him.

It was Austin!

I had never been so glad to see someone in my life before. My toes dug into the soft dirt as I scrambled over the top of the hill and caught up with him just as he reached Dalton.

We both crouched over Dalton's body and Austin rolled him over on his back.

Dalton was smiling up at us.

"There you are partner. Thought I was a goner for a moment there."

Austin peeled up the torn fragments where the bullet had caught Dalton in the shoulder.

He tilted his head back and forth as he prodded the wound with his fingers.

Dalton winced with each poke, but didn't say anything. Austin patted Dalton on the back and pulled on his good arm to help him sit up.

"The bullet took a tiny chunk out of your upper arm. You'll have a helluva scar, but you will live."

"There's so much blood," I said with a shiver.

Austin looked at the splatters that covered the side of the library building.

"Doesn't take much to look like a lot. Alt was lucky. If the guy had a rifle with a scope, we wouldn't be talking to him right now."

Dalton sat up and looked over at the unconscious assassin.

"Who is that guy?"

Austin glanced at the man, whose face was starting to swell from his kick.

"Don't know. Fortunately, we have the opportunity to ask him."

I pointed to the van still parked at the end of the street in the distance.

"He came out of there."

Dalton and Austin both looked where I pointed. Dalton

winced as he looked at me. I didn't know if it was from pain or guilt.

"I knew that van looked suspicious but I decided to finish my circuit of the library grounds before I checked it out. When I got back, I found your shoes at the top of the stairs and bullet holes along the side of the building. I thought I had screwed up and lost you."

Dalton held his good arm out toward us.

"Help me up."

Austin and I helped him to his feet. Blood seeped from the hole in his jacket.

"Don't you need to get that checked out by a doctor or something?"

Dalton gave his wound a sideways glance.

"Naw. I just need a new shirt, that's all. And then his eyes rolled up into the back of his head and he crumpled to the ground. Austin guided him down slowly and looked at me.

"Search that guy for the keys."

"What keys?" I asked.

"The van. We have to get Dalton out of here and resting before we can come back. Fortunately for us, our friend here has provided us with some transportation."

I walked slowly toward the man on the ground and looked back at Austin.

"What if he wakes up?"

Austin swung his hand as he replied.

"Just kick him again in the face."

I looked back at the still form of the assassin. I hoped he stayed out cold so I wouldn't have to do that.

"Hurry up," Austin said through gritted teeth. "Dalton's heavy and we don't want to attract attention to ourselves by carrying two bodies around Pittsburgh."

I bent down and felt around in the pockets. I found a bulge in one pocket and reached in, extracting a set of car keys.

The assassin moaned and started to roll over. I jumped up and started kicking him in the face, all the rage of him chasing me, shooting at me, and shooting Dalton boiled over. I kept kicking him in the face long after he was in la-la land.

Austin grabbed my shoulders from behind and pulled me away from the assassin.

"Easy, Michele. We need him able to talk."

I looked down at the bloody face, at the damage I had wrought, and I sunk to my knees about ready to cry.

Austin lifted me up.

"No, no, no. I need you strong right now. I can't carry three of you. Did you find the keys?"

I pointed to the ground where I had dropped them when the killer surprised me by waking up.

Austin reached down and retrieved the keys, holding them out to me.

"You get the van and park it close. I will see about getting Dalton to wake up long enough to walk on his own."

I nodded as he pushed me forward. My feet complied and they kept placing themselves one in front of the other until I was standing next to the black van.

I pressed the unlock button on the remote and climbed in the van. I was sitting in the driver's seat, the keys in my hand, before I realized I didn't remember how to drive a car.

It was such a basic ability of adults in modern society, Austin hadn't even given it a second thought when he had asked me to get the van.

I stared at the dials, buttons, and levers that filled the dash, and realized I had no idea what any of them did or meant.

I was completely out of my element behind the wheel of a car. Not to say I had been anywhere near my element since watching my doppelgänger jump off a bridge, but I was not ready to attempt to drive.

It would take an already bad situation and ratchet it up to a hundred times worse. I didn't think I could handle things if they got worse. Maybe Austin and Dalton were capable of putting up with more, but I wasn't.

I sat in the driver's seat and stared at the keys in my hand. Why hadn't I told Austin I didn't know how to drive? Was it because his trusted associate was lying unconscious at his feet from a bullet wound?

He had been forced to rely on me, without knowing my abilities.

Or my limitations.

While things could always get worse, there was no way they would get better if I tried to drive the van.

I climbed out of the van and ran back.

Austin was slapping Dalton awake. As soon as he saw me, confusion wrinkled his forehead.

"Why didn't you bring the van over?"

I looked at the ground and my face reddened in embarrassment.

"I don't know how to drive."

"It's not that hard. It's like learning to ride a bicycle. You never forget how."

"Maybe. But I don't remember how to ride a bicycle either."

He leaned Dalton against the side of the library wall and stood up, taking my hands in his. His blue eyes pierced right through me.

"Have you ever watched anyone else drive?"

I nodded. I had found myself watching Robert every chance I got. I had thought that someday I would get the "all clear" from the doctor and be able to get a real license, not the identification variety.

He smiled.

"The key is to take it nice and easy. Don't smash your foot on the pedal. Fortunately for you that's a van, which means it's automatic. You won't have to deal with a clutch. Do you know which pedals are which?"

I nodded again. I wasn't a total idiot. Thankfully, I kept that thought to myself and didn't say it out loud. No sense increasing the tension he had to be feeling right now.

"Just keep your foot on the brake when you start the car and shift into drive. It's the big letter D on the stick shift. Can you do that?"

I nodded and he smiled.

"Just park the van as close as you can to here. I don't know how much longer we have before someone notices bodies lying all over the place."

Even in the middle of a stressful situation, he was able to crack a joke. It may not have been over-the-top, like one of Dalton's, but it calmed me to know that he was still very much in control.

I turned and headed back to the van.

"Hurry," Austin said behind me.

I started running, not paying attention to anything but how I was going to drive the van. My subconscious mind registered the problem long before I realized something was different.

My feet had already started to falter as I noticed the second black van behind the first one. I skidded to a halt and gawked at the two identical vans.

The driver's side door opened on the rear van and a man dressed in the same black combat gear as the assassin stepped out, looking around him.

I ducked behind a tree and peeked around as he slowly walked up to the other van and peered through the front window. He knocked on the glass a couple of times and then looked around.

I ducked back behind the tree, but in my terrified panic, I swore we made eye contact right before I was out of sight.

I had to know if he had seen me.

I peeked around the other side.

He was gone.

I slowly moved around the tree, checking frantically for where he had gone.

A chunk of the tree exploded just above my head and I dropped to the ground, scrambling in a crab walk to what I hoped was behind the tree relative to the new shooter.

"Austin!" I screamed.

The tree exploded twice more, but at the edges of the tree on either side of me. I stopped crawling and knew I was safe for the moment. But how long would that moment last?

Chapter 55

I pressed my back up against the tree, flinching every time another piece of tree bark exploded near me.

"Austin!" I screamed again.

I couldn't see him from this angle, so I had no idea if he even heard me.

"Help!" I yelled at the top of my lungs, hoping somebody would take notice. A man jogging along the sidewalk slowed down and pulled out his headphones. He looked at me curiously, then his chest exploded and he pitched backward onto the sidewalk.

I screamed.

A blur rushed into my view.

Austin had the pistol he had taken from the other mercenary and was firing as he ran. The tree had stopped exploding and I peeked around to see the other soldier running away with Austin in pursuit.

Dalton appeared next to me and grabbed my arm, lifting me to my feet.

"Let's go."

"You're okay," I said as we hustled down the sidewalk toward the two identical vans.

"Not quite," he replied. "But I'm moving, and that's something."

We reached the van at the same time as Austin. Austin tossed the gun to Dalton who caught it in one hand. Austin held his now empty hand out to me.

"Keys."

I was more than glad to give them to him. Dalton opened the rear doors and paused, whistling as a smile spread across his face.

I looked into the back of the van and my jaw hit the floor. It was a small armory filled with assault rifles, other assorted guns I had never seen before in my life, and boxes of ammunition.

Dalton stepped to one side and bowed.

"After you milady."

I jumped into the back of the van, careful not to step on the boxes of bullets on the floor, and sat on the bench opposite a rack of military grade weaponry.

Dalton pulled the doors closed behind us just as Austin gunned the engine and pulled out into the road.

Two pings ricocheted off the back of the van and then Austin turned hard, nearly tipping us over as he wheeled around the corner and away from the mercenary who had recovered enough to start shooting at us.

We drove for nearly an hour before Austin pulled over to the side of the road. He opened the back doors and the sunlight spilled in, making Dalton and me blink against the harsh light of day.

Dalton recovered quickly and hopped out, looking around at the trees that lined both sides of the road. He looked at Austin.

"Why'd you bring us here?"

Austin smiled at him.

"You know where we are?"

Dalton looked around again.

"Of course."

"Good. Help me get these guns and ammo hidden off the road. We might need these later."

I looked at Dalton as he favored his one arm, grabbing a box of ammo with his good arm.

"Why are we taking them out of the van?"

Dalton looked at me as he handed me the box.

"The van is probably being tracked, so we can't keep it for very long. But we can always use guns. And bullets. Lots of bullets."

I took the box from him. It was far heavier than I had expected and almost dropped it.

"You think we need all these?"

Austin grabbed a couple of assault rifles from the rack mounted along one side of the van's interior.

"Hopefully we won't need any of it. But if the next two days are like the last two, we will be glad that we can even the odds, even if just a little bit."

I followed them into the woods until we couldn't see the road through the wild brush.

Austin cleared an area under a tree.

"Put everything here. We can come back for it later if we need it."

We spent the next ten minutes emptying the van of all weapons and ammunition and piling it next to the tree.

"What if some kids find all this?" I asked Dalton as we both carried a box that was too big for either one of us alone.

"We are far enough away that it is unlikely. We have also hidden it far enough off the road that nobody will find it unless they know it's there."

That didn't ease my fears about leaving all this behind as we pulled back onto the road and sped away from Pittsburgh.

After another hour on the road, Austin turned up the radio. We remained silent as we listened to the announcer.

"According to police reports, eyewitnesses described a homeless man who opened fire on innocent civilians as they were exercising around Carnegie Library of Pittsburgh. An official statement from the Pittsburgh Police Department verifies that the homeless man was apprehended a few blocks away and that the families of those caught up in this senseless tragedy will be notified when the victims have been identified."

Austin shut off the radio and pulled the van into the parking lot of a small motel and shut off the engine.

Dalton had been working on a machine he had found behind the driver's seat for the past half hour.

"Got it," he exclaimed and looked like a kid who had just received a lollipop as big as his head. "Anybody got a camera?"

Austin looked out the front windshield and pointed.

"I bet there's a photo booth in that drug store."

I looked at Dalton.

"Why do we need to take photos?"

Dalton held up the small machine he had been playing with.

"This is an ID maker. We can create photo ID, credit cards, even social security cards. The newer ones have a built-in camera. This one looks new enough, but I don't see a lens."

I stared at the machine in his hands.

"I didn't even know something like that existed."

"They have very limited uses, but every one of them is illegal."

"Why did that guy have one?" I asked.

"I don't know," Austin said as he took the machine from Dalton and inspected it.

"This one looks Russian made. Probably why it doesn't have a camera."

He and Dalton shared a look.

I didn't like that look.

"What's that mean?" I asked.

Dalton looked at me, his eyes more serious than I had ever seen before.

"It means we might be up against something that is bigger than we can prepare to handle."

Chapter 56

Austin looked me over.

"None of us look our best right now, but you look better than Alt or me."

I regarded myself in the rear view mirror. My hair was strewn around like I hadn't combed it in days, and my face was smeared with mud.

Austin and Dalton took turns making me look more presentable, or at least presentable enough to purchase some new clothes in the drug store and get my picture taken at the photo booth.

Austin handed me a wad of twenty dollar bills. The last time I had held this much money in my hand, I had taken it from Dead Michele's wallet.

"What's this for?"

"Get clothes for us and a first aid kit for Dalton's shoulder."

I looked at Dalton who had broken into a sweat and was holding a hand against his shoulder.

"He needs a doctor," I said.

Austin shook his head.

"Whoever is after you managed to cover up a shootout in a police station and neatly repackaged the attack at the library. If we take Dalton to a hospital, we might as well be turning him over directly to whoever is behind all of this."

Dalton winced as he shifted on the bench seat.

"Austin's right. We have to stay in the shadows right now. Fortunately we have this little treasure. We can make you a new identity along with credit cards. They won't hold up to very much scrutiny, or work for very long, but they should get us a rental car so we can ditch the van and get back to the library before they close for the day."

My eyes nearly popped out of my head.

"Go back to the library? Are you crazy?"

Dalton smiled at my outburst.

"Crazy like a fox, which is why I'm still alive. They won't be expecting us to return to that library, so that makes it one of the safest places for us to be right now."

I looked from him to Austin.

Austin placed a hand on my shoulder.

"Alt's right. There will be plenty of police around the library to make a good show of force and ease the public fears. We would be crazy to go back there, which is why we have to. We still need to know about the newspaper article."

"Can't we go to some other library?"

Dalton shifted on the seat and grunted from the pain, but he continued after letting out a quick breath.

"Which is what they will be expecting us to do. Now that they know we were headed for a library they probably have someone watching every library in a two hundred mile radius. But there is one they will not be watching. They can't, not with the increased police presence."

I closed my eyes and saw the jogger being killed in front of me. The only reason he was dead was because he had stopped to help me.

During one of our sessions Dr. Westcott had mentioned that everything in life was designed to teach us something.

What was the jogger's killing designed to teach me?

That anyone who helped me would die?

I looked at Austin.

Was helping me the same as signing his death warrant?

He had to know what was at risk ever since we fought our way out of the police station. And he knew, personally, who was leading the mercenaries in their quest to locate and kill me.

His experience had made it so that he knew the risks before I did. Then why was he still helping me?

Dalton had been shot, and now their former teammate had added them to the list of targets. Even if I was captured, I had no doubt that Austin and Dalton would still be pursued to the ends of the earth.

They had no other choice but to help see this through.

I watched Dalton wincing as he shifted in the seat. He had nearly been killed already and we weren't any closer to knowing why.

"Michele?"

I blinked, realizing that my mind had been wandering and looked at Austin.

"Just get the first aid kit. We can work out everything else once we get Dalton patched up."

I nodded and glanced over at Dalton. He leaned against the corner of his seat, keeping a hand pressed against his wound.

He looked at me, smiling through the pain.

"Get me some Tylenol and Motrin too."

"How much?"

He looked at me and exhaled sharply.

Austin touched my shoulder.

"Just get one bottle of each. We don't want to trigger any purchase flags."

I nodded and headed for the drug store.

It took me less than ten minutes to gather clothes, new shoes for me, and the drugs for Dalton.

The lady behind the checkout counter smiled at me as I approached. I smiled back, but thankfully, she rang me up, took my cash, gave me change, and the only words out of her mouth were, "Next."

Back out in the car, I changed in the back of the van while Dalton popped two of each of the pills I had purchased. I knew from all the news stories that taking that much of anything was bad for the liver or kidneys. But then again, the long term effects of taking that much medication at once might not come into play if he wasn't capable of defending himself.

Once I was changed, I headed back into the store to have my picture taken in the photo booth. Two hours after I went in, Dalton and Austin went in one at a time, a half hour apart. They had said that they didn't want to cause any of the employees to think we were together in case someone asked.

"Who would ask them that?" I had asked him.

Austin had closed his eyes and shook his head slightly, as if the answer was obvious.

"Everything we do is to provide distance to what we are really planning. By going in separately, the employees will not connect that two men and a woman all came in for pictures at the same time. We don't want to give away that we are using their ID machine or things will become much more difficult for us."

I stayed silent while Austin created Driver's Licenses and credit cards from the machine.

When he handed me mine, I looked at it. While the picture was mine, the name and other information were unquestionably wrong on purpose.

I smiled to myself as I finally held my very own Driver's License. I had wanted one of these ever since that weird guy had propositioned me on the bus, and now I had one.

Unfortunately, it was a fake.

But you know what?

That didn't matter.

I was holding a tiny plastic card with my picture and the words "DRIVER'S LICENSE" right next to it. I didn't know why, but it was as if a burden that had kept me crushed under its overwhelming weight for years had been lifted.

This must be how high school kids felt when they got their first driver's license.

I pressed the card against my chest. This was my ticket to go anywhere I wanted without having to rely on anyone else. It was the ultimate freedom and I didn't care that it was a counterfeit.

I looked at the card again, and then noticed the last name was listed as Janssen. That was Austin's last name. I looked over at Dalton and he smiled knowingly, giving me a small wink. I gulped and looked at Austin, who was watching me, his bright blue eyes twinkling with anticipation.

"Are you ready for your crash course on how to drive?"

I winced, my heart suddenly leaping into my throat as I realized I would be in control of thousands of pounds of steel and flammable liquid. I had seen one too many movies where cars exploded upon impact. I hoped that Hollywood had gotten that wrong just like they had gotten a lot of everything else wrong.

I swallowed dryly.

"I wish you wouldn't put it that way."

Chapter 57

After only hitting the wheel stops in the middle of the parking lot two times, nearly destroying the shocks on the front wheels of the van, I managed to figure out how to avoid them by turning the steering wheel far enough, or just barely. Learning which was which was the tricky part.

The brakes were much more difficult to nail down. After tossing Dalton around in the back like a Caesar salad made table side a few times, he opted to stand on the sidewalk with the comment that he probably wasn't much safer there.

It took nearly an hour to get to the point where I could smoothly accelerate and then stop again. I even managed to back into a parking space and stay within the lines.

Austin smiled at me.

"I could just kiss you now."

My heart accelerated faster than the engine had when I had accidentally pressed on the gas pedal in neutral. Fortunately, my mouth reacted faster than my brain could to stop it.

"Then why don't you?"

Austin's face softened and he leaned over. I closed my eyes, waiting for heaven when something banged into the side of the van.

I jumped and looked out the side window.

Dalton was giving us both a strange look, and then turned away shaking his head.

I looked back at Austin, but he was already climbing out of the van.

It didn't matter.

The mood was gone.

Chapter 58

As we pulled into the rental car place, Dalton was looking much better and had started cracking jokes on a more constant basis again.

I had purchased a long black scarf that he was using as an arm sling. With the pain killers, he was moving his injured arm more than he should as he pleaded with Austin from the passenger's seat.

"I can drive one handed just fine."

Austin shook his head.

"I don't doubt that, but you can't drive hopped up on medication."

"Oh, c'mon. There's no narcotics in Tylenol or Motrin. I'm fine."

"Your arm still needs to rest. Let's just stick to the plan."

Dalton looked back at me. All the confidence bled from my pores and I shuffled forward on the bench seat in the back.

"Maybe he's right. What if the new car is different? If they see me lurch the car back and forth in the parking lot, they might think I'm drunk or something."

Austin twisted in the driver's seat and focused his eyes on mine.

"I have faith in you Michele. Don't let this jerkwad here shake your resolve? I know you can do this."

I wasn't so sure. I looked at the phony Driver's License and credit card in my hands. Austin reached over the back of his seat and lifted my chin back up.

"Alt's going in with you. He will make sure that everything goes smoothly. You have nothing to worry about."

I guess he read the fear in my eyes and his look softened further.

"Don't worry about the credit card. We should have a good twenty-four hours before it won't work anymore. That's part of the magic of the machine Dalton found."

"But what if it doesn't work?"

"You let me worry about that," Dalton interjected. "We are

about to do what I do best. Make someone believe I'm someone else. Believe me when I tell you, I'm really good at it."

"He is," Austin confirmed. "Sometimes, I'm not entirely convinced his name really is Dalton."

Dalton smiled.

"I am the original international man of mystery."

Austin pointed toward the front door of the small rental car building, a one-room sized square box in front of a large parking lot, half filled with shiny new cars.

"Just get me a car mystery man."

Dalton laughed, all indication that he was in pain erased from his face. He opened the door and looked back at me.

"Let's go, Sweetheart."

Dalton had created the phony IDs listing him and me with the same last name. For the purposes of using them to rent a car, we would be husband and wife.

I followed Dalton across the parking lot and up to the small building. He grabbed the tinted sliding glass door with his good hand.

"Are you ready?"

I nodded despite all the butterflies in my stomach battling each other to be the one to cause me to throw up.

He pulled open the door and motioned with his head for me to enter the room first. I swallowed and stepped into the chilled single room that served as the rental office.

The woman with short curly hair behind the counter looked up at us, her face brightening with an unexpected glow of excitement at having customers enter her establishment.

"Hello. Do you have a scheduled appointment?"

My stomach sank and my mouth fell open. We didn't have an appointment and, as I watched, the entire operation was unraveling right in front of me.

Chapter 59

"No ma'am," Dalton replied in a sickly sweet Southern drawl. Did these guys have anything else up their sleeve when it came time to be someone else? Or were Southern accents the extent of their skills?

"Our car is in the shop up the road a bit and my little wife and I were hoping that you might have something for just a day."

The woman looked at him.

"What happened to your arm?"

Dalton lifted it slightly.

"This? It's silly really. I was reaching for a pen. A pen! And my damn fool shoulder decides to give out. Doc says it's from some old football injury. Funny thing is, I never played football. But the doctor didn't need to know that. He was so sure of himself. Let the bastard think his parents spent good money on his education."

The woman's eyes narrowed at him.

"I can't rent you a car with your arm in a sling."

Dalton put his good arm around me and looked at me with a wide smile.

"That's why my wife is doing all the driving. You got anything small in an automatic?"

The woman regarded me and brightened back up immediately.

"I'll just need a driver's license and a credit card."

I pulled them out of a pocket and slapped them on the counter. The clerk took them and started typing furiously into her computer. She frowned at her monitor and swiped my credit card a second time.

She held the card up and looked at me.

"This card is declined."

The butterflies were no longer fighting each other, but were now working together to induce me to vomit all over the countertop.

Dalton slapped another card on the counter. It was Austin's metallic American Express Black.

"I keep telling the missus to stay away from the shopping malls. Try this one."

The woman took the card and inspected it. It was clear she had never seen one before. She looked at Dalton.

"I need to verify your ID."

Dalton paused briefly, gave her a funny look, and then twisted his hips.

"Honey, can you get my license out of my back pocket."

I slid my hands into his back pocket, rubbing his ass cheek as I did. I forced myself not to flinch as I fondled his butt trying to grip the card.

Dalton wiggled and giggled with glee.

"Just the card sweetie."

My face warmed instantly and the woman behind the counter smiled at my discomfort.

I pulled the card out and handed it to the woman. Dalton had made sure that his name matched the one on the no-limit credit card by manufacturing his ID with Austin's name.

The woman handed back his ID and swiped the card. The computer beeped and she placed a set of car keys on the counter.

"Would you like to upgrade to the unlimited insurance? It's only an extra fifty dollars a day, but it covers everything."

Dalton looked at her and furrowed his brow.

"Everything?"

She nodded.

"If you upgrade, you won't have to worry about anything. The car is fully covered and even includes immediate replacement at no additional cost for the length of the rental contract. And it's only fifty bucks a day. You'll spend more than that on a good dinner, but this won't give you indigestion," she said with a smile.

Dalton thought about that for a moment and then grabbed the pen and hovered over the contract, looking at the clerk again.

"So, this covers everything with the car?"

"Yes, everything. If you get rear ended and the car is totaled, don't worry. We will send out a new car to you as soon as possible, no questions asked."

"No questions asked?"

"Sign right there, pay the extended coverage, and we won't even bat an eye if this car's lying in a ditch when we come out with your replacement."

"What if we were to, say, crash it through the side of a library building or something?"

The rental clerk frowned at him.

"That's a new one, but yes. It would even cover smashing through the walls of a library. You might get some funny looks from the librarian, but not from us."

He looked at me and winked, his smile spreading wider as he signed the form awkwardly with his left hand.

"You never know when that will come in handy."

Chapter 60

In the past week, I witnessed a suicide, took over someone else's life, cheated on my husband with my own husband, got arrested, escaped from armed assassins, realized my marriage was a sham, used a fake ID to rent a car, and found my knight in shining armor.

It was so worth it.

My life in the past couple of days had been more exciting than all the years before it rolled up into one Big Bang moment.

Who knew what tomorrow would bring?

I certainly had no idea, but was more than ready to find out. I might even have described myself as anticipating the next big change in my life, no matter what it was.

After renting the car, Dalton made me drive as we met up with Austin around the corner and followed him to the train station in Huntingdon.

I must admit, I did pretty well and only elicited a couple of angry honks from cars when I had drifted too close to them as we traveled down the highway at terrifying speeds. Dalton tried to assure me that sixty miles an hour was not "at terrifying speeds", but I was not entirely convinced and was continually ready to hit the brakes at the tiniest hint of trouble in the lanes ahead of me.

Once we made it to the train station, Austin parked the van as close to the front as possible while directing me to park farther away. I'm sure from a snail's perspective, I was practically standing still, as I slowly inched the car into a space between two other cars. When I didn't hit the other two cars, Dalton nodded his approval. "Nicely done."

We joined with Austin in the main lobby of the station and made a big show of purchasing three tickets together, making sure to point out Dalton's injured arm to the ticket counter clerk, and several porters, as we climbed on the train.

The whole time, Austin and Dalton spoke with thick European accents and would occasionally slip into another language.

They were pretending to be someone else, and it was refreshing to see it wasn't the same Southern drawl I had already witnessed more than once.

Since I wasn't so sure my acting was up to snuff, I stayed quiet while they drew all sorts of attention to us.

After spending so much time hiding and keeping a low profile, it was confusing to suddenly not care who knew what we were up to and that we were together.

Once on board, Austin walked from car to car, looking at everyone as we walked. In the third car, he approached a family still settling in to their two rows of seats.

"Excuse me," he said to the father of two young boys I remembered seeing behind us in line. The boys were still having the same "did too", "did not" fight.

The man looked up at Austin, exhausted from a trip that hadn't actually started yet. He appeared pleased to be distracted with something other than his two rambunctious progenies.

"Yes?" the man said.

Austin pointed to me and spoke with the hint of a foreign accent. "My wife isn't feeling too well, something she ate."

The man looked at me and Dalton pinched my side, causing me to wince and double over slightly.

The man looked concerned as he watched me while Austin continued.

"I was wondering if you could hold our tickets for us. She might be in the bathroom when the conductor comes around, and I want our tickets scanned."

The man looked at the three tickets Austin held up. His face shifted from concern to confusion.

"You want me to hold your tickets?"

Austin nodded. "That would help us greatly."

"Why can't one of you keep them?"

Austin hooked a thumb at Dalton.

"I can't trust my brother with anything, and I need to be in the toilet with my wife or she'll panic. It would help us greatly if you could get the conductor to scan these when he passes by. I could even pay you."

The man looked startled.

"That's not necessary."

"So you'll help us?"

The man slowly reached for the tickets.

"Sure. I'd love to."

Austin smiled brightly and gave the man our tickets.

"Thank you so much."

Austin grabbed my arm and moved away quickly before the man could change his mind, guiding me to the next car as he jabbered at me in a foreign language.

We went back several cars before we disembarked the train and headed for the parking lot.

We were back at the rental car before the train pulled out, but instead of leaving, Austin pulled the rental car to the outer edge of the parking lot and parked again. Neither he nor Dalton had said a word since we left our tickets with the man on the train, and I was getting more confused as to why we hadn't left yet.

I tapped Dalton on his good shoulder.

He angled his head to the side to look at me without turning around fully in his seat. "What can I do for you?"

"What are we waiting for?"

Dalton pointed out the front windshield. "We're watching the van."

"Why?"

"The guys we took it from will be looking for it. When they find it here, they will follow our trail."

"Is that why we were so noisy and obvious when purchasing our tickets?"

Dalton nodded as he continued. "And why we gave our tickets to that family to have scanned. When they find out we bought tickets to Montreal, and according to the computer records, our tickets were scanned after the train left, they will focus their attention on the stations along the line heading north."

"So we've lost them?"

"For the moment. They will discover we're not on the train. Hopefully, we will have enough time to research the clue in the newspaper article."

I leaned back and hunkered down in the back seat. We sat there for several hours, with Austin and Dalton taking turns napping, before Austin sat up in his seat, hitting Dalton lightly with his hand, waking him up.

Dalton was awake immediately and looked in the direction of the van.

These guys were all business and always seemed focused on the task at hand.

If I had been asleep, I would have woken up disoriented and confused before I knew where I was.

Austin looked back at me, saw that I was awake, and pointed at the van. "Our friends have finally shown up."

My heart skipped a beat as I watched several armed men pop up from behind various parked cars around the van at once. They approached from every angle and surrounded the van.

The man they had called Nick walked around the van, peering in through the windows from a distance before holding up a keyless remote and pointing it at the van.

As soon as he pressed the unlock button, the men rushed the van at once and opened every door, shoving the extended barrels of their rifles in ahead of them. From across the parking lot, I couldn't hear anything being said, but it was obvious that Nick was extremely disappointed at finding an empty van.

After his short tirade, Nick sent one of his men into the station and pulled a shiny badge out from under his shirt and let it hang around his neck.

One by one, the men pulled flaps down on the front of their combat vests to reveal the word FBI in bold white letters.

The butterflies in my stomach returned with a vengeance. Was I actually hiding from federal agents of the United States government? Had Austin killed FBI agents back at the library and the police station?

"They're FBI?" I whispered.

"Not likely," Austin replied.

"Not with Nick involved," Dalton added.

"How can you be sure?" I pressed the issue. I had to be certain that I was on the right side of whatever was happening.

Austin turned around and his blue eyes encompassed me. Now my heart was beating for another reason. "They didn't drop those flaps down until after they found the van empty. They need to look official when they go into the station and ask about us."

I pictured our noisy parade through the station, the attention grabbing activities from Austin while we were in line, and the tickets handed to the man with the tireless children.

The man returned and spoke with Nick who reacted quickly and ordered his men with wild arm gestures. Immediately his soldiers fanned out into the train station, guns lowered so as not to cause widespread panic.

"Time for us to go," Austin said as he started up the car and pulled out the nearest exit and onto the highway. Every minute that passed increased the distance between Nick, his elite army, and us.

Austin and Dalton had painted a picture that we were escaping across the border to Canada. Crossing international borders meant that it would be harder for whoever was after us to get us, but then I realized with sudden clarity, we hadn't crossed any borders, international or otherwise.

Not only had we not escaped to safety, but Austin was still planning to take us right back to the library where Dalton had been shot. Their little misdirection with the train might buy us some time.

But how much time would it give us really?

Chapter 61

Austin took us a roundabout way back to the city. The whole time, Dalton kept a wary eye trained on his mirror to check for anybody following us. When he gave the "all clear", Austin headed straight for the heart of the city.

As we crossed the first bridge into Pittsburgh, my heart started beating so loud, I could swear the guys could hear it over the thrum of the tires as we crossed over the seam joints on the bridge.

The sounds of the tires on the bridge brought back a memory I had long forgotten. For a moment, I was back in the car with Robert. We were coming back from somewhere. In my mind's eye, I saw the floral print shirt he was wearing when we were coming back from our Florida vacation.

My mind shifted to the picture on Dead Michele's mantle. She had returned from that same vacation, probably even in the same manner I had.

Robert was a creature of habit. He kept returning with each Michele to the same places and recreating events in stark detail. He had done it with me, and with the next one in line. He had probably done the same with every Michele before me.

Discovering that he was replicating my life with a new Michele only accentuated his habits as bordering on sick.

My mind focused on the house Dead Michele shared with her roommate, Simone. Was she as innocent in all this as I had been?

The world shimmered around me and I was moving through Dead Michele's house, watching myself and Simone fighting with the sliding glass door when she was trying to keep me out.

I hadn't paid much notice to it then, but the plastic bag on the counter she had knocked down had been emblazoned with bright red letters on a ribbon of yellow.

Scouring my memory of that event, I focused all my energy on that one moment, bringing it into sharp clarity as if I were there again.

I pictured the bag as it fell off the counter and landed label side up. My heart skipped a beat as I recognized the label. The last time I had seen something like that was in the motel room, when Austin had lined up a bunch just like it on the bed.

My eyes popped open and I startled even myself as I yelled out too loudly in the silence.

"I know where Evidence Bag C is!"

Chapter 62

Dalton spun around and winced. The pills he had gulped down to ease the pain had to be wearing off by now. He ignored the shooting pain and gawked at me. "What?"

I could barely contain my excitement at being able to finally provide input. "The missing evidence bag! I know where it is!"

He frowned at me, but it was Austin's eyes staring at me in the reflection of the rear view mirror that made me begin to doubt myself. "It's…" I stammered nervously. "It's at the Dead Michele's house."

Dalton squinted at me. "Are you sure?"

I nodded enthusiastically. "It was on the counter when I went back there after she had been taken to the police station to identify the…"

I couldn't bring myself to say the word "body" out loud.

Dalton and Austin exchanged a look, and then Dalton looked at me again. "If you think you're sure, then this might be the break we are looking for."

I thought back to Simone brandishing the fork at me like it was a two-foot-long machete. "I'm sure."

Austin nodded and returned his attention back to the road. "Then we go there after the library if we don't find anything."

Dalton spun back around, grunting from the pain that evidently accompanied his every movement. "We have to see what the article attached to that picture says."

"What about the missing evidence?" I asked.

Austin broke into the conversation as he turned onto a side street. "That's important too, we don't know if there's anything significant in the evidence bag, since it was released to the roommate. But a picture of you, looking as young as you do now, from over twenty years ago? That takes priority over anything else."

I hated to admit it, but he was right. I still didn't feel comfortable returning to the place where Dalton got shot, but Austin had a point.

I wanted to know how I ended up in a newspaper photo from

two decades ago as much as he did. And the library was the best, and probably the only, place to do that.

Austin pulled onto the side of the street and shut off the car.

"We can walk the rest of the way on foot."

"Walk?" I said.

Austin spun around in his chair to face me. "Dalton will go in first, then you. I want you to head to the back where the periodicals are kept. The computers are back there too, and as soon as we get one, we search for the article."

Dalton held a hand up. "We don't know when the article came out."

Austin let out a quick breath of air. "Use the ad on the back to narrow it down. Start the weekend of the gun show and work your way backward."

"Oh, right. Sorry Austin. The pain is making it hard to concentrate."

Austin gave his friend a long hard look and then his face set as he made a new decision. "Alt, you stay in the car. I'll go in first."

Dalton shook his head. "No way. You gave your orders…"

Austin placed a hand on Dalton's good shoulder. "I hadn't realized how much pain you were in. You need to stay in the car."

"Are you sure?"

Austin smiled. "If something happens, I'm counting on you to come in and get me out. Are we clear?"

Dalton smiled back, his grin forced as he gritted through the pain. "Crystal."

Dalton sat back in the chair, plainly relieved that he could sit this one out. As Austin climbed out of the car, he dropped the keys on the driver's seat. "If we need to get away in a hurry, start the car."

Dalton snatched the keys up and dropped them in his lap. "I think I can handle that, Control."

Austin smiled and then adopted a more serious look as he turned to me.

"Give me five minutes, then walk two blocks that way and go into the library. Meet me in the back by the periodicals."

I nodded and smiled at him.

He didn't smile back as he stood up straight and walked briskly away from the car.

My heart sank as I watched him walk away. Had I done something to make him mad at me?

Dalton must have read the look on my face. "Don't read too much into it, Michele. He always drops into serious mode in the middle of a mission."

I turned and watched Austin run across the street and disappear around a corner. I looked back at Dalton who was fiddling with the Tylenol bottle again. He popped off the top and downed a couple more, swallowing them dry.

We sat in silence, staring out at the street until Dalton shifted in his seat. "Your turn," he said.

I wiped my sweaty palms against the legs of my pants and climbed out of the car. I ducked down before I closed the door. "Tell me everything is going to be okay."

Dalton looked into my eyes without blinking and adopted the quaint Southern drawl he had used on others to get what he wanted. "There ain't nothin' to fear, darlin'. You just get on out there and make me proud."

I wondered, as I closed the door and made my way to the corner, if I would still be headed for the library if he hadn't used his charming Southern accent on me.

Chapter 63

As I neared the library grounds, I could hear the distorted chatter of numerous police radios. As I rounded the corner, I slowed down and gawked at the police cars, officers, and hundreds of yards of police tape strewn all over the side of the library.

An officer approached me quickly. "I'm sorry Ma'am, this area is off limits."

I pointed at the building that had been cordoned off and excluded from public access. "I need to get to the library."

"You'll have to use another entrance."

I spun around slowly, lost as to what to do next. I had never been here before this morning, and I had no idea how else to get in to the library.

The officer noticed my confused expression and looked around him before he motioned for me to follow him. "Stay close to me, Ma'am. I'll get you through this and into the library."

I followed him as he took me across the street and down half a block before cutting back across the grass and leading me to the steps where I had abandoned my shoes the last time I was here.

"Be sure to use another exit when coming out."

I smiled at the officer. "I will. Thank you."

He moved away quickly and I wasn't even sure if he had heard me.

I looked around at the heavy police presence. The space that previously held the dark van contained police cars with flashing red and blue lights.

It made me feel safe to have so many police around. At first, I had been nervous because the mercenaries had been willing to attack an entire police station.

But this was more than just a few policeman. It looked like half the department was here, along with all the additional support crews of evidence gatherers, photographers, and dogs smelling every inch of the outside of the library.

For the first time since Austin said we were coming back here, I felt conformable with that decision.

My trust for Austin grew with each passing incident that proved he was doing everything in his power to keep me safe and find out what was going on.

I turned back to the library entrance and headed for the massive doors. This time, they opened easily when I pulled on the handle. It made a big difference when you showed up while they were open.

I opened the door just wide enough for me to slip into the cool darkness that waited for me inside.

As the door clicked shut behind me, I stood still and waited for my eyes to adjust. While I waited, my hand felt in my pocket for the newspaper article.

My heart skipped a beat.

It wasn't there!

My heartbeat quickened and I dug my hand deeper into the pocket.

Where was the article?

I checked the rest of my pockets, but the newspaper clipping was missing.

I felt all around the outside of my pants, as if I could feel the bulk of a paper-thin piece of newspaper.

My panic grew as I looked around me on the floor, thinking I had dropped it. I scanned the dark floor, but it was nowhere near me.

I didn't know when I had lost it, but it wasn't here. I considered going back out to look for it, but the wind had been kicking up ever since I left the car several blocks back.

If it had fallen out of my pocket outside, it was long gone.

Chapter 64

With the article missing, I made my way through the library feeling absolutely defeated. How were we to find the original article without any of the bits of information on it that gave us clues as to when it was printed?

My head was down, and I didn't notice the rolling cart with books stacked too tall on it until I bumped into it.

I stopped sharply, the books teetering back and forth. I stuck my hand out to stop them from toppling over, but as soon as I touched them, I upset their delicate balancing act and they clattered noisily to the floor.

Every face turned in my direction at the sudden disturbance. I looked around with a sheepish grin, and my eyes fell on Austin's.

He was shaking his head as he approached me. At the same time, a young man with a goatee and wire frame glasses, looking barely older than a teenager, suddenly appeared from among the shelves with a small stack of books in his arms.

"What did you do?" the man-boy hissed at me.

"I'm sorry," I whispered back. "I didn't see them."

Austin was at my side and bent down to help pick up the books. The man-boy waved his arms and frowned.

"Leave them. I'll do it."

He pushed his way past Austin and started gathering the books into another small stack on the floor.

"I really am sorry," I whispered.

He looked up at me, his disappointment with me written all over his face.

"Just be careful."

"I will. Sorry."

He waved us off.

Austin grabbed my elbow, electric sparks rushing through my body at his touch, distracting me from being able to think about anything else but his warm lips against mine.

He led us to the corner of the library where there was a line of computers along the wall. He sat down at the far left, in front of a computer with an "Out of Order" sign taped to the monitor.

"I think I found the article."

I was about to tell him that I had lost the only copy when he pressed the power button and the screen flickered to life.

"Isn't this one out of order?"

"I made that sign. I didn't want anyone to lose my place."

The screen displayed the same picture as the one in my lost newspaper clipping. He pointed to the full picture and my mouth fell open.

I focused on the person attached to my arm.

It was Robert. At least it looked like Robert, but he had to have been twenty years younger in this picture while I looked to be the same age.

Now that we could see the entire article, the name on the building behind us was mostly visible.

I looked closely at the words above the door to the building we were apparently just coming out of.

"UPMC Braddo" was all it said. The rest of the name was cut off.

"Where was this taken?" I asked.

"I was just about to look up the name on the building. But before I did that, I read the article."

He picked up a sheet of paper and held it.

"This is the article."

I took it and read it, the voice of a Roaring Twenties radio announcer echoing in my head.

"New York Socialite Robert Black, billionaire heir to Black Flame Industries, the multi-national corporation started by his father after World War II, assists his wife, Michele Black, from the hospital after she collapsed at a dinner party celebrating her safe return from African kidnappers. Mrs. Black had been taken by African militants during a trip with Mr. Black's family to investigate allegations of abuse in the company's diamond mines."

I stopped reading. There were a couple more paragraphs, but they meant nothing to me. They were about some billionaire I had never met.

Was Robert a billionaire? How was that possible? He worked

as a salesman for someone else, and was always at their beck and call. He certainly didn't act like someone in charge of a multi-national company. And he certainly didn't act like someone worth billions of dollars.

I looked at Austin. He understood my silent questions and held up more sheets of printer paper.

"I checked into Robert Black. His personal net worth is just under ten billion dollars."

My mouth fell open.

I had no idea who my husband really was. But I knew who he was going to be. My ex-husband. Just as soon as we figured this all out.

Austin leafed through the pages and relocated one to the top of the stack in his hand as he looked at me.

"What?" I asked, not liking how he was looking at me.

"I don't know if I should tell you this."

I looked at the pages in his hand and then back to him. "What is it?"

"This is an obituary column from a few months after the article was written."

I tried to read the printed paper upside down, but wasn't able to make it out.

"Whose obituary is it?"

He looked at me, his face serious.

"Yours."

Chapter 65

I snatched the page from Austin and scanned it quickly, that funny over-the-top radio announcer voice echoing in my head again.

"Beloved daughter and wife, Michele Black, passed away early this morning from a rare disease she contracted while on vacation in Africa. She was only twenty-five and is survived by her parents, Albert and Rosa Gardner, and her husband, Robert Black."

I read one specific section again aloud.

"She is survived by her parents, Albert and Rosa Gardner."

Parents?

I looked at Austin, tears welling up in my eyes. His face was still all kinds of serious as he shook his head.

"I looked them up. Your father died the very next year and your mother passed away five years ago. From what I have been able to discover, they did not even know you were alive."

I looked at the obituary column and then into those startling blue eyes that made me want to ignore everything and run away with him into the sunset.

Austin held up the pages he had printed out and waved them in my face.

"If your husband has this much money, we are seriously outclassed. It may be time to get in touch with him and see how badly he wants to get you back."

I couldn't believe what I was hearing. "You want to give up?"

He shook his head.

"Not give up. But we need to make contact. We are flying blind, and if there's even millions of dollars being spent to find you…"

He looked at the pages in his hand.

"We can't hide indefinitely from anyone with these kind of resources. It does, however, explain how Nick can have his team of hired thugs pose as an FBI strike force. Somebody is funding him."

He tapped the picture of Robert in my hand.

I looked at it.

Was Robert, the billionaire Robert, the one I knew nothing about, paying to have me killed by a team of ruthless mercenaries?

It didn't fit the picture I had of him. Sure, he had become distant ever since I had almost died in the hospital, but he had never once showed malice or anger toward me. For the life of me, I couldn't even remember him raising his voice at me.

My heart skipped a beat and I looked at the picture of a young Robert leading me out of a building, and then at the obituary column.

Robert had lost this Michele, the one in the picture. Was he using plastic surgery to recreate her? Was that why he had become distant after I had almost died in the hospital? Was it too eerily close to what had happened to his original Michele?

I saw his actions in a new light. In his mind, I had died, and would do so again soon.

I looked at the picture again.

A shiver ran up my spine and I could taste the sudden rush of adrenaline in my bloodstream.

Was he causing the death of every Michele after the original to make his recreation of their life together complete?

I looked at Austin in a panic.

"I can't call him."

Austin stood up quickly and engulfed me in his arms.

"Don't worry. Alt can make it so he can't trace our call, but it's important. We have to find out how serious Robert is in pursuing us."

"Why?" I said into his shoulder.

He held me tightly.

"I need to know if the only way to stop him is to kill him."

Chapter 66

I tensed in his grip.

Had I heard Austin correctly?

He held me tightly. It was a feeling of safety and security. I never wanted him to let me go, but he was also talking about cold-blooded murder.

Up until this point, I hadn't done anything that would result in life imprisonment. I think that, having a look-a-like steal my life, would cause any jury to go easy on me.

Austin pulled away from me, holding me at arm's length, and looked deep into my eyes. He spoke softly so as not to be overheard in the still of the library.

"He's been trying to have you killed."

"We don't know that."

"He hired Nick. Nick was the Delete button in my little group. His task was to get rid of any roadblocks in our way to achieving the primary objective. He was the sniper, the assassin, the cold-blooded killer who took out his target from a distance without warning; or remorse."

Tears welled up along the edges of my eyes.

"I don't want to hear this."

Austin gripped my shoulders in his hands and peered into my eyes, penetrating straight through to my soul.

"You have to know who is coming after you. After us. I know him, intimately, and I know that it will come down to him or me. I'm ready. Are you?"

I wasn't sure I was. Despite being there when Dead Michele had killed herself, all I really saw was someone diving into the river. People did that all the time and lived. I hadn't actually witnessed her die.

I couldn't erase the visuals of when Austin had killed the men trying to take me at the police station. But that was self-defense.

Austin was talking about taking someone's life. He was planning it.

There were two men in my life, and it seemed that both of them were killers with hearts of stone.

Maybe Austin and Dalton were prepared to kill, but I wasn't.

I shook my head and let the tears flow.

If it came down to someone else dying, or me dying, I feared it would be me.

Austin pulled me close again and stroked the back of my head as he spoke in soothing tones.

"Maybe it won't come to that. Dalton and I will put our heads together and come up with a plan. I just want you safe."

"Why?" I said, muffled into his chest.

I listened to the steady rhythm of his heart beating for a few seconds before he answered.

"I don't know," he replied quietly.

I pulled away from him and looked him in the eyes. It was my turn to peer deep into his soul.

"Why are you helping me?"

"I don't know," he replied again.

"That's not good enough," I said a little too loudly and was rewarded with numerous "Shh's" from people around us in the library.

Austin sat us back down in the chairs in front of the computer and looked at me for a long time before responding. He finally let out a long breath and dropped his shoulders in defeat.

"Okay. At first, having the exact same person in both the morgue and in custody was intriguing to me. I really wanted to find out how that was even possible. But when I went in on my day off and found a black bag strike team removing the dead one, I knew they would be going after you next, I reacted out of instinct."

He lowered his head. I let the silence stretch out for as long as he wanted.

He raised his head again. For someone who had lied so easily to get what he wanted ever since I met him, I could see he was having a hard time with the truth.

"After we escaped and found the tracking device behind your ear, I knew that I had made the decision to protect you. I was determined to see it through and make sure you were safe."

I searched his eyes for any hint he was lying to me. I found none.

"What about the kiss?"

His eyes smiled slightly even though the rest of his face remained stolid.

"It was a mistake."

"Was it?"

His shoulders drooped.

"Not really. I wanted it. I guess it was the adrenaline and excitement. It always makes me frisky. You should have seen some of the sprees I would go on after a deep cover mission."

I flinched and he suddenly remembered who he was talking to.

"But that's not what this is. I've developed... feelings for you."

"How do you know?"

"I... I'm not sure. I just know I don't want anything to happen to you."

"How come?"

His eyes shifted and I saw a hint of pain in them despite his face never showing any emotion.

"I just have this primal need to keep you safe. The last person I felt this way about died in my arms. I will not let that happen again. Not to you. Not to me."

"So, you consider me a helpless little girl."

His forehead wrinkled at my comment.

"Of course not. I've seen you keep it together long after some of the army recruits fresh from boot camp would have cracked. I don't think you are weak at all. You are strong, smart, and beautiful."

I felt my face warm as it reddened. I couldn't let him distract me from my mission of finding out how deep our connection went.

"And what happens if we can convince Robert to leave me alone? No more guys chasing us with guns. No more impending threat of death. Then what?"

He rubbed his earlobe, lost in thought before focusing those stark blue eyes on mine.

"I guess I'll ask you out for coffee and we see what happens."

I leaned forward, closing my eyes as I made my move. Our lips met and stayed connected as we pressed into each other. I opened my eyes long enough to see that his were also closed as we kissed.

At the end of the kiss, which was neither too long nor too short, but absolutely perfect, we both sat back and stared at each other for a long moment until someone said, "Get a room!", only to have them quieted with another round of "Shh's" from the other patrons.

That broke the mood and we both smiled as I looked around embarrassed.

Austin cleared his throat and flipped through the pages, holding one up.

"I googled UPMC Braddo, the name of the building in the picture. It turns out it's a hospital named UPMC Braddock here in Pittsburgh. I printed out the address. If I can get a look at the hospital records, we can find out where the Michele in this picture lived. Maybe that will give us some more clues as to what is happening."

"They aren't going to just let you look at hospital records."

He smiled.

"They will after Dalton makes me the proper ID."

"So, you really think we will find what we are looking for at this hospital."

Austin nodded.

"The trail is leading us there."

"And if we don't find anything?"

"We'll worry about that when it happens."

I admired his positivity, but neither of us were prepared for what we would find when we arrived at the address on his printout.

Chapter 67

We stood at the address of 400 Holland Avenue, Braddock, Pennsylvania and looked at the vacant lot that was overgrown with untended weeds.

Dalton squinted at the empty lot, stopping a man who walked past us.

"Excuse me. What happened to the hospital that used to be here?"

"They tore it down."

"Why?"

"The man don't care about us. Claimed there was no money to keep it open. We pay our taxes just like everybody else. Instead, they closed it down and gave us a shuttle service to another hospital. Lot good it does us. We had a perfectly good hospital right in our neighborhood but they decided it would be cheaper to send us half an hour away. Cheaper my ass. They just wanted to line their own pockets with the money they saved. Greedy bastards."

The man spat on the chain link fence surrounding the lot and walked off, muttering to himself.

Dalton whistled as he stared out over the empty space.

"While conducting your research, Austin, do you think maybe you could have found out that the hospital had been, oh I don't know, demolished?"

Austin stared out at the flat ground, the foundation having been dug out and filled in so that there was no trace of the once grandiose red-bricked multistory building that kept watch over the lives of this neighborhood.

I stared at the last chance we had at finding out what happened to Michele twenty years ago before she died.

No, that wasn't entirely accurate.

She wasn't my last chance at the truth.

There was still someone else who had been in that picture.

Someone who knew the truth.

I realized that Austin was right.

We needed to make contact with Robert.

I turned to let him know I was ready to do what was necessary when I came face-to-face with an elderly black woman who was standing way too close for comfort.

I took a startled step back when her face broke out into a wide smile.

"Why, as I live and breathe. It is you!"

I blinked at her as Austin and Dalton moved in behind the old woman, ready to take her down should she try anything; my ever vigilant protectors.

The woman nodded her head vigorously, waggled a crooked finger at me, and laughed. It sounded like the cackle of a life-long chain-smoker.

"I told Enos it was you when I saw you from the window!"

She glanced back at the two men who had taken position behind her.

"New bodyguards, eh?"

She looked back at me and then up and down the sidewalk.

"Where is that dashing husband of yours, what's his name again?"

"Robert?"

Her eyes lit up.

"Yes, Robert. Is he still inside?"

"Inside where?"

She pointed behind me. I turned and looked at the empty lot, and then back to her.

She jabbed at me with an overly thin finger several times, clucking her tongue.

"You're too skinny. I keep tellin' that husband of yours that you won't be ripe for chillins 'til you get some meat on your bones. Doesn't mean you shouldn't keep practicin' though," she added with a knowing wink.

"Gran!" someone hollered from up the street. We all turned to see a young man heading down the hill toward us.

"Fuck!" the old lady said when she saw him and started to shuffle away, leaning heavily on her cane.

Austin stepped to one side to let the young man pass, but I could tell by his movements he was ready for anything should this be a distraction by the armed mercenaries waiting in the shadows.

The man easily caught up to the old woman and tenderly gripped her arm, turning her around.

"Let go of me! I don't know you," she hissed.

"Gran. It's Kevin, your grandson."

"I'm too young to have grandbabies as old as you. Wait until Enos gets to you. Then you'll be sorry young man!"

"He's gone, Gran. Remember?"

She looked at me, pleading with her eyes to save her from the stranger who was abducting her in broad daylight.

The man looked at us as they got closer, clearly embarrassed to have to chase her down in the street.

"I'm sorry she bothered you," he said as they passed.

"Wait a minute," I said.

He stopped and turned back to me.

"She said she remembered me."

The man closed his eyes and shook his head.

"My Gran's suffering from Alzheimer's. She barely recognizes me most days."

"But she knew my husband's name."

"Did you say it first?"

I thought back to our quick conversation and realized she had prompted me for his name.

"Yes."

"She does that all the time. You supply the name and she agrees with you. I'm sorry she made you think she knew you. I'm usually able to get to her before she leaves the yard. I can't have her wandering around the streets like this."

"I'm just trying to get into the hospital," the old woman muttered as she pointed at the empty field.

"They tore it down, Gran."

She blinked again at the fenced-off area and her face drooped.

"So they have."

She looked back at me as Kevin lead her away, their conversation starting to get lost to the wind as they walked up the hill.

"I do remember her," she said.

"Yes, Gran," Kevin replied.

"We shared a room. Even had the same lady doctor. What was her name?"

"I don't know, Gran."

"Her name soundin' like a piece of clothing or somethin'."

"I'm sure it did, Gran."

"A Ms. Waistcoat. No. That's not right."

My ears perked up and I started up the hill after them, Austin and Dalton falling in place behind me.

As we got closer, the old woman stopped and jabbed a finger into the air.

"Dr. Westcott! That was her name!"

Chapter 68

I caught up to the old woman and her grandson.

"Excuse me?"

They both turned around.

The woman's eyes lit up when she saw me.

"Michele! Are you here for your weekly treatment again?"

My mouth fell open in shock and Kevin grimaced, misunderstanding my expression.

"You'll have to excuse Gran. She does this a lot."

The old woman looked back and forth and then leaned toward me.

"I don't trust that doctor. She looks at me funny every time you leave, like I done somethin' to her. She gives me the willies."

Kevin indicated his grandmother with an open hand.

"See. She thinks we are in the hospital."

He leaned in front of the old woman's face and spoke to her loudly.

"They tore the hospital down, Gran."

She looked at him with a confused expression.

"Kevin?"

"Yes, Gran. I'm right here."

She looked around her, clearly disoriented.

"What am I doing outside?"

"You left the house again, Gran. You have to stop doing that."

She frowned at him.

"But I thought I saw someone I knew."

"There's no one out here, Gran. Let's get you back inside."

She looked around again and focused on me.

Her face contorted as she seemed to struggle with some memory.

"I know you."

I smiled at her.

Kevin moved in-between us and stared me down.

"Please don't encourage her. You're only making things worse for me."

He turned and took his grandmother's arm, starting back up the hill and patting her arm while speaking in hushed and soothing tones.

I stood still, Austin and Dalton thankfully stayed silent behind me as we watched them leave.

Had she known the Michele in the picture? She knew about Dr. Westcott. That meant Westcott had been involved from the very beginning.

But the beginning of what?

The woman suddenly yanked her arm out of Kevin's grip and spun around with a renewed energy. Her eyes found mine and she lit up.

"I almost forgot. I still have that letter you asked me to hold for you."

Chapter 69

My heart hammered in my chest as I ran to the old woman. I could hear Austin and Dalton keeping one step behind me.

Kevin's eyes grew wide as we approached quickly. His gaze cycled between me and my two silent shadows.

"What letter?" I asked her.

Kevin came between us again.

"Please stop. Who the hell do you think you are?"

I ignored him and tried to see around him to the old woman.

"What letter?" I repeated.

"The one you asked me to hold until you came back."

Kevin stood up straight and puffed out his chest, adopting an aggressive stance between the old woman and me.

"If you don't leave, I'm going to call the cops."

Austin moved so fast, the air blurred around him as he grabbed Kevin and held him from behind. Dalton moved forward and pressed a hand against Kevin's mouth, leaning in close.

"Let the ladies have their little chat."

Kevin's grandmother didn't notice that two large men had grabbed her grandson on the street. She was too focused on me.

"Come with me. I kept it safe."

Dalton glared at Kevin.

"If I let go of your mouth, are you going to keep it shut?"

Kevin nodded.

Dalton released his mouth while Austin released the rest of him.

Kevin gave Austin a scowl and rolled his shoulders once he was free of his grappling hold. Together, we followed the old woman to the house at the top of the hill overlooking the open field that used to be the hospital.

She led us up the stairs to the front of the house. Kevin looked worried when we followed her into the house as his grandmother ushered him inside and closed the door.

She looked at her grandson.

"Kevin, will you be a dear and get these gentlemen some tea?"

She looked at Dalton.

"Or would you fellas like something stronger?"

Austin shook his head.

"No. Tea will be fine, thank you."

Kevin looked at us warily as he went to the kitchen and left us alone with his grandmother. My guess was, he was headed straight for a phone to call the police. It was best not to waste any time.

"You mentioned a letter?"

The woman looked at me, her face a blank.

"A letter?"

Oh no.

We were losing her.

"Yes. You said I gave you a letter to keep for me."

She started looking around the room, as if this was the first time she had ever been in it. Her finger shot in the air.

"Yes, the letter. I gave it to Enos for safe keeping."

Uh oh. Based on comments from Kevin earlier, I knew that Enos was a dead relative.

She shuffled across the living room and removed the metal jar from the mantle that had been etched with the name "Enos" on the side.

She popped off the top and reached into the jar. She removed a plastic Ziploc bag, spilling some of the contents from the jar on the carpet.

"Those men were so rude. They made a right mess of my home, but they never found it," she said with a big smile as she held the baggie out to me.

I hesitated.

"It's okay," she said. "Enos was my dog."

I didn't care whose ashes it was. I wasn't going to touch them. Dalton reached forward and took the baggie, continuing the conversation in my silence.

"You said men came looking for this. What men?"

She looked at him in bewilderment.

"Men?"

"Yes. You said they messed up your house."

She looked around at the tidy room.

"It doesn't look messy."

She looked back at me and smiled uneasily.

"Oh dear. This is awkward. I should have called you before you showed up. I hired new cleaners. My memory isn't what it used to be."

She was lost in her own world again.

Kevin returned to the room. Missing from his hands were a tray filled with cups, biscuits, and a steaming pot of tea.

He saw the baggie in Dalton's hand.

"You have what you came for. Just leave."

I looked at him.

"Did you call the police?"

"What do you think?" Kevin replied with a sneer.

I looked at Austin and he nodded.

Kevin was right. We had gotten what we came for. It was time to go.

Chapter 70

We were already in the rental car down the street when the first police car screeched to a halt in front of the old woman's house.

Austin fired up the rental and pulled away, turning around the corner and out of sight of Kevin who had stayed outside to watch us walk all the way back to the car.

He had extracted a promise from us to never come back in exchange for him not giving our actual descriptions to the police.

Dalton inspected the Ziploc baggie closely and then handed it over his shoulder to me in the back seat.

"Looks safe to open."

I took the baggie and held it in my hands. Inside it was a letter written by my former self.

I looked at the tattoo on my wrist.

There had to have been at least six others before me. Which one of them wrote this letter?

All I had to do was open the baggie and find out. I realized it was harder to open it and read the letter than I had originally thought.

My hands trembled as I pulled apart the gripping zippers, broke the seal on the baggie for the first time in years, and slid out the folded piece of paper.

Dalton's eyes watched me intently as I unfolded the letter. A smaller piece of paper started to fall out and I caught it.

It was the obituary notice of Michele Black's untimely and tragic death.

I started reading the letter.

"Out loud please." Austin said.

I cleared my throat nervously and started over.

"Dearest Robert,

If you are reading this, then you believe me to be dead. My only hope is that you visit the hospital one more time and run into my roommate, whom I have given this letter to for safekeeping.

Let me be absolutely clear.

I did not die.

I wasn't even sick.

Dr. Westcott has been giving me medication under the pretext of suppressing whatever mysterious disease I contracted in Africa, but I have secretly stopped taking the medications and feel better than I have in a long time.

Do not trust her, Robert. I don't know what she has planned, but one time when she thought I was asleep, I overheard her explain to someone that I was the perfect specimen for their trials.

I didn't know what she meant.

For the first year, they kept bringing me back to Braddock for testing. It was during one of these visits I managed to sneak this letter to Jasmine.

It is my sincerest hope that you find this letter, and come get me. I am in a private compound on one of the islands in one of the Great Lakes on the United States side of the border. I don't know which one, but with access to your father's company resources, it shouldn't take you long to find me.

Hurry my love.

I don't know how much longer they will keep me alive.

Michele."

I looked up and only then noticed Austin had stopped the car on the side of the road and had turned in his seat to listen.

"When was that letter written?"

I checked the page, flipping it over a couple of times.

"There's no date."

Austin and Dalton shared another of their single-look conversations before Austin looked at me.

"It's time we gave Robert a call."

Chapter 71

Not much had been said after Austin convinced me to call Robert. Dalton and I stayed in the car while Austin went inside the Family Dollar store to purchase a no-contract cell phone for my important call.

Dalton had given him grief that they wouldn't need to do this if they hadn't been forced to smash his phone through Austin's carelessness.

Once while we were playing at the beach during one of our first extended dates, Robert had asked me to memorize a special number for extreme emergencies only.

It had seemed strange, but he had held me in his arms lovingly as the surf crashed noisily against our thighs. Back when things between us were perfect.

"What kind of emergency?" I had asked.

"You'll know it when it happens," he had replied cryptically.

So, Robert had known from the very beginning that something like this might take place and had prepared for it.

In hindsight, I noticed he had only discussed the special phone number with me when we were far away from anyone else, and in an environment that was inherently noisy. He must have known someone was always listening to everything we said, and the crashing waves provided enough cover to impart his important message to me without being overheard.

I had never used the number.

There had been no need before now.

In fact, I had nearly forgotten about it until Austin had asked me if there was a way for me to contact Robert directly.

Austin walked out of the discount store with the prepaid cell phone, ripping it out of its plastic clamshell retail packaging as he approached the car.

Austin climbed in the car and held the phone out to me.

"There should be enough charge for this one call. After that, it doesn't matter."

I took the phone and looked at it.

"Why not?" I asked.

He held up the thin plastic shopping bag.

"I bought a couple more in case we need to make additional calls. We toss each one after use."

I nodded and punched in the number from memory and placed the phone to my ear. Would it still work after all these years? Had whoever he was trying to hide the number from found out about it? Even if they hadn't, would he answer?

Austin reached forward and pulled down my hand, touching the screen on the phone with his other hand.

"Let's put this one on speaker."

We all listened as the phone on the other side of this number began to ring.

Chapter 72

My hands trembled with fear and anticipation at the same time.

After everything I had learned, I knew I never wanted to speak with Robert again.

At the same time, Robert could provide the answers we needed. Maybe he even had enough influence with the people chasing us to call them off.

I wanted Robert to pick up the phone and tell me everything would be okay; that I could live out the rest of my life without having to look over my shoulder.

I wanted him to let the call go to voicemail so I could say what I wanted without interruption.

The phone rang some more and then stopped abruptly.

I waited for the voicemail message to trigger when I heard heavy breathing.

"Michele?" Robert half whispered.

I froze. The last time I had heard his voice, he was leaving for his business trip, even though I knew he was headed over to his new Michele.

Austin rolled his hand in the air, prodding me to respond.

"Hey, Robert."

"Oh my god. Where are you?"

I looked at Austin for guidance on what to say.

He shook his head.

"I can't tell you," I said.

"I know that you are confused. But if you come home, I can explain everything to you."

"Which home do you want me to come back to?"

There was a short silence before Robert spoke again.

"Come to the home we have lived in for years together as husband and wife."

The anger I had no idea was deep inside me boiled to the surface and spilled over as I gritted my teeth, trying not to yell into the phone.

"Wouldn't you rather have the sexually adventurous Michele?

Maybe we could invite her ebony roommate in for a threesome?"

Another pause.

"You need to come back, Michele. If you don't, you will die."

I laughed out loud.

"I think you have that backwards. I was at the police station when your friends came for me. I saw the video of how you entered Dalton's house."

"Who's Dalton?"

"Don't change the subject!" I screamed. "You hired the worst of the worst to find me and kill me. I'm lucky to still be alive."

"That's not true."

"Then tell me what is true."

"Come home and I promise I will tell you everything."

"Tell me now."

"I can't."

"Can't? Or won't?"

"Will you come back to me if I tell you?"

"That depends on what you have to say."

There was another long pause before Robert finally spoke.

"I take it you already know about the other Michele?"

"Yes. What are we?"

"What do you mean," he asked.

"You know exactly what I mean."

There was a short pause before he answered.

"You're clones."

It was my turn to remain silent. Austin and Dalton exchanged a look, and then Austin motioned for me to keep the conversation going. I decided it was finally time to get the answer that had passed over Dead Michele's lips right before she ended her life.

"How many more?"

"More what?"

"Don't act stupid, Robert, or I will fucking hang up!"

"You're the only one."

"Goodbye, Robert."

I reached with my thumb to hang up the phone when Robert's pleading voice came in loud through the speaker.

"Wait! Wait! I'm not lying! The other Michele killed herself, leaving only you."

I looked at the seven dots of the tattoo on my wrist. I looked at Austin and he silently mouthed "hang up or talk" to me.

I decided to get as much as I could now that Robert was being honest for once in his life.

"What happened to the ones before me?"

Robert fell silent.

"What happened to them, Robert?" I demanded again.

"They all died," he said quietly.

"You mean you and your bloodhounds killed them."

"No. It's not like that at all."

"Then enlighten me, Robert. What's it like?"

"Omega designed a method to rapidly age cells so that they could produce a fully adult human clone in a matter of months. But there is a flaw with the original source DNA that is compounded exponentially with that process."

"And what is that flaw?"

"You all terminate within five years."

I gave Austin a panicked look.

"Within five years of what?" I finally gathered the courage to say.

"Of being created."

"When was I created?"

"Every clone is initially aged to twenty years old before being woken up."

"The accident that took my memory?"

"There was no accident. You have no memories from before you were twenty years old, because you didn't exist until you were twenty years old."

I stared at the phone. It was surreal to be discussing clones grown immediately as adults; skipping childhood completely. It was even more incredible to think that I was one of these clones. The technology just didn't exist.

"But... how?"

"I don't know how, but when you fell sick, a research scientist that worked for one of my father's labs said there was a way to cure you, so I agreed to create a new company and fund them."

"Them? Who them?"

"Omega."

"Does Dr. Westcott work for Omega?"

"She's the research scientist. She is the inspiration behind the technologies developed there. For all intents and purposes, she is Omega."

I thought about the implications of being a clone.

"Is what you're doing even legal?"

"No."

"Then why?"

"I couldn't bear to lose you, Michele."

I thought about my five year expiration date. I suddenly realized my twenty-fifth birthday was just around the corner and my heart hammered in my chest. And then I thought about the six Michele's before me.

"How is that working for you?" I asked with a hint of sarcasm.

I could hear the pain in his voice when he finally responded.

"I did this so I wouldn't have to let you die. It was a chance to finish the life we had started."

I thought about the pictures of our life together that he had replicated with Dead Michele.

"Instead, I sat by your bedside and held your hand while you died on me over and over."

Tears welled up in my eyes. This was not how I had expected this conversation to go. I thought about Dr. Westcott and the medication she had insisted I keep taking. And how I improved drastically when I had decided to stop.

"I stopped taking the medication."

"What? No! Without it, you will die in a matter of days."

"I stopped taking them last year."

"What?! How is that possible?"

"I felt stronger and healthier once I stopped taking anything Dr. Westcott prescribed. I'm not going to die, Robert."

"But I almost lost you last year in the hospital. It's why I authorized the creation of Michele eight."

"How many more times were you planning to do this?" I asked.

"Before she took her life, I had already decided to tell Westcott that Michele eight was the last. I couldn't take losing you anymore.

Besides, what twenty year old would even want to date a fifty year old? It has taken so long to bring you back that we are no longer right for each other."

I remembered the reason we had decided to call Robert in the first place.

"I found a letter from the original Michele."

"What?"

"She left it with her roommate at the hospital where they were treating her."

"What are you talking about?"

"Do you remember Braddock hospital?"

"That's where I first met Dr. Westcott. She was a specialist brought in to treat Michele's illness. The one she got in Africa."

"She had a roommate at the hospital. A black woman."

"Right. I remember her. What's she have to do with any of this?"

"Michele, your original Michele, left a letter with her for you."

"How do you know this?"

"I have it."

"Have what? The letter? How?"

"I followed the trail your eighth Michele started before she died. It led me to the hospital, the roommate; and the letter."

"So what if she wrote a letter? It doesn't change anything."

"I think it does."

"Why?"

"Because, she's not dead."

"Who's not dead?

"Michele."

"I don't understand?"

"Her letter came with a copy of the obituary notice. She knows you think she's dead, but she wrote the letter to prove she's not."

The silence on the other side of the phone dragged on for nearly a minute before he spoke again.

"She's alive?"

"She was when the letter was written. It's not dated, so I don't know how long ago that was."

"Where is she? Does it say?"

"She is…"

We were cut off by a loud voice interrupting our conversation from Robert's end.

"What is this?!" someone demanded.

"It's my phone," Robert replied.

"I provided you with your phone, and this isn't it. I will only ask you one more time; what is this?"

"I told you, it's my phone. My private phone."

"You don't have a private phone."

"Clearly I do."

"It's on? Who are you talking to?"

The voice suddenly became louder.

"Who is this?"

Austin took the phone from my hand and held it close to his mouth.

"Hello, Nick."

Chapter 73

The voice on the other side of the line adopted a calm demeanor immediately.

"Hello, Control. You know you can't hide from me forever. Turn over the girl now and I will see about making your death quick and painless. That is, of course, after we have settled your personal obligations to me."

"I don't think so, Nick. You won't be able to delete us so quickly."

"Us?"

Nick paused only briefly before he continued. "Hello, Alt."

Dalton leaned toward the phone.

"Hey, Nick. How's it hanging?"

"Low and to the left. You know you are siding with the losing team."

"No. I'm not." Dalton replied.

"What makes you think that?" Nick asked.

"Because I'm not on your team."

Nick laughed and then quieted down, the sound from the phone muffled as someone spoke in the background.

Nick returned to the phone.

"I can understand your allegiance, but it is misplaced. How much is Austin paying you?"

"I'm not doing this for money."

"Then you're a fool. I will give you one chance to switch sides before you suffer the same fate as your cohorts. Trust me, you do not want to be suffering for Control's past mistakes."

"Go to hell," Dalton spat at the phone.

"After you," Nick said; and then the phone clicked a couple of times before going dead. The silence was broken by a distant thumping sound that grew quickly.

Austin and Dalton exchanged another of their glances.

Dalton grabbed the phone and threw it out his window as Austin started the car.

Dalton struggled with his seat belt, yet took the time to look at me.

"Put your seatbelt on, missy, and pray to every god you believe in. It's about to get hairy."

Chapter 74

I grabbed at my seat belt when Austin whipped the car around a corner, sending me sliding across the faux leather back seat.

"Easy," I said.

"Sorry," Austin replied, and then did it again.

I finally wrestled my seatbelt on, but Austin kept up the sudden direction changes.

"What's going on?" I asked.

Dalton grabbed the overhead handle above his window to keep from ending up in Austin's lap as we performed another Baja off-road racing maneuver, the car lifting up on two wheels before slamming back down.

"Nick tracked the signal."

"But you bought a brand new phone," I reminded him. "To keep that from happening."

Dalton clenched his teeth as his injured shoulder banged into the side of the car while Austin skidded around another corner.

"We just found out you were born in a vat five years ago. At this point, I'm not putting anything in the impossible category."

"But why is Austin driving like a maniac? No one's behind us."

Dalton pointed skyward and then gripped the handle again as Austin took us around another corner on two wheels.

I twisted and looked out the back window, spotting the helicopter keeping pace with us above the city buildings.

I spun back around.

"How did he find us so quickly?"

"Probably not the only helicopter in the sky, just the closest one." Dalton replied as Austin was focused on slipping between two large trucks stopped at a red light, slicing off both side view mirrors in the process.

Horns blared and tires screeched as we raced through the intersection, narrowly missing several cars turning left.

Dalton looked at where the mirror used to be on his side of the car and looked back at me with a bemused expression.

"Good thing we got that extra insurance."

Austin angled the car into a controlled skid around the next corner.

I glanced out the back window and craned my neck to check the sky.

The helicopter was gone.

I turned around to tell them we had lost it when I saw the helicopter skids lowering down in the road ahead of us.

"Look out!" I screamed and pointed.

"I see it," Austin replied and I was pressed into my seat as he stomped on the accelerator.

My eyes grew larger.

He was planning to ram the helicopter.

I ducked as we impacted with the helicopter, the roof of the car denting in as it scraped along the underside of the skids.

The car bounced and jolted as we shot out from under the helicopter. I twisted in my seat and looked behind, seeing the helicopter pilot struggling to remain in the air after being knocked around by Austin's bold maneuver.

He lost his battle and the helicopter rotated sideways and the blades impacted with the ground, slamming the helicopter into the side of a building. It exploded in a massive fireball, the shockwave blowing out every window on both sides of the street.

Austin careened around the next corner and the destruction disappeared from view.

"I'd like to see them try to keep that under wraps," Austin said as he twisted the steering wheel and turned onto the road leading toward the Fort Pitt Bridge.

Once we were on the bridge, I looked out the side window and my heart stopped beating.

I pointed at the helicopter that was tracking alongside us as we sped around the light traffic on the lower span of the bridge.

"There's another one!"

Dalton pointed out the other side of the car as Austin whipped around a slow moving van.

"We got a second one. I hope you have a better plan than trapping us in the middle of a mountain."

Austin stayed focused on the road.

"Don't worry. We won't be trapped."

Dalton looked back and forth between the two helicopters. One peeled away from the bridge and rose out of sight.

"Good. 'Cause it looks like they are planning to leave one at this entrance while sending the other one to the exit."

"They won't be picking us up on the other side."

Austin turned on the hazard lights and weaved back and forth, causing the cars behind us to slow down in response to the maniac swerving back and forth ahead of them.

Still traveling faster than we should have, Austin slammed on the brakes as soon as we entered the bridge tunnel.

Our car skidded to a halt, the cars behind all crowding into the other lane to go around us without stopping.

He ignored the blaring horns as he shifted into reverse and backed the car into an alcove just inside the entrance to the tunnel.

He jerked to a stop and shut off the engine, pointing at another car parked in the alcove next to us.

"Our new chariot awaits."

Dalton had to kick his door open; it had become stuck from the car being sandwiched between two trucks.

"I didn't know you had another car waiting for us."

"Neither did I," Austin replied as he hopped out of the car.

Dalton frowned at him and pointed at the mid-nineties model Ford Mustang.

"Then what's that?"

Austin headed for the Mustang.

"I wasn't sure if it would be here today. I've noticed it parked here most days. I think it belongs to a transit employee. I tried to ticket it once while on patrol and was reprimanded the next morning."

Austin gripped the door handle and squeezed his eyes shut as he pulled up on the lever. The door opened and he looked at us and smiled.

He crawled on the floor under the steering column and yanked at some wires. Within moments, the engine roared to life.

He sat up and shut the door as Dalton and I packed ourselves into the back seat. I regarded Dalton, who looked extremely uncomfortable, smashing his large frame into the cramped back seat next to me.

"Why are you in the back seat? Wouldn't you be more comfortable up front?"

"Don't remind me," he said as he adjusted his injured arm and winced. "In case anyone is watching everyone who drives out the exit, it will look like Austin is alone and they will ignore him subconsciously since it's a different car anyway."

Austin honked his horn a couple of times, slowing down the traffic, and pulled out into the lane. Other cars responded with horn blasts of their own, but they let him in and we were soon on our way through the tunnel.

As we burst out the other end, and into the bright sunlight, I checked the skies for the helicopter. I spotted it hovering low along the side of the highway.

Dalton spotted it too and pushed down on my head as he ducked low.

We passed by where the helicopter floated in the air. After a minute, Austin checked every mirror and looked out the windows.

"We're clear."

Dalton released me and I sat up, only to be thrown forward against the front seat as Austin suddenly skidded to a stop.

Ahead of us, the traffic was being funneled into a single lane. A helicopter rested by the side of the road and a dozen heavily armed men in military combat uniforms were inspecting every vehicle as it passed through the hastily constructed checkpoint.

Chapter 75

I looked at the road ahead. There was nowhere for us to go. Horns honking behind us drew the attention of the blockade personnel. Half of them focused their attention on our car, one of them waving us forward.

Dalton grabbed me and pressed my head against his chest, face down.

"Pretend you're asleep."

I closed my eyes to tiny slits, leaving me just enough of a gap to see what was going on, and pretended to use him as a human pillow.

Austin rolled forward and, as he approached the closest soldier, rolled his window down and stuck his head out.

"What's going on?"

"Just a routine checkpoint."

"Routine? I've never seen you guys do this before."

"Random check for drunk drivers. It's for your safety, sir."

"Who drinks at this hour?"

The soldier ignored Austin's comment and looked in the car, squinting at Dalton and I both pretending to be asleep in the back seat.

The soldier indicated us with his head.

"Who are they?"

Austin glanced back at us and then back at the man who looked in at us.

"My brother and his girlfriend."

Dalton kept his eyes closed as he spoke aloud.

"Wife, Jake."

Austin slapped his forehead and looked back at us.

"It's gonna take me a while to get used to that."

He looked back at the soldier.

"My mistake. That's my brother and my brand new sister-in-law."

"Where are you headed?"

"New Castle."

The soldier squinted at us.

"Kinda far from home."

Austin shrugged.

"We wanted to party and there's not much going on at home. We just spent the night tearing up Pittsburgh, if you know what I mean."

The soldier didn't smile but looked back at Dalton and I.

Austin angled his head to get the soldier's attention.

"It's been a long night, I haven't been drinking, designated driver and all. I'd like to make it home before I get too tired. Is this checkpoint going to take long?"

The soldier looked at the line of cars ahead of us.

"Shouldn't be more than ten minutes. We'll have you back on the road in no time. Just be patient."

Austin nodded.

"Thank you."

The soldier walked away and headed for the next car behind us.

Austin rolled up his window. I started to sit up, but Dalton kept my head in place.

"Let's just stay like this until we are through."

We slowly crawled forward as each car in front of us was thoroughly inspected. Every now and then, they would force the occupants out of the car and search it fully.

Finally, it was our turn.

Austin rolled to a stop in front of the temporary gate.

Soldiers surrounded the car, the one closest to Austin yelling at us to get out.

Dalton looked around at the soldiers surrounding the car. Their guns weren't pointed at us; yet.

"Do you recognize any of them?"

Austin shook his head.

"No. I don't think we've worked with any of these guys."

"Me neither," Dalton replied. "Maybe they won't recognize us."

"That's a big maybe," Austin said as he opened the door after being prompted again to exit the vehicle.

Austin climbed out and leaned awkwardly to one side, keeping his head tilted at a slight angle and one shoulder lower than the other. I marveled at how that made him look shorter than he really was.

He also looked nonthreatening.

The soldier looked in at us.

"You too," he demanded.

Dalton slipped off the sling and grunted as he pushed his seat forward and climbed out the other side. I followed him out the passenger side and then clung to him, his injured arm wrapping around me protectively.

I let my hair fall across my face, not pushing it out of the way in an attempt to keep from being immediately recognized in case they had been provided pictures of us.

Once we were out of the car, the soldiers approached and inspected every nook and cranny, even lifting the hatchback to make sure nobody was hiding in the tiny area the dealership marketers advertised as storage space.

Neither Austin nor Dalton spoke while the soldiers inspected the car.

The lead soldier had never taken his eyes off of Dalton and I while the rest of his men searched the car.

He studied my face as the wind blew my hair around. A big gust lifted most of the hair away from my face and the soldier's eyes grew wide.

Austin had seen his reaction and made his move in that same instant, grabbing the gun by the barrel and shoving it down while simultaneously jabbing the heel of his hand into the soldier's face, the only part of his whole body not protected by armor.

The soldier's head snapped upward sharply and he fell backward. Despite the sudden and violent action, it had happened swiftly and silently.

Austin grabbed him in both arms, while yelling out and looking around at the other soldiers.

"Hey! This guy passed out!"

Soldiers immediately ignored the car and came to the rescue of their comrade.

"What happened?" one of them demanded.

Austin set the unconscious soldier down on the ground as blood poured from his nose.

"I don't know. He made this strange sound and then his eyes rolled back into his head and his nose started bleeding."

Two other soldiers pushed Austin back as they moved in to check on the fallen soldier.

Austin stepped back, looking around him in a panic. Only, I knew he wasn't panicked. I had never seen him panic, not even when bullets were flying all around him, so it had to be an act.

As every soldier rushed to see what was going on, Austin stopped one of them.

"Do you need me to stay and give a statement or anything?"

The soldier looked at him, and then cast a cursory glance at Dalton and I before focusing back on Austin.

"That won't be necessary. You may go."

Dalton shut the hatchback and followed me into the backseat.

Austin climbed in and shut the door.

"That was ballsy," Dalton said quietly. "Someone might have seen you."

Austin glanced back at us in the rear view mirror.

"I didn't have a choice. He recognized Michele and was about to alert the rest of the squad."

Dalton settled in the seat, massaging his shoulder that obviously hadn't enjoyed being removed from the support of the sling.

"Still ballsy. Makes me glad you're on our side."

Austin smiled back at him as he started the car and we left the blockade behind us.

The adrenaline seeping from my pores made me drowsy, and I laid my head on Dalton for real and fell asleep.

Chapter 76

The car turned wildly and I woke with a start, almost falling off the seat. I sat up and blinked my eyes, disoriented for only a brief moment before I remembered who I was with.

I looked out the windows of the Mustang.

"Where are we?" I asked.

Dalton was tracing a line with his finger on a paper map. I don't know where he had gotten it from, but it looked brand new.

"Just outside of Cleveland. You know, this would be easier with GPS."

Austin checked the rear view mirror as we turned a corner sharply. I grabbed the handle built into the side to keep from sliding off the slippery seats and onto the floorboards.

"Why don't you use one of the phones? They should at least have Google maps on them."

Dalton shook his head.

"The last time we turned on one of the phones, a helicopter appeared out of nowhere. I don't know how, but they are tracking us through the burners whenever we turn them on."

"The what?"

Dalton looked up at me.

"Disposable phones. You burn 'em up and throw 'em away."

"Oh," I said, as if that had made everything clearer.

Dalton gave me a serious look.

"If we hadn't turned them all off, we would have been captured by now."

"That is why we are going old school with a map I picked up at a gas station," Austin added.

"Yeah," Dalton continued. "About that. This only shows the roads. It's not helping with the islands."

"Islands?" I inquired.

Austin checked the rear view mirror, then slowed down, refocusing his attention on me.

"In the letter, the real Michele said she was on an island somewhere along the U.S./Canadian border."

Real Michele?

It suddenly hit me, based on Austin's comment, that I was somehow not a person. I hadn't even considered what being a clone made me.

Was I real?

Or was I somebody's property?

Is that why I never had a job or got a driver's license? I wasn't a real person and Robert had known it all along.

"Michele?" Austin said with a hint of concern.

I looked at him.

"Sorry. You just said real Michele, and it got me to thinking."

Austin's forehead wrinkled and he turned to look at me directly.

"I didn't mean that…"

I shook my head.

"It's okay. I know you didn't mean anything by it."

He returned his focus to the road.

"We need to see if the Michele who wrote that letter is still alive."

"How do we do that?" I interjected.

Austin smiled warmly at me through the rearview mirror.

"You like boats?"

Chapter 77

When Austin had asked me if I liked boats, I pictured a large ship, a yacht really, where I could go inside to stay warm when the wind picked up on the open water.

What we walked out to after Austin flashed his American Express Black at the Boat and Jet Ski rental office clerk was nothing more than a step up from a floating dock with an engine stuck on the back. It looked more like a dentist's waiting room on long metal pontoons.

Austin looked at it.

"This is perfect."

The clerk, still gawking at the metallic American Express card in his hand, nodded.

"She's real steady when the water chops up. So, you say you only need it for the rest of the day?"

Austin herded me onto the boat. Dalton was pulling up the mooring ropes and tossing them into the boat.

"That's right. Is there any penalty for keeping it overnight?"

The clerk looked at the wad of cash in his other hand and looked up at Austin with a smile.

"You have her until closing time tomorrow."

Austin smiled and plucked his credit card from the man's hand.

"Excellent. We'll take good care of her."

The man eyed Dalton's sling. "The weather reports indicated some high winds later today, so be careful. If you stay out too long, the lake can turn on you in the blink of an eye."

Austin thanked him for the warning, and then pushed us away from the dock, jumping on board skillfully like he had done it a thousand times.

"Remember," the rental agent yelled out as we backed away. "Boat return is no later than seven tomorrow night."

Austin waved at him and then pushed on the throttle, sending us up the river toward the open waters of Lake Erie.

"What's our first stop, Alt?"

Dalton was thumbing through a travel and tourist guide he

had picked up at the boat rental place.

"Kelleys Island. About an hour away due west at top speed."

"Top speed it is," Austin replied as he pushed up on the throttle. I was pressed into my seat by the sudden acceleration.

Dalton held the book up, reading out loud as we bounced along the small waves.

"According to this, Kelleys Island is a major vacation destination with thousands of visitors each summer. Several ferries provide regular transport to and from the island."

"No good," Austin said. "Too much activity to try and keep someone prisoner on. What else?"

Dalton flipped through some more pages.

"Let's see. There is a small group of islands on the U.S. side called Bass Islands."

"Tell me about them," Austin said.

Dalton tried to hold the book steady as he studied the pages while the boat bounced roughly as it skimmed along the tops of the waves.

"The first is South Bass Island located just under five kilometers from the south shore of the lake. It's another touristy spot with about six hundred residents year-round. It also hosts the annual Inter-Lake Yachting Association regatta."

Austin shook his head.

"Still too busy. It would be hard to hide someone there without attracting attention. Next."

"Okay. There is Middle Bass Island with about a hundred or so permanent residents and up to a couple thousand people living there during the summer."

"Still too busy. Next."

Dalton gave me a funny look before sticking his nose back in the guide book.

"The last is North Bass Island. At last census, there were a couple dozen permanent residents in only twelve private residences. Most of the island is left undeveloped as a state park."

"With government employees working there. No good. Find me something else."

Dalton held the book up, as if that helped his plea.

"We're running out of islands, Austin. We don't actually know if she's on any of them. We don't even know if we're in the right lake."

Austin turned to face Dalton, keeping his hand on the wheel. He looked so majestic standing at the wheel of a speeding boat. Like George Washington crossing the Delaware.

"Just read me the rest. There has to be one that fits the bill. Find me something out of the way."

Dalton returned to the book. As he read the data out loud on each island, Austin kept shaking his head urging him silently to keep reading.

"West Sister Island. Jointly owned by the United States Coast Guard and the U.S. Fish and Wildlife Service. Sugar Island, six hundred eighty-three people, and daily ferry service to Michigan."

Dalton leaned forward.

"Here we go. Ballast Island is a small, twelve-acre private island northeast of South Bass Island."

Dalton looked up from the book.

"It's private and secluded. No tourists, and no government employees. Says here there are only seven houses on the whole island. This could be the place."

Austin nodded.

"I agree. It has potential. We'll check it out first. Keep reading."

Dalton rolled his eyes and made a face.

"I saw that," Austin said without turning around.

Dalton flipped to the next page. He read quietly to himself for a moment and suddenly jumped up.

"Found it!" he yelled excitedly.

Austin looked back.

"Better than Ballast?"

Dalton was smiling from ear to ear as he held the book out in front of him.

"Much better."

"Read it." Austin said and returned his attention to the front of the boat.

Dalton cleared his throat and spoke in a snooty British accent.

"Rattlesnake Island is an eighty-five-acre playground accessible only to the sixty-five members of the exclusive Rattlesnake Island Club. There are currently only about fifteen private lots on the island and the summer staff, mostly brought in from Eastern Europe, are trained to recognize each member and their families on sight and by the yacht they came in on."

Dalton sat back down as he continued reading quietly to himself.

"Holy shit! Jackpot!" Dalton exclaimed.

Austin looked back.

"What?"

"Non-members are turned away by armed security guards in one of the island's two boats before the trespassers even have time to dock."

Austin faced forward and smiled mischievously.

"Jackpot indeed."

Chapter 78

Austin checked the GPS built into the dash and steered the boat around Middle Bass Island.

As we neared the island, I looked at Dalton.

"Are we going there now?"

Dalton shook his head.

"Nope. Just verifying what the guidebook said."

I frowned at him and he elaborated.

"It said they had two boats with armed security that would turn away anyone who got too close."

I sat back and watched as the island came into view. From this distance, it didn't look very big. Was this where they were keeping the original Michele?

I chuckled to myself.

I had been upset when Austin had referred to her as the real Michele, like I was some faded photocopy or something.

Now I was doing it.

There was no doubt that there was an original Michele. And I wasn't her.

But was I really just a copy of a human?

Or was I still a human in my own right?

The boat turned sharply and bounced on rough waters. It jarred me out of my mental self-doubting spiral.

"Here they come," Austin said.

I focused on the island and spotted a speedboat headed straight for us. It looked like a long cigarette sports boat, the kind shown on the front of all those boating magazines.

Only this one had a mounted machine gun on the front. And the man standing with his hands on the gun handles made the hair stand up on the back of my neck.

A loudspeaker crackled to life from the speedboat.

"You are entering private waters. Turn back now or you will be detained."

Austin waved at the speedboat and cranked the wheel, turning our pontoon boat around in place before speeding off the way we had come.

Dalton stood up and conferred quietly with Austin. I couldn't hear what they said over the roar of the motor, but I could tell by the look on their faces that things were getting worse, not better.

Chapter 79

The sun was just setting when Austin pulled us in to the small marina on South Bass Island. Austin jumped off the boat and tied us down.

He then waited as Dalton and I stepped off the rolling boat and onto the swaying dock.

Austin handed Dalton his credit card.

"Find us a couple of rooms in a nearby hotel."

Dalton took the card with a big smile.

"How much longer do you think this will work?"

Austin regarded the metallic card and shrugged.

"The rental car company will probably take action to find their missing car by tomorrow or the next day. It should still get us a room for tonight before I'm cut off."

Dalton gave him a funny look.

"Does the CIA really just cut off their credit cards like that?"

Austin smiled.

"I guess we'll find out soon enough."

I looked from one man to the next.

"CIA?!" I said. "You work for the CIA?"

Austin's head snapped in my direction.

"Not in any discoverable sense."

"What's that mean?"

Dalton took my shoulder and turned me away, leading us down the dock.

"It means he operates off the books. They were keeping him in reserve should they ever need him."

I looked at Dalton like a deer in the headlights.

"If Austin works for the CIA, why have we been running around like chickens with our heads cut off? Why didn't he call in the cavalry to save us?"

Dalton was shaking his head.

"Off the books, means, there is no record of him working for the CIA."

"I don't understand."

"It is very much a one-sided relationship. They can call on

him when they need him, but he doesn't have the same option."

I looked back, and Austin had already untied the boat and was pushing off into the water again.

"Where's he going?"

"He's going to see how good the security really is on Rattlesnake Island."

"Why aren't we going with him?"

"He'll be back before sun-up."

"And if he's not?"

Dalton looked at me without a hint of a smile anywhere on his face.

"We turn ourselves in."

"Turn ourselves in? To who?"

"The FBI."

I looked out over the bay and watched the lights on Austin's pontoon boat blinking smaller and fainter as he sailed away.

"Then let's hope he comes back."

"Don't worry. He'll be back. But it never hurts to have a Plan B."

It didn't take long before I could barely see him in the distance of the fading light.

I wasn't prepared to lose him.

I closed my eyes and prayed that he would remain safe and come back to me. I made a silent promise to myself that when he came back, I would tell him how I felt about him.

I would tell him how I felt about us.

Chapter 80

Dalton rented us two adjoining rooms in a hotel a couple of blocks from the marina. I would have preferred if there was a hotel overlooking the marina, so I could keep vigilant watch for Austin's return.

I thought about the mariner's wives who built their coastal houses with a platform on the roof, called a widow's walk.

I looked around my room, noticing how empty and vacant everything seemed without him.

Dalton had said Austin was going to test how good the security really was on that island. What was he planning to do? How big of a risk was he planning to take to find out?

We had no idea if Michele was on that island. A chill went up my spine as I realized we had no idea if she was even still alive after all this time.

Was Austin risking his life for nothing?

I couldn't let myself believe that. He was smarter than that. He had to be smarter than that. After all I had seen him capable of, I believed that he could gain access to Fort Knox and walk out with a gold bar in each hand before anyone even knew he was thinking about breaking in.

If there was a way past the armed guards onto that island, Austin would be the one to find it.

I could hear Dalton moving furniture around noisily in the other room. He must be setting up the fold-away bed he had ordered after the front desk said they only had one option if we wanted two rooms side-by-side. Each room had but a single queen-sized bed, so Austin would be sleeping on a portable mattress tonight.

Unless I could convince Austin to spend the night with me.

Then the doubts began again. I stood up, stamping out the feelings of being less than human, and walked to the doors that separated my room from Dalton's.

Dalton must have been rearranging the entire room with the amount of noise he was making.

I knocked on the door and it fell instantly silent in the next room.

"Dalton? Can I come in?"

There was no response.

I knocked again.

"Dalton?"

I jumped when something heavy pounded against the front door to my room.

My head snapped back to the dividing doors when I heard a pained howl followed by Dalton's single-word command shouted urgently from the other side of the locked doors.

"Run!"

Chapter 81

My heart thudded against my ribcage as heavily as whoever was on the other side of the doors to my room. Both of them were starting to give under the constant impacts.

I ran to the window in my room. It looked out over the parking lot and was sealed permanently shut. Dalton had rented second floor rooms, so I wasn't going out that window, even if it could open.

The metal door frame bent inward as someone continued to throw all their weight on the door. My choice was to stay where I was, or break through my window and jump for it.

I picked up the small wooden chair at the desk and threw it at the window.

The window shattered noisily, the chair disappearing through the newly formed jagged hole. I ran to the window.

The chair had shattered in several pieces when it hit the parking lot blacktop.

If the chair had broken, there was no way I would survive.

The main door to my room buckled inward noisily.

I spun around, looking around me for something I could use as a weapon. I snatched up the telephone off the table. It must have weighed a grand total of two ounces, it felt so light in my hand.

The man who had busted down my door pointed a handgun with an extended barrel at me.

"Drop it," he demanded.

I tossed the phone to the floor and raised my hands in the air.

He smiled at me, then a blur tackled him from the side, causing his gun to go off. It spit quietly and a bullet whizzed past my ear.

I dropped to the floor with a scream and heard scuffling in the hallway outside my door.

The scuffling intensified as blows were exchanged followed by two sharp puffs of air that were immediately followed by silence.

I crouched next to the bed, my eyes glued to the broken down door, waiting for my killer to come through it and finish me off.

Austin appeared in the door, the other man's gun in his hand. He saw me and ran in.

I reached up to give him the biggest hug of his life.

He wrapped one arm around me in response and lifted me to my feet. He twisted out of my grip and raised the gun, pointing it straight ahead as he faced the door

"Let's go," he said over his shoulder as he moved swiftly forward.

I followed him out of the room and out into the hallway. Austin handed me the pistol.

"If he makes a sound, shoot him."

I gripped the gun and pointed it at the man lying prone on the floor. My finger gripped the pistol and my hands shook so much, I didn't think I would hit him even if I did shoot despite being only a few feet away from him.

Austin kicked the body swiftly a couple of times. When there was no response, he grabbed the man's feet and dragged him into Dalton's room.

Inside, Dalton was lying on the floor next to two more bodies. Blood pooled around him and soaked into the carpet.

Austin took back the pistol and coldly shot all three men in the head, before kneeling down to help Dalton.

He lifted Dalton's head up.

"Can you hear me, Alt?"

Dalton coughed up blood and his eyes slowly opened. They focused on Austin's face.

"Hey, Control. Is Michele safe?"

Austin smiled down at his dying friend.

"Yeah. We saved her."

"There's more coming. Get her out of here."

"Not without you."

Dalton coughed up more blood.

"Forget about me. I'm done for, Con…" he coughed some more, his whole body spasming.

Austin half-stood, preparing to muscle Dalton onto his shoulders.

"Negative, Alt. I've never left a man behind, and I'm not

about to start now."

He tried lifting Dalton, but Dalton cried out and pushed him away.

"It's too late for me, Control. Backup is on the way and you have to get her out of here."

Dalton's eyes closed and Austin shook him awake.

"Stay with me, Alt."

Dalton's face registered the pain racking his body, but through it all, he managed a smile. His eyes sought mine out.

"Michele," Dalton croaked.

I knelt next to him and placed a hand on his blood-soaked chest.

"I'm here, Dalton."

He reached up, grabbed my arm, and pulled me closer.

"Take good care of Austin."

I winced.

"I don't think I can. I've never fired a gun before."

Dalton coughed some more as he shook his head, trying his best to ignore the pain.

"That's not what I mean."

I felt my face flush as it reddened.

"He needs you as much as you need him. I can die happy knowing that you two found each other."

The tears fell from my face onto his.

"You're not going to die. We can get you out of here."

"No," Dalton said, his voice coming in-between rasping breaths. "I told you, I would die for Austin with a smile on my face. What do you think this is?"

He pointed a finger at his smile, and then his smile faded and his head lolled back.

He went slack in Austin's arms, Austin shaking him roughly.

"Alt? Alt?! Dalton!"

Outside the room, the second floor hallway railing rang with the sounds of heavy feet rushing up the stairs.

Austin dropped Dalton, his lifeless body hitting the floor with a squishing sound, and snatched up the pistol, pointing it at the door at the same time two men appeared.

Austin fired twice, both men's heads exploding as they collapsed on top of each other, wedging into the open doorway.

Austin grabbed my hand, pulling me after him as we stepped over the bodies and into the exterior hallway of the hotel.

There were shouts from below, and the ceiling rained debris down on us as bullets tore into it.

I ducked, sobbing, following Austin's lead, and ran in a crouch as we headed for the top of the stairs. Austin rounded the corner gun first and fired twice. I heard a pained grunt followed by something heavy falling down the stairs.

Austin pulled me after him as we ran down the first set of stairs to the middle landing. We stopped at the railing and he pointed to the small cultured grassy spot next to the parking lot below.

"Jump!" he instructed.

Without giving it a second thought, I launched myself over the railing and fell the six feet to the landscaping below.

I hit the ground and fell to the side, but there were no shooting pains. I hadn't twisted an ankle or broke my leg.

Austin fired twice more over my head into the parking lot before jumping after me.

I was on my feet when he landed next to me. He grabbed my hand and pulled me to a large black SUV idling in the parking lot. We ran past a man rolling around moaning on the ground next to the open driver's side door.

Austin tossed his gun on the ground and scooped up the rifle the other man had dropped. I thought to myself that we could really have used all those weapons we had left back in the woods. But there was no way we would have survived the blockade, or been able to carry them on the open boat.

Austin shoved me in ahead of him. I shuffled sideways to the next seat as he climbed in and stomped on the accelerator, letting our sudden change in velocity shut the door for him.

As he pulled out of the parking lot, another SUV slammed into ours, shattering every window on the one side and spinning us out of control. Austin cranked the steering wheel all the way around and kept his foot on the accelerator, continuing the spin as we laid down rubber in a big donut on the street.

He let go of the steering wheel and it spun back to its natural center as he kept his foot on the accelerator.

The SUV straightened out on its own and he grabbed the wheel again, narrowly missing a parked car.

I looked out the side window and saw another SUV pulling up next to us as we raced down the street. It shot forward and pulled in front of us.

The back rear window lifted up and my heart leaped into my throat.

All I could see were the barrels of two rifles pointing at us.

"Stop!" I screamed.

Austin replied by pressing down on the accelerator. He reached over and pulled my head down as the windshield fragmented in spider web patterns repeatedly, but did not shatter.

"Bulletproof glass," Austin yelled as we slammed into the back of the lead SUV.

One of the men fell out and onto our hood. Austin slammed on the brakes, tossing the man airborne to land on the street in front of us.

Then Austin punched the accelerator again and bile rose in my throat as I felt the tires bump over something big in the road.

The other man sat back up and ejected his spent magazine, grabbing a fresh one. I had no idea if the windshield would survive a second assault. Austin handed me the rifle he had taken from the previous driver.

"Shoot them!" he yelled.

"What?! How!" I yelled back.

He pointed in front of us.

"Lean out your window and shoot that way."

I hit the window down button and waited the interminable five seconds it took to go all the way down.

"I don't know what I'm doing," I complained.

"That's okay. They don't know that."

I leaned out the window and the man ahead of us had just finished reloading his rifle.

We locked eyes and I pulled the trigger, the gun bucking

wildly in my hands as I screamed and held down the trigger.

Sparks exploded all around the back of the vehicle and one of the rear tires exploded with a flash right before my gun ran dry.

The lead SUV careened to one side, and then slammed into a parked car, flipping over it like kids playing leap frog. It landed on its roof behind us and slid across the road, sparks flying in its wake.

I fell back into my seat.

Austin was smiling at me.

"Nice shootin', Tex," he said.

I looked forward and pressed both hands against the dashboard instinctively.

"Look out!" I screamed.

Austin slammed his foot on the brake pedal.

We skidded to a halt in the middle of the road. Ahead of us, two SUV's were parked at an angle to each other, yet still facing us and blocking our escape.

Austin and I both rocked violently back into our seats. Stopping so quickly had stalled the engine and we sat there, the hot engine ticking away against the cool night.

I looked out the windows as heavily armed soldiers in full combat gear surrounded us.

The headlights were blinding and I could barely make out the shadow that stepped out from between the two vehicles and walked toward us.

Austin and I looked at each other.

I held up the rifle and the soldiers on my side of the car started yelling for me to drop it.

"It's empty," I said, as I dropped it out the window, the panic rising in my voice.

Austin reached over to rest a hand on my thigh. My leg was hot under his tender touch. I looked back at him and he smiled warmly at me.

"The important thing is that we never gave up. We were defeated. There's a difference."

I didn't understand what he was talking about until I saw who walked up to Austin's window and peered in at us.

Without taking his eyes off of me, Austin let out an exasperated breath.

"Hello, Nick."

Nick leaned on the side of the window.

"Hello, Austin. So nice to finally see you again."

Austin turned to face him.

"I wish I could say the same."

"That really hurts me, Austin. And after everything I did for you, everything she did for you, I was beginning to think that you were trying to avoid me."

"Nick, I..."

Nick cut him off. "Where did you think you were going to run?" he chided. "This is a tiny island. You put on a big show for nothing. It makes me wonder who you were trying to impress."

Nick leaned to one side and looked past Austin at me. "So this is the prize?"

He looked back at Austin. "I hope she was worth dying for."

"Dalton thought so," Austin replied, his voice level and monotone.

Nick's face grew somber.

"Yes. I saw what happened on my monitor. A shame really. I would have liked to have dealt with him personally. It would have been so much more satisfying."

"I guess you are stuck with killing just me," Austin said.

"Yes, well," Nick continued, moving back from the window. "That will have to wait. Please step out of the car. Both of you."

Austin looked back at me and patted my knee. "Giving up is forever. Defeat is only temporary."

He forced open his door. It groaned in protest as the bent hinges tried diligently to accomplish their one purpose in life. He stepped out to join Nick and was immediately rushed by several soldiers that forced him to lie face down on the pavement.

I opened my door and stepped out, only to be rushed and forced to the ground as well.

Just like eating and sleeping, when presented with an opportunity, you had to take it. I had almost missed my chance to let Austin know how I felt. We might never be this close again. It was now or never.

I twisted my head and looked under the SUV at the face of Austin, who was facing me, both of us pressed against the asphalt on either side of the car.

"I love you," Austin mouthed silently before he was yanked to his feet and out of view.

Chapter 82

I really couldn't believe that it had been less than two days since Austin and I had met under, shall we say, less than ideal circumstances.

In that short time, I had fallen in love with him. I had no idea · if he felt the same or if I was just another mission for him.

Just someone to protect from the bad guys.

But now, as we lie facing each other on either side of the SUV, our faces pressed against the pitted gravelly road, he mouthed, "I love you."

I didn't have the chance to return his sentiment before he was yanked roughly to his feet and out of sight.

The dust all around kicked up as a helicopter landed on the road near us. I watched Austin's feet as he was led toward the helicopter.

I was roughly pulled up and my eyes sought out Austin. I called out his name, but the fast spinning rotor blades drowned me out and he never looked my way as the metal flying beast lifted off the ground and tilted away sharply.

I was spun around and led to one of the waiting SUVs. I struggled, but it was a futile gesture as I was shoved inside and the door slammed shut, the window smacking me in the head.

I ignored the shooting stars behind my eyes and screamed obscenities at the tinted window, banging my balled fists on the tempered glass; my own spittle sprinkling the inside with foamy droplets.

"Hello, Michele," a familiar voice said behind me.

My head snapped around and, to my amazement, I found myself looking at the last person I had expected to see. What the hell was he doing here? "Robert?"

He smiled weakly. "Michele, I…"

"You fucking asshole!" I screamed as I vaulted across the small space and attacked him with a blind fury.

He grabbed my wrists in his hands and held them tightly. It was impossible to kick him in the confined area, and the door behind me opened quickly and someone moved in behind me, grabbing me in a headlock and started to squeeze the life out of me. I went slack and stopped my tirade.

Once I had calmed down, Robert looked over my shoulder at whoever had me in the headlock.

"It's okay. You can go. She'll be fine now."

Robert looked at me. "Right, Michele?"

I nodded slightly, the arm around my neck making even that movement difficult.

Robert smiled to the man behind me. "See? She'll be fine."

Slowly the pressure on my neck released and the soldier slowly backed out of the SUV.

Robert nodded to him. "You can close the door. I'll be fine."

"I'll be watching," a gruff voice said, I assumed more for my benefit than Robert's.

The door slammed shut and Robert and I were alone again.

I glared at him. All the feelings of betrayal and lies flooded my whole body. I didn't want to be anywhere near him, but I also didn't want to be choked unconscious by the ape standing outside either.

Robert placed his hands together as if he were about to pray. His eyes looked into mine and he seemed to be wrestling with his own flurry of emotions before he finally spoke.

"I had to give up a lot to get these few minutes with you."

"I'm all broken up about it."

"What you said on the phone. Is it true?"

"I said a lot of things."

"You said you had a letter from…"

He swallowed loudly. The look on his face I had seen only once in the four years I had known him, and that was when he visited me in the hospital after I collapsed on vacation.

"A letter from Michele. Yes."

He held out his hand, palm up. "Can I see it?"

I looked at his hand, and then back to his face. What could it hurt? But then again, I needed something in return. "Let me see Austin first."

Robert's shoulders dropped. "I can order the man outside to search you and take it."

"I don't have it on me," I replied, jutting my chin out in defiance.

He regarded me coolly. "I know you better than you know yourself, Michele. You can't lie to me."

"Like you've been doing to me all these years."

"Please give me the letter."

We scowled at each other for a few moments before I leaned to one side and retrieved the letter from my back pocket.

I unfolded it and held it up.

He reached for it, but right before he took it I snatched it back. I needed to get some form of leverage if I had any chance of getting what I wanted. "I still want to see Austin."

He gave me his sincerest look. "I will see what I can do."

"Don't lie to me," I spat.

"Apparently, he has some history with the mercenary Omega hired. You have my word that I will try, but I can't guarantee anything. Despite what you may think, I'm not the one in charge. The letter?"

I handed it to him and he unfolded it the rest of the way, reading it quickly.

I could see the tears welling up in his eyes. It wasn't a long letter, but he must have read it several times because it was a while before he looked up at me again.

I felt the pain radiating from every pore on his body. "Who was she?" I asked.

He smiled, and his eyes flickered as the tears flowed freely. "She's you. Or, more accurately, you were supposed to be her." He held the letter up and stared at it. "Dr. Westcott told me she had died. But if I could redirect some of my father's resources her way, maybe she wouldn't have to stay dead."

"So you did."

He looked back up at me and laughed through the tears. "So I did. And you came back to me."

His bottom lip quivered as memories flooded his face. "And then you left me again. Westcott said there was a problem with the accelerated growth process, but with more money, they could solve it."

I held up my wrist, showing him my tattoo. He saw it and looked back out the window. I let the silence fill the interior of the SUV until he was ready to talk again.

"Every one of you died by age twenty-five. So I kept funding Omega to bring you back. Each time, each one stayed healthier longer than the last. I honestly thought that you would be the last, you were so strong."

He looked back at me. "But when you collapsed on vacation, I knew it was happening all over again. Westcott assured me that she was close to solving the problem that made all of you terminate."

I clenched my fist involuntarily. "You mean die."

He nodded and frowned at me. I could tell he was struggling to have this conversation with me.

"Yes. Die."

I crossed my arms and stared him down. "I'm not a science project. And I'm not your plaything."

His eyes watered. "I never once thought that. I love you, Michele. I've loved every one of you as much as I did my Michele. It's why I worked so hard to keep you alive."

"Speaking of that, I stopped taking the medication last year in the hospital."

He shot me a concerned look.

I indicated myself by stabbing a pointed finger into my chest.

"And I'm fine. You said all the ones before me died within five years."

He nodded; clearly not pleased with the direction our conversation was headed.

"I've never felt better, Robert. I flushed everything down the toilet; every day."

"That shouldn't have been possible. It was the only thing keeping you alive."

I reached out and touched his hand. "Do I look like I'm dying to you?"

He looked at my hand like it was an alien claw, and then back up at me. "You said on the phone you were doing better. I thought maybe you were experiencing some form of euphoria, but you don't look sick."

"I'm not. I've been giving it a lot of thought, and I believe Dr. Westcott was poisoning me."

He was shaking his head. "No. She said that you would be dead in a matter of days if you stopped taking the medication. She was keeping you alive."

"If I had collapsed at home instead of in Florida, I would have been under the care of Westcott, and she would have finished what she started."

"I can't believe that. Why would she do that?"

"Maybe bringing your Michele back was not her main priority."

His eyes looked into mine. I was getting the same thought he was at the same time.

His forehead furrowed. "But if she wasn't working to keep you alive, what was she spending all my money on?"

Chapter 83

Robert studied the letter again. "Dr. Westcott was the one who told me Michele had died and, because of the risk posed by the African virus, her body had been cremated." He looked at me, a new fire in his eyes. "But she didn't die. This letter proves that."

He refocused his attention on the folded page in his hands. "But is she still alive after all this time?"

I pointed at the paper. "What island is she talking about?"

He was staring out through the front window, focused on the distance with a tear running down his cheek. "I have an idea."

"Is it Rattlesnake Island?"

His head snapped in my direction and he looked at me in shock. "How do you know about Rattlesnake Island?"

"It's the one that we decided was the most likely place, based on her brief description."

He looked away again, his eyes not focused on anything. "If she's still there, we need to get her out of that place."

I finally had my leverage. "I know one person who could get her off that island."

He looked at me, the glimmer of hope reflected in his eyes. "Who?"

"Help us, and we can help you."

"Are you talking about the cop?"

I laughed softly. "He's so much more than a cop. And if anyone can get Michele, your Michele, off of that island, it's him."

He shook his head, the paper crinkling as he gripped it tighter. "I can't guarantee anything. My hands are tied, and besides, he was taken away, most likely to be tortured for what he learned about you, before they kill him."

My mind replayed the last moments with Austin in my head like a movie. He told me he loved me.

And I knew how I felt for Austin, after only two days. My feelings ran deeper than I had ever felt for Robert. But I could tell by the pain mirrored in Robert's eyes, he had never stopped loving Michele.

The clones that had been created were nothing but shadows of the real Michele. They had her looks, but none of her mannerisms and none of her memories with him. He had tried to recreate those memories, but those were only static images. They would never be good enough to replace the real thing.

If it was at all possible, he needed to be reunited with his Michele. He had proven his love for her time and time again. I couldn't fault him for what he was trying to do, no matter how misguided it had been.

In a moment of clarity, I knew that he had been lied to as much, if not more, as I had been. And those lies had all come from a single source.

Omega.

And from what I gathered in my first honest conversations with Robert, the driving force behind Omega was Dr. Westcott.

While I couldn't believe the words that came out of my mouth next, I knew the motivation behind them. "If you can get Austin and me out of this, we will find your Michele, and bring her back to you."

My only hope was that I had convinced Robert enough to get one last chance to see Austin before I died.

If I couldn't have my happily ever after, then maybe I could help Robert get his.

Chapter 84

In the back of the SUV, Robert had promised that he would get to the bottom of everything, and would demand the release of Austin and myself.

After he had left, another helicopter had descended to the street and I was ushered to it. We took off as soon as I was in my seat and we tilted wildly and shot out over the water.

I watched out the window and saw Rattlesnake Island come into view as the helicopter dropped toward it.

It was still pitch black when we landed and I was ushered into my cell without any explanation.

I had thought that the week following my double doing a back-flip off a bridge had dragged on endlessly. But the next several hours felt like an eternity in the cramped space.

I sat on the small bed with my knees drawn up under my chin. Robert had lots of money, but he had admitted that he wasn't in charge.

I always thought that the one with the money was always in charge.

There was a loud awful moaning creak as the door swung open and Dr. Westcott stepped into the cell.

In the stark light of the single bulb hanging from the middle of my ceiling, she looked particularly evil as she glowered down at me. Her teeth shone a stark white as her mouth broke out into a wicked grin. "You've been a bad girl."

Trapped, alone, and knowing that there was nothing left she could take away from me, I felt bolder than I probably should have.

"You tried to kill me."

She scratched at her chin. "True."

I was taken by surprise by her honest answer as she continued with more brutal honesty.

"I've also been lying to you ever since we met."

My mouth hung open in shock. She looked around at the tiny cell with its solitary harsh light swinging from the ceiling and then back at me

"If you promise to be nice, I can move you to better accommodations."

I nodded and she unleashed her wicked smile again.

"Good girl."

Chapter 85

I followed her through several corridors and up several flights of stairs, the two armed guards behind me keeping their distance should I try anything.

It seemed they confused me with their other prisoner.

Westcott stopped in front of an ornately carved door and opened it with a flourish.

I looked into the room. It was brightly lit and the bed was a four-poster with a thick mattress that came up to the middle of my chest.

Westcott smiled again. "I would like you to be comfortable."

I shot her a sharp look. "For my last hours on earth?"

She shrugged, but I took note that she didn't deny it. "Robert informed me about your request."

My heart skipped a beat. Had Robert been stupid enough to tell Westcott that he knew about the first Michele? Had he told her that I wanted him to release Austin and I in exchange for finding out what happened with his first love?

I decided to fish for information rather than make any rash assumptions.

"What request?"

Westcott looked at me over the top of her glasses.

"I have decided to let your new boyfriend join us for breakfast. I promise to answer all your questions without hesitation. You will be given your chance to say goodbye to him then."

"What are you going to do to me?"

"It doesn't matter, does it? Just be satisfied that you will be given unfettered access to the truth. Isn't that what you wanted? Isn't that what you asked from Robert?"

"What about Austin?"

"He became involved in something that is way above his pay grade. He will be terminated along with you after breakfast."

"Terminated! Why?!"

"In any war, there is collateral damage."

"War? What war?"

"It was a war started long before you and I were born. But this is a war that I intend to win. You are my secret weapon, and I plan to use you before I die."

"Weapon?"

She waved away my question with a hand.

"I will answer all your inquiries during breakfast. For now, you need your rest. You really do have a big day ahead of you tomorrow."

"Why won't you tell me who you are fighting against?"

She smiled again, her eyes gleaming.

"My dear, I am fighting death itself."

Chapter 86

I lied in the massive feather bed, sinking into the softness and letting it embrace me. I couldn't even see the floor over the mountains that had formed around the little valley created by the weight of my body.

I probably should have turned off the lights before climbing into bed. Now, I would have to figure out how to leave the warm comfort of the feather bedspread and plunge my last night into the same darkness that would soon surround me forever.

After delivering her chilling proclamation that Austin and I were both going to be dead after breakfast, I was unable to sleep anyway, so I just rested there with every light still burning brightly in my room.

I thought about Dalton, who had already given his life for mine. He had said that Austin had needed me as much as I needed him.

After Austin had told me that he loved me, I realized how true Dalton's final words had been. I hadn't even realized that my feelings for Austin ran so deep until they took him away.

I had become so used to having him next to me through everything, that to have him missing now was more than I could bear.

The door to my room suddenly opened and Nick stepped in, looking extremely angry.

Had he come to punish me for keeping them from killing Austin? Austin was to join us for breakfast so, it probably put a big kibosh on what Nick had planned.

He scowled at me and scanned the room. Satisfied we were alone, he stepped aside and two men carried in Austin between them and tossed him on the floor.

I was out of bed immediately and rushed to Austin's side as Nick stepped backward out of the room and slammed the door, locking it again.

I helped Austin off the floor and onto the bed. His face was bruised and blood seeped from fresh cuts on the side of his face.

"Oh my god. What have they done to you?"

He smiled weakly at me. His mouth was slightly swollen on one side, making the smile look more like a pained grimace.

"Are you kidding?" Austin quipped. "Seeing as how I trained Nick myself, I'd say he's slipping in his interrogation techniques."

He sat up in the bed and felt the side of his swelling eye with light fingers.

"Man. I was sure he was going to break an eye socket or something."

He looked at me. "Are you okay?"

I frowned. "Don't worry about me. Let's get you cleaned up."

"I'd rather just rest."

He tried to lean back into the bed, but I knew once he had sunk fully into it, it would take an act of God to get him back out, and I was all out of favors from him.

"We should get you cleaned up so that none of those cuts become infected."

I guided him to the bathroom attached to the room. Once inside, I dropped the lid on the toilet and helped him sit down.

I started up the bath and pulled the stopper. Once I verified that water was filling the tub, and the temperature was just below scalding, I returned my attention to Austin and began unbuttoning his shirt.

He tried again to smile at me, but the swelling had increased and he looked more like something from a low-budget horror movie.

"If I knew this was all it took to get you to rip off my clothes, I would have found a bunch of guys to beat me up days ago."

I smiled slightly, unable to ignore his attempt at lightening the mood.

"Let's get you cleaned up and worry about what comes of this later."

I pulled his shirt off and couldn't keep myself from wincing at the bruises forming along his ribs.

"That bad huh? I knew I shouldn't have joined that donut of the day club."

I pulled his socks off and removed his pants.

I couldn't help but notice his boxer briefs struggling to do their job at containment.

I looked at him. "Really?"

He tried to smile again. "Hey, I'm not the one taking off my clothes. I think the little guy is just a bit confused, that's all."

I went into full nurse mode and stood him up, pulling down his boxer briefs, ignoring his obvious interest in me.

I helped him to the bathtub. He yelped as he put a foot in and yanked it back out.

I touched the bath and pulled my hand back out slowly, shaking off the excess water. "It's not that hot. Don't be such a baby," I said and pushed him down into the tub.

He slowly lowered himself into the hot water, jerking back up a little bit as it got too much to handle before continuing to submerse himself.

Once he was fully settled into the bath, he looked at the clear water around him. "What? No bubbles?"

I grabbed a washcloth from the rack on the wall and dunked it in the water and began scrubbing his back roughly.

"Easy," he said as I continued to scrub away everything we had collected in our final bid to escape, the water around him became clouded with blood, sweat, and dirt.

I moved to his neck and finally to his face, cleaning him off expertly, leaving only the man who had come to my rescue when I had needed him the most. As I wiped the dried blood from the cuts on his face, he looked up at me with a twinkle in his eye.

We were already close, so the kiss happened naturally. In the middle of our extended kiss, my hand slipped on the edge of the tub and I almost fell in.

We both immediately laughed. Austin's eyes grew intense as they looked deeply into mine.

"Care to join me?"

My heart thudded deep in my chest.

Of course I did.

Instead, I tossed him the washcloth as I stood up. "You can take care of the rest, right?"

His smile never wavered as he scrubbed himself under the water.

Chapter 87

I must have sat in the chair by the vanity mirror in the room for what felt like an hour before Austin drained the tub and switched to taking a shower.

I looked at myself in the mirror.

"What?" I said to my reflection.

My reflection indicated the bathroom door with her eyes and then looked at me with a mischievous smile.

"I can't," I said to her.

"Why not," she said back.

"Because. It's not the right time."

My reflection laughed. "You have very little time left. If not now? When?"

She had a point.

Now I knew I had finally cracked. My own reflection was trying to talk me into joining a man in the shower.

I looked back at my reflection, ready to give a list of why I shouldn't, but my reflection was nothing more than that.

My own reflection.

She was still me. And she knew what I wanted, even if I was unable to admit it.

I stood up and undressed slowly, giving myself time to talk myself out of it. I looked at my reflection again. Why was I looking at her? She was the one who had convinced me that it was ridiculous to wait.

We had so little time left.

Why not make the most of it?

I stepped into the bathroom, the steam from the shower fogging up the mirror and filling the room with a low haze.

I made my way to the shower and pulled aside the curtain that surrounded the tub.

Austin spun around in surprise, and then froze, a smile slowly spreading across his face.

His body didn't look so bad after all the grime and dried blood had been removed. The swelling in his face even seemed to have gone down, returning the chiseled features back to his jawline.

His eyes looked up and down my body, and I suddenly felt self-conscious, placing an arm demurely over my breasts.

He held out his hand and helped me step into the tub.

Taking both my arms, he draped them over his shoulders and pulled me close, pressing his body against mine as he kissed me deeply.

The tension that had built up in my body released all at once and I pressed my mouth against his, drinking in his passion with wild abandon.

His hands moved over my back and slowly worked their way down to firmly grab my butt. I pressed myself against him, feeling him hardening between us.

He kissed my neck, and worked his way down to kiss my breast, his tongue playing with my nipples, stoking the fire burning hotly inside me.

He kissed his way back up to my mouth and I reached down to grab him.

He let out a soft murmur, and I knew the time was right.

I raised a leg to perch it on the side of the tub and guided him into me. His hot breath came in ragged gasps that matched his steady rhythm.

I wrapped my arms around him, both for the closeness and the support as his thrusts grew stronger. My world compressed down to the space that occupied the two of us, the rest of the world fading away to irrelevance.

My entire concentration was on keeping him hard and complimenting his thrusts with moans and cries of ecstasy.

Several times, we almost slipped and fell in the slippery tub, but he had incredible balance, and a control over his body that was derived from years of combat training.

Not to say that sex in a bathtub was akin to hand-to-hand combat, but those skills definitely helped him keep us safe as we tried everything we could to topple us out of the tub.

His strong arms gripped me tightly and his breathing increased to a fever pitch as he forced himself deeper into me.

Suddenly, he gyrated against me as he pulsed. I clung to him, not wanting this moment to end, and my whole body shuddered in blissful release as we climaxed together.

He let out a sharp breath and I felt every muscle in his body relax.

We stayed under the spray of the water until it started to cool, having exhausted the limits of the hot water heater.

Austin reached over and shut off the water before it chilled us, even though I knew that wasn't possible after how hot things had become between us.

We kissed again, but it was apparent that Austin would need a moment before we could attempt to couple again.

I stepped out of the bathtub ahead of him and snatched the only towel off the rack and wrapped it around my slick wet body.

I spun around and smiled at Austin. "Don't move," I said.

He froze. "What?"

"I just want to burn this moment in my mind and keep it with me for eternity."

Austin rolled his eyes and stepped out after me, grabbing a corner of the towel and wiping off his body. "That's kind of corny, don't you think?"

I frowned at him. "Don't spoil the moment."

He smiled and hugged me. "Sorry. I just meant that we have our whole lives ahead of us. We don't need to worry about this moment. There will be plenty more."

My heart sunk. He didn't know. "Austin?"

He pulled away and looked at me. His forehead furrowed and his smile faded when he noticed the look on my face.

"What's the matter?" he asked.

"They are going to kill us after breakfast."

He nodded slowly. "That's what I heard."

"Don't you understand what that means? This is our last chance at happiness. Our last chance to be together. That's why I wanted to burn this moment into my soul. If I only remember one thing from my life, I want it to be this."

He encompassed me in another warm hug and clung to me. "So do I. But we're not dead yet. We might get lucky and have many more moments like this."

"How can you say that? We are trapped on their island with nowhere to go. No way to escape."

"If they kill us, we have clearly been defeated. But since I am not dead yet, I refuse to give up."

It was my turn to pull away and look up into his face. "You have a plan?"

He looked down at me and I felt the muscles tighten up on his back and shoulders.

"Not really so much as a plan as a hope that I still have the chance to swing the odds into our favor."

I searched his eyes for any indication he was appeasing me and putting on a brave front to keep me at ease. Instead, I saw the confidence I was used to seeing in those piercing blue eyes.

"You do have a plan."

"It's sketchy at best, but if we take full advantage of it we might get lucky."

"What do you want me to do to help?"

"I can't give you any details since I will be improvising every step of the way, but tomorrow morning during breakfast, when I say run, you run."

We spent the rest of the night in each other's arms in the bed. I was pleased he had the energy to join with me once more before we fell asleep.

I had loved Robert, and we made love several times a week. But it was more intense with Austin and I knew that he was the man I was supposed to spend the rest of my life with.

I only hoped the rest of my life wasn't just long enough to eat a hot buttered croissant.

Chapter 88

Austin and I were fully dressed before they came to get us in the morning. Despite our closeness throughout the night, now that the sun had risen, Austin kept his distance and had stayed silent ever since we woke up.

I let him keep to his thoughts since he had to be working through a multitude of scenarios and possibilities as to how we could escape.

It was enough to be in the same room with him, despite not a word being said beyond "Good morning" when we first woke up.

The door clicked and opened. Dr. Westcott stepped into the room and smiled knowingly at the both of us after seeing the bed sheets strewn about on the bed.

"Did you two enjoy your night together? I trust you managed to get some rest at least."

Austin puffed up his chest. "I can rest when I'm dead."

Westcott laughed. "Yes. I suppose you will."

Westcott turned her attention to me. "But first, I promised you some answers."

My heart thudded loudly and my pulse raced.

I knew she had promised to answer all of my questions, but she had also told me this knowledge would precede my death.

Now that it was time, I didn't know if I wanted any answers because, getting those also meant I had to die.

I looked at her, tears welling up.

She gave me a concerned look and pursed her lips.

"Don't cry, dear. I can guarantee you that what you are about to find out is worth dying for."

Chapter 89

Several armed guards in black combat armor rushed into the bedroom and pointed their rifles at Austin and me.

Austin instinctively placed his arm around me.

Westcott smiled mockingly. "Aww. He wants to protect you. I'm afraid those times are over."

She nodded to the guards on her left and they broke from the rest of the group and grabbed me, pulling me out of Austin's protective grip.

Austin moved forward and grabbed my hands as the guard wrapped his powerful arms around my waist and pulled me across the room.

A second guard appeared and slammed the butt of his rifle into Austin's face, sending him to his knees.

"Austin!" I screamed as they pulled me out of the room. I tried to struggle, but the man who held me was twice my size and I flopped helplessly in his massive arms.

I sunk my teeth into the meat of his arm and he dropped me in the hallway with a roar that echoed throughout the entire house.

I hit the ground running, but as I neared the closest corner, an arm shot out from around it and grabbed my throat.

I gagged as the hand pressed on the sides of my neck and lifted me off the ground. I clung to the hand to keep from being strangled by my own body weight when the arm came fully into the hallway.

The arm was attached to Nick who smiled up at me.

"Where do you think you're going?"

"Put her down!" Dr. Westcott commanded from right behind me.

Nick gave me an odd look before releasing me and letting me fall to the ground. My knees buckled and I collapsed to all fours as I coughed and gasped.

Behind me, Austin was led out of the bedroom, a muscled guard on either side of him holding their respective arm behind his back.

I gripped my throat and tried to speak, but it came out more like the croak of a frog.

"Let him go."

Westcott crouched beside me and looked into my eyes with her cruel and clinical gaze.

"That was stupid. Even if you managed to get out of the house, where were you planning to go?"

I tried to muster up even a tenth of the courage I had seen from Austin as I returned her steely gaze with one of my own.

"You may defeat me, but I will never give up."

Austin snorted a laugh only to be rewarded with a punch to his gut. Westcott spun around and yelled at her guards.

"That's enough. Bring them both to the patio."

Two guards lifted me off the ground and carried me between them. Behind me, Austin was still laughing as his two guards forced him ahead of them.

I knew why Austin was laughing. I was here, and not the other Michele who had jumped from the bridge, because unlike her, I had not given up. She had taken the way out when she only had a glimpse at who, or what, we were.

She had not been defeated. In fact, her life had really only just begun.

I was here because I took the baton from Dead Michele and ran with it. While I may be defeated, and killed in a matter hours, I had never given up.

While I had thought that Austin had taught me that, I realized that I had acted that way from the very beginning.

It was why I was not satisfied to keep taking the medication and let the world just happen to me.

I took action.

Is this what made me unique among all the Micheles that had come before me?

Was I the only one not willing to accept the world at face value?

Had any of the Micheles before me ever discovered who they were? Had any of them been invited to breakfast with the promise to receive all the answers?

We broke out into the bright light of the morning and I blinked against the harsh sunlight.

Today was not happening like the day before it. Ever since I had uncovered the cameras in my house, no day had been like the one before it.

I looked across the lawn and saw a large patio set with a dozen tables fully occupied by men and women, all dressed in tuxedos and evening gowns as if this were a dinner party in some grand ballroom instead of breakfast in the backyard. Three chefs tended to the outdoor kitchen while servers brought plates to everyone sitting at every table but one.

Every face was watching me intently as we made our way across the freshly cut grass. What did they know about me? What had they been told?

They certainly didn't seem surprised to witness me being carried by two armed guards across the lawn to join them. They had to already know what was going on, or else they wouldn't be here.

My guards set me down roughly in a chair at the head table. Westcott took her seat next to me, with Austin being directed to the other chair on my right.

I searched the faces at the other tables for one in particular. Westcott noticed me checking out the rest of the guests at this strange morning party.

"You're looking for Robert, I presume?"

I nodded.

"He's not here."

"Why not?" I said, looking at her in surprise.

"He has no place on this island. He is not one of us."

The look I gave her must have been amusing to her. She smiled and said the very same question running through my mind. "We are the one percent of the one percent. I'm afraid your billionaire husband is just too poor to belong to our exclusive club."

At that moment, a server placed a plate of poached eggs over sliced potatoes drizzled with a yellow cream sauce in front of me. Fresh cut baby carrots framed everything like a work of art.

My stomach somersaulted. It dawned on me that I was staring at my last meal.

I was suddenly not very hungry.

Chapter 90

I looked at everyone seated around the patio eating, laughing amongst each other, and occasionally casting furtive glances in my direction.

I glanced over at Austin, who had dug into his last meal like there was no tomorrow.

He looked at me and his expression became pleading.

"Remember what Dalton and I said about eating," he said through a mouthful of potatoes as he indicated my plate with his fork.

I picked up my fork and stabbed at a single slice of boiled potato.

I really wasn't hungry, but I poked it in my mouth and chewed anyway.

Loud cheers and jeers took place at a table to one side, drawing my attention to it. Several of the younger men were exchanging money. The men who received the money from their friends mouthed "thank you" to me while those giving it away scowled at me, like I was the reason they had lost their money.

Westcott was shaking her head. "We should really have better standards for membership."

She indicated the men still laughing between themselves. "How much do you want to wager that they bet each other on whether you would eat or not?"

I looked back at the young men. They all watched me intently until I noticed that my second forkful of food was still hovering just above the plate.

I set down the fork and pushed my plate away from me.

Half the table jumped up and cheered while the other half tossed rolls of bills at the obvious winners.

I suddenly reached forward and grabbed the fork, stuffing the eggs into my mouth.

The table in the corner erupted into chaos as those who had already paid tried to get their money back. I looked over at Austin who smiled and gave me a little wink.

He understood my motivation. Just because we were about to

die, didn't mean we couldn't have a little fun at the expense of those who held our lives in their hands.

Westcott shook her head. "I really must be more careful in the future who I let into Omega."

I looked at her. "I thought you were Omega."

She smiled. It was not evil, or condescending, like all the other times she had smiled at me.

"No. Everyone here is part of Omega. We are the last."

"The last of what?"

Her smile widened. "I thought that was obvious. We are the last to die."

"I don't understand."

Westcott let out an exasperated breath. "Rather than try to explain it to you, let me show you."

She raised a hand and the entire crowd fell silent. A man walked up with a small wooden box and placed it on the table in front of Dr. Westcott, opening the lid as he took a step back.

I craned my neck to look inside.

Embraced in red velvet sat a polished hand gun with the omega symbol engraved in the ivory handle. I knew from watching all those action movies on Netflix that I was looking at a Desert Eagle, point-five-oh. But I hadn't realized how big that gun was in real life.

She nodded in my direction and rough hands grabbed me up, knocking the chair over backward as they lifted me in the air.

"What the hell!" Austin shouted as he stood up and was immediately surrounded by several barrels of assault rifles.

The men drug me to the center of the open space that all the tables had been arranged around. They held me tightly as Westcott wandered to the edge of the space, closest to the tables.

I saw the gleam of bright metal reflected in her hand.

She had the gun.

She turned away from me and faced the crowd of eager onlookers. Despite their absolute silence, there was electricity in the air as if they knew they were about to witness something special.

Was it my death they were all here to see?

Technically, I had taken a bite of my breakfast, so Westcott would be keeping her word if she decided to kill me now.

But I didn't want to die.

I wasn't ready.

I twisted my head and looked at Austin. He was being restrained by three heavily muscled soldiers, and yet was still able to inch toward me before a fourth hit the back of his legs with the butt of a rifle, sending him to the ground.

He fell on his knees and craned his neck up to look at me. We were out of options, and out of time.

Nothing was going to save us now.

Chapter 91

Dr. Westcott faced the silent crowd as she began speaking. "And I saw an angel coming down out of heaven and holding in his hand a great chain. He seized the dragon, that ancient serpent, who is the devil, or Satan, and bound him for a thousand years."

She walked back and forth, using the empty space as her stage as she continued. "The devil. Satan. The Grim Reaper. These are all names people have given to that specter who hovers over us from the very moment of our birth. We are destined to die the moment our first cells burst miraculously into life."

She looked at me briefly before looking back at the silent crowd. "Everyone starts life the same. Naked, alone, and with nothing. But we are different. We didn't obtain our wealth by following the rules or doing what everyone tells us what we should do. We saw opportunities where others saw limitations. We bent and broke every law that got in our way. But there was one law we struggled with. One law that we were bound to with no choice. I invited you all here today to show you that we now have a choice."

She spun around and focused her full attention on me.

Her voice fell quiet, causing everyone to lean forward in their chairs to hear her.

"We have been given a gift. Not by some benevolent superior being. Like always, we have become our own god and taken the reins of destiny to make our own gift."

She pointed the gun directly at me. As opposed to when I had last pointed a gun at someone, it didn't waver or shake. At this range, and with how steady she held the gun, there was no doubt she could hit me. "Behold, I give you the future of Omega."

I struggled against the two guards who held me in place. The end of the gun barrel flashed a split second before the crack of exploding gunpowder echoed throughout the open patio.

Chapter 92

Time decelerated to a snail's crawl.

I watched in slow motion as the gun flashed and the bullet tore through the air toward me, waves of turbulence rippling outward from the speeding cone of copper-plated lead. There was nothing I could do to stop it. Nor was there time to move out of the way.

I felt the burning sensation enter my chest at nearly the same moment the gun had flashed. The bullet had taken less than a second to travel the dozens of feet from the gun to me.

I cried out as the most intense pain I had ever felt expanded throughout my whole body.

I looked down to see the bloom of red on the front of my shirt where the bullet had entered my chest.

I collapsed in the guard's arms.

As I slowly crumpled to the floor, my eyes sought out Austin's. He was straining against the hold of his three guards and screaming my name, even though I could hear nothing over the pulsing beat of my slowing heart as my life's blood drained away.

My vision tunneled and I blinked slower, each time my eyes staying closed a little longer.

Dr. Westcott was smiling as she waved her arms wide, everyone seated at the tables staring at me in shock. As promised, Dr. Westcott had killed me after breakfast.

I thought I had more time.

I looked over at Austin who was on his hands and knees, tears streaming down his face as he tried futility to crawl toward me.

I thought we had more time.

His guards suddenly let him go and he rushed toward me, scooping me up in his arms as he knelt beside me.

I smiled up at him.

The pain was gone now, and the world seemed brighter and more colorful.

I tried to speak, to tell him that I loved him, but blood gurgled from my mouth and I lost control over my muscles.

I went slack in his arms as the sun seemed to grow brighter, washing everything in a brilliant white light.

Was this the light at the end of the tunnel that was supposed to be heaven? Was I going to meet the rest of the Micheles when I got there?

Would the other Micheles even be there?

Did clones have souls?

Did I have a soul?

Would I even be allowed entrance to heaven?

The tunnel grew darker as the light faded and I felt warmer, not colder.

I should be feeling colder as every part of my body failed one organ at a time. The darkness was slowly being replaced by a deep red hue and it was getting warmer.

I wanted to cry, but I couldn't.

I realized with a sudden panic that I was not going to heaven.

I was going someplace else.

Chapter 93

The first thing I perceived was the deep red hue that filled my vision. All around me was the murmuring of distant voices, punctuated by sobbing. My entire body felt hot as if I had entered a steam sauna set on high.

Just like hell was described.

I was alone in a pit of fire and darkness; my only companions the murmuring and cries of tortured souls.

The next sensation was of something gripping my body tightly accompanied by a slight rocking motion.

Had the devil found me?

My eyes popped open and I looked up into the tear-streaked face of Austin. I found my voice.

"Austin?"

He looked down at me and his face contorted in terror and he let me go. I sat up and heard audible gasps from the rich bastards sitting around the tables.

Well, they weren't so much as sitting anymore. They were standing up quickly, some of them screaming as they pointed at me.

I looked down at my blood-soaked shirt. I probed inside the shirt with my fingertips, but I couldn't find any trace of the bullet hole.

I took a deep breath and looked at Austin.

He was backing away from me while shaking his head, his facial expressions shifting quickly from confusion, to horror, and back to confusion. Before he got too far, he was grabbed and forced back to a kneeling position.

He didn't fight them this time.

Dr. Westcott yelled above the panicked crowd. "This is the first resurrection. Blessed and holy are those who share in the first resurrection. The second death has no power over them, but they will reign for a thousand years."

Suddenly the gasps and screams were drowned out by growing applause. Everyone who had been running, stopped and turned to face the stage. They looked at me again and then joined in on the applause.

The two guards next to me grabbed my arms and lifted me back up to a standing position while Westcott approached me, her smile stretched from ear to ear. "Good job, Seven."

I looked back down at my bloody shirt, then at the seven dots on my wrist tattoo, and then back at her. "What happened?"

"I shot you, and you died. But you will only stay dead if I destroy enough of you before you have the chance to heal."

The men and women that made up Omega crowded around me. They were all smiles as they took turns touching my face as if I were some interactive hands-on exhibit in a museum.

I tried to shy away from their grubby hands, but one of the guards grabbed my chin and held me in place.

Westcott looked me in the eyes. "The same process that enabled us to grow you to an adult in a manner of months was also the key to a longer life. Your accelerated healing capabilities can easily keep you alive for a thousand years."

My eyes burned into hers. "You told Robert that I would die within five."

"I just said that to him so we could keep making more of you until we figured out how to suitably copy the memories from the original Michele into a clone. You see, the integration process must be done on a sleeping clone prior to being woken up. We could not know if it worked until we brought you out of the coma."

"But I didn't have her memories. I didn't have any memories at all."

Westcott nodded. "That's true. We were not successful with you, and since we couldn't try again after you had been woken up, we grew your replacement. I am pleased to say that we were successful in installing Michele's memories into Eight."

My mind flashed back to the moment on the bridge that had started the path I was on now.

"Is that why she killed herself?"

Westcott's face grew somber. "Sadly, the memories were not integrating properly, resulting in some dementia and psychosis. But I was able to perfect it over the next two attempts, and

Omega no longer requires your services."

"Robert said I was the only one still alive."

"It was convenient for him to believe that."

My eyes widened. "Are the rest still alive?"

She shook her head.

"Sadly, no. It wouldn't have been a smart move to keep them around. As it stands, there are only three of you left. You, Eight, and Ten."

"Ten?"

"She is three more iterations after you, Seven."

"You made three more right away?"

"We were so close; I decided we no longer needed to wait to appease Robert. I mean, I won't live forever."

She laughed as she held up her arms. "At least not in this body."

"What happened to her?"

"Who? Ten? She was the first successful transfer of a complete consciousness into a clone, but we need to know if there are any long term effects, so she is alive, for now. Unfortunately, she's in a lab in Europe and doesn't get the chance to have a normal life like the one you rejected."

I remembered the conversation with the coroner about the body's temperature rising. I looked at Westcott. "The next Michele, the one who jumped from the bridge. She isn't dead, is she?"

"Oh, she died when she drowned. But she wasn't going to stay that way once they fished her out of the river."

"So, that's why you took her."

"That, and I couldn't have someone poking around my stuff. She was an advanced clone, and if someone looked too closely, they might have noticed some discrepancies between her and a birthed human."

"Was?"

Westcott smiled, the warmth gone. "I'm sorry, Seven. Ten will be the only one alive after we dispose of the two of you. I can't risk either of you getting back out into the real world now that you know what you are."

"But you said so yourself. You can't kill me."

"Not by traditional methods, no. But I can destroy you faster than you can regenerate. It will be quick, and a lot less painful than being shot. I promise."

"You bitch!" Austin hollered from the side.

Westcott spun around, the group parting like the sea parting before Moses, so that she could see Austin.

"What did you call me?"

"You heard me," he retorted. "You can't go around playing God."

Westcott approached him. "And why not? You do it every time you draw your service weapon in the line of duty."

"That's different. I don't choose to kill. I only draw my gun when forced. I never choose death unless there is no other choice."

"I'm not choosing death either. I am choosing life."

"For who? Your elite friends?"

"I didn't say I was choosing life for everyone. Somebody still has to break their back to make my life better. I only wish I could let you live long enough to see us become masters over all the earth."

He spat on her.

She wiped it off and then looked back at me before turning back to him.

"I get it. You and Seven had sex last night. You are only protecting the baby you believe might be forming inside her. I won't fault you for running on instinct, but your hatred is being misguided. She's not pregnant."

"How do you know?"

"I made her. I plan on making a clone of everyone in Omega so we can take our rightful place as gods. But I couldn't have a new generation of indestructible teenage shitheads deciding it was time to overthrow us, so I made the clones sterile. There will be no progeny of yours springing from her loins."

"You're a monster," he spat angrily.

"That's one way to look at it," she replied calmly. "The other way is to realize that I have achieved what mankind has sought since the beginning of time. Look around you. These are the new leaders of humanity. And every thousand years, I will provide them with a brand new body and they will rule for another thousand years."

"You're sick!" he screamed at her. Then he looked at the entire group. "All of you!"

Westcott turned to the silent crowd and pointed at Austin. "This is how we will be received in the beginning. But rest assured, when they try to kill us and we keep coming back, they'll realize that they have no choice and grow to accept us. They will welcome us as their chosen leaders."

The members of the exclusive club cheered loudly, every one of them taking turns to shake Dr. Westcott's hand as she made her way back to her table. She sat down and addressed the group all still standing on the stage, with me at the center.

"Now, if we can all finish our breakfast, I have a present for each of you that will be ready in about nine months."

Chapter 94

Austin and I were forced back to our seats at the breakfast table. I stared down at the plate in front of me. My cold eggs and potatoes had been replaced with a fresh, hot stack of pancakes.

I still wasn't hungry.

Did I need food?

If I couldn't die, did the everyday mundane activities of life still apply to me?

No, that couldn't be right. I remembered getting hungry all the time.

I looked over at Austin. He was eating again, diving into the short stack of pancakes and keeping to the rules that had kept him alive this long.

I decided that I should eat, if nothing but to keep my strength. I was virtually immortal, but I wasn't invulnerable.

I cut into the top pancake and held the fork in front of my mouth, casting a glance over at the far table. I couldn't help but smile as every eye was glued on me to see if I was going to eat or not.

What the hell?

I stuffed the pancake into my mouth and watched the money change hands.

As I ate, Dr. Westcott watched me as she chewed on her own small bite.

"What?" I asked, not enjoying her stare.

She set down her fork and turned in her chair to face me. "I was just wondering. What does it feels like to know you can live for a thousand years."

I shrugged. "I don't know."

"Think about it for a moment. This is not some mental exercise for you. I can think about the possibility all I want, but it's not a reality for me. Not until I have moved into my new body. But you. If nobody interfered, you would be able to see generations come and go. Civilizations rise and fall. You could decide to observe the evolution of humanity or take an active part. How does that make you feel?"

I set my fork down and faced her. "But you are planning to interfere. You have said you are going to kill me today. What good is having a lifespan of a thousand years if I won't make it to see the next sunset?"

Westcott pressed her hands together in front of her face like she was about to pray and her eyes sparkled. "But what if I didn't."

"Didn't what?" I asked, narrowing my eyes at her.

"Didn't kill you. What if I let you leave here; alive?"

She pointed at Austin with her praying hands. "Let you leave here with him. What would you do?"

I blinked and looked at Austin. He had stopped eating and was looking at me just as intently for my answer. I looked back at Westcott.

"Will you let me leave? Let both of us leave?"

She smiled and nodded. "Yes."

"Aren't you afraid I would bring back the police, or the FBI, or something?"

Her eyes gleamed. "Who would believe you long enough to storm this exclusive island club. The first thing anyone would do is check our website and see that this is nothing more than a country club surrounded by water. They might even come across the information we planted from supposed former disenfranchised employees who describe this place as a depressed Club Med wannabe with weeds sprouting through the cracks of the tennis court and an empty, unused, hot tub."

She tapped her chin with the tip of her praying hands. "No, I don't think anyone will be re-enacting D-Day on our shores based on your word."

I jutted my chin out in defiance. "I could show them what happens when I get shot."

"And spend the next thousand years in some government lab while they run test after test on you to see why you heal without dying? Maybe even seeing if they could use your ability to their advantage. You don't really want to be a real-life comic book character, do you?"

She had me by the short hairs, and she knew it. And she knew that I knew it.

"So," she continued. "Now that we know I am safe, Omega is safe, and I will be letting the both of you go, what will you do with the next nine-hundred and ninety-five years of your life?"

To be honest, I hadn't had time to give it any thought, what with only minutes before discovering that I could not be killed by conventional means. Dr. Westcott had all but assured me she had ways to kill me that were far more permanent, but now she was giving me the chance to live my life to its fullest.

Is this what the humans were faced with when asked by a vampire if they would like to be given the gift of an immortal life?

Sure, I would die in a thousand years, but a thousand years was a very long time. It might as well be immortality.

Westcott prodded me, always the psychologist, just like when I had visited with her once a week.

"Now that you know you are special, would you stay with Austin? Would you get married?"

I looked at Austin.

"Don't look at him. He will die fifty years from now as a decrepit old man, barely able to keep from shitting his own pants and sleeping twenty hours a day. You, however, will continue to live twenty times longer while retaining your youthful beauty and vigor, right up to the moment when your body stops."

I looked back at her. "I will look like this the whole time?"

"An unexpected, but positive, side effect of the accelerated healing process. Granted, I for one am not satisfied with living for only a thousand years and will be working to break through that limit to live indefinitely at the prime of my life. So, I ask you again. Will you stay with Austin knowing that the two of you can never have children, and that you will look like this when he can barely stand up straight?"

I looked back at Austin. "I don't care about any of that. I will stay with him until he breathes his last."

We smiled at each other as Westcott continued behind me.

"That is very noble of you," she said quietly. "But you have not answered my question."

I turned my head back around.

"What question?"

"Will you live the next thousand years as a spectator, or will you take an active part in human affairs knowing that you, and you alone, have the power to bend the mortals to your will?"

I didn't like how that question had changed.

"I don't know," I replied.

Westcott tapped her praying hands against her chin again and watched my face intently.

"So, given the power of the gods, you would refrain from wielding that power?"

"Who am I to tell others how to live?"

Westcott laughed. "And that is the difference between you and Omega. We are all here because we know how to tell others what to do. We are deserving of this gift. We have earned it."

She turned to the guard standing to her right.

"Take them both to the flash chamber."

I was lifted out of my seat, Austin struggling next to me against the guards that had snatched him up as well.

"Wait!" I screamed.

Westcott held her hand up and the guards froze.

I looked at Westcott. "You said you would let us go."

Westcott's evil smile returned. "I just said that to get you thinking. I can't give you, or lover boy here, the opportunity to upset plans that have taken decades to realize. You have served your purpose and are no longer necessary. Thank you for your dedicated service." She turned her attention to Austin. "And you. All you had to do was follow orders and you never would have been at the police station when my men came to retrieve what is mine."

Austin glared at her. "I have a problem following orders that don't make sense."

Westcott shook her head. "And you wonder why your little combat unit was put out to pasture."

Austin lunged for her, but the two guards that held him were faster and kept him in place as a third kicked him in the face from the side.

Austin's head ricocheted from the impact and the two guards

let him go as he collapsed to his hands and knees.

The man who had kicked him stepped in front of him and I saw his face clearly.

It was Nick. He grabbed Austin's hair, lifting his head up to look him in the eyes.

"I know you will never give up, so just accept that you have been defeated."

He released Austin's hair and looked at Westcott. "You promised I could have him alive."

Westcott stood taller, clearly trying to show her dominance over the mercenary.

"I think it is better that they are put in the incineration chamber together. She wants to be with him for his final breath."

She looked at me. "For everything I am taking away from her, I owe her that."

Had I detected a hint of regret in her eyes?

Nick stepped closer to her, but three guards raised their rifles to stop him. "Ma'am. I was promised his life."

Westcott stood her ground, emboldened by her loyal soldiers. "You may watch if you wish. I might even let you push the button if it will stop your incessant whining."

"He and I have unfinished business. I need him to suffer for what he did."

"You will do what I am paying you to do."

Nick's eyes grew cold and narrowed at her. "You can keep the money. I don't care about any of it. But I want Austin."

Westcott closed her eyes and let out a short breath before she opened them again. "Fine. I was going to keep your money anyway."

Nick turned and sprinted away without warning. The three guards immediately started firing in his direction, but he disappeared through the bushes as bullets tore into them.

The guards stopped firing and started after him.

"Stop!" Westcott ordered.

The guards froze and turned back toward her. The leader of the group pointed to where Nick had disappeared.

"We have to go after him."

"We're on an island. Where's he going to go? Alert the patrols and they will find him."

The lead guard snapped to attention. "Yes, Ma'am!"

"Let me know when he has been captured."

"Yes, Ma'am."

The guard spoke into his walkie-talkie, spreading the new orders to the rest of the guards on the island.

Westcott walked up to Austin and leaned down to look him in the eyes.

"You have developed a very loyal fan club. I guess I must eliminate you as quickly as possible. That should defuse the situation. Your former comrade might still prove useful to me and I want to make sure that there is nothing more important to him than serving me."

Austin spit the blood from his mouth at her feet. She stood upright and waved her hand in a circle in the air.

Two guards lifted Austin to his feet and another two gripped my arms tightly.

The wind picked up suddenly, sending napkins and tablecloths flying into the air.

Everyone raised their arms to shield their eyes against the dust that swirled into the air. It was like a tornado had just formed on the middle of the island.

The wealthy guests all ran around in a panic as the wind intensified. I squinted against the rush of air and looked into the bright blue sky.

A private helicopter was slowly lowering itself over the patio area, knocking over chairs and sending everyone in all directions as they raced to escape the rotor wash.

Westcott ran forward, shouting and waving her arms at the helicopter. I felt the grip on my arms loosen and looked to see everyone's attention focused on the approaching helicopter.

Everyone but Austin.

I couldn't hear anything over the noise of the helicopter blades and people screaming, but I could clearly see what he was yelling at me.

"Run!"

Chapter 95

I broke free from the only guard who still had a hand on my arm and started running for the same row of bushes that Nick had disappeared through. While I didn't want to head in the same direction as Nick, it was the only direction that provided an immediate escape.

I crashed through the bushes, bullets shredding the branches around me.

Hot fire burned my arm, and I looked down to see a slice of red that closed before my eyes, leaving a trickle of blood running down my arm where no wound was visible. I had been shot, but had healed nearly instantly.

Behind me, Austin crashed through the bushes and I paused, glancing back, only to have adrenaline surge through my body.

It wasn't Austin!

A guard had followed me into the bushes. He spotted me and raised his rifle.

I spun and bolted out the other side as bullets shredded the leaves on either side of me. I was so high on adrenaline, I hadn't even felt the bullets that had pierced my back and exited through my chest until my body gave out and I stumbled to the ground.

I gasped in rapid breaths as my internal organs failed one by one. I spat out bile and blood as I crawled on my hands and knees, still trying to put distance between my attacker and me.

My body burned hotly, and I regained my strength faster than I expected as my injuries knitted themselves.

I stayed on all fours and looked back as the guard burst from the bushes and spotted me on the ground. He kept the gun on me as he approached slowly. I crawled away from him, lurching about like I was in pain.

As soon as he was close, I lunged upward and grabbed the gun barrel, pointing it away from me as he fired.

The barrel heated up and burned into my palm. I screamed and kicked hard at his kneecap.

A loud crunching sound emanated from his leg and the guard yelped as he fell on the ground. He let go of the rifle and gripped his back-turned knee.

I spun the rifle around and pointed it at the guard.

"Stay here or I will shoot you!" I commanded.

The guard ignored me, so I spun around and ran full speed back into the bushes.

I had to save Austin.

As I reached the edge of the hedge row, I glanced back to make sure the guard was not following me. He was still rolling around on the ground holding his knee. He looked like an upturned turtle. Just as I turned back, a figure burst out of the bushes looking behind him and slammed into me.

Austin and I collapsed in a heap.

Austin was on his feet in the blink of an eye, grabbed the rifle from my hands, and lifted me to my feet.

"You okay?"

He didn't wait for an answer but instead spun around and pointed the rifle in the direction of new crashing sounds in the bushes. He aimed for the tops of the bushes and fired.

When the gun ran dry, he tossed it on the ground and grabbed my hand, yanking me into a full run.

"Where are we going?" I said between ragged breaths.

"Robert created the distraction so we could escape," Austin replied.

"But this is an island. Where are we going?"

"That way," was all Austin said as he pulled me into a stand of trees.

Chapter 96

From behind us, I heard the clatter of sustained gunfire as it drove away the helicopter. We exited the other side of the trees and Austin changed direction suddenly, nearly pulling me off my feet as we ran.

He stopped just as quickly and looked in every direction before deciding on one and pulling me along with him.

Several times, we would stop and crouch in the bushes, doing our best to breath as quietly as possible as another patrol passed dangerously close to us.

After nearly an hour of alternating between running full bore and crouching down in bushes to hide from another patrol, Austin crouched along the edge of the road and pointed at a small house.

"Michele should be in there."

My heart skipped a beat as I looked at him.

"The Michele?"

He nodded, still breathing heavy from running around the island.

I looked back at the small house that overlooked the lake.

"How do you know?"

"Nick told me."

Now I was confused. I thought Nick was the enemy.

"Nick's helping us?" I asked, not hiding the surprise in my voice.

He shook his head.

"Not exactly. He promised to tell me where she was if I promised to go mano-a-mano with him after we got out of here."

I gripped Austin's hand tighter.

"You can't do that," I said.

Austin smiled warmly and patted my hand.

"It's okay. I taught him everything he knows, and if last night was any indication, he's been letting himself get soft. I'll be fine."

"What if he kills you?"

"If he cheats and brings a weapon, that might very well happen."

My shoulders slumped and I looked into his eyes, silently pleading with him to change his mind.

"That's not very encouraging," I said.

He smiled again.

"I doubt he's going to do that. He wants to prove he's better than me. He can't do that if he cheats."

The bushes parted next to us and I nearly jumped out of my skin. Austin was faster and clamped a hand over my mouth before I yelled out as Nick appeared next to us.

Nick sneered at Austin, yet handed him one of the rifles in his hand.

"I am better than you, and we both know why."

Austin frowned at him.

"We will resolve this after we get both Micheles off the island."

I pulled Austin's hand from my mouth.

"There are three Micheles," I added.

They both looked at me.

"Westcott said they are keeping Michele Eight, the one I saw jump from the bridge, alive somewhere here. I'm not leaving without her, and I think the other Michele will feel the same."

Austin looked at Nick.

Nick shrugged.

"I retrieved her body from the morgue and turned it over to Westcott's people. I don't know where she is or if she's even on the island."

Austin nodded.

"Okay. We keep to the plan but add finding Michele Eight as a secondary objective. If we find her, she leaves with us."

My eyes burned into Austin's.

"We don't leave here without her."

"We don't even know if she's on the island."

"Where else would they keep her if not here?" I pushed and stared unblinking into his eyes.

"Okay," Austin finally said after a short moment of silence. "We have half an hour to locate her."

I relaxed.

"Thank you," I said.

Nick's face grew serious as he stood up and ran across the street.

Austin stood up, ran across the street, and joined Nick along the side of the house. As I caught up, Austin looked at me.

"You stay out here until I give the all clear."

Nick stepped in front of the door and kicked it open. He ran in gun first with Austin right behind him.

I heard several shouts followed by the sharp spit of gunfire, and then silence.

Austin poked his head out the door.

"Clear," he said and then disappeared back inside.

I stepped over the threshold and my stomach flipped upside down as I saw two guards sitting on the couch, gaping wounds in their chests.

In the corner of the living room, Nick was knelt down next to someone who was crying hysterically.

I walked around to see who it was. Despite knowing what to expect, I was still shocked to see myself as an older woman hunched in the corner of the room, tears streaming down her cheeks.

Older Michele looked up at me, her eyes wide as saucers, and froze. We stared at each other for what seemed like forever when she suddenly let out a blood curdling scream.

Chapter 97

I looked at her as she screamed and clawed at Nick in a panic.

"Keep her away from me!"

Nick grabbed her wrists and held her tightly as she tried to keep hitting him.

"Stop it! We are trying to rescue you."

She looked at him, terror mirrored in her eyes as she shook her head violently. He released her hands and she pressed herself against the wall and pointed at me like I was the Grim Reaper come for her soul.

"No. You want to replace me with her!"

Austin glanced at me before he moved closer to her.

"Mrs. Black. Listen to me. Robert is waiting for us."

Her head snapped to him and she gave him a curious look.

"No one has called me Mrs. Black in a long time. Do you know Robert?"

Austin smiled.

"He sent us to find you."

Tears still streamed down her face, but her expression shifted from sheer terror to absolute joy.

"Robert? Robert sent you?"

Austin nodded and held out his hand.

"We have to get out of here now."

She reached out and took his hand, looking over at me.

"What about her?" she asked.

"She's coming with us," Austin said calmly.

She froze, trying to pull her hand out of Austin's grip.

"She has my memories."

Austin gripped her chin with his fingers and turned her head to look at him instead of me.

"You met another Michele with your memories?" Austin asked.

She nodded.

"Do you know where she is?" he added.

She glanced at me briefly with her eyes before focusing again on Austin.

He held her chin and spoke quietly.

"This is not the same one you met before."

Her eyes looked at me again with alarm.

"There's more? How many more?"

I almost laughed out loud. That was the same question Dead Michele had posed right before jumping from the bridge.

Austin looked at me and then back to Older Michele.

"As far as I know, there are just the three of them; and you."

She looked at him in shock.

"Three of them?"

"You. And three clones."

She looked at me.

"Do you know everything about me?"

I shook my head.

"I don't have any memories from before the accident…"

I stopped. There hadn't been an accident. That was the lie that I had come to believe.

She looked at me curiously.

"What accident?"

"I'm sorry," I replied. "There wasn't an accident. That's just what they told me when I woke up with no memories."

"How come the other one has my memories and you don't?"

Austin took over for me when he saw I was having trouble forming a coherent response.

"Apparently, Dr. Westcott tried, but the memory transfer didn't work, so she woke up with no memories at all."

Nick had been standing at the window, looking out while we talked. He spun around.

"We have to get going. Are we searching for this other Michele or what?"

Austin nodded at Nick and looked back at Michele.

"If we can, we would like to rescue all three of you. Do you know where they are keeping the other one?"

She looked at me for a long moment and then nodded.

"I can show you where they're keeping her."

Chapter 98

Nick led the way out of the house. Michele pointed in one direction, but Nick took us an entirely different direction.

As we went the opposite of where Michele had indicated, I caught up to Austin.

"Why are we going a different way?" I whispered.

Austin replied quietly without slowing down. "Nick knows this island better than anyone, and he knows the best way to get there without getting caught."

An alarm sounded behind us. Nick started walking faster between the trees of the forest.

I had to walk even faster just to keep up. "What's happening?"

Austin glanced over his shoulder behind me. "They must have discovered we have Michele."

"How are we getting off the island?"

"Let's worry about getting the other Michele first."

I fell back a step and into line. Nick took the lead, followed by Older Michele, and then Austin and I bringing up the rear. As we moved, Austin continually spun around and walked backward, checking behind us for anyone following.

Nick led us quickly, but quietly, through the forest along one side of the island.

Why was he helping us?

What had happened in their past to make him want Austin dead with every fiber of his being, yet kept him honorable enough to risk his life to help us escape?

I was about to ask Austin if he knew, when Nick stopped and crouched, raising a closed fist into the air.

I knew what that meant and dropped to one knee, keeping my big mouth shut.

Austin scanned the forest around us slowly, like a second hand sweeping across a clock face. As soon as he completed a full circle, he nodded.

Austin looked at Michele and me. We were both crouched next to each other.

"Stay here. We will bring the other one out and then head for the extraction point."

Nick stood up, raised his rifle, and tucked the butt into his shoulder as he walked in a half-crouch out of the forest.

Austin started to stand up when I placed a hand on his shoulder.

He turned back to look at me.

"Stay safe," I said and then planted a kiss on his cheek.

He smiled, and then his face became a mask of concentration as he spun back around and followed Nick, his gun also raised and ready.

I looked at Michele, who was keeping a wary eye on me. I smiled, trying to put her at ease.

"I don't want to replace you. I have my own life."

Michele studied my face for a long moment before she blinked and turned away.

I moved in closer. She shied away when I reached out to place a reassuring hand on her shoulder. I lowered my arm back to my side.

"Robert loves you."

She scowled at me.

"How do you know?"

I thought about the pictures in my house that matched the pictures in the other Michele's house. I guessed that they closely matched pictures first generated with the Michele sitting in the forest with me now.

"I think he was trying to rebuild the life the two of you had before you died."

"But I didn't die. The letter…"

"I found the letter. The woman who shared a room with you twenty years ago thought I was you and she gave it to me."

"She was still at the hospital?"

"No. She lives in a house across the street from where the hospital used to be. It was pure chance that she saw us standing at the vacant lot."

Michele watched me as I spoke. The disdain in her voice softened.

"Does Robert love you?"

I had been giving that a lot of thought after learning what I now knew.

"He has always loved you. But he thought you were dead, and Dr. Westcott convinced him that she could bring you back."

"But I didn't need bringing back. I never died. That whole African virus scare was bogus. I was never sick. It was Westcott's medication that made me sick."

"Then that's something we have in common. I found out she had been poisoning me and had told Robert that I would be dying within five years."

All this talk of death caused an uncomfortable silence that I let hang over us until Michele shifted her weight and looked at me uncomfortably.

"Did you have sex with him?"

I looked in the direction that Austin had gone. What business was that of hers?

Michele shook her head. "Not the soldier. Robert."

I looked back at her, fear written across my face for knowing the truth, but being afraid to tell her.

She nodded. "You don't need to say. It makes sense. Did you love him?"

"I don't know."

"How could you not know?"

"I'd lost my memories; or rather, I guess I never had any in the first place. I had no friends. No family. No one beyond Dr. Westcott."

I swallowed down my heart that had become lodged in my throat as the memories flooded back.

"And then Robert came along. I was so starved for any form of intimacy; I ignored the age difference and agreed to marry him…"

"You married Robert!" Michele burst out and then clamped her own hand over her mouth. We looked around, but nobody came rushing to our position with guns drawn.

We were lucky.

This time.

Older Michele whispered as she continued. "Why the hell did he marry you?!"

I didn't know what to say. Instead, I focused my mind's eye on the pictures on my mantle.

"Did the two of you go to a beach in Florida for Easter vacation?"

Michele's eyebrows raised in surprise.

"Yes. Why?"

"Robert took me to all sorts of places and we took pictures to commemorate our time together. When I... found the other Michele, and entered her home for the first time, I saw the same pictures being replicated. I think Robert was trying to remind us about who we were before."

"But you aren't me."

"I know. But with the next Michele, the memory transfer worked and she must have remembered something that made her question who she really was."

"Why do you think that?"

"She started the quest to find you. Something must have happened and she killed herself."

"Are you talking about me," a voice said behind me.

I turned around, and my mouth dropped open as I looked at Younger Michele, still very much alive, standing bookended on either side by Austin and Nick.

I remembered being shot and then healing enough to come back to life, but it was another thing entirely to see someone else who used to be dead standing in front of you; alive. It made it less believable.

Younger Michele looked at Older Michele, and then back to me, smiling as her eyes welled up with tears.

"You found her."

Chapter 99

Older Michele backed away from the two of us, her head snapping back and forth between us. I could tell this was too much for her and I rushed forward to catch her as she fainted.

I struggled to keep her from falling on the ground when Nick was right next to me and bore the bulk of her weight.

"I can carry her to the docks," Nick said lifting her onto his shoulders with a grunt and positioning her so he could still carry his rifle. Austin ejected the magazine on his rifle and replaced it with a fresh one. He then swapped rifles with Nick and did the same with the second.

They both pulled back on the charging levers of their guns, eliciting a snapping sound from them, and nodded to each other.

I looked at Austin. "The docks?"

"Robert has a speedboat waiting for us," Austin said.

"What about the gunboats," I asked.

Nick strode past me, Older Michele draped over his shoulders.

"We have a ten minute window that is fast closing. After that, we have a problem."

Austin looked at me and Younger Michele standing next to me. "Stay close."

Michele and I both nodded.

"Let's go," he said and then he and Nick fanned out to lead the way, guns first.

Michele and I followed two steps behind.

Chapter 100

Austin crouched and held his fist in the air.

I stopped, Michele following suit.

"What are we doing?" she asked.

I placed my finger over her lips, shushing her silently. She got the message and watched Austin and Nick silently exchange a long conversation, using only their hands, head gestures, and pointed fingers.

They both stopped at the same time and Nick laid Older Michele tenderly on the ground before he disappeared into the forest.

Austin came over to us, keeping careful watch in every direction.

"Nick is going to check out the docks and clear a path if needed. We will follow him in one minute."

"What happens in one minute?" younger Michele asked.

He looked back and forth between us, and then shook his head. As confusing as it was to see two other versions of myself, it had to be exponentially confusing for everyone else.

"Either we have a clear path to the docks, or we don't."

"What if we don't?" she asked.

He shrugged.

"Then we make our own path."

I grabbed Younger Michele's shoulders and looked her in the eyes.

"As long as you are able, no matter what happens, keep going and don't look back until you are on Robert's boat."

"If I make it first," Michele said. "I'll have the boat wait for you."

Austin cleared his throat.

"The boat captain has his orders. He leaves in two minutes, with or without any of us."

Younger Michele perked up.

"Then what are we standing around here for?"

Austin smiled and pointed in the direction Nick had gone.

"He will make the trail easy to follow. I will send... you...

thirty seconds after you."

He looked between us.

"This is… None of my training prepared me for this. What do I call you?"

Michele and I looked at each other.

"We are still both Michele," she said.

"Okay, Michele. Go now. Michele will be right after you. And I will carry… Michele." She ran off, following the trail left by Nick

He laughed nervously and mussed up his hair with a hand. "This is making me sound crazy."

I touched his arm. Austin and I were alone, except for Older Michele, but she was still unconscious and lying on the ground.

Austin's brow furrowed as he studied my face.

"As soon as the three of you are on the boat, go."

"What about you?"

"Nick's not going to let me leave without a fight."

"What's his problem? Why does he want to have it out with you so bad?"

Austin's face grew serious.

"He thinks I did something and won't listen to reason."

"Then fuck him! Shoot the bastard in the back and leave with us."

Austin laughed.

"You know what? That's not a crazy idea."

I smiled at him and moved in closer, placing my arms around his neck.

"I've got plenty of crazy ideas, but every one of them requires your body. I won't leave this island without you."

He smiled back.

We hadn't been this close since the night before and the moment overtook us.

We looked deeply into each other's eyes as we moved closer until we were kissing.

We kissed deeply, the cares of the world melting around us. If I were to die at this very moment, I would die happy.

"Oh, come on!" Older Michele said from the ground. We

both looked down. She was propped up on one elbow, looking at us.

"She's a married woman, you know," she said as Austin helped her to her feet.

I looked at her, still smiling.

"I was kind of hoping you would take over for me as Mrs. Black when we got out of here."

Michele tilted her head and smiled back.

"I think I will take you up on that."

Her face suddenly grew somber.

"Do you think Robert still wants me?"

I placed an arm around her shoulder.

"Believe me, all Robert has ever wanted was to get you back."

Chapter 101

Austin led the way with Older Michele right behind him. I had to wait another thirty seconds before I could make my way to the dock after them.

Austin had already decided that if we traveled together it would increase the risk that, if discovered, it would result in everyone getting caught. His plan to split up and make our way separately to the dock meant there was a greater chance that at least some of us could escape and then bring help back to get the rest.

I wasn't sold on that plan.

Dr. Westcott had convinced me that nobody would believe anything conspiratorial was going on at Rattlesnake Island. Especially something that involved clones, living for a thousand years, and eventual world domination.

It was all too crazy.

Even for me.

And I was one of the immortals.

The implication of what I was capable of suddenly dawned on me.

I was immortal.

I had the power to keep going, even after death.

It took being able to destroy my body faster than it could heal to kill me. Weapons able to do that had to be few and far between.

There was one on this island.

I doubted it was very portable.

Once I had escaped, my chances of survival increased drastically to the point of guaranteed certainty.

I just had to get off the island.

It must have been thirty seconds by now.

I took off as quietly as I could along the same path Austin and the others had taken.

It wouldn't be long now.

Soon, we would all be on Robert's boat and I would be able to put everything that had happened in the past week and a half behind me; forever.

As I picked my way through the dense forest, I wondered if any of the comic book superheroes had ever figured out how to monetize their crime fighting abilities.

I was so focused on what the future may hold, I was barely paying attention to where I was going until I nearly bumped into a small squad of guards who were all facing away from me. They were making plenty of noise, so they never heard me approaching.

I immediately took a step back and ducked behind a tree as one of them turned in my direction.

I held my breath and waited for them to swarm my position and start firing.

Nobody came, so I peeked around the edge of the tree.

What I saw chilled me to the core.

Chapter 102

From where I hid, I could see the dock poking out over the water. Moored next to the dock was a large inflatable raft with black pontoons and a huge motor in the back.

That had to be Robert's escape boat, but it was empty and still tied to the dock.

There were several people standing on the dock in a tight circle, their backs to each other, and I recognized all of them. They stood with their arms raised and were surrounded by guards on all sides.

Two smaller boats in the water motored around the dock; their mounted guns remained directed at the group on the dock as they circled.

Walking out onto the dock triumphantly was Dr. Westcott.

She said a few words to Nick, and then promptly slapped him across the face. I guess she wasn't pleased with his sudden betrayal.

She then turned and pointed at the two Micheles. Two guards split from the semicircle and grabbed them.

I watched as the guards loaded them into the back of the van that had been butted up against the end of the dock. Nobody made a move to get into the van and leave with the women.

From this angle, I could see the glint of keys dangling in the ignition.

All eyes were on the remaining prisoners on the dock. It was in that split second I made my decision.

Austin and Nick were more than capable of taking care of themselves. It was the Micheles that needed my help.

I slinked around the tree and worked my way down to the edge of the forest, staying careful not to make too much noise or be seen by any of the guards who were stationed further up the hill.

As luck would have it, they had decided that watching the scene on the dock unfold was far more exciting than watching the woods behind them, and I was able to make it all the way to the edge of the forest, mere feet from the front of the van.

I watched the back of every guard I could see as I crept out of the woods and made my way to the driver's side door.

I opened it quickly and jumped in, twisting the keys and slamming the van into gear before I heard panicked shouts all around me.

I smashed the pedal to the floor and took off down the thin road, kicking up dirt and gravel as I sped away.

"Are you okay?" I hollered through the wire mesh that covered the window between the passenger and cargo areas of the van.

Younger Michele gripped the wires with her fingers and pressed her face into the mesh.

"Thank god it's you!" she said.

I checked the side view mirrors and saw guards firing blindly into the waters around the dock.

Austin and Nick had taken advantage of the commotion and made their escape. My only hope was that they had succeeded.

I careened around the next bend, stretching the comprehension of my hour of driving instruction I had only just received the day before.

My comprehension couldn't have been that good as the van spun out of control and slammed sideways into a tree.

I cracked my head on the windshield and saw stars. The driver's side door opened, and Younger Michele pulled me from the van.

I regained my senses quickly, almost as quickly as the cuts on my forehead had healed, and the three of us ran into the forest moments before a jeep overflowing with guards waving rifles in the air, reeled around the corner after the van.

The jeep skidded to a halt, guards yelling for us to surrender as they surrounded the empty van.

We kept running, with no clear direction, until we were all breathing heavily and stumbling more often.

I guess being immortal still meant that, while we could thumb our noses at the specter of death, we were still slaves to the laws of fatigue.

Older Michele pointed at a small cement building with no

windows up ahead.

"We can hide in there."

She stopped in front of the building and ripped at a seam on her pants, extracting a key from a secret pocket sewn into the waistband.

She looked up at me and smiled.

"I stole this from Dr. Westcott's desk months ago. Now I get to find out what's inside this building."

As she worked on the rusted lock, I looked at the tiny building. It couldn't have been more than six feet tall and ten feet wide on any side. If this room was empty, we would have officially found the worst place on the island to hide.

We entered the small building and found a single room with circular stairs leading down into the bowels of the earth.

We looked at each other.

I raised my hands in supplication and shrugged my shoulders.

"Might as well see where they go," I offered as I plucked a heavy metal flashlight off a shelf. The thin layer of dust still showed the outline of where the flashlight had rested for who knew how long. I turned on the flashlight, and the bulb illuminated faintly. I knocked it against my hand and the light flared brighter.

I switched it off to conserve what little power was left in the batteries and handed it to Older Michele.

She smiled sweetly and then headed down the stairs and into the darkness.

Chapter 103

As we descended, the metal stairs rang in accord with each step. We froze when the light from above increased as someone opened the door above and let sunlight filter into the vertical tunnel.

We heard voices above us discussing whether or not they should go down to look for us.

"The door was locked, right?"

"Yeah."

"Then, they couldn't have come in here."

"Right. Besides, you'd have to be stupid to climb down these stairs. They must be a hundred years old."

"Yeah," the other laughed. "The salt air has probably rusted half the steps."

Nobody followed us and we were able to continue our plunge down the vertical tunnel carved in bedrock.

None of us said a word as we carefully picked our way down the metal staircase. The light had decreased significantly, and Older Michele slowed her progress to switch on the flashlight and check ahead to make sure the stairs were still there and had not fallen away due to corrosion.

It didn't take long before there was nothing but darkness, with brief moments of a faint glow as Older Michele inspected the stairwell below us with the flashlight.

The only sound was our hollow footfalls on the ancient metal platforms accompanied by our ragged breathing.

We moved at a steady clip for nearly half an hour; spiraling down into the earth. It felt like we were already halfway to China when Younger Michele asked the question I hadn't had the nerve to ask out loud for fear of the answer.

"How far down does this go?"

"I don't know," Older Michele responded as she switched off the faint light and continued down. "This island was used by smugglers during the prohibition. These stairs might be from then. Oops. I think we are at the bottom."

I bumped into Younger Michele and stopped short before we

tumbled down the last few steps.

"Michele?" I said into the darkness.

"Yes?" was the simultaneous reply.

Austin was right. This was going to get very confusing, very quickly.

"Umm, the original Michele?" I said.

"Hold on," came the reply from further away, her dark body outlined by a faint amber glow.

There was a scratching sound, then a loud thunk right before small pale lights hanging from wires slowly bloomed to life around us. Older Michele switched off the flashlight.

"The batteries are almost completely dead. Good thing I spotted the switch to these lights."

The lights continued down a long tunnel that was carved into the rock of the island and led down and away from us.

Water seeped in through the pores of the bedrock, making the walls of roughly hewn rock slick and shiny.

"How far do you think it goes?" Younger Michele asked, her voice echoing down the tunnel.

"Well," Older Michele said. "We have a choice. We go back up, or we follow this and hope it doesn't lead to a dead end."

I looked down the tunnel and thought about what waited for us if we returned to the surface.

"I vote we follow the tunnel," I said.

Both Micheles nodded and Older Michele led the way. Our feet splashed in shallow puddles that had formed all along the floor of the tunnel.

I worried, as we kept walking, that somewhere ahead of us the tunnel might have become flooded. I banished those negative thoughts from my brain and thought instead about the life Austin and I would lead once we were out of here.

The negative thoughts returned as I saw in my mind's eye the guards shooting into the shallow water at Austin and Nick.

I had seen enough movies to know that bullets had trouble moving through water, but how long could Austin hold his breath under water before he had to come up for air?

I tried to think positive thoughts.

He was a trained soldier, and from comments he and Dalton had made, had gotten out of far worse situations than this.

I forced myself to smile. Maybe if I pretended I was happy, my brain would believe me and my mood would improve.

Younger Michele looked back and noticed me smiling in the faint light of the tunnel.

"What are you so happy about?" she inquired.

"Nothing, really. Just trying to convince myself that everything will be okay."

Older Michele laughed.

"Even if I die down here, it's far better that what's been happening to me up there."

Younger Michele caught up to her.

"I've been wondering, if they could create clones of you, why did they keep you alive all this time?"

"I wondered that as well. All I know is they would come at me with needles every five years or so and extract blood and bone marrow."

She shuddered.

"Not pleasant, let me tell you. And then, several months later they would hook me up to a machine with wires trailing from my head and into another room. I never knew what they were doing until I met you a couple of days ago."

"So you were kept here all this time, and didn't know what was going on?" Younger Michele asked.

Older Michele nodded.

"I had no idea why they told Robert I was dead. I overheard them talking about him funding their research, but I had no idea what that research was."

Younger Michele placed a hand on Older Michele's shoulder.

"When I woke up only with partial memories, I was more confused than you could possibly imagine. I couldn't remember everything right away. Only snippets. Dr. Westcott told me about some car accident that had given me amnesia. When I met Robert, and he started taking me out to replicate the things you and he had done before, memories flooded back like a tidal wave. But I never let Westcott know."

"Why not?" I asked as we kept walking.

"I thought I was going crazy. It was like one big déjà vu that wouldn't stop. One day, I had saved enough money to follow Robert. And do you know where I followed him to?"

She stopped and looked at me.

"I followed him right to your house."

"Why didn't you say anything, or approach me?"

"What would I say? 'Hi, I'm another you and I'm dating your husband.' Yeah, I don't think that would have gone over too well."

"But why did you jump from the bridge?"

She looked at Older Michele.

"I remembered the letter you snuck to Jasmine, so I went to the hospital. Only it wasn't there anymore. They had torn it down. My head was so full of conflicting memories. Those you had, and those I was recreating with Robert, I didn't have the ability to conduct this search myself."

She looked back at me.

"But I knew you did. So, I staged myself on the bridge on your day to visit Dr. Westcott."

I looked at her in shock.

"Did you know you wouldn't die?"

She shook her head and started crying softly as she continued.

"No. But there was no way I could go on. But I also couldn't let you continue living a lie. And since we were the same person, I knew that my death was just the push you needed to finish what I wasn't capable of finishing."

Older Michele was looking at us like we were bug-eyed aliens.

"Wait a minute. Did you say you died?"

Younger Michele nodded.

"Yes. Or at least I thought I had. I must have gone into some form of hibernation because of the cold water."

"No," I said and then told them what Dr. Westcott had said about the clones' ability to recover from injuries nearly instantly and how she planned to replace everyone in Omega with clones who would live for a thousand years.

As soon as I finished, Older Michele grabbed Younger

Michele and hugged her tightly.

"It's okay," she whispered softly. "We'll get out of this and make them pay for what they did." Older Michele looked over Younger Michele's shoulder at me. "To all of us."

I moved forward and wrapped my arms around both of them and the three of us stood crying in the middle of an underground tunnel dug by smugglers.

We let the tears flow until we all ran dry.

Sniffling, we wiped our noses and then started laughing at the absurdity of everything. Despite not having to say a word, we knew what each other was thinking.

Forget the debate on nature versus nurture.

We were more alike than not.

Older Michele turned back down the tunnel and we followed her silently.

As we walked, I noted tunnels branching off randomly in other directions. Heading in the direction we were going, it was an easy straight shot to keep going. But anyone coming the other direction might not know which way was the correct one.

The smugglers must have designed the tunnel to be an easy path from Rattlesnake Island to wherever it let out. But anyone coming back the other way would quickly become lost; not knowing which way was the correct path.

We continued on in silence for what seemed like an hour before Older Michele stopped.

"Uh oh," she said.

"What?" I asked.

She pointed ahead of us. The tunnel angled downward again, only this time, it was filled with water all the way to the top of the tunnel.

The path ahead was completely flooded.

Chapter 104

Younger Michele crouched next to the water and touched it. Ripples expanded out across the surface of the inky black liquid, the water having shorted out the bulbs in that section of the wire.

She looked up at us.

"No way to tell how far this goes before it comes back up again to another air pocket, if it does at all."

She stood up and wiped her wet hand on the sides of her pants.

"I've drowned before. It's no picnic."

Older Michele looked back down the way we had come. She suddenly looked at Younger Michele.

"Are you willing to risk drowning again?"

"Not if I can help it. What do you have planned?"

Older Michele pointed to the hanging lights.

"We can tear a section of the wire down and tie it around your waist. If you make it to the other side, you can tug on it and we'll follow you."

"And if I don't make it?" Younger Michele asked slowly.

Older Michele put out her hands, palm side up.

"We pull your lifeless body back and wait for you to come back to life?"

Younger Michele looked into the inky blackness and took a step backward.

I thought of the pain my body experienced when I had been shot. Drowning couldn't be any worse than that. And there would be nowhere else for us to go but back, and the branching tunnels meant we might become hopelessly lost down here.

I stepped forward. "I'll do it," I said.

I offered to pull on the cables with the light bulbs attached to them. If anyone was going to get electrocuted, it should be me. I could just wake up again and keep going.

Older Michele held the flashlight, ready to illuminate our path once I pulled the lights out. She turned on the flashlight and nothing happened. She hit the side against her hand a couple of times, and it bloomed to life.

We all looked at the faint light and knew we didn't have much time left before we would be working in absolute darkness.

I took a deep breath and wrapped my hands around the electrical wire that also served to hold the lights suspended along the low ceiling. I pulled, the lights flickered, and every muscle in my body surged with unfiltered electricity and then my heart stopped beating.

"Aw, shit," I said as I collapsed to the slick floor and the world went dark.

Chapter 105

I felt someone slapping my face as my body grew hot and I looked up at the faint outline of Younger Michele in the glow of the flashlight as she held my head in her lap.

She smiled down at me.

"Ready to try again?"

"Let's get this over with," I replied.

I rolled to my hands and knees and stood up with their help. I reached up and gripped the wire again.

I yanked with all my strength, the electricity coursing through my muscles as I pulled. Bulbs exploded one by one as they overloaded and I pulled the wire out of the ceiling mounts.

Thankfully, the voltage wasn't strong enough anymore to kill me, and I watched in the faint light as the burns on my hands cleared up right before my eyes.

Older Michele tied off one end of the hundred-foot length of continuous wire I had torn down around my waist.

As I lowered myself into the chilled water, I knew we were all silently praying the same thing.

We all hoped the cable was long enough and that the tunnel opened up again on the other side.

Right before I took my last big breath, the flashlight went out for the last time. In the silence and the darkness, I knew that it was up to me to find the other end of the flooded underground tunnel.

I took a big breath and sunk into the ice-cold water, the freezing water urging my body to suddenly expel the air I had taken in.

It had only been a few seconds since I had submerged, but as I swam forward through the darkness I could feel my lungs already craving their next breath of fresh air.

Chapter 106

I felt my way through the darkness as I swam, being careful to stay close to the ceiling of the flooded tunnel at all times. If there was a pocket of air anywhere in the pitch black water, I wanted to find it right away before my lungs gave out.

The wire around my waist dug into my hips, making it difficult to swim quickly. This was compounded by my lack of experience in water.

In the darkness, with nothing to see around me, my mind's eye replayed the time when Robert taught me how to swim during our first vacation in Florida.

With the vast crystal blue ocean less than a hundred feet from us, we spent an entire afternoon in the shallow end of the hotel pool while Robert kept assuring me that he wouldn't let me drown in four feet of water. By the end of our impromptu session, I could flounder my way from one side of the pool to the other on a single breath.

But I could always lift my head and take a breath if I needed it. That was not a choice in the flooded underground tunnel where I thrashed my way forward through the pitch black water.

My lungs ached as I pulled myself through the water; each stroke burning up precious oxygen while slowly advancing me further through the tunnel.

If I didn't get to the other end soon, I wouldn't be able to keep my body from taking a deep breath of water.

I exhaled the last of my air through my nose and my body started to spasm.

I knew I wouldn't stay dead if I drowned. But if there was no way forward, it meant we would have to go back. I had seen the flashlight fail just as I entered the water and knew the other Micheles were waiting silently in the dark for me to tug on the wire and let them know I had made it.

But I hadn't made it.

I fought against my lungs' desire to expand. I clawed at the ceiling with both hands while floating on my back, trying to keep me moving forward.

This had to be the way out.

I kicked at the ceiling with my feet and wanted to scream, but I had no more oxygen in my lungs to make it happen.

My last kick angled me downward. With no air in my lungs for buoyancy, I sank through the water.

My back bumped against the floor of the flooded tunnel and stopped my forward progression.

I wanted to just let the water fill my lungs and let the others pull me back.

Back to what?

There was no life for us going back.

Austin's words echoed in my head, drowning out every other thought.

"You can be defeated. But never give up."

I arched my back and saw his face. Then it faded away as a faint light shimmered above me.

I remembered this.

It was the light at the end of the tunnel.

I was dying, and my body was showing me that light again.

I frowned at the light.

It was as brilliant as I remembered from the first time, but it didn't remind me of the last time exactly. However, it did remind me of something else.

As I watched the shimmering light, I was once again back on my trip to Florida with Robert.

But instead of learning how to swim, it reminded me of the shimmering moonlight reflecting off the surface of the ocean that same night.

My lungs tried to suck in the water, but I wasn't ready to give up just yet and covered my nose and mouth with a hand.

I wanted to hold on to this memory just a little longer before I succumbed to the inevitable.

I pushed off the floor and shot up toward the sparkling light. I was on my way to heaven.

Or was it hell?

Who knew where my soul would wait as my body was pulled back to where the other Micheles waited in total darkness.

I broke through the surface at the same moment my body rebelled against my wishes and took a big breath.

My gasps echoed in the hollow space where the tunnel rose up out of the water. I glanced at the ceiling. Faint light streamed in between the warped wooden boards that lined the ceiling.

It took me a moment to realize what I was looking at. It was the underside of a poorly constructed wooden planked floor in one of the abandoned homesteader's houses that dotted the lake islands.

There was just enough light coming in through the closely spaced wooden slats to see that the tunnel ended a few feet away. I crawled out of the chilly water and flopped onto my back. I had reached the other end of the tunnel.

I calculated the distance we had walked in my head. I must be under a house on one of the other islands near Dr. Westcott's private complex.

It was time to tell my sisters that we were almost free.

I grabbed the wire and gave it three strong tugs. When I felt the responding tugs, I dug my feet into the soft dirt floor and held the wire tightly so the other Micheles could use it to pull themselves quickly through the water to where I was waiting for them.

Bubbles broke the surface of the water moments before Older Michele popped up and took a big gasping breath.

I helped her out of the water and then pulled three more times on the cable, letting Younger Michele know we were ready for her to join us.

In half the time it took Older Michele to cross the same distance, Younger Michele popped up from the water and crawled quickly out of the water. She looked back at the inky blackness with a pained expression on her face, no doubt still unable to shake her past experiences.

Once we were all three together, I took the chance to look around the end of the tunnel. At first, I thought the end had collapsed, but upon closer inspection, the room was too well defined to be an accident.

It looked like we were in a basement that was nothing more than a square hole cut into the ground below the house that was sitting on top of it.

Unfortunately, the ceiling for this small space was several feet above our heads.

Younger Michele was on her tiptoes and doing her best to peer through a gap between the boards in the ceiling. She finally gave up and looked at us.

"I can't see anything. Maybe it's a summer rental and nobody is around."

I nodded.

"That would make it easier for us to get out without scaring anyone. If I stand on your back, or you stand on mine, we can just reach up enough to push on one of those planks."

Younger Michele dropped to her hands and knees and shuffled closer to me.

I started to step up when she sat up quickly and pointed at my feet.

"Take your shoes off first."

I used my toes against the heels to force my wet shoes off my feet.

Once I was no longer going to kill her back with the tread of my shoes, Younger Michele dropped back down.

"That's much better," she said and kept her arms rigid as I climbed onto her.

I pushed up against the boards. They flexed only slightly, dust settling down as the boards creaked against each other.

I pushed up again. The boards groaned as they flexed under my pressure.

I thought I felt one of the boards starting to give when the platform under my feet gave way and I fell in a heap on top of Younger Michele.

Younger Michele rolled to one side and sat up, her face wincing.

"Sorry. My elbow just gave out without warning."

We had decided to switch positions when Older Michele held up a rusted shovel that she had found lying by the water's edge.

"Maybe we can use this to break through."

I took the shovel and flipped it over, jabbing the spade up into the widest gap in the ceiling. It hung there, the end of the handle a few feet off the ground, but at least I didn't need to climb up on anyone's back to manipulate it. I worked it back and forth, the gap widening in the floorboards above us.

As the gap enlarged, I shoved it deeper into the space and worked it back and forth harder until I heard the wood splinter. I looked away as sawdust sprinkled down on my head and filtered into my hair.

Some of the dust tickled at my nose and I sneezed.

Loudly.

I froze when I heard something shift above us, like a chair had been scooted across the floor abruptly in response to my monster sneeze.

I held my breath and listened.

The other Micheles were also staring up at the ceiling as if they had heard something too. We looked at each other. Younger Michele pointed in the same spot I thought I had heard the sound come from.

I nodded and we remained silent for nearly ten minutes, breathing as quietly as possible and straining to hear above us.

When nothing else happened, Older Michele walked quietly over to me and leaned in close to whisper in my ear.

"Keep trying. If someone's up there, we can just deal with it."

I nodded my agreement and pulled on the shovel, stopping as soon as I heard the floorboards creak again above us from the pressure.

I stopped and listened.

Nothing else moved around upstairs.

I would have doubted I had even heard something in the first place if it weren't for the fact we had all heard it.

After another minute of silence, I continued pulling on the handle of the shovel until the first floorboard gave way with a crack.

I fell backward, catching myself before I landed on my butt on the hard ground.

With one of the boards gone, Younger Michele snatched up the shovel and used it like an axe to cut away more of the old and brittle boards until there was a hole big enough for us to climb through.

With nothing to stand on so we could give ourselves a boost

up through the hole, I looked at Younger Michele.

Her shoulders dropped, but I put my hand out and kept her from climbing on all fours.

"You go first, and then we both help Michele up."

She looked at me.

"Who will you stand on to reach the hole?"

I shrugged.

"I'll jump, I guess."

She nodded her agreement and I got onto the floor. She removed her shoes and tossed them through the hole ahead of her.

She climbed on my back and I nearly collapsed when she launched herself up.

Skillfully, she pulled herself up through the hole, then spun around and reached a hand down, looking at Older Michele.

"Your turn."

Older Michele repeated Younger Michele's actions and climbed up on my back, grasping Younger Michele's hand to steady her as she vaulted up through the hole.

My muscles screamed in protest, but she was up and through.

I stood and looked up as they both reached down toward me.

I jumped up and fell short without even reaching their outstretched fingers.

I crouched lower and jumped again.

This time, our hands touched, but gravity overcame me before any of us could get a grip.

I was bending my knees in preparation for one final big jump when bubbles broke the surface of the water at the far end of the tunnel.

I looked toward the sound and my heart hammered wildly in response to the head that popped up out of the water.

I snatched up the shovel and held it like a baseball bat as the head in the water kept coming, trailing a large body behind it as one of Dr. Westcott's guards exited the water and rushed straight toward me.

I swung the shovel and was rewarded with a heavy thudding sound as it connected with the guard and he went down at my feet.

I threw down the shovel and looked up.

The two Michele's were both staring dumbfounded at the guard at my feet.

I reached up.

"Catch me," I yelled as I stood on the guard's ten-inch barrel chest and jumped up.

The guard's body gave me those few extra inches I needed.

They wrapped their hands around my wrists and both pulled simultaneously, hauling me up through the hole.

They both fell backward, with me collapsing on top of them, laughing.

We had made it.

We had escaped from Dr. Westcott and were finally free.

We all stood up and tried to dust ourselves off, which didn't work out so well since our wet clothes had converted all the dust into a thin layer of mud.

Younger Michele looked around her and swatted at the air around her face.

Older Michele looked around as well; confused.

"Do you hear that?" Older Michele said.

Younger Michele looked at her in alarm.

"You hear it too?"

Older Michele nodded her head, and then looked at me with a shocked look on her face.

"You don't hear that?"

I listened, but didn't hear anything.

I shook my head.

Younger Michele was looking around her in a panic.

"It's so loud. How can you not hear that?"

By the time they were covering their ears, I realized what was happening. Before I could say anything, both Micheles dropped to the floor unconscious.

I knelt next to Older Michele and shook her.

"Michele?"

She was out cold.

They both were.

Footfalls echoed across the floor and I heard someone enter the room right before a shadow fell across the three of us.

Slowly, I looked up to see the smiling face of Dr. Westcott, flanked by guards.

Chapter 107

She looked at me and smiled.

"How could you possibly think I didn't know about the old rum runners' tunnel that went from Rattlesnake Island to this house?"

She pointed at the two Micheles lying on the dust encrusted floor.

"Bring them."

Two guards rushed forward, slung their rifles over their shoulders, and each lifted a Michele. They disappeared out the front door leaving Westcott with only two guards to protect her from me. One of them moved in behind me, his rifle pointing at my back.

Westcott regarded me coolly.

"Out of all the clones, you have been the most trouble."

I sneered at her.

"You're welcome."

Her smile faded and she nodded to the guard behind me.

A jab in my back sent me stumbling forward. I spun around and smacked the gun barrel away. I would like to say that being immortal was liberating and made me fear nothing, not even death.

But the reality was, with Austin gone; I no longer cared about being alive.

The guard hit me across the face with the butt of his rifle. The impact sent me sprawling to the floor. I started to get up when both guards pointed their rifles at me.

I stayed on the ground, pressing the heel of my hand against my nose to stem the flow of blood.

"Do it." I said.

The guards inched in and I could see the murder in their eyes as their fingers flexed on the triggers. Maybe they could make death stick this time.

"Do it!" I screamed.

"Stop!" Westcott hollered.

The two guards lowered their rifles and took a step back.

Westcott looked down at me, and then did something unexpected. She held her hand out to help me up.

I took it and stood.

She shook her head.

"I know you better than you know yourself. Your friend isn't dead. He's waiting to be reunited with you right now."

I looked at her, my heart thudding heavily in my chest.

Could it be true?

Or was she lying to me?

I realized she didn't have the best track record for telling me the truth.

She smiled again, warmer this time.

"Here, look out the window at the dock."

I slowly walked over and peered out the window. The two unconscious Micheles were being loaded onto a boat sitting at the nearby dock. Next to the boat, a single guard stood with his gun held on a lone figure.

When the captive turned to the side, I recognized his face in profile.

It was Austin.

I looked at her in alarm.

"He's alive?"

"If you behave, maybe you can keep him that way."

She waved her hand at the open front door.

"After you."

I left the house and, as soon as I was off the porch, began running.

Austin saw me coming and held his arms wide to accept me into them.

He hugged me tightly and I kissed his face repeatedly.

We stayed in each other's arms until Westcott caught up to us standing on the dock. As she approached, Austin pushed me back, positioning himself between us.

Westcott laughed. It was a harsh barking sound.

"If anybody should be sheltering the other with their body, it should be her. She's the one who can't die."

Austin "You won't get away with this."

Westcott rolled her eyes in response to his outburst.

"How cliché. So what is it I am supposed to say now? Oh, right."

She cleared her throat and looked at him sternly, adopting a British accent as she spoke.

"But you see, I already have."

Just then, one of the guards yelped and toppled backward off the dock and into the water.

A second guard yelped and collapsed on the dock, sliding several inches from the impact of a sniper rifle bullet.

The remaining three guards were taken down before they could do anything.

The only people still standing on the dock were Westcott, Austin, and myself. All the guards were lying in pools of their own blood or in the water with a ring of red forming around them.

Westcott was looking around in a panic at her dead guards when her cell phone rang.

She looked at Austin as she answered it.

Despite not saying anything when she put the phone to her ear, it was evident that the caller on the other side knew she had answered.

She listened without saying a word. Her eyes smoldered as she glared at Austin, trying to kill him with a look.

She jerked her head to suddenly look out over the water.

I followed her gaze and saw a boat in the distance heading this way.

Westcott looked back at me and her eyes narrowed, not liking what she was hearing.

Her eyes snapped to Austin and she listened some more. After several minutes of silence, she finally spoke into the phone.

"Yes. I agree to those terms."

She lowered the phone and tucked it back in her pocket, a smile spreading across her evil face. It was a wicked smile that sent shivers up my spine.

She tilted her head at Austin and held her hand up, waving her fingertips up and down at him.

"Goodbye," she said.

Austin jerked back at the same moment I heard the impact of the bullet. He spun sideways off the dock and into the water with a loud splash.

I heard myself scream his name as Dr. Westcott rushed forward and grabbed me from behind, keeping me from jumping into the water after him.

"Let me go," I yelled as I struggled against her unusually strong grip.

"It's too late," she said soothingly in my ear. "He's gone. But it's not too late for you."

"No!" I yelled and my legs lost their strength and Dr. Westcott lowered me carefully to the dock just as a boat pulled in, cutting off my view of Austin as his body floated away from the dock.

I sat there, practically in Westcott's lap, and looked through the haze of tears as several armed men jumped from the boat and surrounded us.

They parted slightly to let someone walk into their midst. I looked up to see Robert smiling down at me.

Then his gaze shifted to Westcott behind me and his smile was gone in an instant.

"Where is she?"

Westcott indicated the other boat tied to the dock. Robert pointed and several men removed the other two Michele's, still unconscious, from the other boat.

He watched as they were brought carefully onto his boat and safely secured.

When that was done, he looked back down at us. Westcott's grip on me tightened.

He leaned over and pried Westcott's hands off my arms and helped me to my feet.

He placed his arm around me. As he led me to his boat, I looked back at her. She sat on the dock, watching us go. There was no malice or hatred in her eyes. Only sadness.

"It's okay," he said calmly. "Everything's okay now."

As we climbed on the boat, I looked over the side and saw my whole world lying face down in the lake. Austin was ringed by a thin film of red that had been disturbed by the wake created when Robert's boat arrived.

Robert's driver started up the boat, and ignoring everything in the water, throttled the boat past Austin's body and then took off into the lake. Austin's body sunk under the surface when the boat ran him over and my heart went with him.

"Is it really her?" Robert asked.

I turned and saw Robert hovering over the sleeping form of Older Michele. One of his guards was tending to her. Robert looked at me.

"What happened to her?"

I pointed to the space behind my ear.

"Westcott installed some kind of stunner device behind our ears that renders us unconscious."

Robert frowned at me.

"Why didn't it knock you out too?"

I looked back at the island that retreated quickly into the distance, the tears welling up.

I didn't answer him as I watched my future recede away.

Chapter 108

The boat ride lasted less than half an hour before we were shuffled onto a private jet on one of the larger islands. As we took off into the sky, I looked down at the small grouping of islands that had given me life, and then just as indifferently, took it away.

With the other Michele's still out cold, Robert focused his attention on me once we were in the air.

He sat down in the seat across from me and smiled.

"How are you doing, Michele?"

I looked at him.

"How do you think?"

His expression became pained.

"This wasn't how this was supposed to happen."

I shot him an angry look and couldn't help raising my voice.

"Oh really, Robert? How was this all supposed to go down?"

He paused briefly before replying.

"When I thought she was dead, you were supposed to remember who you were and we could live out our lives together."

"But those memories would have been false. I'm not the real Michele."

"You are her clone. There is no discernable difference."

I scowled at him.

"Is that the bullshit Westcott's been feeding you?"

"Not bullshit. That's science."

"Maybe scientifically we are the same. Same DNA. Same genes. Same fingerprints. But let me clue you in on a little secret. Up here."

I tapped my temple.

"We are not the same."

"Westcott said she could copy your memories over…"

"They're not my memories!" I yelled a little too loudly. "God, Robert! Are you even listening to yourself?"

I pointed to Older Michele sleeping in the seat across the aisle.

"I am not her. I never was. I never will be."

He looked at her, and then back to me.

"I just thought…"

"No, Robert. You weren't thinking. Maybe if you had, none of this would have happened. To any of us."

"But… but, I had lost her."

I leaned forward, placing my hands on his knees.

"And now you have her back. The real her. Not some copy or attempt at recreating what you once had."

He sat back and stared at me. I could see the tears welling up in the lower part of his eyes.

"I'm sorry."

I let out a breath.

"For what exactly?"

"You will be dying soon."

I laughed. His face became confused.

"Why are you laughing?"

"I'm not dying, Robert. In fact, it's quite the opposite."

"But the clones. They all die within five years."

"That was another of Westcott's lies. She was killing us so she could keep working to perfect her memory transfer process."

Robert was shaking his head.

"No. Every one of you got sicker, and then died."

I looked him deeply in the eyes.

"No, Robert. Westcott was poisoning us so that we looked sick. I had stopped taking the medication last year, and was getting better. But you were too blinded by past experience to recognize it."

"That's not true."

"Westcott lied about a lot of things. She lied about that too. Look."

I pointed at Older Michele again.

"Westcott told you she had died from some African virus. There was no virus. How much do you want to bet, the people who kidnapped her while you were in Africa worked for Westcott."

Robert studied his original Michele.

"How could I have let her lie to me for this long?"

"Because you wanted to believe that there was still hope. There was still a future for love. Even after death. You loved her so much, you were willing to do anything to bring her back. And you did. There she is."

"I'm still sorry," Robert said and then stood up to move to another seat at the front of the plane.

"I know," I whispered silently to myself. "I'm sorry too."

Chapter 109

As we circled the Pittsburgh International Airport, Older Michele finally woke up. As soon as she saw Robert, I watched the years apart melt away. They embraced and I knew they finally had their happily ever after.

They talked quietly the whole time we were landing, and finally she stood up to walk out of the plane. I couldn't leave just yet. I had one more thing to do. I gave Younger Michele a long hug. She returned it with a warm embrace that encompassed me lovingly. "Thank you for being the stronger one," she said. "Thank you for doing what I was too afraid to do." I held on to her tightly, holding the tears back as she continued. "Despite being clones, we are both unique with our own strengths and weaknesses." She finally released me and held me at arm's length, smiling sadly. "Are you sure you don't want to come with us? We are going to try to find Michele number ten and rescue her. I don't think it would take much convincing to get Robert to wait for you."

I shook my head and headed for the front of the plane.

"I would only get in the way."

Older Michele joined me at the open door. "You would never be in the way."

"Still, I think its best I separate from the group. Find my own way."

We stopped at the bottom of the stairs and stood together on the tarmac next to the plane.

"Where are you going?"

"I just want to pick up a couple of things from the house. After that, I don't know. But thanks to Robert's generous gift, I can afford to go anywhere. I can even afford to be someone else. I kind of like the name Athena."

Older Michele smiled.

"Ahh, the Greek goddess who sprang to life fully grown."

We laughed together.

It felt good to laugh.

Older Michele faced me and held my shoulders gently. "Please don't fault him for what he did."

I smiled at her. "Meeting you told me everything I needed to know to understand why he did it."

A limousine, accompanied by two SUVs, one in front and one behind, pulled up to the plane. It was there to take me back to the home that Robert and I had shared for several years. He had promised me that the cameras had all been disabled and that I would be safe there for a little while.

"Last chance, Athena," Older Michele said with a smile. "The other one is staying with us. Once we save the last Michele, we will find a place that even Westcott and her people can't reach."

"That's the thing," I replied. "I don't want to be thought of as one of the other ones."

Her face fell.

"I'm sorry. I didn't mean…"

I smiled warmly and reached up to place a hand softly on her shoulder.

"I know. But I need to make my own life. And I need to do it alone."

It's not that I wanted to be alone, but Austin was gone and I no longer had that choice.

"Okay," she replied. "If you ever need us, you know how to get in touch with us."

I nodded.

I waited by the side of the limousine and waved one last time as Robert met Older Michele at the top of the stairs and they waved to me. I stayed perfectly still until Robert's private jet lifted into the sky. I stood motionless next to the limousine, my vision blurred from the tears that welled up and wouldn't stop.

My life was empty.

Not because Robert was gone.

Not because the other Micheles were gone.

But because Austin was gone.

My life was a blank page.

I could write anything on it I wanted. But there was one thing I could never write. There was no happily ever after among those pages for me.

A soft voice interrupted my downward spiraling thoughts. "Excuse me, ma'am?"

I turned to look at the limousine driver whose eyes were filled with concern. "Are you okay?" he asked.

I wiped away the tears and did my best to smile. "Yes. I'm sorry. I'm ready, let's go."

I climbed into the limousine and the driver immediately pulled away, the two SUVs moving into position to protect me. I felt like a Hollywood star or political dignitary in my own little motorcade.

There was no way Westcott could know where I was headed. Even Robert had no idea where I was headed despite what I had told him about stopping by our old house. There was nothing there for me and I had another destination in mind.

I rolled down the interior divider and told the driver I wanted him to take me to a different place.

"Are you sure, Ma'am? I was told a different address."

"Yes," I said. "That is where I really want to go."

Chapter 110

The limousine pulled up in front of Simone's house and stopped. I looked through the tinted glass at the place where I first met Austin.

It was my desire to warn Robert that had brought me back here when I knew it was risky. And it was after Simone had called the police that Austin came into my life.

Most relationships started with the man pursuing the woman, and ours was no different.

He had pursued me until he caught me.

I smiled briefly, thinking about how excited he had been that I had proven to be a worthy adversary. I wondered if his attraction had started from that very moment. I remembered the look in his eyes as he arrested me.

Then my thoughts focused on how much he had risked keeping me safe when Westcott's mercenaries had come for me at the police station.

He had gambled with his own life, and lost.

My smile faded and I fought back the tears.

So many innocents had lost their lives in Westcott's war. The very thing she had been fighting against, she had caused in so many.

I saw the blinds spread open on the front window, then close again just as quickly.

Good. She was home.

I lowered the divider and spoke with the driver.

"Can you please ask Simone to join me?"

He turned in his seat to look at me.

"Ma'am?"

"Just ask the woman in that house to come to the car."

"Yes, Ma'am."

The driver climbed out of the car and walked up to the front door. As he raised a finger to ring the bell, the door opened. While I couldn't see Simone standing directly behind the driver, I could see her orbit of hair poking out around the head of the driver.

He turned and pointed at the limousine.

Simone frowned and then shook her head "no", her hair taking a moment to catch up with her movements.

The driver walked back and stood next to my window. I rolled it down just enough to talk with him.

He bent down and peered into the open slit.

"She refuses to come out. But, she says you are welcome to go inside."

I looked through the crack of the window toward the house. Simone was still standing in the doorway. That was a good sign.

She hadn't run.

Yet.

I opened my door and stepped out of the limousine. As soon as I stepped out, the two men in the rear SUV climbed out and looked around them as they both took positions on the sidewalk. The two men in the front SUV did the same thing.

Simone's eyes widened, but she stayed by the open front door.

"Thank you," I said to the driver. "I won't be long."

He closed the door and took his position next to it.

"I will be waiting right here for you, Ma'am."

I looked at the large men in tight black business suits and dark sunglasses that stood alongside the SUVs. It was like they were advertising that someone important was at this very spot.

I walked slowly up the front walkway and stopped just before the porch.

"Hi, Simone," I said.

She placed balled fists on her hips and looked at me judgmentally.

"Why do you keep on coming back here?"

"I thought you should know the truth."

"What truth? The truth about the non-existent cameras in my house or why you took over Michele's life after she died?"

She looked at the limousine behind me and then back to me.

"Are you some kind of rich bitch that likes to experience living other people's lives? Do you get your kicks seeing how the other half live?"

"It's not like that at all."

She squared her shoulders and leaned toward me.

"Then, pray tell, what is this shit about?"

"If you'll let me inside, I promise to tell you everything."

She looked at me curiously.

"Everything?"

I nodded.

"Everything."

"What is there to tell?"

"A lot."

She squinted one eye at me.

"Is it good?"

I smiled as I remembered what she had said to me the last time we actually talked like civilized human beings.

"It's better than good. It's delicious."

Chapter 111

I spent the next two hours telling Simone everything, leaving nothing out; not even what happened to Austin.

The full cup of tea in her hand had gone cold. She hadn't shed a tear during my entire monologue, not even when I described the death of Austin, and just listened like I was telling her about some movie I had seen on the Syfy channel. I had to admit, telling it all at once like this made it sound like science fiction; and I had lived it.

She squinted at me.

"You're telling me that you can live forever."

"Not forever, just a thousand years or so."

Simone laughed.

"Might as well be forever. That's incredible."

"It's a curse, let me tell you."

"So, which one are you?" she said coolly.

"What do you mean?"

"You said there were several clones. Which one were you?"

I held my hand up and showed her the tattoo on my wrist.

"I was number seven."

"And they killed the rest?"

"All but Eight, Ten, and myself. They kept the original Michele alive so they could keep working to improve us. I guess their process required the original to be alive for the memory transfer."

Simone set her tea down and leaned over, poking and prodding at my face.

"You popped out of the test tube as an adult?"

I let her finish and sit back before rubbing my face and stretching my jaw.

"That's what they tell me."

She studied me silently for a long time before startling me with her outburst.

"Bullshit."

"Not bullshit," I countered.

She looked around the room.

"Now I wish there were cameras in my walls. It might explain why you have been lying to me all this time."

"I'm not lying."

"Bullshit!"

I stood up and headed for the kitchen.

"I'll show you."

I scanned the countertop, found what I was looking for, and yanked the largest knife out of the knife block.

I spun around and Simone jumped up from the couch.

"Easy, Michele, I'm just saying that everything you told me is a little hard to swallow, that's all."

"Relax," I said. "I'm not going to hurt you."

I spun the knife around and stabbed myself in the chest.

I screamed.

Simone screamed.

I pulled the knife out and blood spurted from my punctured heart.

Simone kept screaming.

I dropped to my knees, the knife clattering to the floor next to me as my vision tunneled.

Simone regained her composure and rushed for the phone on the wall.

"Stop," I croaked. "Wait."

She paused, the phone in her hand.

I shakily stood up, stretched my arms out wide, and arched my back as I let out another scream.

Simone backed up, the phone still clutched in her hand.

I let out a huge gasp, feeling the warmth spreading through my body as it dealt with the injury until the pain subsided.

I straightened myself and walked closer to Simone. I looked down at my blood-soaked shirt and pulled the collar down. Wiping away the blood, I showed her that my skin had healed completely. I looked up with a disarming smile on my face.

"See. I can't be killed."

She gawked at my chest, and then her eyes sought out mine right before they rolled up into her skull and I had to grab her to keep her from hitting her head on the floor as she passed out.

Chapter 112

Simone's eyes fluttered and she looked up at me. I had her head resting in my lap and a cool washcloth draped across her forehead.

"What happened?" she asked.

"You fainted."

She sat up quickly, catching the wet cloth as it dropped from her forehead.

"Not that."

She pointed at my chest.

"That."

"I told you. I'm a clone. Not only will I live for a thousand years, but it is damn near impossible to kill me."

She looked back at me, the fear written in her eyes.

"If I promise to believe you, will you not do that ever again?"

I smiled.

She calmed slightly and smiled back uneasily.

"I don't blame you. It came as an even bigger shock when Westcott shot me. When everything went dark and my body heated up, I thought I was bound for hell. It was just my body going into overdrive for the healing process."

Simone looked at me.

"So, what are you going to do now?"

I let out a long breath before responding.

I had given this plenty of thought, but really didn't have an answer that made sense since all of them had included Austin in my plans.

"I really don't know."

"Why did you come back here? This wasn't your place."

"I thought you deserved the truth. The last time we spoke…"

"Spoke?" she laughed. "I recall a lot of screaming and waving about of kitchen utensils, but not a lot of talking."

"I couldn't leave it like that. You were so sad when you thought your Michele was dead. And then when you saw me."

She nodded.

"That was the most terrifying experience of my life."

She looked at my chest and then back up to me.

"Well, second most terrifying experience."

"I thought you deserved to know everything."

"Weren't you afraid I might tell someone?"

"Without me around to stab myself to death, who's going to believe you?"

"Good point."

We stared silently at each other for a long time before I realized I had done everything I had come for.

I clapped my hands on my thighs and stood up.

"Well, I guess this is goodbye."

She stood up with me.

"You're leaving?"

I nodded.

"Robert gave me enough money to live out the rest of my life."

Suddenly I laughed at that absurd notion with who I was now.

"Although I don't think it will last me a full thousand years. But maybe long enough to let anyone who still remembers me to pass on. Then I can go anywhere and be anyone."

Simone looked at me strangely.

"Have you ever seen Highlander?"

"What is a Highlander?"

"The movie starring a hunky Christopher Lambert. Well, he's getting old now, but he was apparently hot as shit back when they made it."

"Is it on Netflix?"

"I don't know. But it was about a man who was immortal. And it dealt with him staying young forever while everyone around him aged and died, including his wife. The movie came out before I was born, but it's a timeless story."

She winced at her comment.

"No pun intended. But you might want to check it out if you have the time."

She slapped her head and shook it.

"Listen to me. I think you have more time than anyone has ever had before. See that movie if you are interested in a preview of what to expect."

I didn't think I wanted to know, but I smiled anyway.

"Thanks. I will look for it."

After another protracted silence, I turned toward the door.

"Thank you for listening to me Simone. I doubt anyone else will be bothering you about this."

I noticed the spray of blood all around her kitchen.

"Did you want me to stay and help clean this up?"

"No. I can handle that. You should go."

I smiled weakly at the disgusting mess I was leaving for her.

"Are you sure?"

She nodded.

"If you stay, it will just get too awkward around here. I think it best we say our goodbyes and leave it at that."

I hugged her.

It was a stiff and uncomfortable hug.

As I headed out the door and down the walkway to the waiting cars, Simone leaned against the edge of the open door and watched me.

I looked at the three cars that made up my tiny little motorcade. I had half expected the men in tight suits to still be standing outside their vehicles where I had left them.

But then again, I had been inside the house with Simone for a couple of hours, and I really wasn't so important that they had to treat me like the Queen of England and stand at attention without blinking for hours on end.

I saw the two guards in the rear SUV sitting in the front seats, still wearing their sunglasses and staring straight ahead. It must be difficult to have a job where you always had to be serious and couldn't just sit and chat with your coworker.

I stopped at the door to the limousine and waited for the driver to get out and let me in. I didn't think I was too good to do it myself, but I had already been conditioned to be let into a limousine by someone else.

The front window rolled down and the driver called out.

"Go ahead and get in!"

I guess the honeymoon was over. I was no longer going to be

treated like a VIP.

I let myself into the limousine, the driver starting the car up as soon as I settled into my seat.

I lowered the window and waved one final time at Simone. She didn't wave back, but faded back into the shadows of her house and closed the door.

I sat back and realized, for the first time since I could remember, that I was truly alone. I realized how empty my life had been without even noticing. There were only a few people who knew I existed, even before my replica had jumped from the bridge.

I mentally ticked off the players in my small world as I thought about them.

Robert and the other Micheles had flown into the sunset, never to be seen again. They would most likely find Michele Ten and take her with them into hiding.

Dalton had died keeping me safe as a favor to Austin.

Austin in turn had died face down in one of the shallowest lakes in the world in order to save me.

Dr. Westcott had been defeated and I had enough money to build a new life and stay hidden from her forever.

Simone was the last of the old life that needed to be resolved. There was no one else to deal with from my old life.

I was finally free.

And it was lonely.

The limousine turned and I watched out the window as we accelerated down the street. I absently watched the corner, waiting for the rear SUV to follow us around the corner.

But it never did.

As we turned another corner, I looked down the street ahead of us, but the SUV in the lead was also missing.

Where were they?

I lowered the divider between my section of the limousine and the driver.

"Excuse me, driver?"

"Yes, Ma'am?" came the gruff reply.

"Where are the other cars that were with us?"

"I decided they were no longer needed."

"No longer needed? Didn't Robert order them to stay with us?"

"I really wouldn't know what Robert asked for, Ma'am."

I suddenly recognized the voice of the driver. It wasn't the same man who had picked me up at the airport.

My heart sank as I realized my error. There was still one person unaccounted for from my old life.

Nick turned his head and glanced at me sideways with a smile.

"Just relax, Michele. There is one more stop to make before this is over."

Chapter 113

Nick locked the doors and raised the divider.

I was trapped. I could have easily survived a jump from a speeding car, but the door refused to open when I pulled on the handle.

The limousine sped down the street and away from the main part of the city.

All I could do was watch out the window and wonder where Nick was taking me.

He must have promised to return me to Westcott as long as he was allowed to kill Austin.

That must have been the deal they had made when he had called her while we all stood on the dock.

But what use was I to her?

She needed the original Michele for her cloning process. I was only good to her dead.

A chill ran up my spine. I crawled to the front of the limousine and rapped my knuckles on the thick tinted glass of the divider.

Nick lowered it an inch. Enough for us to talk, but not enough for me to reach through it and wrap an arm around his neck, choke him, and climb from the wreckage after we crashed.

"Yes?" he said.

"Where are we going?"

"I'm not taking you back to Dr. Westcott, if that's what you are worried about."

"Then what do you want with me?"

"I need you for bait."

"Bait?"

"There is someone out there I want. The only way to get him to come out of hiding is to dangle the thing he wants most from my hook."

"Who wants me?"

"Austin."

My heart fluttered.

"He's dead. You shot him."

Nick laughed.

"I only slowed him down for a little while. My shot only took off the skin of his arm."

"You didn't kill him?"

"Of course not."

"I thought you wanted to kill him?"

"I do but not through a scope. That's too impersonal. No. I want to look him in the eyes when the life fades from them. I want him to know exactly who beat him."

My elation at finding out that Austin was still alive was short lived. I was going to be bait to draw him out so he could die anyway.

I didn't think my heart could live with that kind of guilt, I don't care how long my lifespan was supposed to be. I had lost Austin before because of me.

I wasn't about to let that happen again.

"Why do you want to kill him?"

He didn't say anything, so I pressed further.

"What did he do to make you hate him so much?"

He glanced back at me and then raised the divider.

I looked around the limousine for something to break my way out. All I found was a bottle of champagne in the ice bucket. The ice had long since melted and the champagne was warming up.

It didn't matter. I didn't feel like celebrating, but I could use it for something else.

I crawled through the back of the limousine and tried the door again. Still locked, and Nick wouldn't be tricked into unlocking it. But maybe I could trick him into opening the door.

I kicked at the side window that ran along the middle of the limousine.

My shoe slammed into it and it flexed with a loud thump.

I kicked at it again. The window flexed further.

Nick rolled down the divider an inch and yelled to me.

"What the hell are you doing back there?"

I ignored him and kicked at the window again; harder. This time it shattered, but the tinting held the shards of the glass together.

Nick lowered the divider further and craned his neck as I kicked at the shattered window.

The window buckled out with the impression of my shoe.

Nick swerved violently to the edge of the road and skidded to a halt; the tires shuddered on the pavement in a staccato pulse as I flew forward and cracked my head on the edge of the half-open divider.

I heard the door locks engage and Nick jumped out of the car, ran up the side of the long car, and flung open the back door.

"What the fuck are you…" he started, and then froze when he saw me.

As soon as he had stopped, I got into position and was ready for him. I aimed the champagne bottle at the open door while pressing up on the cork with my thumbs.

The cork shot out of the mouth of the bottle with a loud pop and hit him square in the face.

He fell backward and I was out the door. A swift kick to his face sent blood exploding from his nose.

I quickly scanned the area around me. On one side of the road were thick bushes and trees and on the other, behind a fence topped with barbed wire I recognized Dexter Yard, the Union Railroad train yard in East Pittsburgh.

I looked at the thick undergrowth and knew my chances for getting through that were less than acceptable. That left getting away through the rail yard.

I delivered one more kick to Nick's face and dashed across the street, leaping onto the chain link fence. I scrambled up one side, ignored the massive cuts from the barbed wire along the top, and dropped down the other side. As soon as I landed, I heard the sound of a bullet ricochet off the gravel at my feet.

I looked back through the fence at Nick.

He was on his feet and wiped away the blood from his eyes before he sighted down his silenced pistol at me again.

I turned just as the gun spat and the bullet whizzed by my head. I could feel the searing heat from the speeding bullet as it tore through my hair, missing my skin by millimeters.

It wouldn't have mattered overall. I wouldn't have stayed

dead. But being shot in the head would have slowed me down enough for Nick to capture me again.

And I wasn't going to let that happen.

If Nick didn't have me, Austin wouldn't walk knowingly into a trap under the pretext of saving my life yet again.

Now that I knew he was alive, the hope had returned, and I had a chance at my own happily ever after. But that would never happen if I let Nick kill Austin.

My leg burned hot and my foot shot out from under me as I ran. I cartwheeled out of control and fell face first into the gravel, bits of granite and limestone chipping at my teeth and tearing open big gashes on my lips.

I rolled over on my back and sat up quickly.

Nick was clawing his way over the fence. He had thrown his jacket over the top of the barbed wire and was climbing over easily without being sliced into hamburger meat.

I felt the heat increase where the bullet had shattered my ankle and watched dumfounded as my foot twisted back into the proper position and healed almost instantly.

My face burned less hotly, but I ran my tongue over my teeth to find them smooth and whole again.

I wiped the blood off my face and was on my feet, running again when I heard Nick bellow behind me.

"You can't run from me, bitch!"

I ignored him and darted around the edge of a railcar at the same moment a bullet sparked off the corner.

I tripped on a railroad tie and broke two fingers when I hit the ground hard.

I cried out as they reset themselves. This was getting surreal, and a bit unnerving.

If I was capable of doing this, why was I running?

I was no longer a victim in life.

I had a say.

And it was a big say.

It was time to be immortal.

I didn't need to fear injury.

I didn't need to fear death.

I didn't need to fear Nick.

Chapter 114

I realized that I wasn't afraid for myself. I was afraid for Austin. My body couldn't be killed easily, but my happiness was barely hanging on by a thread.

I had been granted the chance to be with Austin, and I was going to do everything in my power to keep it.

For that reason, I had to keep running. The longer I stayed away from Nick, the longer Austin stayed alive. If I could get away completely, Austin would find me, no matter where I was in the world.

Of that, I was certain.

A bullet pinged off the railcar to my left and I dropped down, rolling to one side under the railcar. I pulled myself up out of view and held my breath as Nick ran to where he last saw me.

He panted loudly and grumbled to himself as he ducked, looking under every rail car. I pulled myself tighter against the underside and waited.

Nick stood up and ran off.

Even though he was no longer near me, Nick was still between me and love.

He had to be stopped.

And there was only one person in the world who was capable of stopping him.

But I had to get to him first.

And before I could do that, I had to get away from Nick.

I dropped from the underside of the rail car and got to my feet, looking all around me as I did. I half expected Nick to jump at me from the top of a rail car, like how it always happened in the movies. But fortunately for me I wasn't living in a movie and it didn't happen.

I picked my way through the rail yard, pausing every now and then when I thought I heard something shift the gravel near me. I tried my best to remember what Austin had been trying to teach me about moving silently through my environment.

I smiled at the memory of when we were going through the forest, and he moved as silently as a light breeze while I stepped on every crackling leaf and broken twig. I swore I was following directly in his footsteps, but it didn't make any difference.

I knew that, to a man like Nick, I was probably making as much noise as a herd of stampeding elephants, but I did my best to roll my feet from heel to toe and not disturb the gravel any more than absolutely necessary.

The gravel crunched loudly with each step as the tiny rocks ground against one another. The sounds echoed off the sides of the hollow rail cars all around me making me cringe with each slow and steady step.

As much as I was thankful that Nick hadn't found me yet, I was still surprised that he hadn't. Suddenly, my shoulder exploded with an intense burning pain right before the metal dented in on the rail car next to me with the echoing clang of a gong struck by a mallet. As blood splattered the rusted metal wall, I spun from the impact of the bullet.

I was too quick to determine that I had managed to escape from Nick. I was acting like prey, and he was the ultimate hunter.

I ducked a split second before the next bullet impacted against the metal where my head was a half-breath ago.

I took off at a full run, bullets pinging around me. I darted between two rail cars and ran as fast as I could across the yard, keeping a careful eye on the tracks. I didn't want to get tripped up again and give Nick any kind of edge.

My shoulder burned hotly as I felt the wound seal up and the pain subsided more quickly than before. My body was getting used to the accelerated healing process and was becoming more efficient.

I ran with no destination in mind and followed the tracks toward the river. I knew I could never get away from Nick if I stayed in the train yard. He would be able to hunt me down, no matter where I tried to hide.

I had to get as far away from him as possible.

As I reached the edge of the river, I heard the revving of a motor. I looked and saw the limousine, with Nick at the wheel, barreling down the road that would meet up with the tracks I was on.

The only thing that separated me from the speeding limousine was the chain link fence that was locked with a heavy chain and had the requisite "No Trespassing" and "Authorized Vehicles Only" signs.

Nick ignored the locked fence, and its warning signs, and kept his foot on the accelerator, his face lighting up with glee when he spotted me on the other side.

I spun around and ran faster down the tracks, only touching every other blackened railroad tie as I adopted a steady rhythm and forced myself to run faster.

Behind me the limousine tore through the chain link mesh like it was tissue paper and kept coming.

I glanced back. Nick glared at me through the spider webbed front windshield and steered the limousine onto the railroad tracks.

The car jumped the tracks and the tires beat a steady rhythm on the railroad ties as it caught up to me. If only my immortal life included increased speed, strength, or even stamina. Hell, I would have loved to have been able to fly away at that very moment. Up, up, and away like Superman.

And suddenly, I was flying.

As I pinwheeled into the air, I realized that both my legs were broken and I hadn't really taken off in flight on my own.

I came back to earth to land on the hood of the limousine. Nick slammed on the brakes and I went tumbling over the front of the hood and settled into a crumpled heap across the tracks.

My bones hadn't started to heal yet as Nick jumped from the car and walked over to me.

For some reason, I pictured him wearing a black cloak, stovepipe hat, and twirling his finely waxed handlebar mustache as he looked at me lying helpless across the railroad tracks.

He bent down, scooped me up in his arms, and lifted me.

I cried out from the pain that racked every inch of my body.

"Hush, my darling. Everything's going to be all right. Trust me."

He loaded me into the trunk, making sure to remove anything I might use as a weapon. He looked down at me with his hands on the trunk lid.

"I can see why Austin likes you. But trust me; you'll be better off without him."

And with that, he slammed the lid shut, leaving me to slowly heal from my multiple injuries in the gloom of my mobile prison cell.

Chapter 115

It felt like we had been traveling for hours when the car stopped and I heard the shocks groan when Nick climbed out of the driver's seat. He opened the trunk and then stepped back quickly, holding a shotgun casually pointed at me.

"It's time to get you ready for your date."

I slowly stepped out. He waved the shotgun at me.

"I'm using three inch slugs powerful enough to stop a bear. I may not kill you outright, but trust me, you don't want to be hit by what comes out of this bad boy."

I looked at the single barrel shotgun, and then at the space around me. At first, I thought the sun had gone down, but realized Nick had pulled the limousine into a massive warehouse. I could see the glint of sunlight coming through the bent seams of the overlapping galvanized steel panels.

I had no idea what was outside those walls, or even where we were. I had become completely disoriented in the trunk of the car. For all I knew, Nick could have driven around Pittsburgh for the past several hours and we could only be ten minutes from Simone's house. Or we could be hundreds of miles from civilization.

I looked at the steady grip he had on the shotgun. The barrel barely trembled in time to his heartbeat.

If I rushed him now, or tried to run away, he could cut me down before my first leg muscles twitched. It was no use.

I wasn't giving up, but I recognized easily enough when I had been defeated.

He backed away, never taking the shotgun off of me. He walked sideways, turning in a wide arc to get beside me, yet kept his distance in case I tried anything.

I had already decided not to, but he didn't know that.

He motioned with the barrel of his shotgun toward the stairs that led up to a small room that had been made of the same material as the warehouse walls, but was an upraised office so the foreman could keep a watchful eye on his workers.

"That way."

I walked slowly toward the stairs. When I reached the bottom, I stopped suddenly and turned toward Nick. He took a step back, yet didn't flinch at my unexpected move and kept the shotgun barrel pointed at my head.

He was probably guessing that blowing my head off would take me longer to heal from. I was also guessing that he was right.

"Keep going," he ordered.

"You never answered my question," I replied.

His forehead wrinkled in thought, and then he smiled as he nodded.

"Oh, right. Why do I want to kill Austin?"

I nodded.

He motioned for me to continue up the stairs with the shotgun.

"You're going to have to ask him that."

I stayed perfectly still.

"Why won't you tell me yourself?"

He squinted at me with both eyes, but kept the barrel trained unwaveringly on my head.

"I want him to admit to you what he did. If I tell you, you could forgive him. But if he tells you, himself? Well, let's just say that you will never get the image of what he describes out of your head. You might even want to kill him yourself."

"I would never want to kill Austin. I don't care what he did in the past."

Nick laughed.

"The past? This has nothing to do with the past. He is still doing it every day."

"I get that you are upset that the three of you were kicked out of the Army. Especially after the unique services you provided."

Nick lowered the shotgun and moved closer.

"What happened to the three of us was fucked up, but it's the way of the world. I got a good pension and don't need to work for the rest of my life."

"I thought you were mad at him for letting the team get broken up and each of you discharged."

Nick laughed.

"Oh my god! Is that what he told you? That doesn't mean shit to me. I'm not pissed off for anything Austin did in the past. It's what he's doing to me every day that I can't stand."

"I don't get it."

He pointed the shotgun at me again.

"You don't have to. Now, move."

I climbed the stairs, wondering what Nick was talking about. I went over every conversation I had with Dalton and Austin. From what I could tell, neither of them had been in contact with Nick for a while. If that was the case, what was Nick talking about?

I reached the top of the stairs and pointed at the closed door, silently asking him if he wanted me to go inside.

Nick nodded so I opened it and went in.

There was nothing in there but the broken remnants of a once busy office. Copy paper littered the floor. A rusted metal desk sat on the far side of the room by the windows and a single chocolate-brown filing cabinet rusted silently in the corner with all three drawers half open.

There was an old bankers chair in the middle of the room. The green faux leather had torn along one side of the seat and the yellow foam inside was spilling out through the ragged gash.

I turned as Nick entered the room.

He looked at me, his eyes glistening with excitement.

"Let's get you ready."

He nestled the shotgun into the crook of his shoulder, aimed for my chest, and pulled the trigger.

Every muscle in my body tensed for the raw destructive power in that shot. But all I felt was the impression of a small child punching me.

I looked down and saw a small metal tube with a dark red feather cap on the back end sticking out of the center of my chest.

As I started to fall down, Nick ran forward to catch me.

"Sorry about lying to you."

As the world spun out of control, I wondered if I would be allowed to wake up again.

And if I did, where would I be?

Would Austin be there?

Or would I end up staring into the scowling face of Dr. Westcott?

Chapter 116

As I slowly came awake, I remembered every muscle going tense after Nick had fired and the world faded to black.

Why had he done that? And why lie about it?

I felt a constriction around my chest and tried to move. I could barely move. I tried to move just my arms, but found them stuck to my sides.

I looked down at my chest and my head cleared instantly.

I was tied down to the green banker's chair.

And I was wearing something new over my shirt.

It was some kind of bulky vest. I expanded my chest, barely stretching the ropes.

"I wouldn't wiggle around too much if I were you," Nick said from behind me.

I twisted slowly in my seat. He was perched on the edge of the large desk and watching out the window that overlooked the ground floor of the empty warehouse.

"Those are filled with compacted RDX powder, the military's best high explosives. Westcott said that when something was able to destroy every cell of your body faster than they could heal, you would die."

He pointed at the vest around my torso.

"That can do it with room to spare."

I looked down at the vest, and held my breath, not moving an inch.

Nick laughed.

"I was kidding about not moving. It's stable. I could shoot you and, surprisingly, the vest would actually protect you."

He held up a small device in his hand.

"Only this trigger can activate it. Well, this trigger and the timer on your back. Oh, and if you try to take off the vest. That will trigger the explosives too."

I scooted the chair around to face him without straining my neck.

"Austin won't come."

Nick looked at me briefly and laughed again.

"He'll come. I've got something he wants."

"Who? Me? What makes you think he wants me?"

"I could see it in his eyes through my scope when you were reunited at the dock. He won't be able to live without you. He will come. And then he will die with you. Even if he doesn't come, I will have accomplished what I wanted."

"If this isn't about the past, what is this about? Why do you hate him so much?"

Nick looked at me.

"I don't hate him, per se. But he took something very precious from me. I can't let that slide. Originally, I thought that I would have to kill him to extract my revenge. But now, I know I can do that same thing to him he did to me by killing you."

"How does killing me help you get revenge on him?"

"I thought he only cared about himself. But then I saw the look in his eyes when he saw you. He had done very well to cover it up when we were together. But when he thought I was watching Dr. Westcott, he let his true feelings slip out and I knew. If I hurt you, I would hurt him."

He returned his attention to the window. After several minutes of silence, he looked at his watch, and then powered on his cell phone and watched it intently.

"What are you waiting for?" I asked.

His cell phone rang and he looked at me with a smile as he put it up to his ear.

"I've been waiting for your call," he said calmly.

"Yes," he continued. "I already told you where I would be. You will come if you ever want to see her again," he said and then hung up the phone.

He looked at me.

"That was your boyfriend. I'm willing to bet he's close. He might already be outside."

His phone rang again.

He looked at it in surprise and then answered it on the second ring.

"Who is this?"

He looked at me in alarm.

"You can have her when I am done with her. Of course, I have her with me now. I promised to turn her over to you when I was done."

He hung up the phone and dropped it on the floor, crushing it under his boot. He looked at me with a sneer and shook his head.

"That Dr. Westcott doesn't ever give up. She agreed to let me take you to use as bait as long as I gave you back. What she doesn't know is that there won't be anything left to give her. Those explosives will vaporize every cell of your body in less than a second once Austin is within range."

Austin's voice echoed from everywhere, and nowhere at the same time.

"Let her go, Nick."

Nick hopped up from the table and he gripped the trigger in his hand. A pin flew from the handle as he squeezed, and he spun around, looking in every direction at once.

"Come on out, Austin. If I let go of this trigger, your little whore goes boom along with everything in a quarter mile radius."

The door opened to the office and Nick spun around, holding up the trigger, pointing it at the open doorway like it was a weapon.

Austin stepped into the room and my heart fluttered. Once I saw him, I knew that everything would be okay. I didn't like playing the part of the damsel in distress. I liked being bait even less, but it felt good to have him near me again.

Austin ignored Nick and looked at me.

"Are you okay?"

I nodded.

"I am now."

He smiled and then refocused on Nick.

"Let her go, Nick. This has nothing to do with her."

Nick laughed.

"This has everything to do with her. You gave her the very thing you withheld from my sister."

Austin held his hands up.

"I went on one date with Emily; at your insistence."

"You don't get to speak her name!" Nick screamed and nearly

dropped the trigger. He recovered and held the trigger tightly, his knuckles turning white.

"She was only eighteen, Austin. And you took everything from her. You took her from me."

"I didn't take anything from her."

"You took your love away when you discovered you had knocked her up. You ran away like a coward. Why? Didn't you want the responsibility of being a father? Of being a husband to my little sister?"

"I'm not the one who got her pregnant."

Nick waved the trigger in the air. My eyes were glued to it. He seemed to not be paying attention and his grip relaxed on it repeatedly as he spoke.

"Hah! My sister was a virgin when she went on that date with you. You got her drunk and forced yourself on her. You assaulted her you bastard!"

Austin frowned.

"No, I didn't. Who told you I did that?"

"She did. Right before she miscarried your child and went insane. You destroyed her, Austin, and now I'm going to destroy you."

"I swear to you, Nick, I never touched her. She became angry with me when I didn't feel the same way for her that she felt towards me."

Nick glared at Austin.

"Stop feeding me shit. You took her home and attacked her."

Austin was shaking his head.

"No. I took her home and waited until she was safely in the house. And then I left. I never saw her again."

Nick held out the trigger, waving it back and forth.

"Don't fucking lie to me. I want you to admit what you did to her. What you did to my whole family. We were friends. We were family. And you took advantage of that."

"I swear, Nick. I never touched her."

Nick was trembling with rage.

"I thought you were a stronger man than this. I guess I was wrong. You were a coward then, and you are still a coward.

Admit your mistakes, Austin, and maybe I will let the both of you live."

My heart pounded faster as Austin's eyes turned into narrow slits.

"If I apologize for what happened to Emily…"

"You don't get to say her name," Nick seethed, spittle forming along the edges of his mouth.

Austin took a step back.

"I'm sorry about your sister."

Nick stared hard at Austin.

"That's the sorriest apology I've ever heard. You have to admit what you did. And I have to believe you are sorry."

He held the trigger above his head.

"Or we all die right here, right now!"

Austin took a deep breath and his shoulders dropped.

"I'm sorry I forced myself on your sister."

Nick's smile expanded, but instead of brightening his face, it seemed to darken it instead.

"And?"

Austin let out another long breath.

"I'm sorry I ran away when she became pregnant."

I looked at Austin in shock. This was not the man I had grown to love. He never once seemed like the kind of person who would ever do such a thing. So why had he?

"And?" Nick prodded.

"And I deserve to die," Austin added.

Nick laughed.

"Finally. All I ever wanted was for you to be a man and take responsibility. It was all you ever expected from Dalton and me when we were on a mission. I'm only sorry I had to do all this just to get you to admit the truth."

Nick suddenly looked around him and then back at Austin.

"Do you hear that?"

I strained to listen, but heard nothing other than the wind whistling between the gaps of the metal paneling of the warehouse.

"That buzzing sound," Nick continued. "It's getting louder."

Austin and I looked at each other in alarm. We both knew exactly what it was. Austin took a step forward and held out his hand.

"Give me the trigger, Nick. Now!"

Nick took a step back and held out the trigger in front of him. Not to give it to Austin, but threatening to let it go.

"Stay back!"

He looked around him again.

"What is that sound?"

I watched the look on Nick's face and knew exactly what he was experiencing, the memory of how much it vibrated throughout my skull, making me wince along with him.

The moment he moved to cover his ears with his hands, Austin vaulted himself forward and grabbed Nick's hand and held it tightly on the trigger.

Nick fell backward against the wall. His eyes were wild as he looked at Austin in a panic.

"What the fuck," he said and then his eyes rolled back in his head as the device implanted behind his ear rendered him unconscious and transmitted our location to Dr. Westcott.

Nick slid down the wall, Austin staying with him and keeping both hands closed around the trigger hand.

As soon as Nick was on the floor, Austin slowly worked the trigger out of his grasp and kept the spring release from popping out.

Austin stood up as he held the trigger in his hand. He rushed over to me and knelt down.

He went behind me and stuffed the trigger into my hand.

"Hold this. And don't let go."

"Don't worry," I replied, my hands already sweating profusely. I didn't know if I could keep holding it without letting it slip right out of my grasp, but I ignored the negative thoughts and focused on the fact that Austin was here and was untying me from the chair.

He could have easily run away, leaving me here to blow up, but he was risking his own life to save mine. How could the man before me be the same as the one who abandoned Nick's pregnant sister?

I clung to the trigger as Austin tugged on the ropes. I licked my lips, contemplating what to say and finally decided on the direct approach.

"Why did you leave her?"

"Leave who?" he said as the ropes dropped away. I flexed my arms to relieve the cramps caused by being restricted in the same position for so long. "Nick's sister."

Austin grabbed my head in his hands and directed my eyes to peer deeply into his.

"I never touched her. I saw pretty quickly she was cut from the same cloth as Nick. No way in a million years would I let myself get caught up in that kind of crazy, let alone bring a child into the world with someone like that."

"But you just said…" I started.

Nick locked his gaze with mine. "I told him whatever he needed to hear to keep us alive for one more minute. And speaking of keeping us alive…" He let go of me and turned his attention to the vest, tugging and poking around for several seconds before he sat back on his heels, shaking his head.

"I trained Nick too well. He set this up to explode if we try to cut through any of the wires."

My heart thudded so hard in my chest, I was worried I might detonate the explosives all by myself.

"What do we do?"

Austin tilted his head to one side and studied the vest.

"We can probably work you out of it without breaking any of the connections if we're careful. But it will take some time."

"We don't have that kind of time. Westcott's probably on her way here right now."

Austin ignored me and looked around the room. He searched Nick's body and found a small knife.

Austin returned and bent down next to me, holding the knife up.

"I want you to hold very still. I'm going to cut away at the vest material, hopefully without breaking any of the wires."

"What happens if you break a wire?"

Austin gave me a stern look.

"We won't know if I do."

I swallowed hard and then reached out one arm, hooking my hand around his neck and pulling him in for a long kiss. When we finally parted lips, I rested my forehead against his and looked deeply into his eyes.

"Be careful," I said.

He smiled briefly and then was all business as he started to work on the vest. I wondered if that was our final kiss.

If it was, I knew I could die happily.

Chapter 117

As Austin worked on tearing through the fabric of the vest without cutting the wires that were embedded and crisscrossed all throughout the material, I ignored the cramping in my hand as I kept a tight grip on the metal cylinder. Several times I wanted to ask Austin how it was going, but I remained silent. He would be done when he was done, and I didn't want to distract him from his task for even a second.

Westcott was coming, and he needed to work as fast as possible without interruption if we planned to be gone when she arrived.

He tugged on the vest, caught me by surprise, and I almost dropped the trigger.

"Easy," I said.

"I think I got it," he replied.

He pulled on the vest, repositioning wires around as he did. It looked like he was playing a game of cat's cradle with all the brightly colored wires stretched out. Only this cat's cradle was a much deadlier version than the one kids played with ordinary string.

"I think I can work this off you now. Just put your arm through there. Be careful. Don't let go of the trigger."

As Austin held the vest open, I twisted my torso around and pulled my arm in tight against my side. As I pulled my hand into the vest, the trigger handle caught on a wire, nearly pulling it out of my grasp.

"Easy," he said. He reached in with one hand and slowly worked the wire out from under the trigger lever.

"Okay," he said once the wire was free. "Keep going."

I pulled my arm through the tangle of wires and fully out of the vest. Austin lifted up on the vest and raised it above my head. I angled my other arm and slipped easily out.

Austin stood up, holding the vest in his hands. He stood there for a full minute, holding his breath. I gripped the trigger, unwilling to be the first to break the silence.

When the vest didn't explode, he looked at me and laughed.

"It worked," he said.

I frowned.

"You didn't think it would?"

He shrugged.

"There was always the chance Nick set up a proximity sensor inside that would be triggered when we removed it. I guess not."

He set the vest gingerly on the top of the desk and turned to me with his hand out.

"The trigger please."

I held it out and let him manipulate my fingers as he switched the trigger to his hand.

He looked around the room, and then back at me.

"Run."

"What?"

"Get out of here. Run as fast and as far as you can and don't look back."

My heart sunk. What was he doing? I couldn't keep the tears from welling up. I puffed out my chest in defiance.

"I'm not leaving you."

His brow creased.

"I'm not going to kill myself. I'm just going to leave a little surprise for Westcott to find when she gets here."

"Then do it with me here."

He regarded me with a half-smile.

"If they show up before I'm ready, I can run faster on my own."

"The only reason you caught me was that I stopped running, remember?"

His smile widened.

"I remember. Okay. Get some paper and a pen or something."

"Why?"

"I want to give Westcott one last chance to redeem herself."

There was plenty of copy paper littering the floor of the room, so that was taken care of. While I looked for something to write with, Austin hunched by the door to the office.

I finally found a pencil in the desk drawer and took it to

Austin. He looked up at me and I could see that he had wedged the trigger under the door.

He pointed at it.

"If someone pushes on this door, it will trigger the vest and level the entire warehouse, and probably the buildings around it."

I looked at Nick sleeping peacefully on the floor.

"What about Nick?"

"If he wakes up before anyone gets here, he can remove the trigger without setting it off."

I looked at our only way out of the room. Austin had blocked it off with the trigger.

"What about us?"

Austin smiled.

"We will climb out the window. It's not that far of a drop, so we should be fine if we roll on landing."

Austin used the chair to break out the glass of the window.

He pointed to the floor below us.

"When you land, bend with your knees and do a forward somersault to discharge the momentum from jumping. Watch how I do it."

He jumped down and dropped into a roll, popping back up to a standing position with a hop.

He looked up at me.

"Your turn."

I slowly climbed into the window and perched on the edge of the frame. It looked much farther down than it had before now that I was about to jump.

What if I broke my leg?

So what if I did?

I was immortal.

I launched myself into the air.

I hit the ground and my legs buckled under the momentum. Rather than rolling gracefully like Austin had, I hit the ground in a puff of dust and crumpled into a heap.

Austin was instantly at my side.

"Are you okay?"

I rolled onto my back and looked up at his piercing blue eyes full of concern for me. I flexed my muscles and sat up.

"I'm fine. The ground came up a little faster than I was expecting."

He helped me to my feet then took the paper he had written on and ran up the stairs. I followed him up and watched as he stuck the note on the door, using a metal pipe to hammer it on with a nail.

As he stepped back, I was finally able to read what it said.

"Westcott. This is your final chance. Do not open this door. If you leave us alone no harm will come to you."

We looked at each other.

"Do you think she will heed the warning?" I asked.

Austin shrugged.

In the distance, I heard the thumping of helicopter rotors beating the sky. Austin heard it too and grabbed my hand as we ran out of the warehouse and into the setting sun.

Without looking back, we kept running.

We made it to the edge of the forest that surrounded the small complex of dilapidated warehouses when my eardrums popped from a sudden change in air pressure.

Austin reacted quickly and pulled me to the ground right before the shockwave hit.

Dust and debris engulfed us immediately and my ears compressed from the massive explosion that trailed the leading shockwave.

My ears were ringing, and it sounded like Austin was talking to me from under water as he pulled me back to my feet.

The air was choked with fine dust.

Dr. Westcott had failed to heed our warning. While it meant the end for her, it was a bright beginning for us.

Austin pulled my shirt collar up over my mouth and nose and supported me as we walked through the thick brown haze into an unknown future.

Chapter 118

The next three months went by in a blur as we went from one place to another, always changing our identity and purchasing multiple destinations under multiple names at the same time.

Austin always wanted to be the last to board any plane. And he always insisted on watching the other passengers boarding before us. If he missed even one person, that trip was scratched and we were suddenly headed somewhere else.

A couple of times, after we were already on the plane and settled in our seats, he took us back off again and we left the airport in a taxi.

After nearly a month of constant travel, never staying anywhere for more than a few hours, we finally settled on the island of Guam, one of the last remaining colonized U.S. territories. I initially worried that, because it was still technically part of the United States, someone would find us.

Austin assured me that we were just as safe there as anywhere. Besides, he had said, nobody could have followed the trail we had left, what with all the sudden course corrections and decoy travel purchases.

After nearly a month of looking over his shoulder, Austin had finally decided to settle into the relaxed pace of island life.

We spent the days walking the beach hand in hand, and the nights watching the sun set from a small table at various outdoor patio restaurants.

The rest of our time was spent learning every inch of each other's bodies in the bedroom. After another marathon session of lovemaking, I was in the bathroom and, for some reason, Austin was back to his old self and in a terrible hurry.

Austin knocked on the bathroom door and his voice came through muffled.

"Are you ready yet?"

I glanced again at the object in my hand before setting it on the edge of the sink and looked at myself in the mirror, trying desperately to keep the smile off my face. It faded quickly when he knocked again.

"All right, I'm coming!" I yelled as I threw the object in the trash and opened the door.

Austin was standing there and mocked a glance at the non-existent watch on his tanned wrist.

"It's about time. Jeez, woman. You don't look any different."

I punched him in the arm and he pretended that I actually hurt him as he grabbed his bicep.

"Ow!"

"Oh, c'mon. A tough guy like you didn't even feel that."

He smiled and grabbed me by the waist, spinning me around in the small hallway and planting a kiss on my lips. I wrapped my arms around his neck and clung to him, drawing him in deeper.

After nearly a minute of making out, he finally broke our lip lock and held me out at arm's length.

"Are you ready to go?"

"You still haven't told me where we're headed."

He smiled.

"It's a surprise. You like surprises, don't you?"

I smiled back coyly.

"Only if you promise to love them as much as I do."

He kissed me again and then rushed us out to the car. I didn't know what the big hurry was, but I had barely gotten into my seat when he started the car and pulled out of the driveway of our rented beachside bungalow.

As the wind whipped through my hair, I looked over at Austin as he drove. The wind barley affected his short hair. He had promised to let it grow now that we no longer needed to run, but that was still yet to happen. One of the first places he sought out after we settled in Guam was a barber.

He drove up the hill and finally pulled into the small parking lot adjacent to an even smaller building.

He hopped out and opened the door for me.

As I stepped out, I looked around.

"Where are we?"

"Puntan Dos Amantes. Two Lovers Point," he said and ushered me quickly to the small gift shop where he purchased a bright red heart-shaped combination lock.

"What's that for?" I asked.

"Just wait," he said and then led me to a wall with hundreds of similar locks, luggage tags, and foam hearts all hanging from it.

He grabbed a pen attached by a string to the wall and wrote "A+A 4EVR" on the back of the lock and then smiled as he held it out to me.

"If you'll do the honors?"

I took the lock and stared at it. He had finally remembered to refer to me by Athena instead of Michele. The lock with our initials on it was physical proof that the life we had led before was finally behind us.

"What am I supposed to do with this?"

He pointed to the wall.

"Lock it on the wall as a symbol of our undying love."

I held the lock in my hands and tears threatened to burst forth. I grabbed Austin's hand, and together, we placed the lock on the wire fence.

Austin became excited again and led me up the steps to a platform that overlooked the cliffs below; and the ocean beyond.

He pointed at the stone carvings that showed the dramatization of the lovers who gave these cliffs their name.

"A girl who lived on this island long ago was arranged to marry a powerful Spanish captain. She ran away and fell in love with a young warrior. When her father discovered this, he and the captain pursued the two lovers to the top of this cliff. Trapped, the lovers had nowhere to go, so they tied their hair together and kissed one final time before leaping over the edge to be together for all of eternity."

He turned to me.

"Does that story remind you of anyone?"

I tilted my head to one side.

"If you reach for my hair, I'm going to just push you on over. Screw dying together."

He laughed and wrapped his arms around me.

"We are already together. We don't need to die to be complete."

My heart fluttered as I looked into his eyes.

"We're not complete yet," I said.

His forehead wrinkled in confusion.

"What do you mean?"

"Well, at least not yet. But we should be in about seven and a half months. Give or take a month."

Austin frowned and looked at me, his smile fading. I thought my heart was going to burst through my ribcage, it was beating so hard. The last time I felt the adrenaline pumping this strongly through my veins, I was staring down the barrel of a gun.

"But Dr. Westcott said you couldn't..."

He didn't need to finish his sentence.

I shrugged.

"I guess she got it wrong."

His smile slowly returned and grew wider than I had ever seen it before.

He grabbed my face in his hands and planted the biggest kiss on me. Then he wrapped an arm around my shoulders and we faced out over the ocean together.

"Do you think he will take after you? Or more after me?" he asked.

"I hope she takes after me," I replied.

"Oh, most certainly. That would be preferable," he said with a chuckle.

I wrapped my arms around him in a sideways hug. "I think Dalton will be a good name for him or her," I said softly.

He gave me a comforting squeeze as we stood on the edge of forever and looked out into eternity.

Tomorrow will not happen like today.

Other Books by the Author

A is for Apprentice (Fantasy)

Oliver Twist: Victorian Vampire (Fantasy Horror)

A Tale of Two Cities with Dragons (Fantasy)

Shade Infinity (Science Fiction Thriller)

Peacekeepers X-Alpha Series (Thriller)
Inherit the Throne
The Warrior's Code

Steampunk OZ Series (Science Fiction Novellas)
Forgotten Girl
The Legacy's World
Emerald Shadow
The Future's Destiny
The Dangerous Captive
Missing Legacy
Shadow of History
The Edge of the Hunter

Fugue: The Cure (Science Fiction Short Story)

Jason and the Chrononauts (Kid's Adventure)

Be the first to know about Steve DeWinter's next book.
Follow the URL below to subscribe for free today!

http://bit.ly/BookReleaseBulletin